America's Diplomats
The Road To Attleboro

by

John W. Huffman

5/5/2012

ACKNOWLEDGMENTS

My heartfelt thanks to Leonard Jordan, Louis Smith, Jerry Nealy, Jackie Neely Jansen, Don Shrader, Guy Shuford, John Morgan, Captain, US Army (Ret.) and Doug Meadows, Lt. Col. USAF (Ret.) for their invaluable input, advice, and recommendations into the early drafts of this book.

I give special recognition to Whitney Brock for the unique cover design, and Fay Sprouse for the meticulous proof reading.

To each, I extend my deepest gratitude and appreciation.

To my adorable wife, Misty, and three sons,
Dennis, Chris, and John Westley.

CHAPTER 1

I was cold and clammy after countless hours under the plane's stale air-conditioning. When brisk chimes illuminated the no smoking and fasten seatbelt signs, I leaned eagerly to the tiny window as we descended through a layer of clouds more than ready to end this infinite journey. A million fog-shrouded lights appeared out of the darkness outlining Saigon, mysterious and alluring to the unknowing in search of adventure.

"Good morning, gentlemen, and welcome to Vietnam," the pilot intoned. "The time is 0435 hours. We've had a change of destination and will be landing at Ton Son Nhut Airbase in approximately fifteen minutes. Thank you."

The soldier on my left elbowed my arm in the annoying manner I had grown accustomed to after an eternity of sitting together, his dark brown eyes staring at me from his short, stocky frame topped by the shaved head of a recruit. "Why Ton Son Nhut?"

I pointedly ignored him, making no attempt to hide my disdain for his sloppy uniform complete with billowing shirt and baggy pants, or the fact that he was not wearing jump wings, which in my book relegated him to the status of a common, straight-leg soldier deserving of little more consideration than one would give a bug.

"Aren't we supposed to land at Bien Hoa?" he persisted.

"What does it matter?" I sniped, admiring my gleaming jump boots below the perfectly bloused boot tops planted next to his smudged low-quarter shoes.

"There must be a problem if we're landing at Ton Son Nhut," he reasoned. "Do you think they're being attacked or something?"

"How the hell do I know?" I replied, thinking the little jerk could irritate a grandmother.

The bell chimed again. "Well, lads, looks like you're getting the royal welcome. Bien Hoa is receiving a little rocket fire this morning and Ton Son Nhut's on alert, so we'll just cruise around and let them settle down. I'll turn off the smoking lamp, but due to possible turbulence at low altitude the seatbelt sign will remain on. Thank you."

The ragbag nudged my arm. "I friggin' *knew* it! They *are* being attacked!"

I grimaced, thinking, *Christ, all I need is to get killed before I even get there!*

"Look!" He pointed a stubby finger at the weak glow of the city wedged by a purple band below orange filtered sunrise threatening to emerge. Blinking amber lights floated soundlessly high above the outer fringes of the metropolis as thin lines of red chased themselves downward in a silent, ghostly scene, the graceful lines gliding from one sector, then another, converging and dying out in the void below. Other blinking amber disks hurried to join those already in the area to send their own red lines down in a sinister torrent. "See? See? *Friggin' gunships*! Those are tracers! I told you so!"

My stomach clutched as the jet continued its slow bank to the left panning the city and the eerie scene delineating our first glimpse of war from my vision.

Ratchet Jaws elbowed my ribs again. "Hey, do you think rockets can reach us up here?"

Damn! Could they?

"We've been up here a long time," he mused fretfully. "I sure hope we don't run of gas!"

I closed my eyes, thinking straight leg soldiers were the dumbest critters on earth. I dreamed of home a lifetime away now, a sleepy little town in east Texas nestled deep in the heart of the piney woods referred to as the *Jewel of the Forest*, almost hearing the wind whispering through the tall green pines and feeling the deep shade beneath. An overpowering urge to return there engulfed me as I realized that in all the months learning to kill, they'd never once taught me how to die.

———

I'd always dreamed of being a soldier. As a young lad, I huddled at my grandfather's knee before his wood burning stove on winter nights as he spun his tall tales of the men and times of World War I. Bathed in yellow flickering light from his kerosene lamp, I listened to the old gentleman regale the magic of France and Belgium and whole nations mobilized against the mighty Hun amid his occasional wheezes from lungs burned by mustard gas.

Though my father never spoke of his war, I found his Bronze Star and Purple Heart secreted away in our cedar chest along with a faded picture of him and his cronies sitting around a table covered with beer bottles somewhere in France. He and his comrades struck an adventurous chord within me as I viewed his devil-may-care grin captured from some twenty years distant and imagined his courageous deeds in stopping the Nazis cold in World War II.

As a youngster, I watched my uncle march off to Korea to withstand fanatical human wave attacks across the frozen Pusan perimeter, and ultimately emerge from that conflict with a Silver Star and occasional blackouts from shrapnel embedded in his head.

In my rush to enlist after our president announced his intention to commit American troops to Southeast Asia I didn't even ask why. It didn't matter really. I stood on the threshold of my generation's challenge and it was my time to serve. After meeting with a recruiter I hurried home and pulled my father out to the front porch.

"Dad, I volunteered to be a paratrooper today."

He sank down in the swing on the porch as sadness settled in eyes. "Why, boy?"

I drew my slim, five-foot, eight-inch frame up proudly before him as he looked me directly in my blue eyes. "Because they're the best soldiers in the world and I aim to be one!"

He sat staring at me until I began to wonder if he had heard me before finally expelling a slow breath. "Are you set on this thing, boy?"

"Yes sir, dead set," I replied firmly, as I ran my hand nervously through my mop of thick blond hair.

"Why?"

I searched for something convincing to say, to relay my need within to just *do it*! "I-I want to be a soldier!"

He looked out across the field in front of our house. "Son, it's not what you think. Those paratroopers are always the first ones in, you know. Sometimes, in the second war, we couldn't get them back out again." He cleared his throat. "But they always gave a good account of themselves. I expect you will too. You just think about what it would do to your mother if ..."

I felt closer to my father at that moment than I ever had before and wanted to throw my arms around him, but was afraid it would seem unmanly.

Over the next week I said goodbye to all my friends, drank a tubful of bootleg beer, and accepted as my just due the envy and special attention lavished upon me, the local boy going off to war to suppress the forces of evil as generations before me had proudly done. In a strange, far-off country the communists were trying to subjugate a simple, peace-loving people, but America was coming to their rescue. I was already a hero and didn't even have a uniform yet.

Betty Jean and my mother viewed my action with tearful misgivings. B.J. wanted us to marry and for me to settle down in a solid job at the sawmill our small town was built around. Though I rarely knew what I wanted, I always knew precisely what I did not want. My mother was, well, the universal mother—Betty Jean and a parcel of kids were what I needed more than gadding about sampling the evils of a corrupt world. The two eventually came to accept my wanderlust with tearful resignation and mama got B.J. a job at the bakery where she herself worked part-time to supplement dad's meager income. There, the two could offer each other comfort through the interminable wait for their Jay to come back home from a distant place somewhere in the mystic Orient called Vietnam.

———

I found myself in Ft. Polk, Louisiana, for Basic Combat Training, where they placed us airborne volunteers in a special platoon. The drill sergeants went out of their way to make life difficult for us by requiring us to do everything the rest of the recruits did, and then some. For normal trainees an infraction of the rules led to a penance of ten push-ups. "Gimme *ten*, roach!" was heard the day long. For us, it was "An *airborne* ten, swine!" which automatically doubled the punishment and required every man in the platoon to suffer the penalty along with the perpetrator. Our fellow non-airborne recruits held us in awe—or considered us just plain stupid—and in general stayed away from us for fear of drawing double punishment by mistake.

We became a *gung ho* platoon and developed an inner pride while busting our guts to be better, faster, and stronger than the regular soldiers. We were prone to swagger, when the drill sergeants weren't looking, and spent hours on our uniforms and boots to outshine the rest by a wide margin. We won every platoon competition flat out, demonstrating our expertise on the rifle range, land navigation exercise, obstacle course, and the physical training test. On the twenty-five-mile forced march, carrying full field packs and rifles, we jogged over half the route nearly killing our drill sergeant in the process, and beat the nearest platoon time by two and a half hours. In eight grueling weeks of basic training we lost over half of our platoon to dropouts, but they weren't missed. We did not want men who lacked stamina or conviction in our ranks and felt no empathy for those fallen by the wayside. If anything, watching them slip quietly back into the regular's ranks, we were even more scornful of them for admitting failure. We were the honor platoon on graduation day leading the rest of the company in the Pass in Review with arms swinging, every man in perfect step, emulating the pride of the United States Army—*Airborne,* of course.

Advanced Airborne Infantry Training at Ft. Gordon, Georgia, was next on our agenda, twelve of the most miserable weeks I'd ever spent in my life. There, we were all airborne candidates and the only thing unique about us was our ability to survive each day. The competition became fierce and the discipline unforgiving amid our constant fear of washing out and being assigned back down to a *leg* unit. Failure loomed before us each demanding day as we searched deep within to find a strength we never knew existed. Pain and fatigue became our daily rations until we reached the point of collapse. Then the instructors cajoled us into one last mile. Many did not make that mile. In steadfast silence we watched them pack their gear in tears and depart. We kept ourselves going by pulling together and molding into a team united in our desire to succeed. When the point was reached where I could take no more, one of my buddies shamed me out of quitting. The next day I performed the same service for him. On graduation day we were a considerably smaller force than when we began and there were no honor platoons—every man who marched across that parade field was an honor graduate and knew it. Among ourselves, we were equals with no doubts of being the toughest, best-trained troops in the world.

At long last we were shipped to Ft. Benning, Georgia, and the culmination of our dreams—*Jump School.* There we purchased the famed Corcoran paratrooper boots, which we spit-shined to a brilliant gloss, and tailored our uniforms to fit our bodies like gloves, removing every ounce of excess material.

Ft. Benning was awful and made our training before seem soft in comparison. It seemed the instructors hated us and spent every day with everything in their power to break our spirit. Rumor circulated that they were required to buy the silver wings out of their own pockets for each man they graduated, and after the first week I was sure no money would be spent on me, but rumor also had it they had to personally bury each of us they killed in the iron-red clay of Georgia, so I resolved to die trying just to get even with the rotten bastards.

But by now we were rock hard, tough minded, fiercely determined, and had victory in sight. Three weeks and five parachute jumps later, after losing only a handful of men to injuries and dropouts, by God's grace, we made it. At last we were *Airborne*: elite, proud, and ready.

Most of us received orders the next day assigning us to the 101st Airborne Division, Republic of South Vietnam—the famed *Screaming Eagles*. The world was again a beautiful place. The few of us left had faced the worst the Army could dish out and excelled. Now the small task of sallying forth in our country's name to toss out a few pesky commies was all that remained.

My biggest fear was the war would end before my two weeks of leave was up. Saying goodbye to my parents, brothers and sisters, and B.J. was difficult. I was going to war, maybe never to return—or perhaps worse—returning a coward. With damp eyes I boarded a plane for Oakland, California, processed through the overseas station, and took my place on this cramped jet for the eternal journey across the vast Pacific Ocean, unbelieving the months had slipped by so quickly.

At last I was off to seek my fame and fortune. With six months of paratrooper training behind me, Private John Joseph Sharpe, RA-18753477, Airborne Infantry, was the toughest combat trooper the world could produce and prepared for any contingency. In a vague fashion I sought all life offered with my greatest fear set aside—I would *not* grow old without ever having *lived*.

———

G.I. Joe nudged my arm. "Hey, we're on final approach."

I slid my seat into the upright position and tightened my seatbelt as the aircraft began a gradual descent. Bright shafts of sunlight streamed through the small windows of the darkened fuselage in intermittent pools. Dark green walls of vegetation rose up to meet us with whispery tendrils of fog clinging to the treetops. Motion moved at a lazy pace as the morning sun chased my chilly apprehensions away. The pace picked up as we drew near the ground. The green became a misty blur interspaced with scattered buildings rushing by. Two bumps and a jolt followed by a tearing roar and we were down, our speed dropping rapidly and propelling me forward in my seat as the engines reversed. A loud cheer started up front with the officers, swelled in power as it rolled back across the noncommissioned officer section and into our enlisted ranks in the rear. As the plane taxied to the parking area the pilot told us how he and the crew had enjoyed serving us and wished us luck, but no one was listening. When the door opened we jammed the aisles in a squirming throng.

Officers dismounted first, with quiet dignity. Then the sergeants strolled out taking their sweet time. At last we enlisted rabble elbowed our way down the aisles. When I barged through the door at long last the humid smell of rotting garbage left me gasping in the blinding sunlight as I stumbled down the steps on wobbly legs with others trampling on my heels. The heat rising from the pavement engulfed me like an oven as the ground rose and fell in undulating motions.

I groped my way to a cluster of men milling about in what was supposed to be a formation before a sergeant in jungle fatigues carrying a clipboard, the ultimate badge of authority in the army. He directed us to a large hangar on our right, where we collapsed on benches grateful for the shade and the opportunity to gather our wits. A short time later, a convoy of olive drab buses pulled up in front of the hangar. Under the sergeant's direction, we collected our duffel bags from the pile dumped on the pavement in front of the hangar and filed aboard.

The heat was like a blast furnace inside the transport, where I noticed with some trepidation sandbags layering the floors and wire screens covering the windows. As we waited, the sun climbed higher and the stench of unwashed bodies grew overpowering. My parched throat ached for moisture as sweat drenched my shirt, and I no longer cared about the creases in my pants. Eventually, two gun-jeeps roared up with M-60 machine guns mounted on metal posts, with the drivers and gunners wearing steel pots and flak-vests. I watched with misgivings as they positioned themselves to our front and rear, and at last, we began to move. The flow of tepid air brought a small measure of welcoming relief from the suffocating heat as we wound our way around the hangars and buildings of the base and out through a large gate surrounded by circular strands of barbed wire and sandbagged bunkers manned by guards carrying automatic rifles.

That was it. We were in enemy territory. And unarmed! Peering out of the window expecting an attack at any minute, I released my pent-up breath in despair.

Vietnam, I am here and I am yours. Please don't tell my mother I died cowering on the dirty floor of an Army transport bus, my last thoughts of home and sweet, cool water!

CHAPTER 2

We became entangled in the damnedest mess I'd ever seen.

Bicycles, motor scooters, ancient cars and trucks of foreign manufacture, and strange three-wheeled contraptions resembling a cross between a motorcycle and a pick-up truck littered the streets in a swarming tide of disorder amongst milling hordes of strange looking men dressed in black or white silk pajama-type pants and shirts and females wearing oriental *sarongs* in a mixture of colors. There seemed to be no orderly plan to the flow. Everyone beeped his horn and stomped the throttle to dart for the fleeting openings with the biggest or bravest winning as the mass of people evaded them with commendable dexterity. Old women shuffled along in quick, tiny steps balancing long poles across their shoulders with baskets connected by cords swinging from the ends. Men squatted by the close packed, dilapidated buildings with iron bars covering the doors and windows smoking cigarettes as they watched our passage with narrowed eyes. High stonewalls pitted with metal spikes or broken bits of glass embedded in mortar surrounded a mixture of corrugated tin and red tile roofs. Rolls of barbed wire and sandbags manned by Vietnamese soldiers carrying rifles distinguished the occasional government buildings.

As we powered through the chaos, hawkers held wares up to our window extolling their cheap prices in broken English. Droves of dirty, ragged children scrambled beside our bus shouting, *"You number one, G.I., you number one! You give Baby-san, G.I., you give! You number one!"* With their empty palms outstretched, eyes pleading and voices wailing, it was agonizing to have nothing to offer in the face of their desperation. Each break in the traffic allowed us to outdistance them, only to have a new mob replace them at the next bottleneck.

Families squatted in cluttered alleyways with their possessions bundled in rags and wicker baskets beside them. Women cooked meager meals over open fires built on the broken pavement as hungry children huddled close by while men shouted others away. Blowing horns, gas fumes, spicy smells, and loud, discordant singsong chatter enveloped us in this alien world, our fascination marred only by the underlying anxiety that out of that mass of surging humanity a hand would hurl a grenade to turn our transport into a burning skeleton of twisted steel.

We eventually left the city behind and traveled a well-maintained road resembling a stateside freeway, where the bus seemed to fly after the creeping city pace. Oil storage tanks and buildings under construction dotted the country on each side of us. An interminable time later, we passed through a small settlement and pulled up to a large concentration camp encased in rolls of barbed wire with towering guard posts and an arched sign reading:

21st REPLACEMENT DEPOT
REPUBLIC OF VIETNAM

Vietnamese guards stared from the sandbagged towers with disinterest as the lead bus negotiated our entry. Behind the protective barrier on the left side of the road dissecting the perimeter were low wooden buildings with rusting tin tops and two old Vietnamese women scrubbing garbage cans beside one with a sign proclaiming 'Officers' Open Mess.' Another miniature prison within the larger detention center simmered in the rising heat waves on the right, where a sign read 'Women's Army Corps,' with an American military policeman sitting in a chair in the shade guarding the entrance through the wire to the WAC complex.

My heart sank as we motored through this dismal shantytown and approached slum city some three hundred yards across an open area on the backside of the compound. The impression was a turn-of-the-century mining camp with hundreds of tents strewn about in a haphazard maze with their dusty sides rolled up for ventilation below the scorched tops. These miserable structures crouched around a single row of stately wood-and-screen buildings with canvas covers. Board sidewalks with planks broken or missing ran in crooked lines between the structures bordered by pools of moldy green water between patches of cracked earth. Listless troops stumbled about indifferently in the heat as our transports lurched to a stop. Red dust drifted over us saturating our sweat-dampened uniforms as we dismounted dragging our duffel bags behind us. A sergeant formed us into squares as two sergeants watched from a small viewing stand. One raised a bullhorn to his lips and an artificial voice boomed out at us.

"*Let me have your attention*! During your brief stay here, all problems with our facilities should be brought to the attention of one of my cadre assistants, each recognizable by their distinctive head gear." He indicated the shiny black cover with white bands on his head. "The buildings to your rear are processing centers. They are off-limits unless the cadre directs you there. The area you passed through on your left upon entering the compound is the Officer's Quarters and off-limits. The small compound on the right is the Women's Army Corps Quarters and off-limits. Once you have completed processing you will select a tent within the area. The normal stay here is four days, give or take a day. Do not annoy the cadre with questions about your assignment or departure date.

"The mess hall located in the center of the compound serves at 0700, 1200, and 1700 hours. There are four shower points and latrines throughout the camp, one of each clearly marked NCO only. The Post Exchange operates from 1000 until 2200 hours. Alcoholic beverages are restricted from sale or consumption until after 1900 hours.

"Three formations are held daily, at 0800, 1300, and 1600 hours, here in the assembly area. Protective enclosures are located next to each shelter." He indicated the slimy mud holes full of putrid water and flies. "At the continuous wail of the camp siren you will proceed to and remain in their protection until three short blasts of the siren signal the all-clear. You will now complete your in processing. NCOs will move to the first hooch to the rear. The remainder of you will take a break in place until directed otherwise by the cadre." He clicked off his bull-horn and dismounted the stand.

I mopped my sweat-laden brow and dug for my crum-pled pack of cigarettes in the suffocating humidity rising at my feet as distant objects shimmered in nauseous pat-terns. Empty canvas water bags hung from tripod poles to each side of us, their dusty pouches mocking my misery. Time passed in a slow-moving fog as the cadre sergeants led each formation to the processing sheds. Eventually a sergeant summoned my group to the beehive of activity inside one of the structures for formal in processing. With the tedious administrative chore finished, I stumbled out into the blinding afternoon sun in search of a home.

The broken boardwalk proved difficult to negotiate and forced me onto the beaten path beside it. Raising puffs of dust with each step, I selected the first tent in line and thrust my head through the flaps. One bag occupied a cot by the entrance leaving the remaining eleven barren. I swung my bag to the ground across from the occupied one and stumbled out to the water bag in front to find it dry. I plodded back in, slapped at the accumulated dust on the cot to make it habitable, and collapsed in exhaustion. An uncertain time later, determined prodding on my shoul-der pulled me from my heat induced stupor to stare up in bewilderment at the moron from the plane.

"Hi," he greeted cheerfully.

"What are *you* doing here?" I groaned in despair, thinking this the end, not even in combat yet and I'd died and gone to hell for sure, doomed to swelter for eternity in this ungodly heat and be pestered for the rest of my life by a dim-wit *leg*.

"Want some water?" he offered, extending a paper cup.

I propped up on one elbow and grasped the cup like a crazed man to gulp the warm liquid in grateful swigs, noting he had changed into untailored, baggy fatigues, and now wore boots with the tops sloppily bloused. His chubby baby face watched me eagerly as I drank the warm liquid, which felt like lead in my stomach and left an oily film lingering in my mouth.

I worked the grit around with my tongue. "Look, uh—"

"Delarosa," he supplied. "Most just call me Del."

"John Joseph Sharpe," I acknowledged. "Folks call me Jay-Jay, or just plain Jay. Where'd you get that?" I indicated the cup.

"I watched them fill the tank up at the shower point."

"Do you mind if I borrow your cup?" I swung my legs to the ground and waited for the dizziness to pass before trudging up the hill to the shower point with my heels kicking up powdery dust.

"Where are you from, Jay?" Del asked as he hurried along beside me.

"Texas," I replied as I mopped my sweat-beaded forehead with my handkerchief.

"I'm from Chicago. Ever been there?"

"Nope."

"Do you live on a ranch and have a horse?"

"Nope, I live in a city."

"You know what Chicago's known for?"

I shrugged in annoyance. "Al Capone?"

"It's known as the windy city. How many people live in your city?"

"Two or three thousand, I expect."

"Is that *all*?" he gasped, bug-eyed. "We've got *millions*."

"That's too bad," I sympathized.

"Where do you think we'll be assigned?"

"*I'm* going to the *Screaming Eagles*," I answered, sticking my chest out proudly.

"I thought about going airborne," he mused. "I could sure use the extra dough."

"It's *not* the money!" I replied indignantly, secure in my knowledge he would never make a paratrooper no matter what it paid as we topped the hill and approached the shower point, a tin roof affair with slat-board sides and a large tank perched on stilts off to the side to supply gravity-fed water to the interior. A cement floor sloped downward in the middle forming a narrow trough that drained out the far end. Green mold and broken bits of soap littered the floor amid a dank, fetid odor permeating the air. I hurried over to the row of showerheads, extended the cup under the nozzle, and pulled the chain cord swinging beside it. A gush of water filled the cup to overflowing and soaked half my arm. I chug-a-lugged the sun-heated water in gratitude, again feeling pieces of grit in my mouth and experiencing the lingering oily taste.

Del stared beyond me with a flicker of concern wavering in the depths of his big brown doe eyes. "Ready to go?"

"Don't you want some?" I asked.

He eased to the door. "I had plenty the first time."

"Suit yourself." I extended the cup under the nozzle and grabbed the cord. "Water sure tastes funny over here, don't it?"

"You better not, Jay," he whispered.

"Why not?" I filled the cup to the brim with the over-flow running down my arm as he pointed in despair. I turned in the indicated direction as I drank and faced a large white sign posted on the opposite wall with a black skull-and-crossbones insignia and red capital letters.

ATTENTION!
NON-POTABLE WATER!
EXTERNAL USE ONLY!

I gagged as the putrid water exploded from my mouth. "*Hawaaawkk*! Y-You've *poisoned* me, you *agraahhhh* asshole!"

"I-I didn't see the friggin' sign before!" he protested.

"I ought to *aacckk* kick your *haaauuccckkk* ass!" I sputtered as I collapsed against the wall in a fit of coughing.

"I'm sorry, I was only trying to help!"

"Listen, *jerk*," I wheezed, jabbing my finger in his chest as he squirmed against the wall. "Don't *help* me anymore! Don't *poke* me anymore! In fact, don't even *talk* to me anymore!"

I stomped out the door and down the hill with dust flying from my heels wondering how long I had to live. *How would the Army inform my mother? Would they spare her the sordid details?* I sure hoped so since it was embarrassing as hell to travel all this way only to get poisoned by a *damned Yankee!* I stopped to heave up my insides in great convulsions as tears streamed down my cheeks from the effort. Del stood five feet away watching in misery, not daring to come closer, and then slithered along behind me as I limped back to the tent to die like a wounded animal in the sanctuary of his lair. I considered killing the little fruitcake before

I became too weak or delirious, but watching him standing outside the tent flaps in dejection, I resolved not to,
fretful that if he ended up on the same cloud with me in
heaven I'd *never* get rid of him. I waited for the end, allowing fond memories of home to carry me into the gathering darkness of the hereafter.

———

I awoke in the gloomy shadows of evening to find
the temperature had dropped with the setting sun and
shivered in my damp uniform.

Del sat on his cot in the semi-darkness with his chin
propped in both hands, expression mournful. "You all
right, Jay?"

I dug in my duffle bag for my fatigues. "It appears
I'll live."

"I really am sorry. I never saw that stupid sign. I've
been sitting here watching you the whole time. If you
started dying or something I was going to call a medic."

"Forget it," I growled.

"Want some water?"

I glared at him. "What are you, a *comedian*?"

"Huh? Oh, *no*, I didn't mean *that*! They filled the bag
outside while you were asleep."

I hurried out with Del close on my heels and opened
the canvas top to inspect the contents with grave suspicion.
Satisfied with the clarity, I took a flat paper cup from the
container on the side, drew it full from the tap at the bottom, sniffed it for odor, and took a sip to see how my insides would respond. They seemed to like it just fine so

I downed several cups in quick succession as Del watched in delight.

"That's an improvement," I allowed in satisfaction.

Del hung his head morosely. "Jay, I'm *really* sorry—"

"I *said* forget it!" I snapped.

"We can still make chow if you feel like it," he suggested.

"I'm starved," I agreed and turned to lead the way.

When we slipped into the line of hungry men strung out in front of the mess hall, I noticed the man in front of me wearing spit-shined Corcoran jump boots and tailored fatigues.

I tapped him on the back. "Hey, you airborne?"

"Bet your ass." He turned with the silver wings shining on his left breast pocket standing an inch or two taller than my five feet eight with wide shoulders and narrow hips. Jet-black hair matched deep almond eyes complementing his dark complexion and high cheekbones, which gave his face the hint of a heart shape that women would find attractive.

"I'm Jay, headed for the Eagles." I extended my hand, thinking he could step into a recruiting poster and feel right at home as the perfect specimen of an airborne soldier.

"So am I, name's Jerry." He pumped my hand eyeing my own silver wings and tailored uniform appreciatively. "How long you been in this dump?"

"Since noon. You?"

"Two days," he replied. "I should be getting my call tomorrow."

An immediate wave of dread washed through me as I considered the time I had left in this god-awful place.

Del shoved his hand at Jerry. "Hi, I'm Del ..."

"Don't shake hands with *legs*," Jerry declined in disdain as he wiped his hand on his shirt at the mere thought before looking at me suspiciously. "He with you?"

"He shares my tent," I explained. "Came over on the same plane with me."

"Where's he going?"

"Don't know," I replied as Del lowered his hand with a pained expression. "Legs don't get direct assignments like us, they go into a pool and get shipped to units by the pound."

Jerry and I traded stories of jump school as we shuffled through the door and filled our trays with Del continuing to dog our heels in sulky silence. Other leg troops joined us at the table, where we learned the rumor mill had the 101st Screaming Eagles kicking ass somewhere up north while some leg unit was getting their ass kicked down south. Jerry and I exchanged knowing smirks, the superiority of the airborne again proven as we listened to other bits of rumor involving a large number of Vietcong thought to be moving in our direction, finding this particularly vexing because we were unarmed and sitting ducks encased in our own barbed wire encampment. All in all, the war appeared to be moving along while we sat in this hellhole.

Let's grab a beer at the PX," Jerry suggested as we departed the mess hall.

"Suits me," I agreed as we cat walked through the darkness searching for the dangerous tent pegs with our feet as Del continued to tag along.

"I can't wait until we get to the Eagles, Jay," Jerry mused.

"Me either, Jerry. *Ouch!*" I sucked in my breath as I stumbled over a tent peg.

"Do you think you'll ever come to Chicago, Jay?" Del asked.

"Don't rightly know," I answered.

"I'll feel a lot better when I have a rifle in my hands, know what I mean?" Jerry mused.

"Yeah, me too," I acknowledged wistfully.

"You'd love it, Jay," Del insisted. "I could show you things in the big city you'd never see on your own."

"Maybe we can get in the same unit," Jerry speculated.

"That'd be great," I replied to the both of them.

"What kind of food do you like? *Oops! Uhnnn!*" Del grunted as he tripped over one of the tent ropes and sprawled on his face in an eruption of dust.

"You okay?" I pulled him up and slapped the dirt off his uniform.

"You should be a couple of days behind me," Jerry continued as we fell in beside him again. "I may be able to pull a few strings when I get there to get you assigned with me."

"Those friggin' things are dangerous!" Del swore indignantly.

"That'd be super, Jerry. They sure are, Del." *This is getting wearisome*, I thought peevishly.

We arrived at the PX to find the place little more than a long room containing a scattering of toilet articles and a limited selection of canned goods. The beer was a humidity-induced, rust-encased foreign type called Ballentines selling for a nickel a can. Jerry and I purchased a six-pack apiece along with a can of mixed nuts as Del followed along buying nothing. We paused at the door to scrape the larger flakes of corrosion off the cans before returning to my unlit tent.

"So, where you from, Jerry?" I asked as I sipped my beer and squinted at his dark outline in the interior, enjoying a welcoming breeze blowing across the camp.

"Minnesota. I'm part Indian," he replied. "I lost my parents when I was three in a traffic accident and was raised by my aunt and uncle."

"Why'd you join the Army?"

"For the veterans' benefits so I can go to college when I get out. Why'd you join?"

"To see the world," I offered lamely. "You know how that goes."

"Why'd *he* come in?" Jerry inquired of Del's dark outline sitting quietly on his bunk.

"What's your story, Del?" I relayed the question.

"I was friggin' drafted," Del replied frigidly.

"Does he have any family?" Jerry asked me.

"Tell him I lost my dad last year, but I still have my mom and a married sister."

"How'd he lose his father?" Jerry asked in the darkness.

"Tell him cancer," Del answered.

"Does his mother live with his sister?" Jerry asked.

"Tell him no," Del instructed. "I send most of my money home to help support her."

"Is that why you didn't buy any beer?" Jerry addressed him directly.

"I gave her all the money I had before I came over," Del acknowledged.

"Damn, why didn't you say something?" Jerry demanded. "Here, have some of mine."

"Have some nuts." I offered the can to his silhouette.

"Thanks, guys." Del opened a beer and shook out a handful of nuts.

"So what are you going to do when you get out?" Jerry asked Del.

"I've got me a job lined up in a factory." Del took a long pull from his beer and I heaved a sigh of relief with the awkward conversation thus ended.

As we drank, the wind grew stronger and soon brought lightning and rumbling thunder as a storm descended upon us like an avalanche. In an instant, torrents of water slammed the canvas overhead as the wind howled and threatened to pull the wildly flapping tent down around our ears. Rivulets of water trickled across the dusty floor growing into streams in the flashing light and forced Del and me to pull our duffel bags onto our cots to save them from being drenched in the lake that became our floor as we sat wide-eyed before nature's might.

"This is the end of the *monsoon* season," Jerry shouted over the roar.

The storm passed as quickly as it came, leaving a light breeze and trickling streams of water gathering into puddles. Jerry dashed for his own tent, skidding through the standing water with mud splattering from his heels, as Del and I drank our last beer in relative solitude and then used our duffel bags for pillows on the coarse canvas cots, thus ending our first day at war.

CHAPTER 3

The latrine, a narrow structure with slat-board sides and a wide plank containing rough heart-shaped holes running the length of one side, with half of a fifty-gallon oil drum positioned underneath to catch the refuse, was not an engaging place. In the early morning hour Del and I settled down to do our business amidst twitching nostrils and occasional swats at the more troublesome flies. Too late, we discovered there was no toilet paper and sat in discomfort discussing our predicament until another trooper wearing silver jump wings entered.

"Hey, Airborne, you better hold up," I cautioned as he unbuckled his trousers. "There's no toilet paper. We're stranded here."

"I brought my own," he advised, digging a roll from his pocket.

"Can you spare any?" I wheedled with as much dignity as I could muster.

"Help yourself," he offered, tossing the roll to me.

Del flashed a winning smile. "Can I borrow some too?"

"A buck for ten sheets, *leg*," the sky trooper grunted without hesitation.

"Are you friggin' *serious*?" Del implored.

The man shrugged. "Use your finger."

"Two back?" I offered, handing Del a dollar.

"Done," he gritted.

The paratrooper peeled off ten squares of his precious hoard and passed them to Del. As we started out the sky-trooper grabbed my arm.

"Hey, Bro, a word to the wise, there ain't never any shit paper in this hole," he advised in a conspiratorial voice, and then winked knowingly. "Got mine from the NCO latrine last night."

"Thanks," I acknowledged.

He held out his fist in the airborne salutation. "You take care, Bro."

"You know it," I replied, bumping my fist to his before exiting.

"*Two* dollars back!" Del bristled as I drew abreast of him.

"I *had* to make it look good," I explained.

"You airborne guys are real friggin' jerks, you know that?"

"We're a *fraternity*!" I retorted. "You dumb assed legs wouldn't understand that!"

At the shower point, we cleansed our grime-encrusted bodies as other troops joined us in the communal bath and afterward migrated to the mess hall for breakfast before hurrying to the morning formation. Jerry linked up with us as we stood in the escalating heat, his mood buoyant as the garbled voice called a hundred mangled names, with each eager trooper running in jubilation to join a second formation behind the stand, one man even executing a hand-standing cartwheel as the rest of us roared in laughter to the sergeant's glowering disapproval.

With our dismissal, a disappointed Jerry grabbed his duffel bag and moved to our tent, where we whiled away the morning as the heat intensified and dried the mud left by the storm into cracked patches of parched earth around us. By noon, we were too miserable to eat, and stood the formation on rubbery legs in the blinding midday sun. We returned to our tent afterwards to collapse in listless heaps as the compound turned into a ghost town with nothing moving but small dust devils and withered away the afternoon in our patches of shade with the empty water bags a haunting reminder of our growing thirst.

At the evening formation, none of us was called and we shuffled to the mess hall where Jerry's depressed mood set the tone for a gloomy meal.

"Hey, guys, give me a minute," I advised as we exited the dining facility. "I'm going to swing by and grab a roll of toilet paper from the NCO latrine."

"The NCO latrine is off limits," Del reminded me.

I stared at the forbidden structure doubtfully. "Yeah, it might be best to wait until everyone's asleep," I speculated, observing the structure from a distance.

"We could strike around dark-thirty before the storm hits," Jerry offered.

"What if you get caught?" Del asked nervously.

I shrugged as we made our way to the PX for beer. "No big deal. Who really cares?"

"No big deal my ass!" Jerry argued. "I bet the NCO latrine's been raided a hundred times and they've got some sort of a security system to protect their toilet paper."

"Well I sure as hell didn't see any sign of a security system," I allowed as Jerry and I bought a six-pack apiece.

"That doesn't mean it ain't there," Jerry insisted as we made our way back to the tent. "We probably need to post a look out. What do you say, Del, you in?"

"Why don't we just ask the cadre for some?" Del wondered tentatively.

"Let's make a pact," Jerry offered as he settled in on his cot next to me and tossed a beer to Del. "If one of us gets caught he doesn't rat out the others. Agreed?"

I shrugged. "Agreed."

Del swallowed. "What would they do to us?"

"Stealing toilet paper from an NCO latrine can't be all that bad," I scoffed.

"Stealing is *stealing,* and being in an off-limits area is *off-limits,*" Jerry argued. "And this being a war zone and all, we could possibly face a court martial and even a firing squad."

I sneered. "Over a roll of *toilet* paper?"

"Hey guys, let's just friggin' forget it, okay?" Del begged from the near darkness.

I was inclined to agree with him until Jerry jumped up righteously. "If you ain't got the balls, Jay and I'll go it alone! Right, Jay?"

That sealed the fate of all three of us *and* stopped conversation as we sat contemplating our impending loss of life and liberty.

Jerry clapped his hands. "I got it! We'll raid the officers' latrine up at the entrance to the compound instead of the NCO one down here. Think about it, *everybody* raids the NCO one, right? But no one in their right mind would raid the officers' latrine way up there, therefore it won't be as closely guarded." Del and I gaped in stunned disbelief as he began pacing. "Another thing, under the maximum punishment theory, we may as well go for the best, right?"

"Best?" I squeaked.

"It stands to reason the officers have a better grade of toilet paper than the NCOs," Jerry explained. "They've probably got the soft-scented stuff instead of the coarse Army-issue junk."

"You're friggin' nuts!" Del exploded. "I won't have any part of it."

"Count me out too!" I exclaimed as I gathered my wits.

"Chicken shits!" Jerry taunted.

"Oh, yeah?" I challenged, springing up. "How would you like *this* chicken shit standing in your *chest*?"

"Hold on, guys!" Del leapt between our tense forms as Jerry braced to meet me.

"*He's* the dude creating a problem," Jerry insisted, fists balled.

"*You're* the one overloading your ass with your *mouth*, Jack," I swore back.

"Come on, guys!" Del urged. "We're friends! You didn't mean it *personal*, right Jerry?"

"Not unless that's the way *he* wants to take it," Jerry blustered.

I locked eyes with him. "Okay, if you didn't *mean* it personal, I won't *take* it personal, as long as we *understand* each other in the future when it comes to shit labels."

Jerry clapped his hands across our shoulders. "Great, let's get down to business then." He plunged ahead as if we had agreed to his insane plan, which in the reestablished harmony we soon, with great reluctance, found we had.

After awaiting full darkness, we crouched in the shadows on the edge of tent city three hundred yards from the unlit officers' quarters. Jerry scooped mud from one of the slime-covered puddles and smeared it on his cheeks and the backs of his hands. Del and I dipped our fingers in the mud and followed his lead. Jerry darted in a zigzag crouch and faded into the shadows beside a bush. I took a deep breath and charged to a bush beyond him. Del slipped by like an ink spot in the night as we leapfrogged our way across the danger zone and fell prone in the deep shadows of one of the unlit hooches on the edge of the forbidden tract.

"I don't see an outhouse," I whispered. "That means the officers have private showers and toilets inside, so let's get the hell out of here."

"That looks like a latrine over there," Jerry whispered, indicating a small building behind the cluster of WAC's quarters off to our left where a single dim light bulb outlined the entrance through the wire with the MP tilted back in his chair reading a rolled up magazine.

"So much for not being guarded," Del whispered. "There's no way we're getting in there."

"We've come too far to turn back without at least making a recon of the area," Jerry insisted as he surveyed the barbed wire enclosed mini compound closely.

"Come on, guys, this is friggin' madness!" Del urged.

"Wait here if you're too scared," Jerry offered as faint voices and the drum of boots approached along the boardwalk.

"*Scatter!*" I urged and rolled into the deep shadow beside the hooch.

Jerry snaked backwards and Del slid under some bushes lining the boardwalk as the two forms drew near, their footsteps loud in the hushed darkness and slurred voices growing distinct in a heated debate about something to do with an iron fist wrapped in a velvet glove. I dared not blink a sweat-laden eyelash as they drew abreast of the bushes Del disappeared into, staggered to a stop, and turned, shoulder to shoulder, over his hidden form. A terrible comprehension swept over me as they fumbled with their crotches and I lowered my head in anguish as twin streams of water splattered against the bushes, the hearty gush seeming to go on forever before the two shadows grunted, shook themselves off, and tromped on down the walkway zipping their pants, still arguing. For a seeming eternity, all was quiet after they passed.

"*Pssst! Del! You okay?*" I finally whispered.

"*Awe, geeze, they peed on me!*" Del wailed from the bushes.

I collapsed in a fit of suppressed hysteria, the effort tearing at my throat as Jerry squirmed over beside me throttling his own mirth.

"It ain't friggin' funny, you bastards!" Del sputtered as he crawled over to us.

"*Sheeeeeee,*" Jerry choked, convulsed in racking spasms of suppressed hilarity.

"*Sheeeee your own friggin' self!*" Del swore. "*Screw you guys, I'm out of here!*"

"You're a hero for not giving us away!" I gasped.

"You can't bail on us now, we need you," Jerry gurgled. "I'll work my way around to the right and you two work your way around to the left."

Del reluctantly followed as I hugged the darker areas while keeping a wary eye on the sleepy guard at the front. Behind the smaller building at the rear, Jerry emitted a low hiss and his dark form emerged from the deep shadows.

"There's only the one guard," he advised. "I didn't see any movement inside. That small building to our front is a latrine, there's no mistaking *that* smell."

"So how do we breach that?" I waved at the six-foot barrier of coiled barbed wire.

"In Basic they taught us to cross barbed wire entanglements with one man throwing his body across and the rest using him for a footpath," Jerry mused.

"Oh, *hell no,* I *ain't* throwing myself across no friggin' barbed wire!" Del insisted.

"I saw some boards on my recon," Jerry soothed. "We'll use those. You move back along the fence and watch the guard while Jay and I go inside. If the guard moves, throw a pebble against the side of the latrine to warn us. Got it?"

"You guys better get a roll for me!"

"Get going." Jerry pushed him off before slipping away in the opposite direction. When he returned, we laid the short board across the top strand of wire and checked Del's form crouched in the shadows halfway around the small perimeter to ensure all was as it should be. As we applied pressure on the board to bring down the wire it creaked and groaned something awful, which I feared the MP and all the Vietcong between Hanoi and us could hear, but Del remained immobile. With Jerry's full weight suspended on the board in a narrow valley of barbed wire three feet off the ground, I checked Del's position for reassurance the guard was still in place, and then worked my way up beside Jerry to the accompaniment of another round of protesting screeches from the strained wire as we clung together for balance.

"It'll be better if only one of us goes inside," Jerry whispered. "You stay and hold the wire in place for a quick getaway."

I lurched to the middle as he dropped to the ground inside the enclosure, the loss of his weight sending the wire springing upward in a loud protest and me flapping my arms for balance like a ruffled jay hawk. Jerry gave a thumbs-up when I regained my poise and settled the wire down, his teeth flashing white through mud-streaked cheeks before he slipped around the corner of the latrine. The door squeaked open and closed softly as he eased inside.

I looked over my shoulder to check Del and picked him out of the shadows closer now and waving both hands over his head. *What the hell, that isn't the signal!* I thought as female voices reached me. I froze as two women picked their way along behind the weak beam of a flashlight playing before them, realizing that balanced on the board behind the latrine I was in no danger of being seen, but in no position to warn Jerry either. I frantically dug a coin from my pocket and hurled it against the side of the latrine, receiving a small thud as my only reward for innovation and nearly falling off the board again amid another round of squeaks from the wire as I flapped my arms.

"What's that?" a female voice exclaimed.

"I don't hear anything," the other replied.

"Why don't they have lights, for heaven's sake?"

"Because this is a war zone, silly."

I held my breath waiting for the inevitable as they entered and the door banged shut behind them. The beam of light played along the slat-boards as each selected a cubicle and settled down amid the individual doors squeaking on rusty hinges. I breathed again realizing Jerry had slid into one of the end stalls as they approached and that we could still get away with this hare-brained scheme. I stood frozen, listening as they carved up someone named Cathy, daring not to move in my cramped position atop the wire to wipe the sweat trickling down my face blinding me.

"Linda, can you pass me some paper?"

"Sure." Scuffling accompanied the beam of light inside. "There's none in here either, Judy. I'll check the next stall."

Visions of Jerry crouching wild-eyed in the last stall clutching rolls of soft scented toilet paper to his chest framing his mud-streaked face flashed before me. Even as I watched the light flicker along the wall to the last cubicle I wasn't prepared for it.

"*Yiiiiaaaeeeee! RUN, Judy, RUN! Ahhh-eeee! V-C-eeeeeeee!*"

I almost suffered a stroke as light flashed through the slats at an astonishing rate accompanied by the slap of feet mingling with the second one's terrified scream.

"*What! Linda, wait for me! Yiiiieeeeee! Help! AAH-HEEEEEEeeeeeeee!*" The door crashed against the side of the building followed by an ear splitting *CROOAMMMM!*

The combination was too much. As I executed a swan dive into the barbed wire, I bleakly realized Del had thrown a large rock onto the tin roof instead of a small pebble against the wood side. I also realized the guard was coming in our direction as Jerry's boot stepped in the middle of my back and his flashing shadow vaulted over me entangled helplessly in the wire. Jerry grabbed an arm and a leg and yanked, ripping my clothing and skin as my body dislodged from the entangling barbed wire. I hit the ground running with his and Del's shadows hot on my heels.

"Halt! *Dung lai!* Halt or I'll shoot!" a voice shouted from our rear followed by a deafening *boom-boom-boom* reverberating across the compound. An instant later, the camp siren wailed in nerve-rippling savagery.

I fairly flew across the open area like an unleashed banshee and sailed into tent city with Jerry and Del's footsteps beating rapidly behind me. I estimate I was doing sixty miles an hour when I hit the tent rope. Bright light exploded in my head as my chest caved in and my feet went straight up into the air before my body slammed flat into the dirt below. I was vaguely aware of the tent rope humming like a guitar string as dust rose above me, and strange animal sounds coming from far away as the stars overhead turned in slow circles in the broken sky. I realized the animal sounds were my throat gurgling for air to fill the empty sacks that were my lungs as someone pulled me to my feet and draped me over a shoulder. The dark world spun in crazy gyrations as the man under me ran amid excited voices and other running men as the camp siren continued to blare. The man dumped my limp body on a cot and a cigarette lighter wavered before my eyes as two mud-streaked faces stared down at me.

"Are you all right, Jay?" Jerry's garbled voice demanded from far away.

"Uagggah," I gurgled.

He pulled me upright and pounded my back until I could breathe again. In the weak light, I took inventory of myself to see what parts were missing, finding my fatigue pants torn half off and my shirt missing all the buttons, as well as having numerous rips and tears. I had cuts on my face, chest, arms, and legs. One ear was mangled and bleeding profusely. My chest ached from a great red whelp, which started at my left shoulder and crossed diagonally down to my right side below the rib cage from the tent rope. My head pounded, my ears rang, my nose bled, and every breath I took was liquid fire.

"You okay?" Jerry knelt beside me as Del held the lighter before my crossed eyes.

"Sure-thing," I gasped, trying to figure out where I hurt the most.

Del raced outside to the water bag and soaked one of his undershirts to wash my wounds as Jerry held the lighter aloft. He then made a compress bandage of the wet shirt and wound it turban-style around my head to staunch the flow of blood from my ear.

"You ... guys ... alright?" I whimpered.

Jerry reached inside his shirt and extracted a roll of toilet paper for my inspection, his crooked grin stretching wider as he pulled three more rolls out. We exploded into laughter as three short bursts of the camp siren signaled the all clear and the troops around us extracted themselves from the slimy mud holes to move grumbling back to their tents.

"I can't believe it," Del gasped. "We raided a women's shit house!"

"You almost got our ass shot off," I wheezed at Jerry.

"You look like a friggin' wildcat got hold of you!" Del shrieked.

"If you could've seen those guys pulling their peckers out," I choked in helpless fits.

"And those broads un-assing that shit house with their panties down around their ankles!" Jerry folded over in racking sobs.

Del opened cans of beer and passed them around as we lay giggling. Soon the storm hit bringing lightning, boiling thunder, and sheets of rain around us. Unable to converse in the fury, we cowered meekly until sleep claimed us, thus ending yet another successful day at war.

CHAPTER 4

I looked worse than I felt the next morning.

At the latrine, Jerry sold the extra roll of toilet paper to another patron who appreciated the finer things in life. After showering and changing into fresh fatigues, I returned to the tent to hide out while they checked to see if they had launched a massive manhunt to find us desperados. They returned with a bacon and egg sandwich, iodine, and Band-Aids.

"What's the scoop?" I asked as I gobbled the food.

"Word is a small team of Vietcong penetrated the compound last night with intentions of bombing the officers' quarters, but an alert MP beat them off," Jerry said as he played doctor on me. "Also, the large battle we heard about was fought by the 25th Infantry Division. Seems an entire company blundered into a trap laid by a North Vietnamese Regiment in a place called the Boi Loi Woods. You're fixed as good as I can do. Let's get to the assembly area."

I imagined myself part of an out-manned, out-gunned outfit fighting savagely to the death on all sides as we converged on the assembly area in an impatient mood, where I received curious stares from every quarter, but asked no questions. Halfway through the assignments they called Jerry's name. Del and I cheered as he ran yelping like an Apache to the back of the podium to slap palms with the other troops there, a part of us going with him.

Del and I returned to our tent as the heat began its daily soar and whiled away the morning trying to estimate the exact minutes we had left in this septic tank, but the mathematics were beyond us. Near midday when the heat had risen to unbearable and we lay wasting away in a mindless limbo, Jerry burst through the tent flaps.

"I'm not leaving until tomorrow morning!" he raged as he kicked a cot over on its side.

"Hey, that's no big deal," I soothed as he stood staring down at his boots. "You can take another day of this shit hole standing on your head, right?"

Jerry strode to the tent flap with glazed eyes. "That's not the problem, Jay!"

"What is the problem?"

"I'm not going to the Screaming Eagles!"

"*What*?" I asked, astonished. "Then where *are* you going?"

He punched the pole supporting our tent. "They're sending me to a *leg* unit!"

I recoiled in revulsion. "It's a *mistake*! Didn't you tell them you're airborne?"

"Of *course* I told them!" he gritted.

"Maybe you and I'll get the same unit now," Del offered. "That'd be great, huh?"

"*Goddamn you!*" Jerry exploded as I leapt up and threw both arms around him in a bear hug. "You asshole! Filthy hairy *leg*! Lemme go!" he raged as we fell over a cot and collapsed onto the ground before I pinned him, gasping from the effort.

Del backed away in mortification. "W-What'd I friggin' do?"

I eased off Jerry and grabbed Del by the arm. "Let's get some air."

I led him to shower point where he brushed the caked grime off me as I washed the blood from my reopened wounds and pinched my ear to stop the bleeding.

"Damn, Jay, what'd I friggin' *do*?" Del begged miserably as I settled down in the shade on some lumber stacked against the back wall of the shower point.

"You didn't really do anything, man," I soothed. "He's not mad at you, he's mad at the whole system. You see, it's all about being *airborne*. We trained for months where nothing but excellence was acceptable. We gave until we had nothing left to give, and then gave more, ever more, until we passed beyond pain into numbness. Being airborne is all about the discipline, dedication, sacrifice, and pride of standing in a platoon where a company started endless months before. We earned the *privilege* to be different. So you see, it's unfair as hell, and he's got to have time to adjust."

"Jay, what would you do if that happened to you?"

I grimaced. "Kill myself."

We lounged in the shade throughout the long afternoon, stood the evening formation in the dizzying heat, made our way to the mess hall afterwards to pick at our food, and then stopped by the PX where I purchased a six-pack of nickel beer with the last of my money. When we returned to the tent, Jerry lay on his cot. I placed two cans of nickel beer on the end of his bunk in the oppressive silence and soon another storm struck as we lay watching its fury until sleep picked us off one by one, finishing our third day at war.

———

Jerry was still uncommunicative the following morning. In the latrine, he gave his roll of toilet paper to a new leg recruit while ignoring the surprised soldier's copious gratitude. We had a tasteless breakfast and moved back to the tent, where Del and I prepared to go to the morning formation as Jerry hoisted his duffel bag to set off for the departure point.

He turned to Del. "I didn't mean anything yesterday, man, you know?"

Del nodded. "Jay explained things to me. I hope the friggin' best for you, you know?"

"You're okay in my book, Del," he said, unpinning his silver jump wings and extending them to him. "You keep these to remember me by. Maybe they'll bring you luck."

Del clutched them in his fist. "Thanks, man!"

Jerry flashed his crooked grin at me. "Thanks for not leaving me behind the wire, Jay."

I shrugged. "Thanks for not leaving me tangled *in* the wire."

"Keep your heads down," he called over his shoulder as he ducked out through the flaps.

"Give them hell!" I called after him.

At the assembly point, my name was the eighteenth called, Del's the twenty-third. I shuffled from one station to another throughout the morning answering questions ranging from my blood type to the legality of my birth in a tiresome, time-consuming ordeal, but to get out of this place I would have suffered through it twice. When I reached the last desk, the clerk snatched forms from the swollen pack, shoved them into my Personnel File, and tossed it at me with rapid-fire instructions to report to table number seven as he reached for the next man's packet. I hurried to table seven and flashed a brilliant grin to the sergeant there—a grin that slowly faded as my heart sank and a growing sense of doom settled over me when I focused on the patch on the man's arm—a scarlet palm leaf with a yellow lightning bolt running through it: Tropic Lightening. 25th Infantry Division. *Legs*.

"Records, please." The sergeant snatched my file as he recited a well-rehearsed monologue. "You are assigned to Headquarters and Headquarters Company, 25th Infantry Division, for further assignment down to a combat unit. You will depart at 0900 hours tomorrow morning from pickup point number seven at the top of the hill. Have all your gear and be in fatigues and soft cap. There will be a roll call in one hour in the assembly area. Be there. Next?"

I stood in shock as the man behind me waited. "B-But I-I'm *airborne*!"

"Move along, Private," the sergeant ordered impatiently.

I turned on wooden legs and stumbled out of the building with ten pounds of lead in my gut. After a couple of steps, my legs refused to move and I stood in a daze trying to fathom what had just happened. I strained to pull my thoughts back to the present as the light grew dim and a row of buttons swam into view eight inches from my nose. My slow-moving mind analyzed the barrel chest framed by bulging muscular black arms with hands placed on narrow hips in a menacing posture. Tilting my head up, I saw rolled-up sleeves covered with yellow hash marks and cold eyes dancing in anger from a huge, age-lined black face with the sun forming a golden halo above gray-streaked curls cropped close to the skull.

"Hey!" he shouted.

"Y-Yes, Sergeant?" My eyes leveled with his chest again as I snapped to attention and focused on the jump wings pinned above his left breast pocket.

"At Ease!" he rumbled. "What yo problem, trooper?"

"N-No problem, Sergeant."

"Thu hell yo say. Yo standin' in thu middle of my road, yo got a problem. I almost run yo dumb ass over."

"Sorry, Sergeant. I-I was j-just thinking—"

"Yo not equipped thu think, boy!" he bellowed. "If yo ain't got no problem, get yo ass off my road fore I gives yo a couple of problems to wear on top of yo head!"

"Yes, Sergeant!" I scurried to the side of the road with a surge of hope as he turned back to his jeep. *He was airborne!* *"Sarge!* They're putting me in a *leg unit!"* I shouted in panic.

He looked over his shoulder as I stood trembling under his fierce gaze, the foolishness of my action beginning to dawn on me.

"Get in thu jeep, boy," he commanded as I considered darting into the maze of tents and disappearing. "I *said* get yo *ass* in this here jeep, trooper!"

I hurried around to the passenger side and hopped in with heart pounding. He grunted in satisfaction and lurched off snapping my head to the rear. We skidded to a stop in front of one of the forbidden hooches with a sign reading NCO MESS.

"Follow me."

He disentangled his hulk from the jeep and crashed through the door as I trailed after him. Without looking back he pointed a thick, dusky brown finger to a nearby table as he clomped to the rear. I slipped into a chair at the appointed table feeling like a cat in a dog kennel as he moved behind the serving counter yelling for the mess sergeant. A fat little man wearing a soiled white undershirt emerged from the rear with a cabbage in one hand, a large butcher knife in the other, and a cigarette dangling from the corner of his mouth to give me an evil look as the big sergeant spoke to him in an unintelligible rumble. With a final withering glare in my direction for defiling the inner sanctum of his domain, the fat man yanked his head to the rear and they moved out of sight. The impulse to run was overpowering, but my legs were too weak to make the effort. The big sergeant returned alone carrying a tray, straddled a chair from the rear, slammed the platter down in the center of the table, and deftly placed a saucer of apple pie and a mug of steaming coffee before each of us before fixing me with a scowl.

"Yo take cow milk or sweetener?"

"N-No, Sergeant," I lied.

"Good! Now spit it out, boy, I ain't got all day," he commanded as he forked a bite of pie in his mouth and lifted his mug.

"T-They're trying to put me in a leg unit, Sarge! I'm *airborne*! I can't go to no damned leg unit! You've got to help me! They can't *do* this to me!" I drew a deep, shuddering breath as he stared wide-eyed at me, his mouth full of pie and coffee mug halfway to his chin. He chewed once and swallowed as he chased the glob with a sip of scalding coffee, the heavy creases in his forehead deepening.

"Well now, boy, yo jus eat yo sweets and drink yo poison while I absorb all this here."

I ate the pie keeping my attention riveted on my plate in misery, and tried to drink the greasy coffee but couldn't manage it without cream and sugar. He finished his pie and wiped his mouth with the back of his hand before leaning forward, elbows on the table, his cup balanced in his fingertips.

"Now, looky here, boy, I done been in this man's Army most thirty years. Been a soldier longer yo been born. Been to thu big war in Europe where we whipped up on 'em Nat'sies under Eisenhower, and made thu little one too, where we beat up on those chinks under MacArthur, yo see. So I been there, boy, and I'm here again. This time we gonna kick slope ass. It all thu same. They done riled thu Uncle, and we gonna teach 'em respect.

"Now, yo aeroborne. That says yo a quality soldier. Up to now, leastways. But yo hafta understand, boy, yo a *soldier* first, yo an *infantryman* second, and yo a *sky-trooper* third. What that means is, a soldier does what he told to do. Don't question why, he jus goes and does it best he can, cause he *is* a soldier.

"Now I be thu first to admit ain't no better infantry in thu world than aeroborne infantry. But don't sell straight-leg infantry short neither, boy. They been kickin' ass long fore us aeroborne types come along. Yo see, it a state of mind—not where yo *at*, but how yo *are*.

"It boil down to this, boy. An infantryman's a fighter. He want to *close with an destroy*. That all he want. He don't care how or where. He just want to get hold of thu enemy any way he can. Don't care whether he jump out of a aeroplane or off thu back of a truck. Once his feet on the ground, he jus wanna close with an destroy. We all the same.

"That what we here for, nothin' more or less. It ain't for glory. It ain't for yoself. It for what MacArthur done said. It for *duty*, *honor*, and *country*. Yo and me, we jus a small part of that. In the long run, we don't even count. We here representin' thu folks back home. We can't forget that for one minute neither, nor let our individual preferences deter it, yo see. Yo think bout it for a while. Yo owe it to yoself an our country." He sat back and sipped his coffee.

I looked into his tired, wrinkled black face framed in gray as a wave of humility swept through me, seeing a hundred battles reflected there, thousands of hard miles, and more pride and determination than I'd ever seen on any monument. "Sarge, I'm going to be the best damned infantryman in that whole damned leg unit," I vowed grimly, looking him in the eye. "I'll show them what an airborne trooper is. I-I'm sorry for sniveling to you like this."

"That's all right, boy. An yo better be good, yo might be workin' for me down there in that damned 25th *straight-leg* Infantry Division." He grinned as I stared up at him. "Yep, I done been signed down there too. Reckon I needed this chat bout as much as yo did."

"I'd soldier for you any day, Sarge!" I swore, offering my hand.

He grinned as he grasped it. "Know yo would, boy, otherwise I'd kick that skinny ass of yo'rn all over this here South East Asia."

I laughed, knowing he would for sure, and winced as his huge paw pulverized my hand.

"Now get on outta here fore I turns that mess-monkey loose on yo. Yo'd never get outta his tater bin."

I hurried out feeling near whole again. He was right, infantry was infantry. All I wanted to do was get on with what I came over here for, to close with and destroy. God, was I ever going to get a rifle?

Del leapt to his feet when I entered the tent. "I answered up for you so they wouldn't know you were missing." He hung his head as I stared at him in wonder. "I'm sorry, Jay, if you want to take a swing at me, it's okay."

"You're going to the 25th too?" I grasped his arms as he nodded miserably. "*Great*, we'll be together!"

He stared at me in astonishment. "B-But, Jay, the 25th's a-a friggin' *leg* unit!"

"Who cares? An infantryman's an infantryman! It doesn't matter if he jumps out of an airplane or off the back of a truck. And even a *leg unit* can't be as bad as *this* hell hole!"

Del was dumb with shock as I danced a jig. In high spirits, I unrolled enough toilet paper to get us through the following morning and struck out for the latrine to participate in a little capitalistic enterprising. In short order, I sold both rolls to grateful troops and from there went to the PX and spent every last nickel on beer and nuts before returning to the tent to throw ourselves a going away party. On schedule, the rain poured and the lightning flashed as we sang every bawdy song we'd learned since Basic and drank ourselves into a proper stupor.

But just before dozing off I experienced one last tinge of regret for my beloved 101st Airborne *Screaming Eagles* as I completed yet another day of war.

I shouldered my bag the next morning thinking a lot had happened in a few short days and that a year seemed a mighty long ways off from this end of it. If the coming months held as much adventure, I wasn't sure I'd survive it. Passing my melancholy mood off as momentary delusion brought on by the heat, I trudged up the hill to the pickup point with Del in tow.

Other troops joined us there and we collapsed into haphazard lines in front of our numbered stakes. A sergeant approached, called our names from a clipboard, and grunted his satisfaction at finding our accountable bodies in the proper location. A column of heavy, open topped trucks lumbered up the hill trailing dust and drew up before us with the floors covered in the by now expected sandbags with a row of benches in the center facing outward behind wood rails running the length of the steel sides. A truck with a canvas cover groaned to a stop behind the column and the sergeant issued us grime-encrusted rifles from the racks inside.

"An infantryman would get court martialed over a piece of crap like this," I swore as I attempted to jack the bolt to the rear. "This damned thing would blow up in my face if I fired it."

"Let's just hope we don't friggin' need them," Del replied as we clambered aboard.

The convoy sergeant heaved an ammo can up to us. "Listen up! I want each man facing out with rifles at the ready. Do not lock and load unless we encounter hostile fire. This convoy will stop for nothing. If a vehicle becomes disabled it will be bypassed. If you are on a disabled vehicle resist if so capable by forming a defensive perimeter around said vehicle until relieved. Don't forget your ammo when you dismount."

"Well, *that* scares the friggin' hell out of me," Del moaned as the sergeant hurried off.

The drivers gunned their diesel engines and belched oily smoke over us as we lurched forward. We obediently poked our useless rifles through the rails in what we hoped was a menacing fashion and kept our eyes as wide as the stifling dust would permit, for better or worse on our way to our new home with the 25th straight-damned-leg Infantry Division.

Our convoy covered the same route that brought us here after passing through the gate with its Vietnamese guards and the small village before angling down the wide road into the outskirts of Saigon. Begging children again swarmed about us in the chaotic traffic, but this time without wire screens to protect us from grenades as we threaded our way through the city. Our tension eased somewhat when we reentered Ton Son Nhut Air Base and joined a much longer line of vehicles containing jeeps with M-60 machine guns, armored personnel carriers sporting .50 caliber machine guns, and trucks filled with troops and mounds of supplies. We sat in the heat as the drivers huddled in groups and kids wandered along the dirt road begging for cigarettes and offering Cokes for sale, which we were reluctant to purchase because rumor had it the Vietcong often put ground glass in them.

Eventually churning smoke and a crescendo of noise announced the departure of our convoy as the long line of vehicles rolled slowly through the gate and down a patched two-lane asphalt highway bordered by rice paddies. Once the last truck cleared the airbase, the pace picked up and we became a rolling train of thunder with two helicopter gunships patrolling our flanks. As briefed, we stopped for nothing. Bicycles, scooters, cars, men, women, and kids all leapt for their lives before our charging mass. That we managed to avoid crushing half of them and the small vehicles we encountered was a direct tribute to their individual agility and panic as they literally drove into the ditches in front of us only to swarm back into the road behind as if a boat had parted water. Power gripped us as we sat high in the air jolted about as we leapt over small bridges and bolted around curves. Old *papa-san* men and *mama-san* women stooping in knee-deep water tending their rice crops ignored our intrusion, but one felt they missed nothing under the shade of their conical straw hats. Often we traversed thick patches of jungle with vines growing next to the pavement amid the oppressive smell of decaying vegetation, which made our mighty armada seem insignificant as the foliage muffled the noise and hid the vehicles to our front and rear. Sensing these were the most probable areas for an attack, we hunkered down behind our thin cover with watchful eyes until we broke out of these eerie tunnels into bright sunshine again temporarily blinded by the glaring sun but empowered anew as we regained sight and sound.

Onward we roared through villages large and small with homes of mud and grass thatch, stucco and cement walls, and some even constructed entirely of flattened American beer and cola cans. In the larger hamlets, half-burned buildings bore bullet marks and larger scars of explosives as proof of their sacrifice to the war. South Vietnamese soldiers sauntered through the streets in sandals, seemingly unconcerned that a war was tearing their country apart. Most used sign language to ask for cigarettes as we passed and offered obscene gestures when we threw none their way. After a grueling two hours, our pace slackened. The two gunships sliced overhead in perfect formation and pulled high in the air at the head of the column before splitting in opposite directions to dive back so low we ducked as the landing gear flashed above our heads. Climbing high into the air at our rear, they floated off in apparent boredom, their escort mission ended, as rows of sandbagged bunkers fronted by long lines of barbed wire appeared.

I looked across at a dust-covered, wide-eyed Del. "Can you believe that?"

He shook his head mutely as we stood to catch a glimpse of the interior of the base camp while paralleling the wire entanglements of the perimeter fence. A mile or more wide and as deep, Dog Patch USA stretched before us consisting of thousands of sagging structures littering a vast clearing. Most had canvas tops, but a few had tin roofs. Low, sandbagged walls surrounded all, with a few command bunkers scattered about completely covered with the dirty brown bags. Black electrical wires sprouting out in all directions draped randomly from any conceivable object offering an advantage in height. Gravel roads divided the encampment into neat squares with dust drifting from slow-moving vehicles in a lazy haze. Laundry of every description was strewn about to dry in a menagerie of positions. Soldiers wandered from one point to another, some shirtless or wearing olive drab undershirts. One group played volleyball as others gathered around smoldering barbecue pits with beers in hand. Booming artillery split the air at regular intervals sending projectiles streaking overhead on swift journeys of destruction to unknown destinations. From the far side of the perimeter a light machine gun chattered in angry bursts, the volleys echoing across the camp, but no one seemed alarmed by its insistent stutter. A string of helicopters lifted out of the compound's midsection to climb swiftly over the far tree line. The image was one of organized confusion, the soldiers oblivious to the happenings around them. I searched in vain for the long lines of grim-faced infantrymen moving into battle, but saw only troops wearing cut-off trousers and sunglasses rubbing suntan lotion on their bronzed skin as they lazed atop the bunkers forming a rough circle around the perimeter of the base camp fronted by the strands of barbed wire.

Inside the gate with its arched top proclaiming *The Tropic Lightning Division,* our convoy split into smaller groups going in different directions. Our truck lurched to a stop in front of a row of wood-and-screen buildings near the middle of the compound. We tossed our bags over the side and dismounted as the sergeant with clipboard in hand approached, called our names from his list, and had us turn in the filthy weapons to another sergeant in one of the nearby buildings. He collected a copy of our orders and waved at a row of tents across the road before wandering off. Del and I found a couple of cots and dumped our bags beside them.

"What now?" he demanded.

I shrugged. "We wait, I guess."

"For what?"

"Who the hell knows?"

We sat through the long afternoon with no one paying us the slightest bit of attention. In late evening, the smell of food revived us from inactivity, a reminder that we hadn't eaten since morning, and we followed our noses to the nearest mess hall to slip into line behind several other soldiers. When no one questioned our right to be there, we filled our trays and found a quiet corner to enjoy the plunder. Afterwards, we returned to our tent and lay in the gathering evening shadows talking to old-timers, which qualified anyone who had been in-country more than four days or in the 25th more than one. We slept at irregular intervals through the night, waking often with hearts pounding when intensive outgoing artillery barrages shook the entire camp without warning. Concluding that a unit was engaged in combat somewhere in the distance, we then dozed again.

The following morning we searched out an empty shower point and stood under the tepid streams to wash the layers of grime from our clammy bodies. After breakfast we sat in boredom waiting for something to happen and listening to other troops discuss the battle that occurred three days earlier between a unit called the Wolfhounds and the North Vietnamese regulars. By early afternoon, we had sunk into the usual stupor from the heat when a long line of helicopters landed beyond the row of hooches behind us. Bored, I decided to investigate, much to Del's annoyance.

We found the choppers strung out down the center of a narrow grassy strip, their idle blades drooping, the crews with their feet propped up in listless fashion. Sprawled troops dressed in ragged, faded jungle fatigues littered the grass on each side of the aircraft forming irregular lines. Everyone seemed to be taking a siesta, with no one inclined to move in the sweltering heat. All wore steel pots with camouflage covers, the cloth fabric covered with black ink depicting every conceivable slogan, the elastic bands holding books of matches, bottles of mosquito repellent, and metal P-38 can openers. Some of the men wore flak vests, all wore web gear. Many had bandoliers of M-60 machine gun ammo crisscrossing their shoulders in golden lines. Weapons of every caliber were visible, all well oiled. The soldiers themselves were lean and tanned with eyes sunk back under their hooded helmets exhibiting a cold, hungry look as they used green towels draped over their shoulders to wipe sweat-drenched faces. A hard, no-nonsense aura surrounded them, their bearing exhibiting a calculated menace to those not of their own kind. We paused near the closest group conscious of a quiet wariness settling over them as they measured us, intruders in their world as yet welcome.

"Hi," Del ventured.

A rangy, unkempt trooper lifted a calloused hand to tip back his helmet where a buzzard feather fluttered from the band below inked lightning bolts. Small festering scratches covered his arms above dirty, broken fingernails as he stared up at us with unblinking, piercing eyes.

"Lo."

"Where you guys from?" I inquired.

"First Hounds," he answered with a note of pride under the otherwise flat statement.

"The Wolfhounds?" I asked.

"No other," he confirmed.

"Heard you guys kicked ass the other day," Del offered ingratiatingly as the veteran looked him over carefully. "Where you headed now?"

"Out," the veteran replied as if that explained everything, a hard edge creeping into his voice as he squinted up at us. "You REMFs?"

Del hesitated, perplexed by the danger signals emitting from the group. "REMFs?"

"Rear-Echelon-Mother-Fuckers." The veteran punctuated the accusation with a derisive stream of spittle that landed within an inch of Del's toe. Not another soul moved or changed expression as a decided rejection swept through them.

I flushed from the contempt directed at us. "We're infantrymen!"

Every pair of eyes looked into mine. My knees wobbled and bumps sprang out on my arms as a chill passed down my spine.

The veteran chuckled without mirth. "You Fucking New Guys then, ain't you?" It was an accusation, but one that sounded forgiving.

"We just got here yesterday," Del admitted.

"Been in-country a week, though," I fudged.

"Yeah, and he's even *airborne*." Del pointed to my chest.

"No shit? So am I." The veteran stood, stooped under his heavy load. "Where they dumping you?"

"We're not sure yet," I answered, taking my first real breath in several minutes as he wiped his face on the end of his towel.

"You guys ask for the Hounds," he suggested. "The rest are okay, but ain't got no real class like us, know what I mean?"

I nodded mutely as if I knew exactly what he meant.

One of the other soldiers staggered to his feet and strolled over squinting through the curling smoke of a cigarette hanging from the corner of his mouth, his rifle dangling by his side, his helmet decorated with *Bewitched* inked above licking flames.

"Hey, Sarge, these are FNG's," the first veteran introduced.

He nodded. "Howdy. Name's Rogers. Where they a sendin' y'all?"

My eyes flickered to his sleeves, as soiled and devoid of markings as the others. "They haven't told us yet, Sergeant," I replied, surprised by his apparent youth.

"Well, y'all ask fur the First Hounds. Our sister company, Ol' Alpha, could use y'all long bout now, cause they went an got their clock cleaned thu other day an gonna be needin' fresh meat." He wiped his face with his towel.

"We heard they fought a whole North Vietnamese Regiment!" Del exclaimed.

"Yeah, found one all right, an chewed it up pretty good, but those suckers have done licked their wounds an are more'n ready fur another scrape by now. We been chasin' 'em ever since," he drawled as if we were discussing a football game. "What part of Texas ya from?"

"East, Sergeant," I answered. "Down around Houston."

"Yeah, thought ya was from that little twang you got there. I'm from Del Rio, myself." He turned to Del. "An ya'd be damned Yankee, I hazard to guess?"

"Yes, Sergeant, I'm from Chicago. Ever been there?"

"Nope, an ain't goin' either," he proclaimed. "What'd y'all hear bout us an those Hard Core Mothers?"

"Just that it was a big battle and that a whole company got massacred," Del replied.

"Yeah," the first veteran cackled. "Old Alpha latched on to them Hard Core Mothers like a bulldog." He paused to wipe his brow. "Then found out they done bit a bear right in the ass. Took us and Charlie Company might near a whole day to get them untangled. Don't know who was the most surprised, the bear or the bulldog. Neither of them dared turn loose." He and the sergeant slapped their knees in laughter as I wondered what could be so funny about a unit shot to pieces in such a valiant effort.

"Y'all ask fur the Hounds now, ya hear?" the sergeant shouted before turning to the growing high-pitched whine of the aircraft. "All-righty now, let's saddle up! Move it!"

The clearing became a boiling mass of active troops stumbling to their feet and shifting loads from their stooped positions as Del and I stepped back from the scrambling confusion.

The chopper blades reached a steady rhythm and the lines of infantry surged forward to enter the aircraft from opposite sides, the lackluster mob of seconds ago now a well-organized operation with every man knowing where to go and what to do when he got there. A moment later the aircraft lifted from the ground on cushions of air, swept forward gathering momentum, and leapt into the clear sky with blades thumping, each in perfect formation with the others. The soldier we had engaged in conversation lifted his hand in salute as they moved out over the perimeter and banked to the left towards the distant horizon in the shimmering heat.

I stood in the empty expanse finding it hard to believe the multitude of men and equipment had really been there. Not a trace remained to show their passage, not a scrap of litter or piece of manmade substance, only trampled grass already springing back into shape to ward off any feeling of delusion. I turned back impressed with the strange men flying off in search of combat, hoping those gaunt warriors would all return safely, preferably with a bearskin trophy.

"You're going to ask for the Hounds, aren't you?" Del accused, mimicking their slang.

"Believe so," I replied, already picturing myself tanned with ammo slung across my body nonchalantly going out to hunt down an NVA regiment.

He sighed. "Me too, then."

After discreet inquiries, we located the orderly room, a half screen sided affair with men in undershirts working at various desks. I knocked and heads lifted.

A man near the front shuffled over to peer down at us through the wire mesh. "Yeah?"

"We want to see the First Sergeant," I announced.

"What d'ya wanna see Top about?" he demanded. "You got a bitch about something?"

"We want to volunteer for the Hounds," Del stated.

"The *First* Wolfhounds," I amended.

He eyed us suspiciously. "Why d'ya wanna go there?"

"Because they're the best," I answered.

"And they've got class," Del added.

The man glanced over his shoulder, grabbed a fatigue shirt with specialists' fourth-class insignia on the sleeves with a nametag reading *Holbrook*, and hastened down to herd us along to the shade of the opposite hooch. "Ya don't wanna see Top, ya wanna see *me*. It sure don't take long for word to get around. Only thing is, that might be pretty hard to do. Everybody's tryin' to get them these days."

My heart sank, making any other unit twice as unacceptable.

He snapped his fingers. "Ya know maybe there *is* a way." My hopes rose, then sank again when he frowned. "Naw, I guess not."

"What?" Del pleaded.

Specialist Holbrook peeped over his shoulder. "Well, I *do* have this guy I know over in assignments ... I'd have to grease his palm a little, ya know. Get him to bump a couple of the others and add ya in, ya see."

"How much?" I asked, remembering Del and I were dead broke.

"About twenty," he suggested.

"We'll pay it," I affirmed as Del gasped.

"Apiece," he countered, watching closely as I sagged in dejection. "Look, thirty total, package deal. But if ya ever let this out to anyone, my shit's weak. Understand?"

"Not a word, right, Del?"

"Uh, right," he confirmed hesitantly.

"Okay, gimme tha dough." Holbrook held out his palm and looked around furtively.

"Uh, look, can you give us a little time?" I pleaded.

He stiffened. "Ya jerks putting me on or something?"

"We haven't been paid yet," I protested.

A gleam crept into his eyes. "Okay, tell ya what, I shouldn't, but I'm gonna trust ya guys anyway. I'll go ahead and make the connections, get the ball rollin', ya know. Ya'll get paid before ya leave here and then ya can pay me. Deal?"

I nodded. "Deal!"

"There's just one thing, though. Gonna cost twenty apiece, working on credit, ya understand. If ya don't deliver, I gotta make it good, ya see."

"Deal!" I confirmed.

"Remember, not a word to anybody or there's gonna be hell to pay. Got that?"

We high-stepped it back to the tent, confident we had just pulled off a coup, and were informed a sergeant had taken our group for processing. We got directions and double-timed a quarter-mile in the heat to arrive covered in sweat. We straightened our uniforms and entered the building to find the sergeant sitting just inside the door tilted back in a chair with an electric fan blowing in his face. "Wondered where you guys were. Start over there."

A PFC in an undershirt took our records and began tapping on a typewriter. Two hours later, paid and processed, we skipped back to the tent area with fresh copies of our orders assigning us to A Company, 1st Battalion, 27th Infantry, clutched in our sweaty palms.

"That Specialist worked a miracle," I said admiringly as we hurried along. "The very first station we passed through was the assignments section." I'd grinned at the clerk when he selected my new unit, but he'd played it cool by looking back at me in wide-eyed innocence, although a little uneasiness did show when I winked at him. He got rid of me fast after that and I figured he must have been afraid I'd give him away.

As we entered the headquarters area, the specialist whistled and motioned for us to join him in the latrine, where he had apparently been awaiting our return. "Well?" he demanded.

"We got the Wolfhounds," I confirmed. "Alpha Company! That's the one that got—"

"Sheeeee, not so loud, ya idiot! Did ya get paid?"

"Right here," I whispered, removing a roll of the military pay currency from my pocket, which the army used in place of greenbacks due to the flourishing black-market and looked like Monopoly money.

"Gimme the dough," the specialist demanded, his eyes locked on the roll.

I peeled off four five-dollar bills of the funny money as Del reluctantly removed two tens from his own wad.

"Look, guys, I hate to mention this," the specialist whined as he licked his lips. "A deal's a deal, and if ya wanna hold me to it, I'll understand, but, well, ya see, it cost a little more than I thought since the time was so short, ya know."

"How much more?" I asked.

He shrugged. "Five more apiece."

"What the hell." I handed over another five as Del handed him another ten and extracted one of the fives from his trembling hands.

"Hey, guys, thanks," he swooned.

"We appreciate what you did for us, especially in such a short time," I reassured him.

He grinned. "Glad to help out, ya know."

"Here, this is for you." I grandly handed over another five dollars as well.

"Sure, have a beer on us for all your trouble," Del mumbled as he handed back the five he had taken as change.

"See you around," I offered as I slapped his back.

We left the poor man standing there speechless with gratitude, hurried back across the road to the tent where a truck waited with the other troops already loaded, grabbed our bags, and scrambled up in the back for the ride to our new unit. As we lurched along, I looked at the other troops expectantly.

"We're assigned to the Wolfhounds," I advised proudly. "Where are you guys going?"

"We're all going there," one of the men advised listlessly.

I looked around and realized everyone grouped around good old stake number seven back at the replacement depot was now part of Alpha Company of the First Wolfhound Battalion.

"*That little bastard!*" I whispered through clenched teeth.

"Oh, but Jay, we're *Hounds* now!" Del chided spitefully.

"Yeah, well *this* damned dog is going to have his day with *that* little asshole!" I grated.

CHAPTER 5

The gravel road we traversed led to the far southern edge of the vast perimeter where perfect rows of trees twenty feet high and spaced ten feet apart with all limbs trimmed near the ground offered a welcoming measure of shaded relief from the open, sun-baked field that housed the majority of the division.

"What are those?" one of our companions asked.

"I think they're rubber trees," another answered.

A column of dust settled over us as the truck lurched to a stop before a stake driven into the ground reading:

A/1/27th Inf.
WOLFHOUNDS

"End of the line," the driver called.

We tossed our duffle bags over the side and dismounted before two rows of long, narrow, decrepit wood-and-screen structures with sagging canvas tops facing each other across a twenty-foot company street. A line of rubber trees ran down the middle with another row bordering the front and rear corners of each building. Boardwalks ran in straight lines on each side flanked by narrow drainage ditches. A waist high sandbag wall enclosed each structure to provide protection from exploding rocket and mortar fragments. Slimy potholes littered the sandy soil with sporadic tufts of grass clinging to less trafficked areas.

"Looks like a shantytown," Del observed.

"Home sweet home," someone echoed sourly.

The first building on our right sported a tin top with a small sign identifying it as the supply room. Behind this, a larger tin-roofed structure housed the mess hall. The first building on the left was also tin topped and had a sign proclaiming it to be the orderly room. Behind this, a smaller structure with bamboo shutters drooping over the screened portion with a small latrine and shower point off to its side denoted the officers' quarters. Farther along, a larger latrine and shower point serviced the rest of the company. To the left, separated by a dirt road and within the brush line, two large bunkers with circular sandbag pits held round-ribbed 81mm mortar tubes marking the fire support center of the heavy weapons platoon. Thick bushes on the edge of the perimeter concealed the bunker line and strands of barbed wire beyond. On the opposite side of the road a similar settlement housed Bravo Company, with an identical group of shacks for Charlie Company just beyond.

"Is this for real?" someone groaned.

A pack of mangy dogs stirred in the shadows under the orderly room and approached us with tails wagging as the driver clattered away abandoning us to our fate.

Seeing no one visible in the lonely stretch of bleak hovels before us, we hesitantly moved into the shade of the rubber trees as one of the dogs began barking, the sound reverberating in the eerie ambiance before the mutt settled down to scratching at his neck with a hind paw.

"Now what?" someone asked.

For lack of a better direction, I slipped through the narrow opening in the sandbag wall up onto the wood steps of the orderly room and cupped my palms to peer through the rusty screen siding. Several desks held typewriters and stacks of paper lying in disarray within the deserted office offering no clue as to where the inhabitants might be.

"*Hello*?" I called. "Anybody on duty in there?"

Bedsprings creaked and bare feet thumped onto the wood floor. A gleaming baldhead pushed through a strand of beads hanging over a doorway revealing hairy shoulders below little pig eyes. "Yo?" the gnome inquired as he glared crossly at me standing on the steps peering through the screen door.

"Sir, we've been assigned here," I explained to the shiny top of its head as it dipped for a hairy paw to scratch at the back of its neck. Beads clacked as the thing entered the room revealing a thick, hairy chest and muscular shoulders above a lower body clad in olive-drab boxer shorts and skinny legs crawling with curls of black hair.

The little fur-ball padded up to me. "I'm the *First Shirt*."

I snapped to attention. "Private John Joseph Sharpe, First Sergeant!"

"You in charge?" he demanded.

"No, First Sergeant," I replied tentatively, thinking he should know privates couldn't be in charge of anything, especially themselves.

"Are now." He rubbed his face and yawned. "Find hooches for this crew. Have them back here in the morning and we'll get you signed in." He padded back through the beads and the bed squeaked in protest as he settled back in again.

I turned to the others. "You heard the man. Find a bunk and come back in the morning."

"What time?" a voice queried from the pack.

"0700 hours," I replied, making my first command decision as a soldier. I shouldered my bag, set out across the company street with Del in tow, and selected the hooch next to the supply room to the rear of the mess hall as one other man followed us inside.

Bunks lined each side of the building, twelve to a row, with a narrow aisle in the center and no other furniture visible. A second screen door was located in the rear. On the outside of the hooch, rough plank shelving ran the length of each side protected from the elements by overhanging canvas and held three footlockers. The cots inside and to the rear of the footlockers had camouflaged bed covering and pillows, the rest were thin barren mattresses. Overhead, two-by-four beams held the drooping canvas roof in place. A single low-wattage light bulb dangled from patched cords on each end of the hooch trailing pieces of string. The plywood flooring sagged in places with various stains showing through the dust and creaked as I walked down the aisle eyeing the rusted wire screen sides. I dropped my bag beside the cot in the back right corner across from one of the three showing signs of use as Del plopped down on the cot next to me, and the other man chose one across from Del next to the occupied bunk in the left corner. I slammed my palm into the coarse fabric of my new bunk and backed away hastily as dust rose in a billowing cloud.

The man who followed us in extended his hand. "Hi, I'm Bernie."

"Jay." I shook his hand, carefully gauging his slim physique, prominent nose, dusky Spanish complexion, fine, jet-black hair parted so perfectly on the left side of his head it looked like a razor cut, and dark eyes, taking special note of his aristocratic manner.

"Del." Del shook and the three of us sank down on our cots, moods as dark as the hooch.

"So where are you guys from?" Bernie asked in the eerie silence of the empty bunks.

"Texas," I replied.

"Chicago," Del answered. "And you?"

"Los Angeles. I was a semi-pro in baseball until I got my draft notice—a shortstop with one of the minor leagues for the Angels."

I sniffed the aroma from the mess hall behind us. "Come on, Del, I'm half starved."

Bernie followed us out the back door to the chow hall. With my mood considerably improved by the best meal since joining the Army, I returned to the hooch with Bernie and Del in tow to find the occupant across from me lying on his bunk clad in baggy new jungle fatigues with his arm draped across his eyes. I eagerly appraised the M-14 rifle hanging by its strap from a large nail over his sleeping form as I sank down on my cot half-listening to Del and Bernie earnestly bemoaning their bad luck in drawing low numbers in the draft system.

"Hey, I'm trying to sleep, for Christ's sake," the man growled from his dark corner.

I leapt up to stare at his hidden face. "Jerry?" When his arm lifted, I charged over with Del hot on my heels. "*Jerry!*"

He sprang up with a wide grin and we pounded each other in jubilation. "I guess it only makes sense you guys would get assigned here as replacements too!"

"Hell, we *bought* our way in," Del replied, much to my discomfort, and proceeded to deliver a less than eloquent rehash of the event via the evil clerk in the headquarters section.

Jerry howled with laughter. "You guys are the biggest chumps I've ever known!"

I grinned weakly. "Finding you here almost makes it worth the price."

"Well, you bought yourself into one bad-assed outfit, for damned sure," Jerry appraised.

Bernie looked around the emptiness. "What outfit—they all got massacred, didn't they?"

"This unit slugged it out with a force ten times their size, which makes them a mighty fine outfit in my book, *Pedro!*" Jerry bristled.

"My understanding is the rest of the battalion had to rescue them," Bernie countered.

Jerry's face darkened. "What are you, a *wiseass*?"

Bernie shrugged. "I'm just pointing out that it appears they got their ass kicked."

"Some are on R&R," Jerry allowed defensively.

"You mean the few who aren't in the morgue or hospital?" Bernie quipped.

"It was the biggest battle of the war—you got a *problem* with that?" Jerry demanded.

"And we're just cannon-fodder replacements," Bernie replied.

Del sighed. "Hey, guys, how we got here doesn't much matter now, does it?"

I cast a warning glance at Bernie. "So what the hell have you been up to?"

Jerry's glower softened. "They issued my gear the day I got here and placed me on the bunker line. I just got relieved and was too tired to eat before hitting the sack. I'm sure glad you guys are here to take up some of the slack."

The three of us talked until midnight while Bernie lay silently on his bunk, wherein having no bedding, Del and I removed only our boots before slipping into dreamland.

———

After breakfast, we reported to the orderly room as instructed, where we found three clerks sitting at their desks. Processing consisted of the usual personnel forms, but an unexpected promotion to Private First Class awaited us at the end.

"PFC in six months," Del exclaimed. "That's twenty more bucks a month!"

"General Westmoreland's policy," the clerk explained. "All privates arriving in the war zone are automatically promoted."

The first sergeant, *Top* now that we were PFCs, directed us to the supply room to draw our combat issue. There, a lean, mean sergeant about sixty years old lined us up, eyed us critically to determine if we were small, medium, or large, and threw jungle fatigues and boots in our direction. We deposited these items in the hooch before returning for our bedding, web gear, and foot-lockers. Returning a third time, he directed us to the company armory, where racks of rifles wrapped around us in cold reserve in a dark room awaiting our bidding.

Bernie chose one with distaste. Del picked one at random. I walked around hefting first one and then another searching for the right balance. In a far corner, I found one unlike any other and carefully appraised its blond stock, distinctively different from the subdued brown and red hues of the others. I snapped it to my shoulder and sighted down its blue steel barrel as the peep sight sprang into view glowing darkly around the thin blade of the front sight, and then jacked the bolt to the rear relishing the businesslike mechanical action. I squeezed the trigger and received a comforting clack from the firing mechanism, enjoying the feel of readiness it gave off, sensing it to be an instrument of death with no desire to shy from its mission and seemingly impatient with its dependence on a mere human to give it vitality.

Jerry clutched the weapon as soon as I entered the hooch. "Man, where'd you find this?"

I grinned. "It was just sitting there waiting for me."

"Give you five bucks and my own in exchange," he begged.

"Not a chance."

I cleaned my rifle with care before hanging it on the nail over my bunk and then joined the others in exchanging my heavy fatigues and leather boots for jungle fatigues and canvas jungle boots to provide a degree of comfort in the heat, which also help removed the stigma of *FNG*. We next stenciled our own personalized graffiti on the fabric of our helmets with permanent black ink. I sketched a ferocious wolf's head on each side facing forward with jaws dripping saliva. Jerry placed an Indian lance with feathers prominent near the spearhead on his. Bernie inked a circle with two dots for eyes and an up-curving smiling face. Del penciled in a dove in flight with distorted claws clutching an olive branch.

"At least we're beginning to look like veterans," Jerry said, admiring our handiwork.

"All we need now is a few Cong for seasoning," I agreed.

When we returned from the noon meal two soldiers dressed in khakis were unpacking at the opposite end of the hooch. "Barney, frum Ohio," the tall, skinny one announced and nodded at the black man. "That there's Johnson, frum Detroit. He don't have much tu say tu white boys."

I judged Barney to be a typical farm boy, down to his sandy hair, freckled face, and tobacco stained buckteeth, as he eyed me speculatively, holding his head slightly askew due to a noticeable eye misalignment. The tall black man with a well-developed torso gave me pause with his direct, unblinking stare. I noted a Purple Heart and Bronze Star in his double row of ribbons below the Combat Infantry Badge and figured him the type who, when he chose, acted decisively and with more violence than most foolish enough to be on the receiving end cared to experience.

"We just got here," I answered.

"We'uns jus gettin' back frum R an R," Barney replied. "Deployed frum Hawaii bout six months back."

"Are there others?" Del indicated the empty cots.

"A few, courtesy of thuh dad-dam' 9th." He spat a stream of brown liquid into a can beside him. "Thuh gooks call 'em thuh *Ghost Regiment*."

"Why do they call them that?" Del asked, wide-eyed.

"Cause they disappear after they strike," Barney replied. "They were thuh furst tu invade thuh South after they defeated thuh French. Thuh ARVNs are scared tu death of 'em."

"ARVNs?" Del questioned.

"Army of thuh Reublic of Viet-num," Barney explained. "Our so called allies."

"Why are the ARVNs so afraid of them?" Del asked.

"Cause ever time thuh ARVNs find 'em, they get thuh shit kicked outta 'em."

"We'll change that," I blustered.

Barney cast a skewed glance in my direction. "Reckon you'll get a chance at 'em soon enough, since you're standing right in thuh middle of their AO."

"That does it, I'm friggin' going home!" Del kidded with a nervous chuckle.

Another old-timer stopped by to talk to Barney and we subtly eavesdropped to learn our new commander was at battalion headquarters, and even got a brief glimpse of the man minutes later when a jeep deposited him on the gravel road and he entered the orderly room.

"Looks hard as nails," I speculated as we peered at a captain of average height with thinning black hair and somber eyes.

"The ideal commander," Bernie added dryly.

"What do you think?" Del deferred to Barney.

Barney shrugged. "Won't know till we'uns see 'em operate in thuh bush."

At the evening meal, the entire mess paused when Top stood and yelled "At Ease!"

In total silence, our new commander walked to the rear and seated himself at the officers' table. He motioned Top to join him after nodding a greeting to the sparsely occupied NCO table and turned to survey us as we quickly became preoccupied with our trays. I watched covertly as the mess sergeant placed a tray before the commander and a cup of coffee before Top, since NCOs did not eat at the officers' table, of course. When I carried my tray to the KP window, I could feel the commander's eyes following me calculating my net worth.

"It's custom tu throw a party when you get promoted," Barney informed us as we exited the dining facility.

"I'm game," Jerry agreed.

"Then let's start at thuh Wolf's Den," Barney suggested as he and Johnson turned to lead the way.

We fell in behind them in a gaggle to find the Wolf's Den was actually the Battalion NCO Club, a medium-size, one-room structure a block away with a window on the side to serve us enlisted types. Wood benches spaced under the trees afforded us seating amid garbled country and western music seeping out from a record player within as we sat under the trees for a couple of hours swatting mosquitoes and drinking beer, the four of us doing the buying and Johnson and Barney doing most of the drinking.

When the mosquitoes became unbearable, Barney stood and stretched. "Bout time tu move thuh party in doors."

"Wher' to?" Del slurred.

"To thuh Dragon's Den, whur else?"

Though woozy, I felt obligated as one of the hosts and stood unsteadily. "I'm in."

"I think I've had enough for one night," Bernie appraised.

"You don't wanna seem ungrateful tu General Westmoreland, do you?" Barney challenged.

Jerry burped. "Yeah, Bernie, thiz iz for ol' Westy himself."

"Come *on*, Bernie," Del insisted, swaying to his feet. "Don't be a spoil-sport."

Bernie reluctantly joined us as we purchased beers to tide us over and struck out for the far side of the compound following the quiet Johnson and garrulous Barney.

"What's the Dragon's Den?" Bernie asked as we scuffled along.

"Thuh club over in thuh 14th Infantry's area," Barney replied as he drained his can.

"Are we allowed in there?" Bernie asked, passing his untouched beer to Johnson when he crushed his empty can in his fist and tossed it into a drainage ditch.

"Who's askin 'em?" Barney demanded. "Golden Dragons 'er nuthin but a buncha gurl scouts! Back in Hawaii we beat their ass in everythin' frum softball tu mountain climbin!"

Although I gathered there wasn't much love between the two units, they did have a great club, an enclosed high-ceiling affair with tables, chairs, and a jukebox. Even more impressive, they served their beer in big frosty mugs instead of rusty cans like our own.

"These guys got class," I observed, having a wee bit of trouble getting my words out.

Barney slurped his beer and sneered. "Bunch of pussies. Ought tu burn thuh place down for poor ol Kolchek."

Del wiped at his chin. "Whooose Cold-seck?"

"Our dawg, thass who," stammered Barney.

"Where is your dog?" Bernie asked.

"He's not *my* dawg, he's *all* our's dawg," Barney fumed over the rim of his mug as rivulets of beer trickled down his chin.

Del tried to focus his corkscrewed eyes. "Whoose dog?"

Barney wiped his chin with the back of his hand, slammed his empty mug down, and picked up one of the spares before us. "*Us*! Thuh Wufhounds! He's our mascot back n' Hawaii!"

"We've got a dog for a mascot in Hawaii?" Bernie asked.

"Yep, an albino wufhound, frum Russia, by gawd," Barney affirmed. "Cost fourteen hunnerd dollars. An they painted 'em gold."

Del gaped. "Whoooose gold?"

"Kolchek, thass who. Oughta' burn thuh place down," Barney complained.

"We, the Wolfhounds, have a fourteen-hundred-dollar Russian albino wolfhound back in Hawaii?" Bernie asked.

"Pain'ed gold," acknowledged Barney. "Wiff his hair fallin' out."

"Whass he talking bout?" asked Jerry, returning from the latrine.

"Our gold dog," answered Del, swaying in his chair.

Jerry grabbed a mug of beer from the table. "I got a shepherd back home," he appraised, growing misty-eyed.

"Duz he have 'air?" quizzed Del as Johnson stiff-armed him back into his chair to keep him from collapsing across the table.

Jerry glared. "'Course he's got hair!"

"Cold-seck don't," mourned Del.

Jerry burped, eyes watering. "Why not?"

"Cause they pain'ed 'em gold!" an exasperated Barney explained.

"An' it made his 'air fall out," added a sorrowful Del, shaking his head.

Jerry's eyes widened in horror. "Who'd do dat?"

"Golden Dragons, thass who," chimed Del, elbows propped on the table, hands supporting his head. "Ought ta burn the place down."

"Apparently our battalion has a Russian albino wolf-hound as a mascot back in Hawaii, which the Golden Dragons painted gold and caused his hair to fall out," Bernie explained.

"Well, that pizzes me off," Jerry fumed.

"Name's Kolchek, an he cost for-teen hunnerd dollars," added Barney.

Jerry drained his mug and wiped his chin. "Why'd day do dat for?"

"Cause they don' like us, thass why," scoffed Del.

"Thuh little pussies," Barney agreed.

Jerry thumped his empty mug down. "Tha's no reason to 'urt our dog!" He grabbed a fresh mug and staggered over to the table next to us. "Hey, why ya wanna 'urt o'r dog for?" he demanded, leaning on the table to keep from falling over.

The four men sitting there looked up in surprise. "What dog?" one asked in puzzlement.

"You kno' wha' dog, *Colsex*!" Jerry argued as Del lurched up swaying behind him.

"Man, we've never even seen your dog," another answered hotly.

"Yu painted 'em gold an made 'is 'air fall ote," Del jeered.

"You're full of shit!" the first man insisted. "We ain't painted nobody's dog gold. You've got the wrong man, pal."

"Hey, you guys talking about that white mutt back in Hawaii?" a soldier from the next table offered. "I remember that!"

"Well, I was never *in* Hawaii," the man from the first table called back. "I just got here two months ago."

"Yeah, that mutt peed on our dragon and some of the guys sneaked over and spray painted him gold in revenge," another troop from the second table chuckled.

"Peed on our dragon?" the man from the first table quizzed.

"Yeah, back in Hawaii, we had this big statue of a dragon in front of our battalion headquarters, see. One day these guys from the Wolfhounds were walking their mutt and he ups and hikes his leg and pees on our dragon, pretty as you please. There was a hell of a stink about it!" The man from the second table shook his head ruefully and laughed as Jerry lurched around the first table to his table.

"Ain't no mutt!" Jerry exclaimed.

Bernie grabbed my arm. "Come on, Jay, let's get him out of here before he starts something."

I drained my mug and rose unsteadily to follow him.

"Hey, man, we ain't looking for trouble now, okay?" the trooper at the second table hedged. "You guys ain't supposed to be in here anyway. This is the 14th's area."

"Sa' 'e ain't no mutt!" Jerry demanded.

"Now look, buddy," the trooper answered, rising to his feet as his face reddened.

Jerry straight-armed him back down into his chair and staggered, spilling his mug of beer down the front of the man's shirt. The man next to him stood and uncorked a punch to Jerry's head.

"*Hold it!*" Bernie shouted as he closed in on the second table and collided with Jerry staggering back from the blow. A soldier from a side table lurched up and punched Bernie in the mouth, snapping his head back. Jerry swung his mug at the man who struck Bernie, missed, and hit the one across the table from him, bowling him over backward.

"No, Jerry! Don't—*agghhhh*," I gurgled as someone jumped on my back and locked an arm around my throat. Another punched Del, who staggered back into me and sprawled across yet another table, sending glasses flying. Through the flurry, I saw Barney and Johnson back-to-back throwing punches as I tried to stomp the instep of the man who had me from the rear and another punched at my head. I collapsed onto the floor pulling the two down on top of me as they hit each other in their eagerness to get at me. In the confusion, I wriggled out from under their squirming bodies and crawled under a table as Bernie landed on top of another in a shower of splintered glass and wood. I staggered to my feet and started throwing punches at a blur of men around me as I tried to maneuver over to the last place I had seen Jerry. Del crawled by kicking a foot back at someone hanging on to his other leg. I kicked the man in the ribs, and Del scurried off, as Barney smashed a beer mug against someone's skull, sending shards of glass flying. I saw Johnson backed against a wall swinging a splintered table leg wildly at men encircling him. I staggered over to a throng of squirming bodies on the floor and kicked them aside to find Jerry curled into a ball on the bottom of the pile with his hands clasped protectively around his head. He crawled off under a broken table as someone tackled me and I went down again with the assailant on top of me.

Thunk. "*OOOhhh!*"

Crunch. "*Oohhhh!*"

Through the thrashing arms and legs, Johnson appeared above me amid the meaty thump of the table leg making contact with flesh. I scrambled under the table Jerry had disappeared under, and when I came out on the other side someone kicked me in the face as another jumped on my back and hammered the back of my head. The body left me on the fly as splinters from Johnson's table leg filled the air. Gasping for breath, I wiped my face on my sleeve to remove sticky stuff and restore my vision to a blur. Johnson grabbed my arm and tried to pull me to the door as whistles blew and men scrambled for the exits.

"Where's Jerry?" I demanded as I shook my head to clear my senses.

Johnson yelled something I couldn't understand with the buzz in my ears and tugged at my arm. I jerked free and turned to a pile of groaning bodies as a mob of MPs burst through the door. I saw Del on the floor holding his nose as blood dripped through his cupped hands and Bernie stretched out near him among other men lying in various positions of agony. Jerry was nowhere to be seen, nor Barney or Johnson.

"Move it! Get over there!" An MP shoved me against the wall and used his boot to kick my feet apart in a spread-eagle stance amongst a wobbly group of dazed men. Another MP shoved Del into line further down, who was still holding his dripping nose with a blood-covered hand. MPs moved along the line frisking each of us before slamming us against the wall. An MP placed a table at the front of our pitiful line and seated himself. Keeping our left shoulders pressed against the wall as other club-wielding MPs patrolled beside us, we shuffled to the table one at a time. Two ambulances pulled up to the door and medics moved amongst us and placed several men on stretchers as others limped along behind them in various stages of pain. A medic took Del out of the line behind me and helped him to one of the ambulances after an MP took his information.

I eventually worked my way to the MP at the table, who took my ID card, wrote my name, rank, and unit on his pad, and then directed me to a table across the room. I figured that wasn't good because all the others had been released to one or another of the many sergeants now standing around the wrecked room. Bernie soon joined me, but the MP standing behind us wouldn't let us talk so we sat in numb silence as the others staggered before the MP at the makeshift desk. A captain joined the room full of mean looking sergeants and walked through the shambles in a menacing mood. When he turned to glare at Bernie and me, we lowered our heads and stared at the floor in earnest. A colonel came in and the captain walked him around the room gesturing and talking in low tones.

Fifteen minutes later Top strode into the room followed by a half-pint sergeant first class. The two paused to stare at the wreckage while shaking their heads in wonder, and then Top went to the MP seated at his table as the little sergeant stalked over to us. I noticed his nametag read *Black* as I rose unsteadily to attention before him and estimated he stood about five-feet-five with his boots on and weighed roughly a hundred pounds with a damp towel wrapped around his bony waist. He snatched a fat cigar from his thin lips below his pencil-thin mustache and jabbed the soggy end at us, his piercing eyes pinning us as readily as a snake.

"You shits belong to me now!" he hissed. "And I'm anticipating a great deal of pleasure in turning your sorry asses into soldiers!"

We stood quivering fearfully before the evil little sergeant as Top signed papers and took copies from the MP before hurrying over. "Let's go, boys," he ordered and turned to the door.

"You heard the man!" Sergeant First Class Black growled. "You shits move your asses!"

We scurried out before the little runt as fast as our battered bodies could move, climbed into the back of Top's jeep, and lurched off.

"What these little shits need is a double dose of discipline to set an example for the rest of the unit," Black allowed, sending spasms of fear through us.

Back at the battalion area, Top dropped us off at the battalion aid station and ordered us to report to him at 0700 hours the following morning. We were inspected by the medics, our cuts and bruises treated, and then released back to the unit.

"Jay! Bernie!" Jerry exclaimed as we limped into the hooch. "What happened to you guys?"

"After *you* ran out on us, the MPs grabbed us," I replied.

"Nobody ran out on you!" Jerry protested. "Where's Del?"

"Could have fooled the hell out of me," I snarled.

"We tried tu get you tu come with us fore thuh MPs busted thuh joint," Barney advised.

"I was busy looking for *him*." I indicated Jerry. "*I* don't *leave* my pals behind."

"We had tu drag 'em away," Barney insisted.

"I'm sorry, Jay," Jerry mumbled, hanging his head.

"*You* start the shit and *I* get arrested!" I grated.

Sometime later Del limped through the door looking like a lopsided walrus with swabs of bloodied cotton sticking out of each nostril below his swollen slits for eyes and broken nose. We grimly settled down to ponder the likely consequences we would face in the morning when we met with Top, with none of the possibilities encouraging.

CHAPTER 6

At 0700 hours Bernie, Del, and I reported to the orderly room, where the diminutive Sergeant First Class Black greeted us with a dark scowl. "Top's in with the Old Man! You shits wait outside till he's ready to deal with you!"

After that cheerful salutation, we lounged under the shade of the rubber trees in front of the orderly room. When Top came out of the commander's office some-time later we snapped to attention as he paused to stare at us sorrowfully through the screen siding before turn-ing in resignation to his desk without a word. Sometime later, the commander strolled out to converse with Top and the three of us again snapped to attention outside, but he turned back to his office without even glancing in our direction, which we figured was not a particu-larly good sign. At 1000 hours, Top finally motioned us inside. With heavy hearts, we filed in, where he led us to the rear and paused to knock on the doorframe lined with beads.

"Come in," the commander's firm, well-modulated voice directed from within.

Top stepped aside and motioned us forward, which sent a jolt of anxiety through me since that put me in the lead. We shuffled in, executed a right face, and at Top's encouraging nod raised our arms and saluted with trembling hands, our voices merging in a chorus as we formally reported to the commander. The Old Man snapped a brisk salute back and bent his head to the papers lying before him on his otherwise clean desk. With my eyes fixed rigidly to the wall over his head I could vaguely discern his head rise to stare at each of us in turn. A full minute passed before his soft voice startled us in the strangling silence.

"This is a hearing under Article 15 of the Uniform Code of Military Justice. You each have the right to request a trial by court martial in lieu of these proceedings. Do you wish to exercise that right?"

My head spun. *Court martial? Dishonorable Discharge? Maybe even jail—or shot with this being a war zone?*

"Do you understand the question?" he asked.

He was talking to me, I realized in near panic.

"Do you want the Commander to conduct this hearing or do you want a court martial?" Top prompted.

My vision blurred. I sure didn't want a court martial, but I wasn't sure about this hearing thing either. If he'd just let us explain maybe we wouldn't have to do either.

"Which is it?" the commander prodded.

At least the hearing thing didn't sound as bad as a court martial. Maybe they didn't shoot people in hearings. "No, Sir," I mumbled.

"No what, Private Sharpe?" the commander inquired. "You don't want me to conduct a hearing or you don't want to request a court martial?"

"No, Sir, I don't want a court martial," I answered, sure I was going to faint.

He looked at Del. "And you, Private Delarosa?"

"No, Sir, me either," Del whispered in a subdued voice as he held his head at an angle to see through the slit in his one half-open eyelid, the stance almost comical as his purple eyes bulged over the blood-dried swabs of cotton protruding from his nostrils.

"Sir, I do not request a court martial," Bernie stated firmly when the commander shifted his gaze to him.

The commander lowered his head and began reading from what he referred to as the charge sheet. I occupied myself with slowing my pounding heart and trying to follow all the bewildering legal jargon, but I did understand the parts about us being in a restricted area and causing a disturbance, though all the *willful assaults* and *willful destructions of government property* were somewhat confusing.

"What do you have to say in defense of these charges?" the commander asked when he finished, again looking at me.

I swallowed. What was I supposed to say? "They started it."

"*Sir,*" Top admonished.

"*Sir!*" I amended.

"That's not the question," the commander stated. "Did you willingly go into an off-limits area? Did you willingly engage in the destruction of government property in said off-limits establishment? Did you willingly induce physical harm to a number of occupants within said off-limits establishment?"

I stood trying to decipher the meaning of all this, searching for a way to explain that I hadn't really *wanted* to do any of those things.

"Answer the Commander," Top instructed.

"N-No, Sir," I stammered.

The commander stared at me. "You did not do *any* of these things?"

"N-Not *willingly*, Sir," I choked out.

"I see." The Old Man turned to Del. "And you?"

Del drew himself up righteously. "No, Sir, me either. Not willingly, Sir."

The commander looked at Bernie. "And you?"

"Sir, I did go there," Bernie answered in a level voice. "I was involved in a fight. But I did not do it willingly, Sir."

"I see." The commander looked at Del. "Would you care to explain the event?"

"Sir?" Del asked.

"Tell the Commander what happened," Top encouraged.

"Oh, well, Sir ..." Del paused, thinking hard. "Well, Sir, you see, they painted our dog gold and that made his hair fall out."

"They?" the commander prompted.

"The Golden Dragons, Sir," I offered, somewhat relieved we could at last clear up this whole silly little misunderstanding.

"So you went looking for these men who painted your dog gold?" the commander asked.

"No, Sir, we didn't know about it until we got there," Del corrected.

"They had your dog there?" the commander tried again.

"Oh no, Sir, he's still in Hawaii," Del responded.

"Hawaii?"

"If I may, Sir?" Top interrupted. "An incident occurred prior to the Division's deployment that resulted in our battalion mascot being spray-painted gold. It was generally believed that soldiers from the 14th Infantry were involved in the incident."

"I see." The commander frowned. "And you identified the men who committed this act?"

"No, Sir," Del explained patiently. "We were just talking about it when everybody started swinging."

The commander sat back in his chair. "Did you know these individuals when you were in Hawaii, or have reason to suspect their involvement in the act?"

"No, Sir, we weren't in Hawaii," Del replied. "We only got here two days ago."

"You were assigned to this unit two days ago?" The commander stared at us uneasily before turning to Top. "When did this event in Hawaii take place?"

"Oooohh, let's see, we've been here since ..." Top studied the ceiling for a minute. "About a year ago, Sir."

The commander leaned forward in his chair. "Let me see if I've got this right," he appraised, his voice taking on a decided chill. "A *year* or more ago while stationed in Hawaii, this battalion's mascot was spray-painted gold by a person or persons unknown. Two *days* ago, you three were assigned to this unit. Last *night* the three of you engaged in a brawl with elements of the *entire* 14th Infantry Battalion because of that incident. Have I missed anything in my summation?" His gaze locked on me again.

Due to his tone, I felt compelled to strengthen our case a little. "Well, Sir, they also called him a mutt."

"Why would they call him a mutt?" the commander asked, his interest beginning to wane.

Del charged to my rescue. "Cause he peed on their dragon, Sir."

The commander's face darkened. "Because he *peed* on their *dragon*?"

Top cleared his throat. "Uh, if I may, Sir, you see—"

The commander waved his hand dismissively. "It's not important, First Sergeant. Now, let's see, someone called our dog a mutt, so you three took offense at this apparent slur and struck the individual, right?"

"No, Sir, they struck us first," I corrected.

The commander gazed serenely at his clasped hands on the desk. "I see. After calling our dog a mutt, one or more of the individuals then struck one or more of you. Was there any provocation for this action?"

"*Provo—?*" Del wrestled with the word.

"Reason. Any *reason* for one of them to strike one of you?" Top prompted.

"Oh no, Sir, none at all—just a little beer was spilt on him," Del assured him.

The Old Man grimaced noticeably. "I see. A little beer. How much beer?"

"Only one mug full," Del answered.

The commander wiped his face in a long, vertical pull, blinked his eyes several times, and cleared his throat as we waited patiently. "Who else from this unit was involved in this incident?" A heavy silence ensued as he focused on me. "Private Sharpe?"

"Um, I-I, it was m-mostly just us, Sir," I choked on the lie.

"Private Delarosa?"

"M-Mostly j-just us, Sir," Del whispered.

He looked at Bernie. "And you?"

Bernie hung his head in shame. "Mostly just us, Sir."

"I see," the commander deadpanned. "So you would have me believe the three of you jumped on the whole 14th Infantry Battalion all by yourselves? I find that a somewhat bold and implausible deed."

"B-But we're *Wolfhounds*, Sir," I explained desperately.

"Yes, Sir, and anyway, they're just a bunch of pussies," Del chimed in as Top flinched.

The commander took a deep breath and expelled. "I find you *guilty* of charges one, two, and three. Do you wish to present any mitigating circumstances as to why I should not impose the maximum punishment on you?"

"W-Well, uh, a-at least we didn't b-burn the place down ..." Del pleaded.

The commander lowered his head and groaned. "First Sergeant, before I pronounce punishment, I would like a word with you."

Top hastened us out of the commander's office into the clerk area and returned alone through the clacking beads as I wondered miserably what had gone wrong, and more importantly, what was going to happen next? Muted voices drifted out as we and the clerks leaned towards the beaded door to decipher their words.

"... classmate of mine ... think I command a rabble!"

"... just high spirited, Sir ... count on me to ... yes, Sir ... no, Sir ... absolutely, Sir!"

"... here again I'll ... be sorry they ever ... this time, but ... counting on you!"

With the parting of the beads, we all jumped and the clerks got busy again.

"Report to the Commander," Top directed with a grim face.

We limped back in and executed a right face as smartly as our sore bodies could manage. With pounding heart, I listened to the rapid speech of the commander, the words flying at me: "reduced to private—fifteen days restriction and extra duty—forfeiture of one-third pay for a period of two months—suspended pending future demonstrated performance." Top motioned for us to salute and herded us back out, this time marching us all the way through the orderly room and out to the shade of the rubber trees.

Del tilted back his battered head. "W-What happened?"

Top sighed. "All three of you are busted back down to private. You are restricted to the company area for fifteen days and will perform extra duty during that period. One-third of your pay is suspended for two months. That means you won't actually lose it, providing you don't screw up again. All in all, it could have been a lot worse. I don't have to tell you I've got my ass out on a limb for you knuckleheads. Don't make me regret it."

"What does extra duty mean?" Bernie asked.

"You will work your normal duty day and then report to Sergeant Black for an additional four hours each day to perform tasks assigned."

My heart sank with the vision of a scowling Black looming over us, whip in hand.

When we trudged back to the hooch Jerry, Barney, and Johnson required us to repeat every word uttered during the hearing. To their way of thinking, we had gotten off light, but then they hadn't met Sergeant First Class Black. Personally, I hated the bust back to private the most. Though I had been a PFC for less than a day, the idea of being a dirt-ball private again was excruciatingly painful.

———

The following fifteen days were pure hell. We reported at the end of each day to Sergeant First Class Black for our dose of humility and soon unanimously elected him "Supreme Asshole of the World." A creature more deserving of that title never crawled from beneath a rock. For those fifteen days we repaired broken boards on the walkways, raked leaves, cut brush, painted anything that didn't move, and worst of all, pulled duty on the fire brigade, which consisted of dragging the half-barrels of human refuse out of the latrines and burning them in a mixture of diesel fuel. Each barrel required

an hour to burn as we held our breath to avoid the paralyzing stench and stirred the contents with a long metal
rod. Then we took buckets of soapy water and scrubbed
the inside of the latrine.

Throughout this period, Black never cut us one
ounce of slack. Each day he assigned specific duties and
a given time he judged adequate to complete them. We
were then on our own until the tasks were finished, at
which time he would reappear to inspect our work. The
first few days we did everything twice before he considered the job acceptable to his standards. The first day we
began at 1800 hours and finished at 0230 hours, eight
and a half *four hours* later. We had to work at near frenetic
levels to complete the scheduled work in the allotted
time, and after redoing many of the jobs, learned to be
thorough in the execution of the others. He never once
complimented us or issued an encouraging word, his
dark scowl when he could find no fault with our efforts
an exhilarating stamp of approval we cherished as praise
coming from the depths of his cold heart—assuming he
had one. He hissed when he spoke, which he did with
his emaciated lips curled around a fat, smelly cigar with
the end chewed into a soggy lump. Essentially all of him
was mean and evil, and we dourly amused ourselves by
inventing colorful adjectives to call him at the end of
each fun-filled day spent with him as we showered and
collapsed on our bunks, too tired to move even if we
hadn't been on restrictions.

Jerry always had a six-pack of nickel beer for us to
split, which we downed before sinking into oblivion.
Once he even tried to help us with a particularly odi-

ous chore, but Sergeant Black appeared out of thin air and raised all sorts of hell. After that Jerry stayed as far away from us as he could while we worked. We ended the fifteen days on a low note, having to redo a job three times before he would accept it as complete. At last, he snatched his cigar from his mouth and jabbed it at us.

"I'm going to be watching you shits like a hawk in the future. You got that? Dismissed!"

As soon as he was out of sight we burst into wild yells—free men again and still alive after working two weeks and a day for the monster.

———

Our regular unit duties proved almost as trying during this period of punishment as we alternated one day of guard duty on the bunker line with one day of unit training while awaiting our company to fill to combat strength.

The instruction involved practical hands-on exercises in everything taught to us over the last six months conducted under the rubber trees behind the bunker line. Some of this we put our hearts into—like zeroing our weapons to obtain battle sights and the explosives class where we rigged actual charges and blew down rubber trees—but for the most part we considered the courses repetitive and beneath our dignity. After all, we were full soldiers now, so to run around with empty weapons yelling *bang-bang* and pretending it was night in the middle of the day was silly. Normally, by mid-afternoon the heat beat us into walking zombies that moved, stood, or fell where told to with little imagination as our instructors admonished our apathy and warned we would soon need to execute these maneuvers without thinking under hostile fire. This generally fell on deaf ears, since anyone could see we were already executing the maneuvers by reflex and without a great deal of forethought.

The bunker line was an altogether different story. Excited at first because *up there* we were *really facing the enemy*, our enthusiasm soon waned. Our company manned ten of the bunkers in the formidable shield surrounding the supporting units within the division. The bunkers themselves were large steel-and-wood fighting positions reinforced with double rows of sandbags designed to withstand direct hits from mortar, rocket, and small arms fire with portholes to provide protection while firing into the flanks of an attacking force. Each was six feet high and built over a three-foot hole in the ground with a large command bunker located fifty yards to the rear centered on our first line of defense. All trees, shrubs, and obstacles to vision were removed from the area to the front of the bunkers for a distance of four hundred yards. Five rows of barbed wire strung eighty yards apart stretched in an unbroken line in this cleared area and connected to each unit on our flank designed to slow an advance and channel attackers into kill zones.

Our fears were never of a large-scale attack. Those within the perimeter were concerned with the weekly mortar and rocket attacks the enemy sent streaming in. We infantry types on the perimeter had little to do during these slugfests other than sit on our bunkers and watch the two sides duel it out overhead. Our bunker-line battle focused on snipers, sappers, and the environment.

The snipers were notoriously lousy shots who caused little harm other than scaring the hell out of us when the unexpected rounds came whizzing by our ears. Devastating fire from a multitude of weapons met such indiscretions and quickly ended the affair.

The sappers were a different story and we feared them like the plague. During the hours of darkness they would strip down to their underwear, smut-blacken their bodies, and attempt to wriggle their way through the five strands of barbed wire, which took hours of patient work and nerves of steel, place a satchel charge virtually in our lap, crawl back out again, and gleefully blow it in our face. They seemed to have a knack for turning into shadows, stumps, and wavering blades of grass in the arching glare of the flares floating overhead as we fretfully attempted to keep them at bay with unexpected small arms fire and randomly lobbed grenades into the no-man's-land before us. Though we rarely caught them in the act, the little rascals were always there waiting for the unwary, making for long nights, taut nerves, and racing hearts.

The real danger of the bunker line was the environment—sunburn, heat exhaustion, insects, and rodents. We maintained the fortifications in a communal world under a blazing sun where nature and man lived in close disharmony and constant confrontation.

We pulled guard in shifts, two men to a bunker, beginning at 1600 hours each day and ending the same hour the following day. We positioned ourselves on top of the bunkers during the hours of darkness for a number of reasons. First, the dug out floors of the bunkers usually contained several inches of brackish water filled with swimming snakes, rats, and other creatures with little red eyes that glowed in the beam of a flashlight. Additionally, the narrow gun ports offered great protection but poor visibility for spotting the devious night-crawling sappers trying desperately to blow us away. The lovable black scorpions also called the dark interiors home and were prone to snuggle up to a warm, sleeping body if they could beat the snakes to it, and all of them got grouchy as hell if you rolled over on them. And the simple tarantulas and other assorted spiders considered an empty pair of boots or draped shirt abandoned property and moved right on in. There they exercised squatter's rights, thereby requiring patience and long sticks to coax them back out again. The VC on the outside paled in comparison to the horrors inside.

In addition to offering greater visibility to spot the night urchins crawling our way, the bunkers' height discouraged all but the most persistent rats and usually kept snakes out of our pockets, scorpions off our chests, and spiders out of our boots. A side benefit was the enhanced ability to remain awake through the long, dreary nights since the penalty for a drowsy guard squatting on top of a bunker was a six-foot drop straight down with a sudden stop at the end.

For all these advantages we had only to pay the small price of being in an exposed and vulnerable position when flares were fired, of offering our bodies in sacrifice to the thirty billion starving mosquitoes circling over-head awaiting their turn, and training oneself to sleep in pouring rain and flashing lightning when not pulling guard shift. And not to turn over in one's sleep since the six-foot drop on the back of the bunker was just as far as the one at the front. Most of us eventually made one or the other of those trips.

The nights weren't that bad. The days were the hard part. Beginning with a bleary-eyed breakfast at daybreak, we spent the remainder of the day repairing all the for-tifications in the frying sun. The occasional sniper that chased us back into the tree line was heaven-sent. We always cheered them on for temporarily ending the monoto-nous, backbreaking, never-ending work and booed our own mortar fire that sent the hapless chap scurrying back home and us back into the endless chain-gang labor force to string the miles of wire, fill the millions of sandbags, and cut and clear the clinging vegetation. At 1600 hours the new guard force relieved us to drag our exhausted bodies back to our hooch to bathe, treat sunburns, blis-ters, insect and rodent bites, and grab a hot meal and a cold beer before the next dreadful tour of duty.

Though the sun and insects usually won the encoun-ters leaving us sick, hurt, and totally pissed off, the day-in, day-out endless repair of the bunker line sapped our spirit. Each time we returned to find bushes re-grown from stumps previously cut, new wire rusted and bro-ken, and the same stacks of sandbags to fill, haul, and replace. Our minds wasted away in this thankless labor and the needless refresher training we endured in the interval between guard shifts.

Our positive outlook on the glories of combat waned considerably as we waited impatiently for our unit to reach combat strength. Slowly troops trickled in, mostly newbies, with a few veterans returning from the hospital or R&R thrown in, swelling our ranks and filling the hooches. Each day we estimated the days remaining before we would be combat effective and get on with the war, eagerly ready to leave this degrading, rotten existence to lesser individuals. We were infantry, by god, not the local coolie labor force.

———

A couple of days after our restrictions were lifted we completed a hot and boring day of refresher training, where unfortunately, Sergeant First Class Black was our instructor, and therefore only perfection was acceptable. He required us to execute a simple drill over and over which he gauged we performed poorly. In the strain of the event, Jerry and I exchanged heated words over a procedure he had performed incorrectly thereby requiring the whole lot of us to rerun the exercise. When we returned to the hooch in strained silence, Jerry and Bernie disappeared without a word. Del and I lay on our bunks in brooding silence. A couple of hours later they wandered through the door grinning like a couple of Cheshire cats.

"Hi, guys," Jerry greeted as he and Bernie seated themselves on their bunks. "You guys should've been with us."

I eyed them sullenly. "Don't recall us being invited."

"It must've slipped our mind."

"Kiss my ass," I offered sweetly.

Jerry stooped to peer at me in mock concern. "Bernie, I think Jay's pissed."

Bernie studied my scornful scowl. "Looks like his own sweet, lovable self to me."

"Knock it off, guys," Del grumbled.

"Bernie, I believe Del's pissed too."

"Think so? Mmmm, lips are a bit thin ..."

"You bastards having a hard time getting the message?" I challenged. "You're poking a rattlesnake with a short stick."

Bernie pretended alarm. "They really *are* pissed."

"Jay's blue eyes sparkle *so* when he's pissed," Jerry admired.

"Contrasts so well with his red face, don't you think?" Bernie observed.

I sat up coiled in fury. "I'm in no mood for your silly games, assholes! You looking for some shit?"

Jerry grew cautious. "Hey, we're sorry for not inviting you guys along. Can you find it in your heart to forgive us?"

I stood and grabbed a fistful of his shirt. "You just don't know when to quit—"

"And as a token of my friendship ..." He held a roll of funny money before my eyes. "A little peace offering because I admire your sunny disposition so much." He removed my clenched fist from his shirt and placed the funny money in my palm.

I blinked. "What the hell?"

"And this is for you, because you're such a swell sport." Bernie tossed Del a roll of funny money also.

Each wad contained thirty dollars, the exact amount we had paid the headquarters clerk to buy our way into the Wolfhounds.

"W-What the hell?" I blubbered.

Bernie shrugged. "Jerry thought we should pay a visit to your Specialist Holbrook up at Headquarters and Headquarters Company. It took a little doing, but we finally found him returning from the shower point. Jerry borrowed the towel wrapped around his waist to wipe his sweaty forehead as he discussed his admiration for you and Del and explained how you two had loaned some jerk clerk some money and that the man was past due paying it back. The guy even offered to pay interest on the loan. We determined five dollars was sufficient, which Jerry and I pocketed as a collector's fee."

I grinned. "Buy you guys a beer?"

In our renewed camaraderie, the next few days were bearable. Even the daily grind of bunker duty and refresher training seemed survivable as we eagerly awaited combat.

CHAPTER 7

The hooches were overflowing with men.

With the increased manpower, we pulled the hated bunker duty only once every three days now, with the other two days devoted to training. After one particularly grueling day of meaningless instruction, we returned to the hooch and collapsed on our bunks in exhaustion. Soon Jerry sat upright and hurried out as we continued to wallow in self-pity and paid scant attention to his return other than directing scowls at his happy shuffle. When he lay back on his bunk with his hands clasped behind his head and began humming to himself it was too much.

I propped my head in my palm. "What?"

Jerry lifted his head. "*What* what?"

"You know what *what*, shithead. *What*, damn it?" I challenged.

"Sorry, don't know what you're talking about." He flopped back on his bunk and began humming again.

I attacked him. Del and Bernie joined in as I sprawled across his chest and tickled him until he begged for mercy and agreed to tell us what-what.

"Okay, out with it," I ordered.

"Only in private," he gasped.

We escorted him outside, where he faced us with a smirk. "We got ourselves a mission."

Del snorted. "*What* mission?"

"To Cu Chi."

"You mean the *village*?" Bernie demanded.

He grinned. "The one and only."

I stared at him suspiciously. "Cu Chi is off limits."

He nodded. "Yep, and according to the veterans, it contains everything a man could want, restaurants, shops, street vendors—"

"And bars, whorehouses, and a rampant black market," Del finished.

"They say if you can name it, they can produce it," Jerry agreed affably.

"And *we're* going there?" I demanded, my limited imagination surging to unparalleled heights. Next to getting into combat, I wanted to go to Cu Chi, figuring it just *had* to be great if it was *off-limits*! "How do you figure that?"

"All *four* of us?" Del demanded.

"*Legally*?" Bernie added skeptically.

"All four of us and totally legal," he affirmed.

We broke into an excited chorus of gleeful yelps.

"Of course, we got to carry Sergeant Black along with us—"

I cringed. "*Do what*?"

"*Oh, no!*" Bernie moaned.

"*Aw, crap!*" Del exclaimed.

"Don't *worry*, guys," he soothed as we plummeted back to earth in unison. "We can *handle* the situation. *Trust* me!"

"*Bullshit!*" I exploded.

"*No way!*" Del yelped.

"*I'm out!*" Bernie insisted.

"*Sheee!*" he scolded as he looked warily over his shoulder. "Keep it down guys! Now gather around and listen to my plan."

We edged around him vigilantly. "See, I overheard this conversation between Black and Top this morning planning a big barbecue for our reorganization party. The mess hall needs charcoal. It seems Sergeant Black's been checking around with the other units trying to rustle some up, but came up empty handed. I remembered one of the veterans telling us the division commander approves missions to Cu Chi on an individual basis."

"Yeah," I scoffed. "Provided they're tightly controlled and properly supervised, which translates into '*don't have any fun or I'll have your ass!*'"

Jerry shot me an annoyed look. "*Anyway*, figuring I stood no chance with Black, mainly due to my regrettable association with *you* three, I approached Top and convinced him that in addition to charcoal the whole unit needs some of the many niceties of life not provided by the Army, such as locks, metal mirrors, wash pans, metal cups, and the like. Top agreed, obtained permission from higher up, and even commented on my initiative when I volunteered to handle all of the details, such as getting a few men to help out in collecting the lists and money from all the other troops."

I scowled. "Was that *before* or *after* he put *Black-beard* in charge of the detail?"

"I figure we can handle that little set back too," he insisted, nonplussed. "See, once we get to the village, we'll need to scatter to get all of the items, right? There's *no way* he can keep his eye on us *every minute* of the time. So are you with me or not?"

I eyed Del and Bernie tentatively. "It *might* work."

"Nothing ventured, nothing gained," Del echoed.

Bernie hung his head and sighed. "Okay, I'm in."

The following morning we compiled a list from the men in each of the hooches before going to the armory to draw .45 caliber pistols and ammo. We next drew a three-quarter ton truck from the motor pool and pulled up beside the orderly room.

Sergeant Black came strutting out, stopped abruptly when he saw Bernie, Del, and me in the back and Jerry behind the wheel, and almost swallowed his stogie as his eyes bulged. "Where the *hell* do you morons think you're going? *Get your ass off that truck!*"

We eased toward the tailgate as Jerry scrambled out of the cab. "But, Sarge, Top told us to go," he insisted, stretching the facts a bit. "We're making a village run for the unit."

He poked Jerry in the chest with the chewed end of his cigar. "Village run, my ass—you four are thicker than thieves and *twice* as suspect. Are you trying to pull some shit on me?"

"Honest, Sarge, we're just doing what Top told us to do, don't you see?"

"Yeah, I see, stupid!" He stabbed Jerry with the soggy end of his cigar again. "I *see* you trying to make a *monkey's ass* outta me. Okay, let me set you shits straight. *I* don't trust you, *any* of you, but especially *you,* cause you're a little *wise-ass.*"

"B-But, Sarge," Jerry protested. "We're just—"

"Shut up and listen! Cu Chi is a dangerous place. Most of the villagers are sympathetic to the VC cause. In fact, they blew up a jeep there just a few months back. One step out of line and your ass *belongs* to *me*! Got that?"

"Yes, Sergeant!" we chorused meekly.

He swept us with glinting eyes, checked the pistols and two magazines of ammo we carried that were standard issue for village runs to satisfy himself with our preparations, strutted around to the passenger side of the truck, climbed in, and slammed the door. Jerry threw us a wink and scrambled in behind the wheel. We growled through the base camp, bounced through the MP checkpoint, and down the road to Cu Chi proper, all eyes and full of wonder.

The one long, muddy street of Cu Chi was lined with shops made of cola and beer cans, cardboard, mud, straw, and anything else that could be had, and filled with people pushing carts or chugging around in the little three-wheeled Lambrettas. Greedy looking merchants and sleazy, half-dressed women lined the doorways, all watching us in hungry anticipation, with the shop owners beckoning to us as the women fluttered their eyelashes in an attempt to look seductive. Some of them did a good job of it too, I admitted to myself as I grinned back at them foolishly.

We lurched to a halt in the middle of the rabble and dismounted, where a throng of children with big, sorrowful eyes, all talking at once in broken English as they jostled for attention, surrounded us clutching at our hands and offering watches and other items for sale or begging for cigarettes and chocolate. One grabbed my leg and propped my foot on a small box and began shining my boots in the melee as Sergeant Black looked around amidst the overpowering stink of unwashed bodies while we braced ourselves for more threats.

"Okay, that's my side over there. You shits got one hour, not a minute more. You know what's off-limits, so don't let me catch you in one of them." He winked over his evil grin. "I want one of you to have this vehicle in sight at all times. Got that?" We nodded dumbly. "Okay, time's now 1015. We depart at 1115 hours sharp. Don't cause me any grief. Here's my list and the money. Make damn sure you get every item on it." Without another word, he strolled across the street, stopped a few doors down to admire a sweet young thing in a flimsy negligee, and followed her outstretched hands as she backed into the room and closed the door.

"*Who* would have *thought*?" Bernie asked awestruck.

"We're wasting *time* and *I'm* already in *love*," Jerry chortled, rubbing his hands together as he rolled his eyes at a little lady motioning to him.

"Not until we get the supplies," I insisted.

"Let's split up to save time!" Del suggested.

In half an hour, we purchased everything on our list without bothering to haggle over the prices unless they were clearly ridiculous. After depositing the goods in the back of the truck, we turned to the small open café in front of us with dirty, rickety tables lining the street, where four young beauties wearing little or nothing accosted us as soon as we entered. We ordered beer for ourselves, and *Saigon Tea* for the lovelies, knowing full well from the veterans that the price was five times the cost of our own drinks and consisted only of Coke. In full view of the open street and the swarm of kids crouching at our feet watching our every move, the bar girls did all sorts of things to heighten our interest. After a second round of Saigon Tea, which disappeared amazingly fast, Jerry called the Madam over to haggle over the price. After a lot of head shaking and arm waving, the two struck an agreeable bargain and she directed us to the rear of the bar where draped blankets divided the back wall into tiny cubicles with straw mats placed on the floor.

"One of us has to keep the truck in sight at all times," I warned.

"Right," Jerry advised as he yanked the blanket closed behind him. "You handle the first shift."

"Don't forget your Trojans," I called after them as they disappeared.

I took my confused sweetie by the hand and returned to our table, which set off another chorus of begging from the kids crouching at my feet at the entrance, feeling somewhat thankful they weren't allowed inside the establishment. I glanced out at the bustling street, satisfied myself all was as it should be, turned to the giggles and swaying blankets behind me, checked my watch to find less than fifteen minutes remaining of our allotted time, smiled hopefully at my rejected love watching me with morose eyes, and turned back to check the truck.

The hair on my neck rose as I stared in bewilderment at the empty street. The throngs of people had disappeared as if they had never been there. Even the kids were gone. I eased to the door and looked up and down the line of vacant shops with their doors now closed as little bumps sprang out on my arms and my stomach clenched. I drew my pistol with trembling hands and backed into the bar, where I noted that even the Madam and my little honey were now missing.

"Guys, get out here!" I called as my heart galloped wildly.

"Almost through," Del grunted.

"*Now,* damn it! Something's wrong!" I jacked a round into my pistol for emphasis, the unmistakable metallic sound of the chambered round getting their full attention. Almost in sequence the curtains parted and three tousled heads popped out. "We got trouble," I whispered. "All the people are gone."

Del stared at the empty street. "Gone where?"

"How the hell do I know?" I replied, trying to look everywhere at once. "They're just *gone*! Let's get out of here!"

One of the girls thrust her head through one of the blankets and chattered urgently to the other two still behind the coverings. In a flash, all three charged out clutching clothing to their breasts and ran off down the street.

"*Holy shit!*" Jerry yelped.

Their three heads disappeared in unison as they dived for trousers and boots. Jerry darted out and jacked a round into his pistol, laid it on a table, and sat down to wrap the laces of his boots around the tops before shrugging into his shirt, his eyes never leaving the front entrance as Del and Bernie joined us. Del drew his pistol and chambered a round as we knelt at the entrance. A little dust devil at the far end of the village was the only movement. Our heads rotated to the left. A piece of paper drifted before a light breeze in the heavy silence.

"You guys cover me," Jerry whispered. "I'm going after Sarge. If you see one head pop up, blast them!"

"*No!* I'll go. Cover me." Bernie drew a deep breath and darted out.

We spread out and watched the surrounding buildings as he ran in a zigzag pattern and flattened himself against the exterior of one of the shops across the street. Nothing moved as he slid along the wall to the door Sergeant Black had disappeared into, spun, kicked it open, and charged inside, the crash causing us to jump. Loud voices trailed into silence. A moment later the girl ran out and down the street, her bare butt jiggling. Black's face appeared near the bottom of the door, took in the deserted street, and disappeared. He reappeared through the door and crouched to one side, back against the building with pistol drawn, as he searched our side of the street. Bernie hesitated in the doorway, and at a nod from Black, darted for the truck. We tried to watch every building at once, pistols swinging before us, as Bernie dove through the open window of the vehicle. The engine roared and the wheels spun mud geysers to the rear in a tight, skidding turn in the middle of the street, veering toward Sergeant Black's position, with Bernie slapping at the steering wheel as he fought to straighten it out. Black ran for the back of the truck as it fishtailed by and dove headfirst into the rear.

BOOM!

We ducked as the windshield of the truck exploded in a shower of flying glass, and then opened up in a terrified mêlée shooting in all directions, the thunder of our weapons ripping the silence and feeding our panic. The truck swerved to our side of the street with the crushed windshield encased in spidery cracks on the passenger side as I dumped the empty magazine from the butt of my pistol and slammed another into the bottom.

"Let's go!" I yelled, leading Del and Jerry out in a wild scramble.

I leapt onto the running board on the driver's side as Del sprawled in a heap in the mud. Jerry jerked him to his feet as Bernie fought for control of the steering wheel and tried to jam the shift into a higher gear amidst a great deal of grinding as the vehicle careened by. Del and Jerry ran after us as I clung to the door and snapped off a round in the general direction of the building across the street. Jerry grabbed the tailgate and heaved himself inside the bed in a jumble as Del ran along behind us. With a mighty effort, he grabbed a handhold and lurched halfway over the tailgate as Bernie found the higher gear and stomped the throttle, almost dumping him back out again as he clawed at the floor for something to hang on to, his legs kicking wildly in the air. Jerry popped up from the tangle and began blasting in all directions.

"*Cease fire, goddamn it, cease fire!*" Black screamed as we tore out of the village.

"*Agghh! Help!*" Del pleaded as his fingers clawed at the smooth metal floor.

Black braced his feet against the tailgate and snatched Del over the rear on top of him as Bernie shifted gears and pressed the gas pedal to the floor, the shrill engine filling our ears as we watched the village grow smaller behind us.

"*Stop, goddamn it!*" Black yelled from the back of the truck. "Stop the vehicle!"

Bernie eased to a stop a safe distance from the village as Black untangled himself from Del and stood. "Anybody hurt?"

We looked at each other and shook our heads numbly.

"Did any of you shits actually *see* a VC?"

We looked at each other and shook our heads dumbly.

He sighed. "I didn't think so. The thing is, my pistol discharged and blew out the windshield when I jumped into the back of the truck—"

"And scared me out of ten years of prime life!" Bernie accused.

"—which is no excuse for you dumb shits to go shooting up the whole village!" Black growled. "Let me think ... okay, here's the deal—finish knocking out the windshield so nobody can tell it's a bullet hole. I'll do all the talking, but for the record, our story is a rock from a deuce and a half's tire spun back and busted out the glass. If I *ever* hear anything else out of any of you shits, your ass belongs to *me*! Got it?"

We nodded.

"Good! Mount up and let's get the hell out of here!" He swung into the cab of the truck as we scrambled up into the rear.

The MP at the gate questioned Black about the shots heard from the direction of the village, but Black said it must have been a nearby patrol or something. Back at the unit we quickly distributed all the goods throughout the company and grabbed six-packs of nickel beer before slinking off under the rubber trees to rehash the event. We deduced we would never know for sure what caused the villagers to disappear, but concluded that one or more of the local VC had entered the village, where the inhabitants, fearing a battle with them in the middle, simply crawled into the nearest hole they could find. It had been a close call, we agreed.

After this event, Sergeant First Class Black didn't seem as evil or threatening to me. After all, he was just like the rest of us, a man who put his pants on one leg at a time and took them off just as fast.

———

At last, we reorganized into a combat unit.

The end result was three infantry platoons for combat missions, one heavy weapons platoon for indirect fire support, and a headquarters platoon, which we officially dubbed the *animal platoon*. This gaggle was made up of all the clerks and jerks who worked in the orderly room, supply room, and mess hall, as well as the lightly injured and misfits. The lightly injured were the sunburn, sprain, bite, sting, and jungle-rot cases that performed light duties as their injuries permitted and bunker guard when the rest of us were in the bush. The misfits were the bums, cowards, and other forms of low life every unit accumulates. These deadbeats pulled fire brigade duty at the latrine, worked as KPs in the mess hall, maintained the shower points, and performed other menial, degrading work fit only for those who couldn't cut it in the infantry. In a weird way, the animals were good for our morale because they pulled the shit details for the rest of us, which they didn't mind because it kept them out of combat. Still, we treated them with justified contempt. They never spoke to us or got anywhere near us if they could help it, and as such, were bunched together with the clerks and jerks in the last two hooches on the end.

Each line platoon consisted of four squads of riflemen, with two machine gun teams in each squad. As is the army way, we were in the first hooch beside the supply room, so we became first platoon along with the hooch next to us. Del and I were on the right side, so became part of the first squad. Bernie and Jerry, on the opposite side, became part of the second squad. Third and fourth squads were in the hooch next to us. They moved the few veterans left around to provide a little *steel* to the rest of us newbies, with Barney and Johnson joining the first squad with Del and me and eight other new men while Bernie and Jerry picked up two veterans from different hooches. For our squad leader we drew Staff Sergeant Thomas, who had been in-country six months and had a quiet, firm disposition. He was tall without being skinny, and seemed the type one instinctively followed in a crisis. He slept in the NCO hooch across the way. Sergeant Lunas, short and dark with bushy eyebrows and a perpetual scowl, and a newbie like the rest of us, became our assistant squad leader and moved into the hooch with us to occupy the bunk at the front entrance.

Our platoon sergeant became the immortal Sergeant First Class Black. I figured it would have been too much to ask of fate for another platoon to have drawn the bastard. A big, six-foot-three inch, two-hundred-pound college type second lieutenant with drooping jaws and a complacent manner became our platoon leader. Our company commander was of course the stern West Pointer.

The head Wolfhound himself, the 1/27th Infantry Battalion Commander, roared up in a shiny jeep the next day at our reorganization party.

"Who's that?" someone queried as we stood in company formation, the first time I'd ever seen our whole unit together down to the clerks and jerks.

"Sheeetttt, that there's ol' *Sky-eye* his-self," Barney sneered.

"Yeah, he thinks we're real magicians," one of the second squad veterans whispered. "The bastard'll look down from his copper at us two thousand feet below him in mud up to our knees and water up to the cracks of our asses carrying a hundred pounds of gear in 110 degree temperature and call on his radio, 'Uh, Mustang Alpha Six, this is Mustang Six, move your element to grid so and so.' Presto, we can trip through the thickest jungle, cross the widest rivers, and tiptoe through mazes of booby traps and minefields to appear on the exact coordinates ready to do battle."

"Sheeeeetttt!" Barney added.

Our commander called us to *Attention* and *Present Arms* as he approached, which we performed rather snappily, having just practiced it for two hours prior to his arrival. He and our commander exchanged salutes, shook hands, and then moved to a small platform erected for the occasion. Our commander instructed the platoon leaders to move us around the podium, where we crowded together in a decisively unmilitary manner, pushing and shoving to get in the best position to hear what this miniature god might have to say to us.

Mustang Six gazed down from his platform, his five-foot-seven-inch skinny frame exuding a stern demeanor as a hush descended over us.

"Fellow Wolfhounds, I address you today because tomorrow we begin a new era when this unit is officially declared combat ready!" He waited as we cheered.

"Over the past few weeks we have infused a proud and highly valorous unit with new blood. The old Alpha Company was one of the Division's finest. Their record speaks for itself. They met the enemy face-to-face and never failed in their duty, resolve, or courage. I take this opportunity to inform you that this Battalion has been awarded the Presidential Unit Citation for Alpha Company's action in combat against a superior force a few short weeks ago." He smiled and held up his hands as we again cheered.

"As you may know, the old Alpha took on a force ten times its size. Although they suffered grievous casualties, veterans of that action can hold their heads up with pride, for none has fought a more glorious action."

Cheers and yells abounded.

"I want to ensure each of you understands the type of unit you now serve with, that there is no misinterpreting of why this unit was reorganized, that no taint of defeat be attached to such a proud and heroic effort."

Taint of defeat? I mused to myself. *What the hell is the dwarf talking about? Clearly any unit that goes one-on-one with a North Vietnamese Regiment has to be the best. Hell, some fools even paid good money to get here.*

"As the new Alpha, you have a powerful reputation to follow, a high mark to match, a score to settle. Not only from this unit's proud history, but also from two hundred years of American fighting history. You are infantry. As infantry, your mission is to engage the enemy in combat and destroy him. You must never falter in that mission. You *cannot* falter in that mission. Two hundred years of American fighting men in every conceivable uniform will rise from their dark, damp graves if you fail in that mission!"

An angry murmur rippled through us as men hissed in defiance.

"You must always remember that you are Americans and represent not only this unit, not only this Army, but also the very Nation you serve. Your war is not only one of bullets and bayonets, but one of words, deeds, and acts of humanity. You must never forget this in your days ahead. You must be more than infantry. As the first point of contact between the people of this unfortunate land and the people of our own great land, you must always be conscious of your diplomatic role in the war for the hearts and minds of these people.

"Everything you say, everything you do, everywhere you go, will be heard, will be watched, and will be evaluated, and a judgment will be rendered. A judgment of not only you, a judgment not only of this unit and this Army, but a judgment of the American people as well. As diplomats, I charge you to consider every action, give every courtesy, and in all instances, conduct yourselves as true representatives of your country.

"You are the finest Army the world can produce. You have the best equipment and logistical support man can devise. You have a nation of proud people counting on you to perform in a manner befitting our country's greatness. The world has never seen the likes of you before and may never do so again. At this point in time, you are unique. I charge each of you to meet this challenge, *for to fail will forever bring down the wrath of history on your generation!*"

We went wild, which caused him to wave his arms for several minutes to calm us down.

"I thank you for your attention. I am proud to serve as your Battalion Commander. I look forward to our days ahead. Now I will release you to your Company Commander, whom I believe has some festivities planned for you. Thank you!"

"*Attention!*" Black screamed in my ear, almost giving me a heart attack in the hush that had fallen over us as the commander spoke. We sprang to rigid postures as the two commanders exchanged salutes and left the platform. The platoon leaders saluted the platoon sergeants and hurried after them. Black marched us to the shade of one of the rubber trees lining the company street and gave us *At Ease*.

He stood glowering, hands on hips, cigar smoldering. "You shits might be *diplomats* to Mustang Six, but you're still *infantrymen* to me, and don't you forget it! And don't go getting no high-flaunting ideas about yourselves. Starting day after tomorrow, we leave the fifth wire and we go out to *kick ass*, nothing more. You shits got that?" He waited while we cheered, a flicker of a grin playing at the corners of his cruel lips as he twirled his cigar. "I think you're ready, but if I get you shits out there and you flounder on me, you'll pull bunker duty for the rest of your tour. Got that?" he threatened, stabbing at us with his stogie as we cheered again.

All I wanted was a chance to do what I had been training to do for months now. *Fail? Flounder?* Dream on! I was a combat trooper, and by god I was finally going into battle!

When Black released us to the pits of barbecue and tubs of iced beer, my spirits soared as I thought of the enemy soon to be vanquished, inwardly wondering if I could match my own high expectations and those of our nation. The training and grinding details were over. At last, I could confront my individual fears and never ending self-doubts. At some point during that marvelous evening, I paused for reflection on our commander's words and the unthinkable thought—*failure*.

I imagined hundreds of ghostly, somber eyes measuring me in the darkness, the gaunt figures wearing tattered uniforms of blue, gray, and olive drab. I saw my grandfather in the muddy trenches of the Argonne Forest, my father atop a tank in Patton's Third Army dashing across Europe, and my uncle grimly hunkered down in the frozen tundra of Korea.

As I watched the carousing men outlined by firelight, I imagined the muted sounds of war drums beating the long roll and a faint bugle trumpeting *Charge!* as in the far distance the growing din of rattling musketry locked men in mortal combat.

The time had come for my test. I stood ready.

Please, God, if death is to be my wretched fate, don't let me die a coward!

CHAPTER 8

"From the moment we cross the fifth wire we are on enemy terrain and subject to attack."

Staff Sergeant Thomas sat back on his heels from where he squatted below us and looked up at our circle of eager faces as he folded his map. "It will get hot, very hot, and for the most part very boring. You will have a tendency to relax. That is when the VC will strike. We are a team. Each of you must cover your assigned area at all times, on the move or stopped. If you fail, the team suffers. It could cost the man next to you his life, as well as your own." He stood and dusted his hands as he surveyed our grim faces. "If you are not sure about something, ask. Call it to my attention, or ask Barney or Johnson. They've been there. Watch them and you'll stand a decent chance of going home with your boots on. Inspection is at 0700 hours, move-out at 0730. Get some rest." He collected his notes and left the hooch.

We drifted to our bunks absorbing his instructions and warnings while glancing sideways at one another, each aware of the trust each man must expect from the other. *No man will ever get injured due to my negligence,* I swore silently as I checked my gear for the thousandth time.

A few held low conversations with Barney and Johnson as the rest of us eavesdropped. From their mannerisms and short answers, it was obvious we newbies were a pain in the ass with all our dumb questions and inability to comprehend the answers. I knew bonds were forged of mutual dependence and trust, of shared hardships and experiences, and that we were as yet untested and unproven as they attempted to impart small tricks of the trade to us. Like putting our ammo magazines in upside down in the pouches so we could draw and load in one motion as well as keep water and dirt out, or to place all pouches to our sides and rear instead of the front in order to get closer to the ground. Both stressed the rationing of our water, cautioning us to take small sips throughout the day and never large drinks.

Sergeant Lunas strutted about informing anyone who would listen to keep their eyes on him and he would let us know what to do and when to do it. From his chatter it was clear he was as scared as the rest of us. We pretended sleep as the night slipped away and were up and about by 0530. By 0630 we had completed breakfast and our personal hygiene requirements and were joking coarsely as we awaited the formation. When Barney and Johnson strapped on their web gear, we followed their lead, even Lunas, who was thankfully quiet for a change. We then filed out behind them to the company street, where Sergeant Thomas distributed to eight of us a one hundred round belt of M-60 machine gun ammo, a block of C-4 plastic explosive, a white phosphorus

Willie Pete grenade, a smoke grenade, two fragmentation grenades, and one C-ration meal apiece. He issued the two men who did not get a belt of machine gun ammo a light antitank (LAW) rocket and a large coil of rope with a grappling hook. Taking our cue from Barney and Johnson, we hurried back to the hooch, selected a sock from our gear, emptied the cans of C-rations from their box, placed selected cans in the sock to form a tube, and tied it to the back of our web gear suspenders. We strung the M-60 machine gun ammo across our shoulder and chest bandito style, strapped the block of C-4 plastic explosive to our web belt in the rear, and hung the various grenades from our harness suspenders.

When we were ready, Sergeant Thomas led us through the rubber trees to a small clearing at the rear of the bunker line where the other three squads soon joined us. The lieutenant and Black approached accompanied by the radioman RTO and Doc, the platoon medic. Black paused before us to light a fresh cigar between his cupped palms.

"Your Squad Leaders have briefed the specifics in the Warning Order. Order of march is First, Second, Third, and Fourth Squads. I will travel with First Squad, the Lieutenant and his RTO will be between Second and Third Squads, and Doc will be with Fourth Squad. First Squad will provide a point man, Second and Third flank security, and Fourth rear security. This will be a search mission against a small settlement ten clicks from the fifth wire code named *Nightmare Village*. The villagers are sympathetic to the communist cause. The surrounding area is saturated with booby traps, mines, and punji pits. You've been trained to locate and bypass all of these obstacles. Today we will find out if you were attentive. There are snipers throughout the area. A known company sized VC element controls this sector. The 9th North Vietnamese Army has overall responsibility for this area of operations. We could encounter any or all of these unsavory characters from this point forward. Any questions from you little diplomats? *Saddle up!*"

I staggered to my feet under the awkward load and shifted the equipment into a comfortable travel position. Thomas inclined his head at Johnson, who moved through the intervening bushes to the bunker line. Barney sent a stream of brown tobacco juice slicing through the air, rolled his bulging wad to the other cheek, and followed him. Staff Sergeant Thomas motioned the rest of us in behind them single file. Second squad fell in behind our last man, with third and fourth following them. We were a tight-lipped group as Johnson set a steady pace, turning left on the road along the rear of the bunkers and right onto the narrow path running in a circuitous course through the strands of wire stretching before us. The men on top of the bunkers looked down in envy as we passed. Tomorrow they would have their day outside the wire. We passed the end bunker as the guard on top picked up his field phone and alerted the command bunker. The command bunker in turn alerted the units to each side of us and placed the mortar section on standby back at the fire direction center.

My heart increased tempo as we negotiated the narrow path through the wire channeling us into our own kill zones. Johnson led us rapidly through the twists and turns as the rest of the platoon strung out behind us. We cleared the fifth wire and fanned out in the rubber trees in protective positions. When the last man in the platoon cleared the wire, Sergeant Thomas pointed at Johnson, who turned and slipped through the bushes. Barney gave him a fifty-meter lead and sent another spray of tobacco juice ground ward as he fell in behind. We slipped into the line at fifteen-meter intervals as our lieutenant's radio crackled in the hush calling us clear. Men from second and third squads moved out to each flank as we assumed the travel position, our formation resembling a huge arrow with Johnson on point and the rest of us forming the shaft. With not a word spoken, the only sounds were the soft swish of brush against tense bodies.

I experienced a momentary thrill. *This was war.* I envied Johnson, barely visible through the trees, leading us into battle. An error in judgment could cost half the platoon. He would be the first to spot the trip wires and the nearly impossible-to-detect subtle differences in the leaves that pointed to a hidden device intended for destruction. Since he covered the ground first, he would find them with his eyes or his feet and pay a grim price if the latter. He would also be in the most vulnerable position if we happened upon an enemy patrol, alone between them and us. His only consolation was that in an ambush the enemy normally allowed the point man to walk through before springing the trap on the main body itself. Sharp eyes, a clear mind, and a reliable instinct for trouble were prerequisites for a good point man, with a great deal of respect bestowed on one chosen for the honor.

I admired Johnson's easy confidence as I watched his head swivel taking in every feature of the surrounding terrain with each measured step, his head cocked as he listened to the stillness, sensing he was as good as they came. He moved at a steady pace, stopping on occasion with upraised hand. During these pauses, we lay prone alternately to the left and right while he checked whatever had piqued his interest. Satisfying himself all was well, he would again sweep his arm forward and we would stagger up, shift loads, and move again. We had performed these actions many times in training and were faultless in execution now while maintaining constant 360 degree security as each man watched his specific area, eyes darting to take in any sign of danger, with the only noise the steady crunch of decaying vegetation underfoot and the periodic clink of gear as heavy loads shifted.

As the morning deepened, the sun built its heat. My load cut into my shoulders and hips, chafing flesh into tender areas of concentrated pain. Sweat streamed down my face and back saturating my shirt and the towel draped around my neck. I found the air under the canopy of the rubber trees stifling and swatted irritably at the millions of gnats swarming about my head and sticking to my flesh, clogging my nostrils and rolling into balls in my mouth. Sunlight impaled the ground in dust-filled beams through the leaves overhead, where it played in patterns in the shade, as the heat took its toll on my overburdened body.

Grunts and wheezes surrounded me as I stumbled along, with often the soft thump of a body and rattle of equipment followed by a curse of pain as others tripped and sprawled on the ground. Two hours of stop-move, stop-move progress found my jungle fatigues streaked white with salt and my eyes red-rimmed with fatigue. I jerked my concentration back to my assigned sector in alarm when my mind wandered. At the brief halts, I began to kneel instead of going down into a full prone position as some around me simply staggered over to the nearest tree and leaned wearily against it.

I fought to focus as the trees swam before me in a haze, knowing I was dangerously close to heat exhaustion. My shoulders ached and I trembled from exertion as I gasped in the thick oxygen depleted air like a beached whale, desperately needing water but unable to reach my canteens in the middle of my back with all the extra gear draped over me, and the interval between us prevented Del to my rear from getting it for me. When I glanced back at him, his dark red face, glazed eyes, and frantic gulps of air showed him to be as desperate as me.

The lieutenant called a halt from the rear through a whispered command sent up the line. I sank by a tree and tore at the layers of equipment, grasped one of my canteens in shaking hands, and gulped in desperate draughts, draining two thirds of the container before I could control myself as Del emptied his canteen and sagged against a tree with his eyes closed. The water felt like molten lead in my stomach and I breathed in measured gulps to control the nausea. Del wasn't as successful and gagged, dropped to his knees, and threw up. I shook two salt tablets from my packet and downed them with a sip of water, fighting the urge to drain the remainder, dragged myself up, and stumbled back to Del as he reached for his last canteen.

"Hey, take it easy," I cautioned.

"I'm dying, Jay," he gasped. "I'm really dying."

"Here, take some salt tablets and a small sip of water," I encouraged as one of the new men behind us named Silverstein approached.

"I need some water," he pleaded.

"Where the hell is yours?" I demanded.

"I filled my canteens with Kool-Aid," he confessed miserably.

"You dumb shit," I swore as I thrust my partly empty canteen into his trembling hands, and then shook out two of my salt tablets and insured he took them before he limped back to his position after draining the last drop of water from my canteen. Soon second squad moved through our position to take the point, with Jerry and Bernie flashing weak grins as they staggered past, faces flushed with heat. Third and fourth squads followed and our first squad fell in behind to take up rear security. I found the trail position much easier traveling and requiring a fraction less caution than the point position as we ambled along regaining our wits. An hour later, we halted for the noon break.

I eagerly removed my equipment before eating sparingly from the C-ration cans stuffed in my sock and took the opportunity to rearrange my gear, bringing the canteens to the sides and placing some of the ammo pouches to the rear. Sergeant Thomas collected a few ounces of water from each of us for the idiot who had filled his canteens with Kool-Aid as the man sat in extreme embarrassment against a tree. The lieutenant and the squad leaders slipped forward to conduct a recon, leaving Black and the assistant squad leaders back with us.

"Delarosa! Keep your head up!" Sergeant Lunas directed in a harsh whisper as he strode by immersed in his own self-importance. "Watch your sector, goddamn it. Sharpe! Move to your right about ten feet there. Stay alert."

"What a pain," I mouthed to Del behind his back as he wandered off to make some other needless adjustment to another exhausted trooper down the line.

Barney rolled his wad to the other cheek and spat a stream of juice at a bug crawling on the side of a tree, encasing the hapless creature in syrup. "He'll learn," he drawled, wiping his chin with the back of his hand. "Ol' Deputy Dawg's doin' a decent job in thuh bush though."

"Who's Deputy Dog?" I asked tiredly.

"Thuh new officer of our'n. Most over here ain't worth their salt tablets."

Sergeant Thomas slipped up to Del and me. "First, second, and third squads will form a wedge around the village. Fourth squad will sweep from the open end. This is for the money, so keep your eyes peeled," he warned in a low, guarded voice before easing off to the next position to repeat the instructions.

My apathy turned to tremors of excitement as we moved out in different directions with caution replacing our prior stumbling advance. Sergeant Thomas swept his arm forward and we raced in a line across a dry rice paddy to fall prone on the side of a hedgerow surrounding a cluster of mud-and-thatch huts. To our left and front, second and third squads rushed into their own positions sealing the village on three sides as fourth squad hurried in a line across our right to complete the box. The villagers disappeared like magic except for one old, wrinkled man who stood before a red tiled hooch with white walls near the middle of the smaller mud structures gazing toward the open end of the village where fourth squad advanced. Several blackened and partly burned hooches sagged in various stages of destruction from previous combat exposure, and I could see where bullets had knocked jagged bits of plaster from the side of the hut nearest me. Fourth squad advanced on the village in a skirmish line, rifles at hip level, as the lieutenant who Barney thought looked like deputy dog followed five yards to the rear with his radio held to ear level, the cord strung back over his shoulder to the RTO crowding his heels. I tensed and searched the hooches strung out before us for signs of danger, but saw only emptiness and silence with the old man standing like a statue. Fourth squad entered the hooches in two man teams canvassing each structure as they worked their way through the village driving the sullen women and children before them to the center.

"Look out!" a member of fourth squad shouted as two men darted from one of the hooches at the opposite end of the village and ran from the approaching fourth squad towards the third squad hidden in the hedgerow to our left.

"Hold your fire!" Sergeant Thomas ordered as we raised our rifles.

I saw they carried no weapons as the two charged into the hedgerow full tilt. One bounced back out amid shouts from third squad and ran at our flanking position as a couple of men from third squad charged out after him shouting '*Dung Lai! Dung Lai! Halt!*' The terrified man sped ahead of his pursuers straight for Del and me. I jumped to my feet with mind racing, wondering what I should do. He darted to the left, his eyes wide in fear, as Johnson charged out yelling like a maniac. He broke stride and flung himself to the ground with his arms covering his head as Johnson grabbed him by the shirt, jerked him to his feet, dragged him over to our position, and shoved him to the ground in a heap of quivering flesh.

"Watch the bastard," Johnson ordered before trotting to a new position nearer the hooch the two men ran out of and training his muzzle on the open doorway, eyes narrowed in readiness.

Shouts and curses reached us from the third squad as the second man led them on a merry chase. Fourth squad renewed their advance through the village driving the villagers to the center to squat around the steps where the old man stood immobile. The lieutenant approached the old man, who began pleading in Vietnamese as two of our men moved around him to search the interior of his home. The frightened man in front of us dressed in black shorts and a peacock-blue shirt appeared to be about fifteen years old. His shoeless feet were thick with calluses as he squatted before us now, hands clasped behind his head, eyes pleading as an animal might who was trapped by a powerful predator.

"It's okay," I soothed as though talking to a frightened child and smiled in a reassuring fashion. "No one's going to hurt you. It's okay."

His eyes darted left and right, and then like a shot, he was by us as Del and I recoiled in alarm at the unexpected lunge, the wind from his passing fluttering against my face.

"*Hey*!" I shouted. "*You can't do that*! *Hey*!"

"Dung Lai! Stop! Stop!" Del yelled.

"Oh, shit!" I yelped as I lunged after the fleeing man. "Let's get him!"

The little slant-eyed bastard could run like the wind. After four hundred yards, I lost sight of him as he streaked across the paddy area and sped through the rubber trees. I sagged against a tree gasping for breath, eyes bulging from the effort, my gear shaken loose and jumbled all over me. Del, coughing and gagging fifteen yards to my rear, collapsed onto his knees wheezing like a locomotive, eyes trying to focus in his swollen red face. I stumbled back, hooked an arm under his, lifted him to his feet, and propped him against a tree as I wiped my streaming face on my towel, conscious of how sinister everything had suddenly become with what seemed a million eyes watching us from the shadowy depths.

"You okay?" I gasped hoarsely as shivers of fear laced down my back.

"I-I think so," Del gasped, his head turning fearfully in all directions.

"We better get back," I panted.

He surveyed the wall of green around us. "Which way is back?"

I indicated the stillness over his shoulder. "This way, I think."

"Are you sure?"

"No."

"Okay," he gasped, satisfied with the choice.

I waded into the shrubbery casting frequent glances over my shoulder trying to pick out familiar terrain, my pace becoming frantic as I regained my wind and then sagged in relief when I saw Sergeant Thomas, Barney, and Johnson threading their way through the trees. From fifty yards away I could tell Staff Sergeant Thomas was pissed.

"Just what the hell do you morons think you're doing?" he demanded as Barney and Johnson moved beyond us to secure our rear, both grinning in wry amusement.

"H-He ran by us," Del explained.

"W-We tried to catch him," I mumbled.

"That's a damned good way to get your ass killed!"

Del hung his head. "Sorry."

"We didn't think," I whispered in humiliation.

"Johnson, take point, Barney, pick up the rear," he ordered, indicating for Del and me to follow the still grinning Johnson as a smirking Barney stood to the side so we could pass.

Johnson led us through the jungle in a slightly different direction than I had been taking when they found us. After glancing back once and getting the snickering treatment from Barney, I kept my eyes to the front for the remainder of the trip.

Back at the village, Black directed us into our traveling formation with third squad leading. As we formed up, we learned third squad had allowed their man to escape also and some of the men grinned sheepishly at Del and me as if we shared some sinful brotherhood. As they passed, I heard their squad leader apologizing to Black. From the lieutenant's muted radio conversation with the rear, I learned the search of the village by fourth squad had produced nothing of value. The women and children, along with the old village chief, watched without expression as we slunk off in a dejected group.

The trip back was more grueling than the trip out, with the heat taking a worse toll on us in the midday sun. At the halfway point, we paused for fourth squad to assume the lead and pushed on. Barney and Johnson were the only two with water now and the rest of us suffered in agony as we watched them take small sips periodically. My tongue was swollen and my mind dizzy when we at last reached our base camp to stumble through the channels of wire and slump to the ground in the assembly area, a silent and beaten group, where we waited for the security teams to join us as we watched Black and the lieutenant conferring off to the side. When we were all together, they rejoined us.

The lieutenant stood before us, his features drawn. "I know you're tired and want to hit the showers, so I'll cut this short. For the most part, we moved well today, but looked a little sloppy near the end. I was pleased with the security throughout, although there were a few lapses near the end. I did not observe you bunched up or straggling, which is outstanding. Some of you learned a hard lesson today in regards to water conservation. We were lucky we lost no one to heat exhaustion. I cannot overemphasize the importance of rationing and taking salt tablets. If you allow yourself to become a heat casualty, you become a burden to the platoon the same as if Charlie had zapped you. The search of the village went well, but as in other areas, lessons were learned. I'm confident Sergeant Black and the squad leaders will cover these areas adequately. Overall, I'm pleased. The important thing is to remember the mistakes made and learn from them on future patrols. A few more times outside the wire to shake out the bugs and this will be the best platoon in Nam. Sergeant Black, take charge." He moved with a tired gait down the trail, his RTO and Doc dogging his heels.

Black removed his helmet and cradled it under his arm as he jammed a cigar in his mouth. We collapsed back onto the ground, helmets plopping down beside us as we dug crumpled, sweat stained packs of cigarettes from our pockets. Black waited until we settled down before removing the cigar and expelling a cloud of blue smoke.

"We let him down today. We'll do better next time out. Learn from your mistakes and don't make them again. But don't carry them like a rock around your neck. No mission is a failure when all of us return under our own power. For a bunch of dumb shits, you didn't do too badly. Squad Leaders, take charge of your girls." He turned on his heel and walked jauntily down the trail after the lieutenant whistling a happy little tune, cigar held between thumb and forefinger. Sergeant Thomas rose and stood in front of our squad.

"Clean your weapons, see to your gear, and grab a beer. Dismissed." He turned down the trail with the other squad leaders as Sergeant Lunas popped up in front of us with his hands on his hips and his bushy eyebrows drawn together in displeasure.

"At ease!" he smothered our groans. "I don't think you did well today. In fact I thought you were pretty sorry overall. *You two.*" He fixed Del and me with a glare. "You made the whole squad look like monkeys with your little screw-up. From now on—"

"Sergeant Lunas?" Staff Sergeant Thomas interrupted from his location on the trail. "I think you'd better come with me."

"I'll get back to you two later," Lunas threatened as he gathered his gear and trotted off.

"That little bastard," Silverstein, the man from our squad who had filled his canteens with Kool-Aid, swore. "Somebody's going to stick a boot in his mouth one of these days." He staggered to his feet and grabbed his gear. "You guys did as well as any of us out there today. None of us were without sin."

The rest of the squad followed him down the trail, each managing to nod or smile at Del and me as they joined the growing stream of men. Johnson leaned against a rubber tree with a piece of grass between his teeth.

"I'm sorry we lost your prisoner, Johnson," I muttered.

"I should have warned you those little mothers are slicker than owl shit." He flashed a mischievous grin. "But I wouldn't have taken the coldest beer in Nam for the sight of you two white boys floundering off after him like that."

"That were a sight," Barney agreed, chuckling as he gathered his gear. "Looked like milk cows chasin' after a thoroughbred. Next time you'll know tu shoot thuh little bastard. Bout a pound of lead slows 'em down considerably." He spat a stream of liquid tobacco as he and Johnson moved down the trail arguing about where to get that coldest beer in Nam.

As other members of the platoon filed past, Bernie and Jerry approached us grinning. I stared hard at the toes of my boots stretched out before me as they paused in front of us, gear clanking around them.

"We heard some little runt beat the crap out of both of you and chased you halfway back to base camp," Jerry teased. "That a fact?"

Bernie snickered and we all burst out laughing. As we stood and limped back, Del and I were forced to repeat every sordid detail of the great escape to the gleeful Bernie and Jerry.

Later, with gear cleaned and bodies showered and fed, we bought six-packs of nickel beer before watching John Wayne in the *Sands of Iwo Jima* at the battalion outdoor theater, finding little consolation in the fact that *he* seemed to be winning *that* battle. Later, in my bunk with the lights off, I relived the day's patrol feeling something less than a conquering hero as I slipped into dream-filled exhaustion haunted by grinning faces in a village called *Nightmare*.

CHAPTER 9

I awoke to a consuming desire to redeem my pride.

At our morning formation, Black covered our errors in water rationing, movement and search techniques, and ended by thrusting his cigar at us for emphasis.

"One other point I want to make to you shits. In the future, you will order prisoners attempting to escape to *Dung Lai*, or *halt*, three times. At that point, you will fire on them, preferably to disable rather than kill. Under no circumstances will you pursue the individual and be led into a minefield or across a booby trap." He paused to fix me with a hard stare as I shrank into a fuzz ball before him. "I don't need to tell you how lucky you and your dumb sidekick were yesterday, Sharpe. Don't count on such good fortune in the future." He shoved the cigar back in his mouth. "Okay, our next mission will be a night ambush patrol in the Golf Course. Square your gear away and get some rest. Inspection is at 1900 hours, move out 2000 hours. Squad Leaders, take charge of your girls!"

Staff Sergeant Thomas briefed us on special preparations we were to make, such as wearing soft caps to break up our outlines, drawing M-60 machine gun ammo in cloth bags to reduce glare and noise, and leaving the C-4 explosives, rope with grappling hook, and LAWs behind. As he departed we clustered around Johnson and Barney.

"Thuh Golf Course is a VC stronghold on tu other side of thuh rubber tree plantation," Barney advised grimly. "It's one bad assed area, for sure. Thuh whole dad-dam' place's covered with booby traps and punji pits." He sent a stream of tobacco juice downward. "Don't recollect ever goin' there without drawin' fire, an if thuh truth be known, ain't excited bout us bein' in there after dark neither."

I shuddered, envisioning the VC possessing super-natural powers when the sun went down, growing from five-foot, five-inch, hundred pound weaklings to six-foot, two hundred pound marauders with the ability to move like shadows as they positioned themselves for attack—and now we were going directly into their sinister habitat at night to hunt them down.

I wrote what I feared might be my last letter home to my mother, mentioning that if anything should happen to me my younger brother should have my most prized possession, a rifle I received for my twelfth birthday, the words reflecting self-pity as, for the first time in my life, I doubted my invincibility. I prepared my gear by dulling every shiny surface to reduce glare and then jumping up and down while tightening each strap to eliminate all possible noise. I dug out my soft cap and sewed two strips of luminous tape to the back so others could identify me in the darkness, and placed strips on the back of my claymore mine to prevent the enemy from crawling up and turning it around to blow in my own face. I ate a light lunch, dozed the afternoon away, and skipped the evening meal entirely due to visions of a belly wound on a full stomach. The day passed faster than I cared for, and I was soon standing in formation remembering many important things I needed to say in my last letter home.

"Black is not only beautiful," Harley, the only black in our squad besides Johnson, observed dryly as Del marked my face with greasy camouflage paint. "It's just downright best."

"Right on, brother," Silverstein quipped. "Think of all the money the army would save on camouflage paint if they'd put only blacks in the infantry instead of us white boys."

"Only a Jew bastard would think such foolishness," Harley scoffed.

Sergeant Thomas led us to the assembly area behind the bunker line and briefed us on a new marvel he carried called a starlight scope, which could turn the night into a soft green haze with up to four hundred meters of visibility on a moonlit night.

Soon Black and the lieutenant, who we now discreetly called *Deputy Dog* thanks to Barney, arrived with Doc and the RTO. Black used a stick to draw in the sand as he briefed formations, casualty procedures, radio frequencies, call signs, supporting artillery and mortar fire, and ominously, actions to take if we, the *ambushers*, became the *ambushees*, which entailed running directly into the enemy fire as our best means of survival. He then divided the platoon into three teams and instructed that the M-60 machine gunner in his position in the middle of the designated kill zone would spring the ambush. Firing would stop when he released a green star cluster. The assault team, which included Del and me, would then rush across the beaten zone to eliminate any remaining resistance and set up security fifty yards on the other side. The search team, which included Bernie and Jerry, would strip the slain of all weapons, gear, and documents. The recovery team would police all of our excess gear from the ambush site and prepare to lead us to an alternate position to set up a defensive perimeter against counterattack.

Black allowed us one last cigarette as darkness settled. Those who spoke did so in whispers even though we were still within our own lines. The day's heat drifted away with the setting sun, leaving me shivering in the cool air as I looked out across the rows of wire to the forbidding rubber trees attempting to still the growing trepidation rising in me. Soon, I stubbed my cigarette out under my heel as nervous shuffling around me announced our imminent departure and strapped on my gear, anxiously wondering if there was an honorable way out of this insane mission. I swatted at the clouds of mosquitoes buzzing around my head and hastily applied a coat of the vile smelling insect repellent to exposed parts of my body. The liquid turned the camouflage paint on my skin to syrup before drying into a crusty shell, but the mosquitoes still bit through my shirt and pants leaving agonizing welts as I gloomily propped against a tree. When the line of men to my front began moving, I followed, keeping my eyes glued to the two bobbing strips of tape on the back of the hat in front of me as my feet searched the invisible ground for stable support, and Del slipped in line five feet behind me.

We halted briefly at the command bunker for Deputy Dog to alert the lieutenant inside we were moving through no-man's land, who in turn placed the bunkers on alert and the reaction force on standby. If the enemy hit us in the twists and turns of our own wire and trapped us like rats between them to our front and our bunkers to the rear, theoretically, our sister units on each side would race through their own exits into the flanks of the enemy to rescue us, a feat none considered appealing or realistic.

Deputy Dog then radioed our departure to the battalion command post, which in turn put our mortar section on ready standby status with their tubes zeroed fifty meters from our fifth wire. If attacked they would fire without command and it was understood we would get short rounds in our ranks and our fair share of sizzling hot shrapnel from the exploding projectiles, but faced with certain death anyway, it was a small comfort to know the enemy would be paying a price along with us.

With all notification procedures complete, we mutely threaded our way into the narrow barbed wire channel and moved swiftly out across the fifth wire to fan out into a defensive posture in the trees beyond, now mere shadows in the night. With the entire platoon through the wire, we moved wordlessly into our travel formation, the only sound that of Deputy Dog's softly crackling radio as he called the all clear to the battalion in a strained whisper. We moved a hundred meters and stopped as the low whine of the starlight scope announced a search of the area to our front. We completed another hundred meter move, steady and methodical, our pace agonizingly slow compared to day movement, mere dark forms gliding silently through the trees with carefully placed boots searching for support while hoping only earth and leaves would receive them. Occasionally we halted for the point to check out an area that had a particularly sinister look to it before moving the platoon across.

I recalled Johnson's motto when I ask him his secret for walking point. *If in doubt, check it out.* Nothing felt right out here. Move, stop, search, and move. With nerves tingling, eyes staring into the void, ears strained to every sound, we slipped deeper into the night, farther away from the safety of our base camp, ever farther into the enemy's domain. The silent line of ghostly figures strung out before me with the head of the column lost in the shadows fifty feet away. The soft glow of the luminous tape on the man's hat to my front faded in and out of view causing me to catch my breath and quiver fearfully when it was excessively long from sight. Hugging the shadows and avoiding patches of moonlight, careful not to scrape a tree or bush, searching the shadows to my flanks, with beads of perspiration trickling down my cheeks, eyes stinging, breathing in shallow gulps as my heartbeat drummed in my ears, I slipped ever forward.

It seemed we had moved forever when I checked the soft glow of my watch and saw that only half an hour had passed, indicating we had covered less than a quarter of the distance to our objective. Already my nerves were ragged and my emotions numb from the tension, my eyes rebelling at being forced wide and unblinking into the nothingness stretching around me as we moved into the unknown. Every step I took could be placing me in an enemy trap that would split the night asunder with hot flashes of light and screaming bullets tearing at my flesh. Every boot I placed on the ground could bring the roar of an exploding mine, or a plunge downward to impale my body on razor-sharp tips of bamboo in a punji pit.

The moon glided out of the clouds overhead, its sudden emergence bathing us in a surreal, murky haze with a hundred-yards of visibility, leaving us exposed to watching eyes. The next moment it tucked back behind its cover and left us groping in the dark to stumble against trees or over dead limbs, the sharp crack slamming against ears strained to the breaking point. As the moonlight teased us, the shadows taunted our senses, one moment frozen and serene, the next flickering and shifting in spurts, snatching our attention about to decipher the lurking forms they created. Fallen branches became the tips of rifles poking around trees, low brush became prone bodies lying in wait, and blackened stumps became crouching men. Nowhere in this lethal environment was anything friendly, all was evil, all was there to destroy.

I loathed the madness of it all, desperately wanting to be somewhere else, where there was light and noise. I wanted to fire my rifle into the blackness on each side to drive the demons back, to yell and scream and disrupt the heavy, choking stillness. Occasional low roars rumbled overhead followed by tiny pops. I moved next to a tree and knelt frozen in place as artillery flares lit the sky overhead and bathed the forest in yellow artificial light as they spiraled down under silk canopies. As trained, I closed one eye to preserve night vision and searched the area around me with the other. With the last sparkle, I moved again with spots swimming in the ruined vision of my opened eye.

Whispering lips pressed next to the ear of the recipient passed all commands to our front or rear, with no explanations given.

"Hold up." *Why*? I wondered.

"Squad Leader back." *What's going on*? I agonized.

The line stops. I face out, cover my area. *What have they seen? Is there something out there? Was that something that just moved?* No, only another shadow. *Or was it?*

Time stood still in our twilight zone. It seemed we would move forever in this purple void and never see the sun again. *Why don't we just stop and crawl under a bush and wait for someone to lead us out of this terror-filled place, lead us back to safety, sanity, and reason?*

CRACK!

My heart leapt as an unwary boot snapped a twig, leaving me wincing at the sudden assault on my raw senses. A limb carelessly released by the man to my front slammed against my face with a swishing thump, leaving me half-blinded.

"Watch it, shithead!" I hissed angrily.

"Sorry," he whispered back.

"Shhhh!" another instructed harshly.

This isn't war! This is inhumane torture. What am I doing out here? I asked for it. No, not this—I asked for an honorable fight, man to man, not this sneaking, groping horror. War is not supposed to be like this! I swallowed a lump of self-pity at my betrayal. *I'd been tricked. I could be killed out here and never even know it.* I trembled, stepped on a twig that sounded like a base drum, and cursed myself for a damned fool as I pulled my thoughts back to the present and paid more attention to placing one foot in front of another while dully watching the darkness even as I knew it was useless.

Two hours later, we halted. Word drifted back for the guides to move forward, signaling we were near our objective and others were scouting our ambush site. *Ten minutes more and we'll be in a strong defensive position,* I coached my tired body. *Just a little longer, we're almost there.* Silent shadows glided back to our line. With seeming deafening noise, teams moved in file behind the guides, the creaking of equipment and the crunch of vegetation underfoot announcing their departure. One of the dark forms approached our team, paused as we struggled to our feet, and led us out of the deep shadow of the rubber trees through knee-high grass into impossibly bright moonlight. I instinctively crouched low to reduce my silhouette as we glided several hundred yards across the flat, open terrain before we halted. To our front, less than a hundred feet away, a dirt road ran parallel to our position. In the center a second road connected with the first, forming a T, just as Black drew it in the sand back in the assembly area. The guide placed a hand on my arm indicating this was my position.

Del and I knelt at the end of a long line of men covering the road and the primary kill zone. I shrugged out of my web gear and placed it on the ground as other men moved in behind us to provide rear security in a perimeter resembling a large capital D. I knew five of the machine guns were in our line, the remaining three in the half-circle behind us. I crawled forward, placed my claymore mine on line with the others a few feet from the road, crawled back to my position next to Del, opened my ammo pouches, removed two grenades from my harness, placed the handheld detonator leading to the claymore mine between us, slid my rifle out to the front, and snuggled it into my shoulder.

I breathed easier when all movement ceased, knowing we were now settled in strong. Anyone knocking on our door would receive a bitter welcome. In the deep silence, the only sound was the low hum of the starlight scopes as the squad leaders searched the night around us. Now we would wait for someone to walk into our trap, knowing that if the enemy observed us setting up we could expect them to ambush us on our return trip. For the moment we had done all we could do—it was Charlie's move.

I motioned to Del that I'd take the first watch. He laid his head down and was asleep almost instantly. I fought to keep my eyes open, exhausted from the fatigue of the march, the relaxing of my tense body coupled with the relative security of our position serving as a strong sedative. I counted the shadows to my front, noting each one's position and shape. The luminous tape on my claymore swam out of focus, bringing on a brief attack of panic until it slipped mercifully back into focus. The hands of my watch crept around the dial so slowly I held it to my ear to ensure it was still working. When my hour was up, I was near the end of my endurance and reached over to shake Del. He stiffened and raised his head, eyes searching the front. I lowered my head and closed my eyes gratefully, aching for rest.

Within minutes it seemed, Del clasped my arm, sending my heart pounding against my ribcage. *Is it already my shift again?* I checked my watch suspiciously, pulled my rifle against my shoulder, and settled in for another long vigil. I checked each shadow, trying to recall if one or another was there on the last shift, watching the suspect ones closer. The night wore on as I alternated each hour with Del while trying to ignore the swarms of mosquitoes attacking me in relentless droves. The occasional snort from a sleeping man, quickly throttled by the man next to him, was the only sound as the night slipped away.

In the early morning hours, a thin ground fog slowly formed a foot off the ground creating an eerie graveyard ambiance. The long night had taken its toll on me. With fifteen minutes left on my shift, I estimated from stars beginning to fade in the deepening black of approaching morning that we had an hour of darkness left. I longed to stand and stretch my cramped muscles as I lay shivering in the chill morning air, the long hours of contact with the ground leaving my body rigid and numb. Small insects crawled under my clothes and I ached to scratch in a hundred places as tiny points of concentrated pain throbbed from their bites and stings. I stared out across the spooky pall of hanging fog searching for my claymore, uncomfortable because its soft glow was lost in the dampness, and grimly lowered my chin to the stock of my rifle in temporary surrender to the heavy fatigue, counting the seconds and fighting to stay awake, to keep my mind functioning. Then I heard it.

My body surged into tingling currents of electricity as my dull senses sprang to full alert. I jerked my head up with eyes wide searching the shifting veil of smoky gray, every fiber of my body tuned to the incisive danger as my heart lurched and then settled into a steady pounding. I lay frozen, listening intently to nothing, and slowly relaxed, thinking it only my imagination. I breathed again while rotating my head left and right to release the tension, blinked my eyes to replenish the moisture and reduce the burning strain, and glanced at my watch to find I had four minutes yet to go on my shift. Then it came again, a muffled voice, louder this time. I grasped Del's shoulder. He sighed and raised his head in preparation for his shift. I squeezed harder, freezing him in suspense. He snapped his head to the front as a voice floated through the haze and arched higher trying to see over the low, silky air as other forms around us stirred, other heads lifted in concentration, and rifles inched forward. The hum of four starlight scopes operating at once filtered over us, all trained to the front. My pulse raced in earnest as a steady, mysterious creaking noise reached us. A low laugh rang out, followed by several voices in muted mirth. My skin crawled as feet scraping along the dirt road became discernible, mingling with the odd creaking sound. I swallowed to stifle the urge to clear my throat of the strangling saliva suspended there as pressure built in my head. Still the noise grew to our front, voices happy and carefree in the darkness.

The air hummed with tension as we coiled for the attack. One by one, the starlight scopes clicked off as they picked out the approaching silhouettes still invisible to the rest of us. In the middle of our line, Black's dark form rose to a kneeling position, stared through his starlight scope, and sank back into a prone position as the low whine of his scope faded away. The muzzle of the machine gun in his position shifted to the junction of the two roads. I eased my trigger finger forward and pressed the safety of my rifle, the tiny click inordinately loud in the stillness. Time stood still. Nothing moved around our rigid, prone figures hunched over our extended weapons. No other sound reached us save the muted, gay voices approaching through the drifting dirty gray veil.

I could not believe enemy soldiers would make such a racket in a combat zone. *Are these the feared shadows of death? Surely, they're civilians blundering into our lethal trap!* I quickly reminded myself there was a curfew over the whole country from sundown to sunup. Anyone outdoors was subject to attack without question. Still, I agonized in the moments I lay waiting, could they be peasants going early to their rice paddies? It would be daylight soon. Vietcong would not stumble along a road laughing and talking the way these men were doing. *This has to be a mistake! We are about to murder innocent people!*

They appeared out of the fog, at first only a dark blob, but growing in detail as they approached the junction. First two figures with rifles slung over their shoulders, and then the darker mass making the strange creaking noise, an ox cart with high rail sides inching along in a slow plod. They reached the intersection and turned right along the road parallel to our grim, waiting line crouching in the mist. Behind the ox cart another group of men trailed along in a disorganized mass, the sound of their sandals scuffing the dirt mingling with their laughter. I hunched over my rifle and pointed its invisible muzzle towards the middle of the bigger group in the rear as Del clutched the claymore firing-device in both hands.

The tension seeped from my body. The enemy no longer unknown. He was here, and extremely dumb and incompetent. *And he was going to die.* I sighted along the top of my barrel through the darkness aiming center mass of the group of dark figures. As the last of the group turned right, streaks of red darted into their midst followed by a deafening *TAT-TAT-TAT-TAT* as a machine gun barked harshly, disrupting the preceding tranquility. My shoulder slammed to the rear as the recoil of my rifle danced back from the bright orange muzzle flash, its discharge lost in the ear-splitting thunder of our massed fire. My senses reeled in the blinding flashes of claymores erupting in rippling booms sending thousands of lethal pellets into the kill zone. I continued to pull my trigger, absorbing the jarring recoil of my weapon amid the tearing roar and reddish-yellow sprouts mixing with converging lines of red tracers sweeping the road in gluttonous determination. In the wavering light, bodies rose in the air, pitched backwards, and spun around.

Wood flew from the side of the cart and sparks cascaded from broken metal as a great terror-filled bellow from the ox surmounted our ripping fire.

I rose to my knees tearing at my web gear for another magazine in the inferno, reloaded, and emptied it into the wreckage to my front. A green streak arched through the night and burst into fragments, ordering us to desist. Another green streak erupted in the air, commanding us to cease firing. The machine guns yammered to an echoing silence as our own fire tapered off into sporadic pops.

"Killer Niner, Killer Niner! This is Mustang Alpha One, over," Deputy Dog screamed into his handset, his voice frantic as he called our direct support artillery. "Roger, Killer Niner, Fire Mission Delta! I repeat, Fire Mission Delta! Request continuous illumination over Delta! We are in contact. I repeat, continuous illumination over Delta, unit in contact, over!"

I felt panicky as I inhaled the burnt cordite hanging in the air and fumbled for another magazine to replace the empty one locked in my weapon as eerie silence settled over us. Parachute flares popped overhead, bathing the area in yellow wavering light, sending shadows dancing around us as they drifted lazily to the ground. Smoke wafted from the end of my rifle and the heat from the metal tinged my fingers as I stared in disbelief at the collapsed bodies and splintered cart in shambles before us. The ox was on its knees now emitting a deep, soulful bellowing from its pain-riddled body. My own spent body shook uncontrollably in spasmodic twitches.

"Assault teams! Move out!" Black yelled.

"Let's go!" I rose to my feet and jogged across the road, sidestepping the spreading pools of blood and sprawled bodies with their torn skin and gaping mouths, praying none of them would move and force me to shoot them. Pangs of anguish rippled through me from their ghastly wounds as I crouched in the grass on the opposite side of the road praying I would not see any one before me.

"Search teams, move out!" Black yelled, his commanding voice a calming balm to me.

Behind me, the search teams sifted through the fallen bodies lifting broken weapons and bits of frayed equipment. Sergeant Thomas walked over to the ox, placed his muzzle against the head of the moaning creature, and fired twice. The beast rolled over on its side with one leg twitching in the air. I tried to convince myself this was real, that we had just killed people. My dazed mind could not accept it had happened and was over with so quickly. It was only a dream. I would wake up any moment now and be thankful. I longed for a cigarette as I fumbled the canteen from my hip.

"You okay, Jay?" Del asked in a tremulous voice.

"Yeah, are you?" I replied, my voice husky and unnatural. I looked over my shoulder as more parachute flares popped overhead. Deputy Dog stood in the middle of the road talking into his handset as his RTO hovered behind him looking like a hump-backed dwarf with its master. Black stalked through the debris directing the search team as they piled equipment into mounds. The recovery team beyond them scrambled to pick up the claymore wires and equipment.

I felt cold and hollow, like the times as a child when caught in a lie or doing something shameful. I struggled to convince myself I had played a part in this tragic event, tried to remember the specifics, but could only recall the images of roaring noise, flashing light, and jitterbugging bodies—and the steady jar of my weapon against my shoulder. I turned back to the front trying not to think.

Sergeant Thomas informed us we were remaining here until morning instead of withdrawing to our alternate position, his voice grave and face drawn. Johnson on my left rearranged his equipment as Barney beside him removed a plug of chewing tobacco and filled his jaw. Harley and Silverstein beyond them huddled together casting baleful looks over their shoulders as if this were all a bad dream. Del, beside me, drank from his canteen, the water spilling down his chin as his hands shook. I watched the search teams drag the bodies along the road and place them in a line near the mound of equipment. Figuring it didn't make much difference with the flares overhead, I lit a cigarette and inhaled deeply while cupping the glowing tip in my palms.

As the sun eased up over the horizon, the steady thumping of blades approached from the direction of the base camp and a helicopter circled down to land on the road near the bodies and equipment. Deputy Dog strode forward to greet the group of men exiting the aircraft and two stopped to talk to him as the others hurried by to the massacre site.

"That's our Commander," Del whispered.

"That's Mustang Six with him," I observed.

Barney spat a stream of tobacco. "Peers thuh brass wants tu inspect our handiwork."

"God, I was scared shitless, Barney," Silverstein moaned.

"So was I, Jew boy," Harley acknowledged softly.

"Sheeettt," Barney sniffed. "When you ain't scared, it's time tu un-ass this place."

"Knock the shit off!" Lunas instructed loudly, mostly to impress the brass behind him. "Keep your eyes to the front, goddamn it!"

"Asshole," Silverstein muttered under his breath.

The group from the chopper rummaged through the bodies while taking pictures and holding up pieces of gear in excitement as they called out to one another. Deputy Dog pointed out various things to Mustang Six and our company commander as he reconstructed the operation. A half-hour later, a truck barreled down the road escorted by two gun jeeps. The equipment and bodies were loaded onto the back of the truck and the convoy roared off, leaving only the dead ox and the broken cart on the road. Deputy Dog and Mustang Six walked back to the waiting aircraft and climbed aboard, though the lieutenant seemed reluctant to do so, and the chopper departed in a swirl of dust, circled once overhead to gain altitude, and then streaked back to the base camp as our company commander stared after them.

"Squad Leaders, round them up!" Black ordered from the road. "Give me a travel formation, two columns, First and Third leading, Second and Fourth in trail. Let's move it!"

We moved back to base camp with our company commander and Deputy Dog's RTO in the center, covering the same ground on the return trip as we had the night before. By day, it seemed open, almost scenic. The company commander ranged up and down between our two columns smiling and nodding his head as he made eye contact with us, letting Black run the formation, unconcerned with the blistering pace we set as we blitzed through most of the areas we normally would have stopped and checked out.

I dully realized how spent I was. My only desire was to reach the safety of the fifth wire, and any enemy who placed himself before me would face a swift and brutal foe.

We held the swift pace all the way through the bunkers and into the assembly area, where we finally slowed and milled about indecisively. Men passed cigarettes around and lit them in silence. I backed against a tree and looked at those around me, stunned at their appearance—haggard faces streaked with grime and camouflage paint framing red-rimmed, bloodshot eyes staring with glazed expressions, each looking like no soldiers I had ever imagined, with none looking another full in the eye.

Del reached for my pack. "Give me a cigarette, Jay."

"You don't smoke, asshole," I reminded him callously.

Barney offered his plug of tobacco. "Here, have a chaw."

"No thanks," Del declined with a despairing sigh. "What I really need is a beer."

"Make that an even half-dozen," Silverstein agreed.

The company commander and Black caught up with us with the RTO panting along behind them, and passed through us without a word. We fell lamely in behind them, moving two abreast down the trail. The mortar platoon poured out of their sunken pits to cheer our passage as we crossed the road and limped through the shower point into the company street, our heads drooping, waves of fatigue weighing us down as fear and tension drained away. Black formed us into a sloppy formation as troops poured out of the hooches in a cheering mass calling out to those of us they knew. Even the cooks and clerks hurried to join the throng as the animals congregated into an awe-inspiring tangle off to one side.

Black crisply executed an about face and saluted the company commander. "Sir, the Platoon is formed!"

"Thank you, Sergeant. Be at *ease!*" our commander ordered.

We sprang to parade rest with as much snap as our numb bodies could muster.

"You men have just conducted one of the most successful ambush patrols this Division has ever recorded." He paused as those around us cheered while we stood mute.

"The Battalion Commander and I viewed the site this morning. Frankly, we could find no fault with any part of the superbly planned and executed operation. Indications from the intelligence teams at the site are that you hit one of the longest sought-after, most vicious terror groups operating in this area, a group known as the *Black Widows*." He paused again as the group around us cheered. "This element has been responsible for many of the executions of the local populace, as well as the emplacement of most of the mines, booby traps, and punji pits in this AO. They have operated with impunity throughout this region for two years. Last night, indications are you annihilated the entire group, including their leader." He waited for the roar of approval around us to settle down. "Your record stands at sixteen enemy soldiers killed, one ox cart filled with explosives and ammunition captured, ten rifles and two pistols recovered, and enough leads to other local guerrilla units to keep our intelligence units busy for some time to come. Gentlemen, you have performed *magnificently*! You have done this Division, this Battalion, and this Company proud. I *salute* you!"

Wild cheering erupted around us as the commander and Black exchanged salutes. When Black executed an about face and released us, we were mobbed by happy troops pounding our backs as we waded through them shaking hands and slapping palms, their excitement beginning to penetrate our reserve. We dumped our gear and went to breakfast, where the mess sergeant met us at the door.

"There will be no routine breakfast for you on this morning!" he proclaimed, beaming.

The KPs served us at our tables, placing heaping platters of steak and eggs before us, followed by mounds of potatoes and cups of coffee. Del, Bernie, Jerry, and I ate together silently surrounded by the smiling faces of our fellow Wolfhounds, and then hurried back to the hooch to clean our weapons and gear in hopes of beating the crowd to the shower point. There we washed the scum from our bodies, letting the water cascade down in streams, and returned to the hooch to learn the general himself had pinned a bronze star on Deputy Dog's chest at division headquarters.

As I stripped and lay on my bunk, I saw the letter I had written the previous day lying on the pillow. I ripped it in half wondering hauntingly if any of our foes had prepared their own letters before entering into the darkness of the night before.

CHAPTER 10

I awoke in the late afternoon flushed with heat and lay on my bunk with my hands clasped behind my head attempting to sort through my jumbled emotions. I analyzed the glory of our return and the pride of our unit as they surrounded us. I tried to recall the horrors of the night before, the terror of the movement in the deep blackness, but the fear I experienced at the time eluded me. I had read somewhere that the mind erases pain. One could recall something hurt but could not reproduce the actual trauma itself. Lying here in broad daylight, I remembered aching with terror, but could not replicate the sensation. It all seemed subdued now. I saw again the jarring light from claymores, the muzzle flashes and red tracers converging in their death dance along the road, the bodies jerking and sagging as metal ripped through them, their screams of anguish lost in the crescendo of our onslaught. These enemy soldiers, I reminded myself as waves of pity stabbed at me, would have gladly done the same to us given the opportunity. This was what we were here for, even if it wasn't the heroic thing I had imagined. No one ever said it was pretty, but no one ever described the ugliness of it either. I recalled the strange calmness and annoyance that settled over me as the enemy moved into our kill zone. Why had I been so disappointed in them? Why even now did I resent their lack of professionalism? I realized I was angry because they died like babies, not like the crafty, harsh enemy I had trained to face. We had practiced the procedures a hundred times in Basic. Last night happened exactly as it was supposed to happen. Sixteen men died suddenly and violently. We did not suffer a casualty. The viciousness and utter surprise of our attack prevented them from firing a single shot in our direction. Men were not supposed to die like that, not battle hardened, experienced guerrillas at the hands of raw recruits like us. Until that moment, with the exception of the half dozen veterans among us, none of us had ever even seen the enemy or fired a shot in anger. I sank deeper into despair trying to make sense of it.

"Jay? You awake?" Jerry asked from his bunk.

"Yeah, sort of," I replied, surprised that he was.

"You kill anybody out there?" he asked.

"It was hard to tell." I continued staring at the ceiling. "Did you?"

"I had to squeeze the claymore three times before it blew. Most everything was over by then."

"We all did," Del interjected from his bunk. "Doesn't matter whose bullet it was."

I recalled the flashes as my rifle jumped against my shoulder but could not remember aiming at any specific person or seeing anyone fall. They taught us in Basic

most men instinctively fired high ... so I had deliberately aimed low ...

Bernie broke the silence. "I didn't."

"Didn't what?" Del asked after a pause.

"Kill anybody," Bernie replied.

Jerry turned his head on the pillow to study him.
"How could you know?"

"I just know."

"Bullshit," Del snorted, raising his head to look
over his feet at Bernie across the aisle. "Like I said, we
all did. Nobody knows whose bullet hit who. It could've
been anybody's."

"Not if I didn't put any bullets out there," Bernie
countered after a long silence.

"You saying you didn't shoot?" Sergeant Lunas
demanded from his end of the hooch, and then sat
up and swung his feet to the floor when Bernie continued to stare silently up at the sagging canvas roof.
"I asked you a question, goddamn it! Did you fire or
not?"

"It don't make no difference no how," Barney said
from his bunk.

"It makes a difference to me!" Lunas insisted, glaring at Bernie.

"In thuh end, it don't mean nothin'," Barney
insisted as he lifted his can and spit.

"It means something to *me*," Lunas insisted.
"Chicken shits belong in the animal platoon, not out
there with us!"

Johnson sat up on his bunk. "That's uncalled for."

"I don't have to put up with any of your shit, John-son, or yours either, Barney, I don't care how long you've been over here!"

"It don't mean nothin'" Barney insisted. "So jus give it a rest already."

"Are you talking to *me*?" Lunas raged, caught up in his anger now and jumping to his feet. "I'm a sergeant and I'll say what I damn well please about gutless cowards that let the platoon down, you understand that, *Specialist*?"

I looked across at Barney in surprise, having had no indication that he was a Specialist Fourth Class since he never wore any rank and always went as slick-sleeved as us privates.

"Gutless cowards?" Johnson rose, looking him in the eye as he reached for Lunas' web gear hanging over his bunk.

"What the hell do you think you're doing?" Lunas demanded, snatching his web gear from Johnson's grasp.

"Helping you search out all the gutless cowards in the platoon," Johnson replied softly.

"W-What do you mean?" Lunas asked, clutching his web gear protectively.

"This morning Silverstein issued replacement ammo to every man in this squad except for you," John-son replied, eyeball-to-eyeball with Lunas now. "That right, Silverstein?"

"That's right, Johnson," Silverstein confirmed. "Everybody but Sarge."

"So?" Lunas croaked. "So I haven't drawn mine yet! So what?"

"So show us your magazines," Johnson challenged. "Show us you're not a chicken shit gutless coward."

"Show us!" Silverstein cajoled as the tension mounted and it became obvious Lunas would not accept the challenge.

"Come on, Sarge, put up or shut up!" Harley joined in.

"Come on, Sarge!" another called.

"Empty your pouches, Sarge!" Silverstein insisted.

"Do it for him, Johnson!" another yelled as Lunas looked around in panic.

"I don't have to show you anything, Johnson!" he screamed and rushed out of the hooch still clutching his web gear.

We lay in stunned silence as Johnson walked down the aisle and paused at the foot of Bernie's bunk. "It's easy learning how to kill," he said so low we had to strain to hear. "The hardest part is learning when to kill. Every man reaches that point on his own." He looked down at Bernie. "You don't hurry it, white boy. Let it come naturally. Because once you've passed that point, you can never go back." He walked out of the hooch with measured steps.

"Sheeeeettt! Tryin' tu analyze this nutty place'll make you loony in thuh head," Barney offered from his end of the hooch and punctuated the statement with a well-placed stream of tobacco juice into the can beside his bunk. "I tell you, it don't mean *nothin*'! You got tu take it a day at a time, an when thuh shit's really flyin', by thuh minute. After that, dad-dam' *forget* it!" He wiped his chin and grinned around his crooked teeth. "All this heavy drama's done made me thirsty. Who'll loan me thirty cents fur a six-pack of Ballentines?"

"I will, provided you pay me fifty back," Silverstein offered.

"Dad-dam' Jew shark!" Barney cried in anguish. "How bout forty?" The two sauntered out the door still arguing the terms as we laughed.

Jerry sat up on his bunk rubbing his hands together in anticipation. "Hell, I'm for a beer. How much money we got?"

"Me too!" Del chorused.

"You guys go ahead," Bernie stated miserably from his bunk.

Jerry, Del, and I had a grand total of seventy cents amongst us. Even at a nickel a can, we couldn't quite muster a six-pack apiece, and with payday only two days away, weren't really in the mood to pay the exorbitant interest rates commonly charged by those who had money, so we politely invited Bernie to join us again. When he again refused, and faced with no other alternative, we mugged him. After a vicious scuffle in which several bunks were overturned, we held him upside down by his ankles and shook eighty-five cents from his pockets as the rest of the men cheered us on. Forced to join us then or watch his hoarded cash squandered on what he insisted were 'the three vilest, no good, rotten sons of bitches on earth,' we headed for the PX with him dancing around a tight-fisted Jerry trying to snatch his money back. As friends, we felt compelled to help those unfortunates among us who had fallen on hard times, and as such, bought him a six-pack along with the rest of us and even shared the can of mixed nuts we purchased. With spirits high and burdens forgotten, we then set out for the battalion theater.

The theater itself consisted of a large sheet of plywood painted white suspended on poles placed in the ground before rows of benches spaced across the grass with no sides, top, or floor. The 16mm projector required the movie to be interrupted every twenty minutes or so when the reels of film were changed. This intermission resulted in a mass exodus to the drainage ditch running along the side where we stood shoulder to shoulder to relieve our beer inflated bladders before rushing back for the next reel. Mosquitoes, curious bats, and miscellaneous large flying insects went to the movie with us and buzzed around madly in the light. It was common to see a man serenely watching the movie one minute, and the next leaping to his feet to dance a wild, foot-stomping, arm-flopping gyration, before returning to his seat, having just shaken out the latest creepy crawler to fly down his collar.

We always cheered the heroes and booed the villains, often throwing empty beer cans at images of the bad guys on the board screen. We also evaluated and rated every woman amid loud, raunchy arguments and spontaneous declarations of eternal love. Though a festive event, it inevitably left us homesick and nostalgic as we viewed scenes of *The World* thousands of miles away. Tonight was no exception. The movie moved us deeply. The hero lost, leaving us misty-eyed, and Jerry fell in love with the hero's wife. Lying on our bunks afterwards, the four of us shared the last three cans of beer as he fantasized.

"She's the most beautiful girl in the world," he insisted. "In fact, she's what all this shit over here is about. Just knowing there are women like her back home makes it worthwhile."

"She's just a stupid *actress*," Del argued sleepily. "She wouldn't give you the friggin' time of day."

"She's a knockout," I said in an attempt to soften Del's harsh rebuke.

"I'll take sloppy seconds!" a voice offered from the darkness.

"How would you like your ass kicked, asshole?" Jerry offered hotly.

"Jerry's in love," Bernie teased.

"And you can be second in line behind the other shit face!" Jerry fumed.

"They're just kidding," I soothed.

"Yeah, well, goddamn it, she's the only decent broad I've seen in this shit hole, and it pisses me off to hear her trash mouthed."

I was becoming a little bored with his tirade, although she did have the all-American girl image and it would not have been hard for me to fall in love with her if Jerry hadn't already claimed her. But when Jerry felt, he did so strongly, and I was learning to indulge him his excesses. Nor would I put it past him to go home a big hero with sergeant's stripes and a chest full of medals and marry his new found flame.

"Listen up, guys," Jerry begged from the darkness. "Really, I could write to her fan club, get autographed pictures of her, and posters with her in bathing suits. We could send a platoon picture to her, one that everyone has signed. Or better yet, if she comes over here on one of those USO shows with Bob Hope, I can present it to her personally as the representative of the platoon. What do you think, guys? Hey, anybody awake?"

Always going for broke, I thought with a smile. As his voice droned on in the darkness, I slipped into sleep dreaming of Henry Fonda's delightful little daughter Jane in the movie *The Chase* which we had just watched, visualizing her crying tears for us as we moved through the fifth wire to face the evil Cong. Dawn would come early.

———

Over the next few weeks, we weathered into a functioning team as we hardened under the rigors of combat. All unnecessary pounds washed from our bodies, leaving us lean and fit as we acclimated to the heat, learned to ration our water, and acquired the basic survival skills in our hostile environment.

Day patrols evolved into little more than pleasant strolls through the countryside. Night ambushes still carried fear and uncertainty, even in the absence of further contact. Bunker duty remained just plain miserable, with rats becoming an increasing problem as the monsoon rains eased away. The creatures scurried over our sleeping bodies at night chewing at fingertips, pockets, and even the corners of our mouth if the smell of food lingered. For those bitten, the awful rabies shots were the price for negligence.

One hot, muggy night the mosquitoes were unmanageable, biting through shirts, pants, and the layers of repellent as we squirmed in misery. At midnight, Jerry woke me for my shift. I applied new layers of oily repellent to my skin as I moved to the front of the bunker and squatted on the edge as Jerry settled down at the rear and wrapped himself in his poncho in an effort to protect himself from the swarms of insects. As my shift wore on, he tossed and turned in frustration as I sat in a fatigued state at the front of the bunker mindlessly counting shadows, my thoughts of home as the night lay in a dark silvery pool around me.

"*Shit!*" Jerry bellowed.

"W-What is it?" I demanded, his outburst scaring the hell out of me, and most likely half of the VC sappers trying to sneak up on us.

"Goddamned mosquitoes! How the hell can a man sleep in this shit?"

"Christ, you almost gave me a heart attack," I sputtered as I searched the front for shadows that might have moved, finding that several seemed to be outright missing. "Keep it down, will you?"

"I can't take this shit anymore, I'm sleeping in the goddamn bunker!" he grumbled as he collected his gear and climbed down the side.

"You've got to be nuts," I warned.

"Aw hell, the woolies won't bother me if I don't bother them," he mumbled as he entered the black pit.

I shrugged. "Lots of luck."

This seemed to work, and within minutes, his snores vibrated from within the cavern below as I squatted on the front edge of the bunker with my rifle across my knees recounting and marking the shadows in the restored harmony of the night. The silence stretched around me again as my mind resumed its wandering and I began to nod, dreaming of home.

"*Yiiiieeeeeee!*"

The piercing scream stood the hair up on the back of my neck as my eyes bulged out trying to look everywhere at once.

"*Yiiiieeeeeee!*"

Goosebumps fleshed out all over me and I damned near fell off the bunker as the scream split the night in bloodcurdling intensity. I jerked my rifle bolt to the rear and chambered a round in panic as Jerry tore out of the bunker below clutching a large black mass in front of him.

"Yiiieeeeeee!" he screamed as he galloped off to his left.

"What is it?" I yelled as I jumped down and started after him.

He made a circle and came back at me full speed. *"Shoot it! Shoot the goddamned thing! Shoot it, somebody!"*

"*Wh-What is it*!" I screeched as I turned and ran in the opposite direction, thinking I obviously couldn't shoot it with him holding it in his hands and that *I* sure as hell didn't want it if *he* didn't. "*Hey, keep away from me!*" I yelled as I scrambled back up the side of the bunker to get away from the both of them.

"What's going on down there?" a voice challenged from the darkness.

"Halt! Dung Lai! Halt or I'll shoot," shouted another in panic from the opposite side as a hand flare flamed into the night and a spooked guard fired a rifle.

The field phone buzzed frantically as I regained the top of the bunker a step ahead of Jerry and his friend and peered back down at them, ready to leap off the opposite side if they followed. The light of the hand flare outlined Jerry wide-eyed below me holding a nasty, fat-bodied rat squirming for all it was worth with its foot long tail twitching madly as it squeaked.

"*Christ!*" I shrieked as more flares erupted and a machine gun's chatter intermingled with popping rifle fire. "Throw the damned thing down! *Throw it!*"

Jerry threw the furry body against the side of the bunker and began growling like a dog as he jumped up and down on it, pulverizing its body in the dirt. He leaned against the bunker gasping as I crawled down next to him on quaking legs.

Deputy Dog charged up from the command bunker, helmet-less and with his boots unlaced, skidded to a halt beside us, and peeped around the corner to the front. "How many were there? Anybody hurt?" He swung his rifle around the corner and fired off six or eight rounds before snapping back against the bunker, muzzle sky-ward, like in the movies. "Sergeant Black's calling up the reaction force!"

Dully I tuned in to all the shooting and the half dozen flares drifting overhead as he peeped around the corner again. "Sir ... it wasn't VC ... it was a rat."

He frowned. "A rat?"

"A rat," I confirmed, pointing to the mangled body lying in the settling dust. "Um, Jerry killed it, Sir."

He stared blandly at the bloody mass of hair in the stomped out hole. "Oh hell, Sergeant Black isn't going to like this," he advised sorrowfully as the sounds of running feet and shouted commands announced the imminent arrival of Black and the reaction force coming up the trail behind us.

"No, Sir, he sure ain't," I agreed.

"I better call the CP." Dazed, he moved inside the bunker to the still-buzzing phone as the reaction force fanned out to our rear intent on blocking the penetration.

The lieutenant and I were right—Black didn't like it. It took him over an hour to get the bunker line settled down again, plus answer all the questions over the field phone from the company, battalion, brigade, and division CPs. And that didn't count the ass chewing Jerry and I got, which covered at least another half hour.

It was a miracle the rodent didn't bite Jerry during the melee, and even more so that the spooked guards didn't shoot him as he ran around screaming after awakening in the bunker with a heavy weight on his chest and something tickling his chin. Out of reflex, he grabbed it. The rest was legend. Several days later I sat in the latrine letting nature take its course reading the graffiti on the walls, where I observed the following inscription:

First Platoon 16, VC 0, Ambush

Scrawled below this in poor taste, read:

First Platoon 1, Rats 0, Hand-To-Hand Combat

So quick in war do fortunes fade, I mused, which proved an old Army proverb: *One aw-shit wipes out a hundred atta-boys.*

Soon another old Army proverb proved true as well: *Familiarity breeds contempt.*

With the continuous visits of one platoon or another to Nightmare, the poor villagers were flooded with GIs. Our platoon was directed to search the village yet again on this particular day for signs of bad guys. We dutifully crept up through the trees with our squad assigned the search mission and the other three blocking. At the preplanned moment, we broke cover and charged to our position to begin our sweep through the village. The smiling villagers immediately formed around the steps of the main hooch as we entered from the opposite end. Every container, box, and sack was open and displayed for our inspection. The children followed after us smiling and holding out their hands for chocolates. Worse, the villagers had erected a small stand next to the main hooch to sell Cokes, tea, and fresh fruit, obviously intent on doing a booming business from our frequent visits. This somewhat took the fun out of our raiding and pillaging, but still, a Coke and piece of fruit were welcome treats after a long march in the heat.

The darker side of this old proverb was burned into our minds a week later as we complacently half checked danger zones on our route of march, and didn't bother with some at all, while using the trails to cover the distance in half the time. We didn't even bother to put out blocking forces around the village and simply marched straight in barely taking the time to search the containers in our haste to get to the refreshment stand, obviously thinking the enemy had moved on to less patrolled areas since this one was *pacified*.

Even the villagers' subdued attitude and diverted eyes and the children clinging to their mama-sans squatting in silence around the main hooch failed to alert us. Disappointed to find the concession stand closed, we hurriedly formed up for the march back to the base camp in hopes of beating the heat. In two fast moving columns, we crossed the open paddies and entered the wood line. Sergeant Thomas directed me fifty yards out on right flank security as second squad took point on this sweltering hot day. The gnats swarmed in waves, sticking to my sweat-streaked face as loud grumbling and hollow laughter wafted from the platoon hidden by the brush on my left. As we moved at a steady pace, an uneasy feeling crept over me. I stumbled along grappling with the unsettling phenomenon as my taut senses hummed with danger.

WHOOOOMMMM!

I cowered as the ground shook under my boots and dark smoke rose in the air.

"*Medic*! Get the Medic up here!" a voice cried in panic as bits of leaves and twigs pattered down around me.

My gut clenched as I realized someone had stepped on a booby trap and frantically searched the area around me for signs of trip wires as someone moaned from the bushes separating me from the platoon.

"Patch Work Control, this is Mustang Alpha One, over!" Deputy Dog yelled into his radio, filling me with dread as he summoned a dustoff. "Roger, Patch Work. We have an *immediate*, repeat, immediate! Grid, Golf Zulu-one-zero six-niner, over!"

"You two rig a poncho litter!" Black's voice ordered. "Johnson, take point, due east!"

On unsteady legs, I changed direction with the platoon while searching every inch of the ground and slipped in closer until I had them in sight. I froze in shuddering panic after stumbling through a single strand of spider web, my imagination seeing the fiber as one of the almost invisible trip wires, expecting an explosion to lift me high into the air minus a leg. With a stomach of jelly, I hurried along beside the platoon placing each trembling foot in front of the other until we stumbled into a small clearing in the rubber trees. The squad leaders spaced us around the edge facing outward into the trees as rotor blades beat the air. Black popped a yellow smoke grenade and tossed it into the middle of the clearing and the chopper fishtailed down a moment later and bounced as the skids touched the ground. Doc and two men ran to the open doors carrying a body on the improvised litter between them.

The first *Crack* pulled my attention back to the front in surprise. The second *Crack* kicked bark off the tree I was kneeling beside and the wind caressed my cheek as the hornet hummed past my ear. I scratched for cover as several enemy weapons opened up in a broken barrage, at least three carbines and one AK-47 automatic rifle, I counted as I groveled in the dirt. One of the enemy guns was directly in front of me I noted as I rolled behind a tree and answered it round for round firing into every bush and likely hiding place in the green tangle before me, my bullets cutting leaves from branches. The whole perimeter erupted in a steady roar as the platoon fought back. I dug for a fresh magazine and reloaded as the chopper behind me flapped into the air pulling maximum power, little more than a sitting duck on the ground, and the VC guns intensified, trying to bring it back to earth in flames.

The ground shook as explosions ripped the trees to my front, and I blasted away in an attempt to suppress the enemy fire as Deputy Dog adjusted the artillery. Billowing smoke filled the air as the thunder rolled in tight, numbing my senses. I covered my head as trees sagged under the pounding, and hugged the ground as chunks of earth fell across my back, the deafening noise subduing the small-arms fire from both sides. When the crushing explosions subsided, I lifted my head to stare into the drifting haze, finding the vegetation a shambles of charred and splintered trees covered with scorched dirt and drifting smoke. I gathered my empty magazines, shoved them into my pouches, loaded a full one into my rifle, and shoved another into my belt in readiness.

"Fire and maneuver!" Black ordered in the lull.

"First team, cover! Second team, move out!" Sergeant Thomas shouted.

We moved in short leaps, our fire teams dashing from one bit of cover to another.

"Here's one of the bastards!" Harley yelled from the far left. "Half of him's in a tree!"

A hand with part of an arm appeared in front of me, the stump wet with blood. "Sergeant Thomas, over here!" I shouted as I shuddered. "Here's part of another one!"

Sergeant Thomas trotted over, glanced at the bloody stump, and moved past me to search the area beyond. "Here's the rest of him," he called after a few paces.

I edged forward to a mass of raw flesh and soggy clothing ten yards from the first piece.

Barney elbowed past me to toe the corpse over onto its back. "Yep, this one's hamburger now," he appraised, rolling his wad of tobacco so he could spit, and then frowned as I queasily looked closer at the torn torso. "You'n ain't gonna be sick, are you?"

"It's him, Barney!" I exclaimed, recognizing the man who had escaped from Del and me. "The one that got away at the village!"

Barney looked closely at the disfigured man. "Well what do you know, got thuh little dickens after all." He spat a stream of brown juice on the lump of flesh. "How bout that shit?"

One man on our side sustained a flesh wound to his left arm during the sharp exchange. Doc patched the wound as Deputy Dog made a fruitless attempt to get the dustoff to return, becoming furious when advised to bring the man back with us since he could walk and the landing zone was not secure. Black ordered the wounded man's gear distributed to others as we formed up. We left the two bodies, but carried the one enemy rifle we recovered as we set out on our journey home, now a far wiser platoon.

Carelessness had cost us. After our first determined battle the tally sheet read one American soldier maimed for life, one wounded, two confirmed enemy killed, and one probable as evidenced by bloodstains found in the vicinity. We had not lost the battle, but we were far short of a victory. A large part of the company turned out for our arrival, but there were no cheers today.

"Here comes *Magnet-Ass First*," a voice from the pack joked.

"Hey, First Herd, can't you guys leave some for us?" a second trilled in a halfhearted attempt at lightness.

We met them with stony stares. Still the only platoon in the reorganized company to engage the enemy, we now had established a second record we would rather have foregone—the first to suffer casualties.

We lay on our bunks in a nasty mood with little to say. Ironically, both of the wounded were from our hooch, one from second squad and one from first. Third and fourth squads, in the next hooch, while not feeling the loss less, were still spared the sight of the two empty bunks stacked in their midst as a somber reminder of our stupidity.

———

We immediately went back to the basics of doing things by the book. We moved quietly, with no laughter or grumbling, and carefully checked each danger zone while taking nothing for granted. We avoided trails altogether, and blocking forces were again posted around the village before we entered. The villagers continued to form around the main hooch since we would herd them there anyway, but now were sullen, even fearful, as they watched our thorough search of their homes. The concession stand disappeared as well to further underscore their resentment.

Increasingly we began to find booby traps and the instances of sniper fire grew, though we took no further casualties. Nor did we inflict any. It seemed we were shadow boxing with the enemy as we clashed in brief, bitter exchanges. The VC seemed to anticipate our every move and slipped around us at will, leaving us feeling ponderous and dimwitted as they feinted and darted, hooked and jabbed in defying our attempts to pin them down for a knockout punch. At times, I could almost sense their mocking laughter.

Bunker duty became less of an ordeal, however, when Jerry appeared on the scene with a 12 gauge shotgun and a box of birdshot. I watched in suspense as he climbed on top of the bunker and tossed a teargas grenade into the dark interior. Within seconds, rats streamed out in all directions while he gleefully blew them away. This captured our imagination and the platoon leaders kept score in the command bunker for confirmed kills, with Jerry topping the list until we were hard pressed to find a single little furry rodent anywhere on the line.

CHAPTER 11

"The Warning Order directs us to the vicinity of the Mekong Delta to protect the rice harvest, where the VC expect to tax the peasants forcefully as they stockpile their crops for market," Deputy Dog briefed as we listened closely. "Over the next several weeks we will operate from a firebase in the middle of the AO and place an umbrella of protection over the defenseless villagers."

We packed our gear amid grand visions of saviors of the oppressed. With morale at an all time high, we tried to drink enough beer the last night in our base camp to last us for several weeks. They trucked our hung over bodies to the pickup zone the following morning, where even our sour stomachs couldn't deny the excitement of our first heli-born operation. With the turbine engines whining, we surged forward to load under the watchful eye of the crew chief and settled into cross-legged positions on the bare floor. The aircraft floated up on a cushion of air, glided across the ground, and lifted into the blue sky spreading a breathtaking panorama below our lofty perch.

Perfect squares of water with dancing sunlight bordered narrow dirt berms and large hedgerows with farmers stooped in the paddies, their hands darting down to pull the stalks. Water buffalo with small kids astride their backs switched their tails at swarms of flies as they chewed their cud. Rutted dirt roads meandered in lazy curves crossing dark rivers lined with thick green vegetation. Three-wheeled Lambrettas hurried along, raising clouds of dust as they intermingled with the occasional ox carts and motor scooters near the hamlets. Small pagodas dotted the countryside, surrounded by graves with rough stone markers. Triangular earthen compounds guarded by moats lined with bamboo spikes and rows of barbed wire marked small South Vietnamese Army outposts, with their flags of yellow with three red stripes fluttering in the clear morning light. Long streams of smoke rose from bundles of burning rice stalks beside the small patches of life supporting mud as our chopper thumped over this serene world like a confident beast sure of its environment. Peace existed below in timelessness wrought by centuries, so remarkably alien to our chattering world far above it seemed unfeasible a war could really exist down there.

I tensed as my aircraft descended with startling abruptness. Gunships streaked by in graceful dives stalking our flanks. A long, grassy field loomed before us bordered by surrounding paddies. The pace increased as we swooped near the ground and trees flashed by in a green blur. The blades vibrated as the engine screamed in a high-pitched whine and wind tore at my face. *Every VC in the world must be watching me*, I thought fearfully as the chopper became a fat, sitting duck in my mind, wallowing along with me helpless inside, giving nothing to hide behind but the thin sheets of aluminum under me holding tons of aviation fuel. I imagined bullets ripping through the floor searching for my flesh and the aircraft exploding in flame, desperately wanting to flatten myself on the ground below, to have mother earth shield me. I edged to the door and placed my feet on the skids underneath as the grass rose up beneath me.

"Let's go!" I yelled, leaping out of the aircraft.

But the ground wasn't there. I plunged down through the tall grass, legs churning, and hit the ground like a sack of coal, pitched forward on my head, and cart wheeled in a stunning, arm-flapping tangle as my gear flew in all directions. I came to rest on my back staring up at a darkening sky. From some vestige of my reeling brain, I realized the aircraft behind me was landing on top of me and rolled over onto my stomach, too stunned to stand and run as the rotor wash whipped grass against my face, and lunged with my last ounce of energy. In my dazed, semiconscious state, legs charged by me as my ears buzzed and my lungs fought for air.

"Sharpe?" Deputy Dog's face swam into view, eyebrows furrowed in concern, as I finally managed a ragged breath of delicious sweetness. "Give me a hand here!"

Del hooked an arm under mine and hoisted me up. "You okay, Jay?"

"Where am I?" I gasped as the sky revolved around me.

"Get him off the LZ!" Black directed as he trotted past.

"Come on, man," Del urged as he lugged me stumbling towards the tree line. When he released me, I collapsed onto the ground and someone thrust my rifle and helmet at my feet.

Sergeant Black positioned our platoon in a narrow strip of trees, bordered on the backside by the LZ, and on the front by rice paddies. As I regained my senses, succeeding waves of aircraft landed in the LZ. Second platoon linked in on our right flank, third platoon our left flank, and the other two companies of the battalion tied into their lines, forming a giant circle stretching around the LZ. Sergeant Thomas placed Del and me in front of a mud and thatched hooch with a dirt floor. To our right were Silverstein and Harley, and beyond them Barney, Johnson and the rest of the squad. To our left, on the opposite side of the hooch, Bernie and Jerry settled in, with the remainder of their second squad strung out beyond them. A middle-aged mama-san watched us with apprehension from the wide opening of the hooch.

"You okay, man?" Jerry called, a twinkle in his eye.

I glowered. "It ain't funny, asshole."

Bernie laughed. "Is that how they taught you to *jump* in jump school?"

"It weren't thuh *jump*," Barney cackled from the other side. "It were thuh sudden *stop* at thuh other end," he declared, and the whole squad obliged him with peels of laughter.

"*Commando Sharpe to the rescue!*" Silverstein howled as Harley trumpeted a bugle charge, and so it went until Sergeant Thomas approached with a wry grin.

"Sharpe, you and Delarosa fall on back and draw your personal gear from the LZ, and be quick about it so the rest of the squad can rotate back for theirs."

Del and I hurried back to the LZ and stood in awe surveying the beehive of activity as hundreds of men littered the landscape constructing bunkers, digging holes, stringing commo wire, and filling sandbags. Others raised tall radio antennas, drove stakes in the ground, and positioned heavy equipment into precise locations. Jeeps, deuce-and-a-half trucks, and tracked vehicles lumbered about flattening the tall grass as walls of sandbags rose in layers around great tubes of artillery with their barrels pointed skyward. Helicopters landed and departed discharging mounds of equipment and soldiers in the center of the perimeter as Del and I stumbled through the sea of men stripped to the waist erecting a miniature city of sandbags. We located our old supply sergeant standing guard over his mound of supplies, and he parceled out our quota of C-rations, five-gallon water cans, empty sandbags, concertina wire, and waterproof bags of personal gear. As I gauged the stack in dismay calculating how many trips across the compound it would take to carry the heap back to our position, a heavy truck lumbered up. The driver jumped down from the cab and looked around expectantly, his expression settling into a heavy scowl as it became apparent there was no one to help him unload.

"Sure got a lot of junk there," I observed as a plan took shape.

He eyed the load. "Yeah, same old shit. I'm supposed to have a team to unload."

"We'll help you unload if you'll haul this junk over to the tree line there for us."

"By god, Ace, you're on."

It took the better part of half an hour to unload his truck. We then drew our entire platoon's gear and threw it up in the back. The driver shifted gears and plowed through the small trees in a shower of leaves and limbs to lurch to a halt in front of a startled Deputy Dog and Black, whose shocked expressions changed to grins when they discovered we had brought the entire platoon's equipment.

"Sergeant Thomas, these two have shown superb initiative," Deputy Dog praised as Sergeant Thomas drifted over to investigate the truck sitting in the middle of the woods.

"The Lieutenant's right," Black leered as Sergeant Thomas looked up at us doubtfully. "You might want to keep them in mind for future details."

Our beaming grins faded quickly with this bit of enlightening news. We lugged our gear over to our position, dug our two-man foxhole, lined it with sandbags, cleared our fields of fire, and stretched rolled concertina wire across our front lined with trip flares. We then erected a small poncho shelter to the rear of our fighting position, which allowed us to slip in and out of our foxhole with enough room to stuff our gear in the rear and place our air mattresses inside. The squad leaders prepared similar positions fifteen yards to our rear centered on their squads, with the platoon command post located thirty yards to their rear centered on the platoon. Commo wire and field phones linked the squad leaders to the platoon CP, which connected to the company CP, and in turn to the battalion CP. With our fighting positions complete, Black called us to the platoon CP.

"First off, I'd like to recognize Private Sharpe for his daring attack to secure the LZ." He held up his palms to calm the applause and catcalls. "I'm sure it was inspirational to the VC scouts who witnessed our arrival, undoubtedly removing any stigma of our professionalism from their minds." The whole platoon convulsed into hysteria. "On a less grand scale, the Lieutenant has a few words to say about our mission here."

Deputy Dog stepped forward. "Beginning tomorrow we will conduct continuous patrols and ambushes in the surrounding area to deny the enemy freedom of movement and access to the peasants. Intelligence reports indicate they are operating in the area in strength and are expected to remain here as long as the harvest is ongoing."

"Sir, are we to take it the Ghost Regiment is in these parts?" a man asked.

"Sheeeettt." Barney spat a stream of brown fluid in contempt. "Nobody knows were thuh dad-dam' 9th's at but thuh dad-dam' 9th."

"No one knows for sure," Deputy Dog replied as my pulse quickened. "This is definitely their AO, so it would serve us well to assume so. Booby traps and mines saturate the entire area. We can expect large-scale sniper actions. We will rotate missions on a daily basis, alternating between patrols in the immediate area, air assaults into outlying areas, and night ambushes. A composite force in our rear will man our lines during the times we are away from the perimeter."

When Black released us, Del and I shared a hurried meal of cold C-rations with Bernie and Jerry in front of the mud hut as dusk descended upon us. We then returned to our fighting positions to settle in for a long night of booming artillery and drifting flares as my imagination conjured up images of little iron men moving into position around us.

———

We were up and going at dawn, splashing water from our five-gallon cans into the shells of our steel pots to wash and shave before visiting the toilet, a slit trench located just outside the wire where low hanging ponchos gave some form of privacy as we straddled the foot wide trench and performed our basic body functions. Afterwards, Bernie and Jerry met Del and me in front of the hooch as Johnson strolled over to join us for breakfast. Under his tutelage, we punched holes in the sides and bottoms of empty C-ration cans and rolled small balls of C-4 plastic explosives from the two-pound blocks, which burned like blowtorches in our improvised stoves, and soon had steaming cans of lima beans and scorched slices of turkey and ham before us, accompanied by hot chocolate and coffee. Johnson produced a bottle of Texas Pete hot sauce to spice up the goodies, which we passed around in delight. Cans of mixed fruit and chocolate bars completed the meal in high style as we watched the sun rise in glorious colors, its rays chasing whiffs of ground fog from the paddies to our front.

"Can you believe the Army pays us for this shit?" Jerry mused in gratification.

"Not much more a man could ask for," I agreed in contentment.

"I could think of a lot," Bernie sniffed crossly.

"Free room and board, lots of fresh air, and plenty of exercise," Jerry goaded. "I ask you, how much would you have to pay for this back in smog bound Los Angeles?"

"Who wants it?" Del demanded.

"You city boys miss out on the best of life," I teased.

"Yeah?" Del argued. "Well, we city boys can live without bugs and mosquitoes and lizards and snakes."

"And we can live *with* air conditioning, toilets, bathtubs, and beds," Bernie added.

"You guys are spoiled," Jerry insisted. "Where's your pioneer spirit? Where's that rugged individualism our great country is known for?"

"In a malt shop on Sunset Boulevard," I accused.

"I wish to *hell* I was in that malt shop right now," Bernie snipped.

"Me too," Del chirped.

Jerry sighed. "Me three."

"Well, I'll let you crackers know how it is in a few months," Johnson teased as he stood and dusted his hands. "Better get your gear organized, we'll be moving out soon."

We sat in silence dreaming of home after he departed as Mama-san puttered about in her hooch behind us making her breakfast of rice and tea, which we watched with casual interest. Soon she picked her way around us through the wire to her paddy, waded in to her knees, and stooped in the timeless fashion of generations past to pluck her stems of rice, glancing back often to ensure we weren't robbing her meager possessions.

"Do you think she's pregnant?" I asked, indicating the bulge in her midsection.

"Not likely," Jerry reasoned. "There doesn't seem to be a papa-san about and a pregnant woman wouldn't be working so hard in a rice paddy, would she?"

Sergeant Thomas called for us, and after we gathered around, pointed to a map with grease penciled lines dividing the surrounding area into a series of pie shaped wedges. "These are the company sectors which we are responsible for day and night. Today our platoon will conduct a patrol from the firebase to this hamlet here. Move out time will be in half an hour. Draw your rations and fill your canteens."

We formed into two columns with the remainder of the platoon to pick our way through the wire. One file, containing third and fourth squads under Sergeant First Class Black hugged the brush covered dike on our left. Our first and second squads, under Deputy Dog's command, took the one on the right a hundred yards away, with Black and the lieutenant using radios to control our parallel advance when we were out of sight of one another. Second squad, with Jerry and Bernie, led our file, with Deputy Dog and his RTO located between the two squads. Each man held the prescribed fifteen yard separation as we navigated the narrow berms and wider, brush-covered hedgerows. Within a mile of the firebase, the point man located several booby traps, which required us to slip into the knee-deep water on each side to bypass. The last man in line placed a grenade beside them and ran to blow them in place.

Chunks of dry land a hundred yards square interlaced the hedgerows at intervals with each parcel containing vegetable gardens, hooches, and groupings of fruit trees. We strolled along in the sun enjoying the scenic rural environment, pausing near midmorning as the column on our left under Black fought a small-scale sniper action, and then pushed ahead.

Old men and women stooped in every plot of mud and water pretending to ignore us as they watched from beneath their conical hats. Small children tended the mammoth water buffalo grazing on patches of grass, but did not approach us to beg as in the villages, choosing to keep their distance as they watched us pass, with the water buffalo lowering their heads and snorting in displeasure at our invasion. I was astonished at how the children controlled the animals with thin switches and a string connected to a metal ring running through their nose, the docility of the towering beasts amazing as they cowered under the tongue lashings of the infants even as they glared at us with suppressed rage. We happily gave them a wide berth while smiling at the children with sincere hopes the little urchins wouldn't unleash the monsters on us.

As we ambled along, I noticed a total absence of young men and women. Everyone seemed to be under ten or over fifty years old, most old wrinkled women with black teeth and red lips from the beetle nut they chewed to soothe tooth decay and gum disease. All wore black silk pants and shirts without collars, with conical straw hats adorning their heads. All stared stoically at us as we searched their homes, approaching to watch from fifty feet away but never interfering. None of us felt like the good guys as they hurried in after our departure to count their sparse possessions and see what we had pilfered from their pitiful hooches. Most of the structures were empty of furnishings, with the exception of straw mats on the dirt floor, a broken cup or two, a bowl, cheap tinsel ware, and a scorched pot or pan stacked around a tiny brick stove built into the ground. At noon, we halted in one of the large squares containing several hooches. Most of the inhabitants nervously converged into their homes and squatted in the wide, opened fronts to watch us as we lounged in the shade and ate our sparse meal of unheated C-rations from the cans.

Security wasn't a problem with several hundred yards visibility across the paddies, so we stared at the villagers as they stared back. Eventually several small children edged closer to Harley in a jittery mob. Harley coaxed them with a can of peaches extended at arm's length, and the little group inched forward with their parents looking on in alarm. The pack huddled together several feet away, unwilling to move closer, their eyes darting about, as they stood coiled to spring out of harm's way at the slightest provocation. Harley continued his gentle murmurings with the can of peaches, tempting them beyond endurance. One of them broke away and approached, trying to watch all of us at once. One timid step at a time he drew nearer to the peaches and then darted forward to snatch the can. We applauded his bravery as he scampered back, and the other kids gathered around the little hero to share his prize, dipping dirty fingers into the can and licking the juice from the tips. Once they devoured the spoils, the same child approached Harley again and stopped just short of grabbing distance. He pointed to his skin and at Harley speaking in his singsong dialect. The rest of the children huddled a step to his rear, their big brown eyes filled with anticipation. Harley extended his arm out to the child, who leaned as far forward as possible, and stretched his own hand out to rake his fingers along Harley's arm. The whole group retreated a safe distance, and we broke into laughter as they gathered around the child to inspect his fingers to see if Harley had rubbed off on him. With the ice broken the children mobbed the rest of us within minutes. To their glee and the parents' consternation, we passed out cans of fruit cocktail, peaches and pears, and bars of C-ration chocolate, which they devoured greedily with lip smacking relish.

Feeling at last like true diplomats, we saddled up and continued our patrol. I was plodding along in the hot afternoon sun with the heat shrinking my mind into a fuzzy little gray ball when I became aware of something odd occurring as we strung out along one of the larger hedgerows with second squad again leading, but out of sight beyond a thick growth of bushes.

"Look out!" Splash!

"Hell!" Splash!

"Ohoooo shit!" Splash!

"Yeowweee!" Splash!

I looked at Del in alarm as the ground quivered and the bushes shook. Suddenly Deputy Dog charged out trailing leaves and twigs, his eyes wide in terror, and dove into the rice paddy on our left. I watched open mouthed as his RTO came tearing out behind him and sailed spread eagle through the air to land in a geyser of mud and water as he belly-flopped into the mire on the opposite side. I gasped in horror as the bushes again exploded and out charged the biggest, meanest looking water buffalo in the world, eyes red, nostrils flaring in rage, head lowered, expelling great bellowing snorts from its depths.

"Yiiipppes!" yelped Johnson, flinging himself sideways into the paddy an instant before being trampled.

"G-God!" squeaked Del, jumping for his life.

"Shit!" I gasped, springing in the opposite direction.

I surfaced to watch the bull charge down the entire column amid screeches and strangled cries, each punctuated by splashes as the men jumped for their lives on alternate sides of the paddy. The enraged bull charged on through the next hedgerow and disappeared as heads began popping up around me in the muddy water. From the bushes to our left a small child emerged, tiny switch in hand, running as fast as his little legs could carry him, yelling frantic commands at the disappearing bull, and vanished through the hedgerow. We looked around at one another, some sitting in the mud, others sprawled on all fours, a few standing searching for lost gear with trembling hands, and then Deputy Dog's big frame surged out of the water looking like a monster with all the mud and bits of grass clinging to him.

"Christ, did anybody get killed?" he sputtered, spitting out water and pieces of straw from his mouth.

We broke up into a hilarious mass, pointing to each other's muddy faces and dripping bodies as we climbed back up on the berm amid peels of laughter. From the mud-caked figure identified as the RTO only by the big backpack and antenna dripping water on his head, we heard Black's crackling voice.

"Mustang Alpha One, this is One Bravo, over. Come in Alpha one, this is One Bravo. What's going on over there, over?"

We doubled over in mirth as Deputy Dog sloshed over and, with white teeth gleaming, attempted to explain the situation. Black's voice reflected concern for the lieutenant's sanity as he and Deputy Dog got our two columns turned around and heading back to the firebase, our passage marked with chuckles and outbursts of laughter as we threaded our way home in the evening sun.

Back in the firebase, we washed ourselves off and cooked a hurried meal. Mama-san returned from her long day in the paddy to prepare her rice supper as we languished in the cool evening air talking of home and anticipating tomorrow's air assault. The second platoon had made light enemy contact on their operation, suffering one wounded in the battle. They had not found any enemy bodies, but two blood trails confirmed they had at least hit something in the exchange.

With the deepening dusk, we drifted back to our positions to settle in for the long night of eternally flickering shadows.

CHAPTER 12

The red hued sunrise promised a serene day in the mystical Orient.

We congregated in front of Mama-san's hooch for breakfast as she hovered in the recesses of the dwelling preparing her rice over a small wood fire in her earthen stove.

Jerry warmed a can of cocoa over his sizzling ball of C-4 explosive, holding the container by its peeled back jagged top. "These folks are so poor they're pitiful."

"Imagine life without electricity or running water," Del mused.

"Hell, these people have never even seen a hospital," Bernie added. "None of them have gone to school or know how to read or write."

I got my fireball going in my improvised stove and placed a can of turkey loaf on top. "It's sad as hell, alright."

"Can you believe the average weekly wage for one of these farmers is only one dollar and fifty cents?" Bernie asked.

"I don't think they even know how bad off they are," Del observed.

I removed my steaming turkey and placed a can of cocoa in its place. "They live in blissful ignorance. Since this is all they've ever known, they don't know what the rest of the world has to offer, so therefore don't miss it."

"Well, by god, we ought to do something about it," Jerry insisted.

"Us?" I shot back. "What the hell can we do, fool?"

"A lot, if we're willing."

"I'm listening?"

"Well, we could, you know, adopt a family or something and teach them," Jerry fumbled.

"Okay, I'll take a couple of eighteen year old girls," Del jeered.

"I'm talking about helping them, not exploiting them," Jerry snapped.

"It's a great idea, but not practical worth a damn," Bernie observed. "I mean, here we are, four dumb ass privates sitting in the middle of a rice paddy roasting cans of C-rats over a fire made of explosives. In an hour, we'll be out there wading around in the mud all day hunting down little men to kill. What can we do for the poor and downtrodden of this country?"

"I agree," I added. "I have enough trouble looking after *one* idiot." I nodded at Del's bowed head. "I can't be taking on any more burdens. Besides, what the hell have they done for themselves in the last thousand years?"

"I'll still take the eighteen year olds," Del offered.

"That's pure selfish bullshit," Jerry argued. "There's a hell of lot we can do. Remember what Mustang Six said about us being the first point of contact between our two countries?"

"Okay, man, the next sniper that takes a pot shot at me gets two more freebies before I blow his shit away," I promised.

"Don't patronize me, Jay," Jerry snarled.

"What do you expect?" I demanded indignantly. "Hell, I'm not trying to be selfish, I just don't know what the shit I'm supposed to do for these people, other than be a designated target for them to shoot at when the mood strikes them."

Bernie sighed. "Knock off the shit, guys, okay?"

"Aw hell, leave them alone, Bernie," Del interjected as he licked his fingertips and snatched a smoking can of beefsteak off the fire. "They can't talk about shit without getting their friggin' feathers ruffled and blustering all over the place like two roosters. They're both dinky dou airborne types, remember?"

Bernie frowned. "*Dinky dou*?"

Del shrugged. "It's a new word I learned. Means crazy."

"Oh."

"Well, we could start right here with *her*," Jerry grated.

The four of us looked at Mama-san, who withdrew nervously with our sudden attention focused on her.

"She's not eighteen," Del objected.

"Okay smart ass, so *start*!" I offered.

Jerry's face reddened. "Alright, by god, I will." He strode to the front of the hooch as Mama-san backed away from him. "Hey, uh, Ma'am?"

"Tell her we just adopted her," I chided.

"Invite her to breakfast," Del sang out as Jerry hesitated in the door of her hooch.

"Uh, ladda, uh, day?" Jerry called gently. "Is that it, guys, 'come here,' Ladda day?"

"I think it's *Lai dai,*" I called.

Mama-san rattled off a long string of dialect as she backed deeper into her hooch.

"Leave her alone, man," Bernie begged. "She doesn't understand what you're doing."

"She'll be okay when she sees we aren't going to hurt her," Jerry insisted. "Hey, Mama-san, it's okay, we're your friends. Want to be friends?" he soothed as he eased in after her, took her arm, and tugged her out to us, where she stood trembling with her head hung in submission.

"Now what?" Bernie demanded.

"Come on, man, let her go," Del pleaded. "She's scared to death."

"Offer her something to eat," I advised.

"Yeah, Mama-san, want some chocolate?" Jerry snatched my can of hot cocoa and turned the jagged handle for her to take as she shied away from the container, her nose wrinkling in distaste. "Hey, gooood, mmm-mm-mmm, try some," he insisted, forcing the can into her trembling hands.

Jerry pretended to hold an invisible can, little finger extended, and blew across the top to cool it. She held the container as if it were acid starring at him in wide-eyed amazement. With a mock frown, he took an imaginary sip from his imaginary cup, swallowed with exaggerated concentration, and then sighed while patting his stomach in pleasure. He then indicated for her to try some, but she wasn't having any part of it and tried to give the witch's brew back. He placed his hands over hers and guided it to her mouth, but she still wouldn't drink the evil potion as she stood frozen in place, her pleading eyes locked to his, her lips trembling. He placed a finger on the bottom of the can and tipped the rim against her mouth. The liquid dribbled down her chin and she moaned with her great belly heaving in spasms.

Bernie groaned as we stared aghast. "Aw man, look what you've done!"

"She thinks you're trying to poison her," Del accused.

"Leave her be, Jerry," I scolded.

"Hey, Mama-san, here, watch me," Jerry cooed, grabbing the can from her jerking fingers and taking a small sip. "Mmmmmmm, gooooood! Go on, Mama-san, try it, it's goooooood!"

She hesitantly took the improvised cup, raised it to her lips, and took a tiny sip. After a brief hesitation, she smacked her lips in satisfaction and rattled off something in her sing-song dialect. She then drank the remainder in rapid swallows and handed the empty can back to Jerry while patting her stomach in approval.

As we cheered in triumph, Sergeant Thomas called for us to saddle up. We grabbed our gear and drifted back to the platoon CP where Black briefed us on the coming air assault.

"Intelligence indicates a VC squad has occupied this village during the night." He pointed a bony finger at a speck on his map. "Second platoon is moving by foot from their ambush site to the village now. Third platoon will airlift in to this landing zone here and link up with them to form a blocking force around the hamlet. We'll go in on the second lift to this LZ and conduct a sweep through the village. Interpreters will be with our company headquarters. Detain anybody who does not have a government identification card regardless of age or sex."

We filed out to the small LZ in the middle of the perimeter, formed into lines behind third platoon, which rushed forward to board the craft and depart in a sea of swirling grass. In our now quiet LZ we waited, ears tuned to Deputy Dog's radio, and cheered when the third platoon leader reported their LZ cold, no enemy contact. Moments later the line of aircraft descended and we surged forward to clamor aboard. My view rapidly expanded into one of orderly squares of sunlight reflecting from the rice paddies as we gained altitude, mesmerizing me anew with the beauty of the country rushing by below.

Moments later Del nudged my arm and pointed to twenty mud and grass structures clustered together. Two hundred yards from the edge of the hamlet soldiers strung out in long lines on three sides, rifles pointing inward. We dipped into a narrow field on the open end as the troops on the ground rushed forward into blocking positions. The gunships glided by protecting our descent as we edged to the doors with our feet dangling out while watching the scrub brush for signs of enemy activity as the ground rushed up to us.

"*WHOOOOOOOM!*"

Dirt and debris showered over me as the concussion slapped me back. Our chopper pitched nose up, wobbled drunkenly, and slid sideways in jerky motions as I clung to anything I could find. When it slammed down and came to a lurching halt, I rolled through the door and ran for the trees as aircraft lifted off in all directions like a covey of startled quail. I knelt next to a tree and looked back at the lead aircraft sitting sideways in the LZ engulfed in billowing clouds of black smoke with its blades still turning. One of the pilots strapped to his seat twitched in the flames, his jettisoned door on the ground beside him. A second aircraft lay on its side with both blades missing, the fuselage warped and twisted. A third aircraft pointed in the opposite direction with its windshield shattered, the big main rotor warped and the skids on the bottom spread so wide the belly was only inches off the ground. Men thrown in all directions stumbled about in shock, almost all without rifles or helmets.

"W-What just friggin' happened, Jay?" Del stuttered.

"I think the first aircraft landed on a mine and the other two collided with each other," I replied, watching in stupefaction as one of the pilots in the third aircraft jettisoned his door and fell out with blood streaming from his face. A crew chief with helmet and visor limped around to the opposite side of the aircraft and jerked at the door of the other pilot slumped over the controls inside. One of our men, his face streaked with blood and dirt, stumbled towards us.

BOOOOMMMM!

I stared in horror as his body rose in the air in thunderous smoke and flame and thumped back down in a shower of rubble minus both legs, cringing as his high-pitched scream faded from his twitching body, experiencing pain the man himself no longer felt.

Sergeant Lunas, rifle in hand but without his helmet, his face blackened and fatigues ripped, stumbled from the back of the second aircraft. "*Don't move! We're in a minefield!*"

All froze and looked in his direction with stunned expressions as Black ran by our position. "Stay put! Nobody moves until I tell you! Keep your eyes peeled!"

I watched fearfully as Sergeant Lunas limped around, carefully placing one foot in front of the other, and led the dazed men to the nose of the third aircraft one by one, his steady voice cautioning them to keep their eyes on the ground to look for metal or bamboo stakes sticking up in the grass. When he had them assembled in a tight, shell-shocked group, he checked three unmoving bodies and lifted one up across his shoulder to transport back to the others. I could only imagine the courage it took to move in a minefield as he was doing, aware that my own legs were trembling so badly I wasn't sure I could stand, let alone walk.

Deputy Dog edged out to the group huddled at the third aircraft, checking the ground before applying his full weight and twisting his boot to press the grass down in order to leave an imprint. He stopped once, backtracked, and picked a different direction before reaching the group Lunas assembled as I watched breathlessly, jaws clenched against the sudden explosion expected with each step. Working as a team, Deputy Dog and Lunas led the men from the aircraft to the tree line, where Black and the third squad leader arranged them into groups as Doc rushed about administering to them. Deputy Dog and Lunas then made a poncho litter and waded back into the LZ twice to recover our two dead as the pilot continued to burn in the first aircraft.

During this period, the gunships thundered overhead in fury searching the vegetation and spoiling for a fight, wanting to strike at something, anything, to avenge their broken sisters below, but nothing dared raise a hand against us in the face of their teeming wrath. Black shifted us around the improvised aid station to provide an added measure of security as third platoon conducted a hurried search of the village. Second platoon secured another LZ near us for our extraction. Black had members of the fourth squad carry the dead and wounded there, where two choppers soon landed and discharged teams of minesweepers with long tubes and flat round disks. After loading the casualties on board, fourth squad escorted the minesweepers back to our LZ to conduct a clearing operation. We provided security as the teams located and placed detonation charges on the identified mines to blow them in place. Two giant Chinook helicopters hovered high over the LZ and lifted out the two salvageable aircraft on slings as the third continued to burn off to the side.

Sergeant Lunas, still missing his helmet, formed what was left of our first squad, which consisted of himself, Del, Silverstein, Johnson, Barney, Harley, and me, on the edge of the clearing. We had one dead, and Staff Sergeant Thomas was one of our three wounded. Second platoon secured the LZ as we lifted out and flew back to the firebase, where we straggled across the perimeter to gather at the platoon CP around an exhausted Deputy Dog and Black.

"We lost two of the helicopter crewmen, along with two of our own, killed in action," Black informed us gravely. "Ten members of the platoon and six crewmen are wounded. I'll pass along any news I get on them as it becomes available. Sergeant Lunas will become the new First Squad Leader. Get some rest."

The four of us gathered in front of the hooch and sat starring out across the rice fields in silence. Mama-san came in from her paddy in mid-afternoon and hesitated as she observed our grief stricken expressions.

Jerry looked up at her grimly. "Well, Mama-san, we got our ass kicked today and we didn't even see the little bastards."

Mama-san clucked her tongue sympathetically, for what she knew not, and placed a comforting hand on Jerry's shoulder as she uttered small crooning sounds of comfort.

"Your Sergeant Lunas had his shit together out there today," Jerry broke the silence as Mama-san left us for her hooch. "That took real balls."

"I couldn't have done it," I agreed.

"He's still a friggin' asshole," Del offered glumly.

"He's just new, like the rest of us," Bernie defended.

"*You're* one to talk, after what he said to you," Del accused.

"That's *my* business," Bernie spat back.

"Well, kiss my ass too," Del snarled.

"Looks too much like your face," Bernie retorted as he stood and stomped away.

"What's eating him?" Del demanded.

"He and Tom were in Basic together," Jerry advised, referring to the man who stepped on the mine in the LZ.

"That's no reason to take it out on me," Del insisted.

"Bernie's a pacifist at heart," Jerry soothed. "He'll be okay."

"Has he fired his rifle yet?" I asked.

"He will when he's ready," Jerry replied.

"Well I wouldn't want him next to me until he gets his shit together," Del growled.

"Cut the crap, man!" Jerry sizzled. "I trust him and that's all that counts. *Right*?"

"Enough already! Christ, have we got to fight each other because we can't catch the shadows?" I argued, trying to stifle my own anger at facing an enemy that chose the time and place to confront us, of the frustration of walking into his mines and booby traps, of taking sniper fire but never having a target, of knowing he was always there, watching for any sign of carelessness as we groped for him. The days and weeks of looking for him in the hot sun, often finding his traces but never him, unless he was ready to be found. The brief, fierce exchanges of fire, of closing with him and finding him gone again, disappeared into thin air, hearing his imaginary mocking laughter echoing in our minds as he made us look like fools. I broke a stick I was doodling with in the sand, imagining it the body of our tormentor.

Jerry took the stick, symbolically broke it in half, and dropped the pieces as his piercing brown eyes met mine. "One day, Jay," he swore in rage.

"Bet your ass," I promised.

Mama-san padded out of the hooch and extended a small, chipped china cup containing a light green fluid with leaves floating near the top to Jerry. He examined it as she pantomimed holding a cup, blowing across the top, and pretending to take a sip as she rolled her eyes and patted her stomach in contentment. He looked helplessly from one of us to the other.

"Goooooooodddd," Del cackled.

"It'll probably give you the shits for a week," I teased, enjoying his acute discomfort.

Mama-san cupped her hands over Jerry's on the cup and murmured as she guided it to his lips, which were grim at the corners, and forced a sip as she tipped it up. He gulped a mouthful and swallowed as his Adam's apple bobbled. Mama-san crooned as he resolutely drank the remainder in short, forced sips, his eyes bland. When she took the cup and returned to the hooch, Del and I rolled on the ground laughing as Jerry grabbed his throat with both hands and made a horrible grimace of distaste with tongue extended, eyes crossed.

"Oh god, please no," Jerry moaned, turning white as Mama-san approached with another cup of the steaming brew, sending Del and me into another fit of knee-slapping hysterics as Jerry shrank back in terror. My giggles were throttled in mid-pitch when she paused in front of me and extended the pitiful cup.

"Drink up, Jay," Del howled as I held the cup in damp palms.

"Be a man about it," Jerry trilled.

"I-I don't like tea," I pleaded.

"Mmmmmmm, gooooooooddd," Del coaxed.

"*Awwww ...*" I sighed and took a swig. I grinned with thin lips, trying to force down the awful, nauseating bile caught midway in my throat as my stomach pitched around trying to get out of the way. Tears sprang into my eyes from lack of oxygen before I choked it down to peels of laughter from Jerry and Del. I discovered that holding my breath killed the taste and gulped the remainder in two passes to end the suffering. Mama-san looked from one of us to the other, puzzled by our mirth, took the cup from my listless fingers, and returned to the hooch. I gagged and spit, my mouth growing fuzzy as my stomach did a rumbling gyration around the warm liquid smoldering down there in the darkness.

Del started to his feet as Mama-san reemerged from her hooch with a third cup of the bitter brew in her hand. "I'm un-assing the premises!"

Jerry tackled him at the knees. "Oh hell no you don't!"

"You're getting your share too, hero," I growled, draping over his twisting form and pinning him to the ground as Mama-san approached.

Del meekly took the cup as Jerry and I hovered over him, grimaced and gulped the whole thing down in one bolt, his eyes bulging as beads of sweat popped out on his forehead. Mama-san clucked her tongue at us, took the cup, and pantomimed that we were supposed to sip it with great relish. We nodded in mock seriousness, and when she turned back to her hooch, split hastily back to our individual positions.

———

We passed another uneventful night alternating between guard and sleep while dreaming of home. At dawn, we attended to our hygienic duties before assembling in front of Mama-san's hooch for breakfast. She joined us with her bowl of rice and watched with hopeful eyes as we brewed cups of cocoa. Jerry presented her with a can, which she accepted with a great deal of bowing and grinning before sipping it with pleasure. Bernie prepared her a can of pound cake with peaches poured over the top, which she took without hesitation and munched with lip smacking delight. When she finished, she grinned and patted her protruding stomach as she rolled her eyes in ecstasy. She then offered her bowl of rice, which we graciously accepted and pretended to eat a small bite of before returning the bowl to her.

We were scheduled to pull the night ambush patrol, thus had the day to rest and prepare for the task. We catnapped until the afternoon as we swatted at the pesky flies, bored beyond endurance, and then the four of us grouped under the shade in front of Mama-san's hooch to watch her work in the paddy. After a time, Bernie removed his boots, rolled his pant legs up, picked his way through the wire out to Mama-san's paddy, stepped into the muddy water, and waded over to her. Under her guidance, he was soon stooping and pulling as if he had been born to it. Curiosity got the best of us, and without a word, we removed our own boots and rolled our pants up. Soon, to Mama-san's amazement, we were standing knee deep in the murky water plucking the green shoots along with Bernie. At Jerry's insistence, Mama-san sat on the low berm watching as we pulled stalks like pros. As we worked, she hummed a soft, haunting melody floating like a whisper on the wind, hugging her round belly as she rocked back and forth in rhythm to her song. She erupted in laughter when Jerry ducked Del's low-bent head under the water and ran for his life, only to sprawl head first in the paddy himself as Del splashed after him in indignant rage.

Deputy Dog and Black appeared at the edge of the wire to watch us in silence before departing with help-less shrugs. We soon learned rice pulling wasn't all it was cracked up to be, and within two hours were lined up on the berm beside Mama-san with aching backs and sore arms from the constant stooping and pulling. Chatting gaily, nobody really listening to another, no one really caring, we propped back on our elbows and let our feet dangle in the water, tired and happy. Jerry began hum-ming Mama-san's song, and the rest of us joined in as she sang the lyrics in lilting singsong harmony, laughing with the rest of us as Del squeaked along a note or two behind, with each of us wondering what her words sung with such tenderness meant.

Under the red ball of the setting sun, we returned to the hooch to gather our boxes of C-rations for the evening meal. At Mama-san's invitation, we moved into her hooch and used her little earthen stove, placing the rolls of C-4 explosives along the bottom of the grill, the fierce burning white clay leaving her spellbound. Jerry took charge of the preparations and combined our meals after placing Mama-san on her straw mat with a cup of cocoa. With the flair of a born chef he soon had the cans steaming before us, which we shared around, each taking a bite or two before passing the can to the next, with Mama-san doing her share of eating and chattering, even though we had no idea what she was saying. From her expressions, we learned she liked tuna fish, ham, pears, peaches, and chocolate. She thought beans and franks were so-so, but didn't care for the roast beef and potatoes or the fruitcake, and hated the coffee until we added powdered cream and sugar. She then perked up and drained the cup while smacking her lips.

We lay back in contentment enjoying C-ration cigarettes yellow with age. Mama-san watched our expressions grow somber, her face growing grave as well, as we mentally prepared for the hours of terror ahead, of groping in the dark, inhospitable environment to kill or be killed.

I visualized the dreaded movement, the dragging hours until dawn, the waiting to see if anyone would blunder into our kill zone, the uncertainty of us becoming the target as the enemy sought us out and moved into position around us. The hour before we moved out was always one of deep thought, fast letters, and silent prayers.

At dusk, Sergeant Lunas called for us to saddle up. The mobile security team moved in and occupied our fighting positions for the night, grumbling about poor fields of fire and shallow holes, invoking our sneering replies. Mama-san watched in silence as we blackened our faces and jumped up and down to test the taped gear for the slightest noise. She reached out a frail hand to touch our shoulders, murmuring one single word, as we brushed by her in the near darkness and moved to the platoon CP.

Black covered the standard actions and contingency plans we all knew by heart, emphasizing each man's position in the designated teams as he sketched the entire operation on the ground with a stick. With everything said we settled back for a last cigarette, cupping them in our palms to thwart sharp-eyed snipers in the fast fading light as the silence deepened and settled into our souls.

CHAPTER 13

Under complete darkness, we slipped past Mama-san's hooch with her ghostly form standing rigid in the open front, past the wire and trip flares, and out into the dark world beyond fraught with danger and sudden death. We stopped often to check danger areas and to search the void with starlight scopes, fear building with each step and nerves frayed by the shadows slipping and darting about us.

I was positive the sun would come up before we even reached our ambush site, but three hours later by the luminous dial of my watch, we finally paused for guides to reconnoiter the position as our tired bodies sagged. An eternity later, they led us forward and placed hands on our shoulders to indicate precise locations.

Del and I were part of the rear security force, with the kill zone behind us covering a road intersection. We faced a scattering of dark bushes at the bottom of a small hill and placed our claymores out before arranging our gear and settling in as fatigue eroded our vigilance. Near morning, a hand grasped my arm and my sluggish mind fought its way back to consciousness thinking a whole hour couldn't have already passed since my last watch. The hand squeezed my arm again and my heart beat rapidly as I grew conscious of the dark outline of a man squatting beside me with his starlight scope humming. I rolled over to get my bearings, remembering the kill zone was behind us. *What was he watching out there in the bushes to our rear?* The enemy was supposed to come down the road, not back here with us. Black leaned down to pull Del's and my heads together, his lips inches from our ears.

"One man, unarmed," he breathed. "Take him prisoner. Keep him in sight while I alert the others." He pressed the scope into my hands and crept off to pass the word to each side of us, who in turn would pass it on to the next position until it circled the perimeter. In theory, this would keep Del and me from getting shot as we moved out of our defensive position to ...

Cripes! The son of a bitch intended for us to go out there and jump the little bastard! Muffle him before he could call out to his ten million buddies lurking around and drag him back to the perimeter. *Holy shit!* I attempted to swallow the cotton accumulating in my throat, pressed the eyepiece to my face with trembling hands and picked out the lone figure two hundred yards away. The trail he traversed led to the edge of our clearing fifty feet away, where large bushes bordered each side as it emerged into the field. As before, the actual sight of the enemy had an immediate calming effect on me. Cool supremacy replaced fear. I knew where he was. I had the upper hand. I was a better soldier than he. I passed the scope to Del with steady hands. As he scanned the area I leaned over to whisper in his ear.

"We wait by the bushes on each side of the trail and take him when he enters the clearing. Bring your rifle. I'll grab him. If he makes a sound, bust him one. If he runs, shoot the bastard." I took the scope and scanned as Del leaned over to cup his hands over my ear.

"I-I can't, Jay!" he whispered in near panic. "I'll blow it, I know I will!"

I pulled his ear next to my mouth. "Follow my lead and be ready to help keep him quiet."

Black glided up to thrust his head between ours. "Ready?"

I took one last hurried look at the figure, less than a hundred yards away now. "Yeah."

"Go." He pulled the scope from my hands and gave me an encouraging shove.

I eased forward leaving all of my gear behind. Del followed, carrying only his rifle. I crouched next to the bushes on the left side of the trail and Del faded into the one across from me. I flexed my hands in readiness and looked back at the platoon, seeing only soft lumps of immobile shadows spaced at intervals in a rough circle. I tensed when a sandal scraped on earth and held my breath, the moment suspended in time. A dark shadow emerged through the opening striding fast. I sprang on his back, locked my right forearm under his chin, and jerked him back.

"*Uhuuugggg!*" His mouth gaped open next to mine and exhaled putrid air into my nostrils as his hands clutched my encircling arm. "*Aggheeee—*"

I jerked my forearm against his throat to cut off his air supply as one of his hands clawed at my face. He bent forward and pulled me up onto his back with my legs kicking wildly for support. *"Clobber the bastard!"* I hissed.

THUD! My left ribcage burst into searing pain.

WHAM! My left shoulder numbed and electric tingles danced in my fingers. I sucked in his foul stench and clung to him as he swung me in a violent circle. *"Christ! Hit him, not me!"* I screeched as Del danced around our gyrating bodies.

WHOMP! *"Ohoooo!"* I sucked air into my collapsed lungs.

WHAM! *"Hold it! Hold it!"* I screamed in agony, knowing another blow would finish me.

My foe stumbled and dragged me down on top of him, his arms flopping against his sides as I pulled against his throat with all my strength, my only thought to tear his head off before I passed out. Strong hands tore at my arms and forced them open as my victim collapsed in a body-twitching heap.

"You killed the bastard!" Black accused as I gasped for breath.

Good, I thought weakly as pain rippled through me in sharp waves. Sergeant Lunas bent over the inert man and slapped his face in an effort to revive him as his head lolled about. When the man wheezed and coughed, Black and Lunas each took an arm and dragged him away with his feet skidding along behind him.

Del helped me to my feet. "Sorry, Jay, I was trying to help," he whispered.

"You bastard, you nearly killed me!" I gritted through clenched teeth as fire seared my body. "I think you busted my ribs."

"I told you I'd screw it up."

"Well, you sure as hell did, asshole!" I moaned as I sank down beside our gear.

Black and Lunas dropped the prisoner off at Deputy Dog's position, where Doc taped his hands behind his back and ran another strip across his mouth before laying him prone next to the RTO to guard. I suffered for a time before slipping into deep sleep as Del kept watch the remainder of the night, afraid to wake me.

At dawn, Doc probed my ribs. "I don't think anything's broken, just severe bruises."

"*Just*?" I whined.

"Can he walk?" Lunas inquired.

"Can you make it back?" Doc redirected the question.

"I-I think so," I grunted as Del squirmed in embarrassment.

"Silverstein, Harley, Delarosa, distribute Sharpe's equipment," Lunas ordered.

"Not my rifle," I insisted, snatching it from Harley's hands.

"Man, you mighty particular about that damned old thing," Harley groused.

"Squad Leaders, give me two columns," Black directed as the rest of the platoon strapped on their gear.

Silverstein and Harley led the prisoner, blindfolded now with his hands still taped behind his back, and I shuffled along, my upper body sore and erect, not missing an opportunity to glare at an obviously despondent Del. At the firebase, we assumed our positions from the security teams and I sank down in gratitude as

Mama-san rushed to greet us. She shrank away as Harley led the prisoner through the wire and kept her eyes diverted as Silverstein removed his blindfold prior to leading him to the company CP.

Jerry helped me out of my shirt and examined the bruises decorating my shoulders, back, and ribs. "What a sight you two made!"

"*That's me! Hit him!*" Bernie cackled, mimicking my pleas.

"It was too dark to see," Del mumbled.

Mama-san clucked her tongue as Jerry and Bernie bellowed callously at my injuries, and hurried to her hooch to return with boiling water and a handful of rags, which she soaked and placed over my bruises as I lay throbbing in pain.

The three of them prepared breakfast and placed my portion of the steaming cans before me since I couldn't move. Mama-san shared in the feast and drained two cans of hot chocolate in rapid succession before gathering her tools to go to the paddy.

Sergeant Lunas approached with bushy eyebrows drawn together. "Sharpe, you're assigned to rear security until further notice. Remain in the platoon area and guard the perimeter until we return."

Del bowed his head as Lunas strode off. "Jay, I'm sorry."

I scowled. "You asshole, you've been saying you're sorry since the day we met." Unable to bear his glumness any longer, I shrugged. "Hell, while you're out there wallowing around in the mud all day, I'll be back here laying on my ass."

"Saddle up!" Black called from the CP.

"See you later," he mumbled as he strapped on his gear.

I settled down for a day of rest with the only interruption Mama-san's return every couple of hours to place hot pads on my bruises. At noon, she presented me with a cup of the hot green tea, which I pretended to sip until she turned her back, and then dumped it over my shoulder.

In late afternoon, gunfire at a distance awakened me. A few minutes later, our artillery began lobbing rounds out as the whole firebase shook under the discharge. I used the field phone in Deputy Dog's CP to call the company CP, where one of the RTOs informed me our platoon was engaging an unknown sized enemy force. A half hour after the firing stopped the RTO called back to inform me the platoon called for a dust-off, which brought on an acute attack of guilt because I was not out there with them as I settled down for a spell of worrying.

Filled with apprehension, I watched them pick their way across the paddies to the firebase backlit by the setting sun. From their plodding pace, it was obvious they were hot and worn out. I slipped through the wire as my anxiety reached a fever pitch and saw the graceful Johnson leading them home, with Barney, Silverstein, Harley, and Del in tow. Relief washed over me as second squad plodded into view with the indomitable Jerry leading, followed by Bernie.

"You guy's had me scared to death," I protested as they straggled past.

"Poor baby, did all the racket disturb your little nap?" Jerry scoffed irritably.

"Hey, Jay, tired of shamming?" Silverstein greeted.

"What did you hit out there?" I demanded.

"Nothing we couldn't handle," Harley groused. "A pack jumped us about four clicks out, but we put them on the run soon enough."

"Who was the dustoff for?"

Bernie shrugged out of his web gear and sank down tiredly. "An old woman got hit by our artillery."

"Nuthin' but a typical day in thuh sun dodgin' booby traps an findin' nuthin' worth findin'," Barney drawled as he limped past.

"Did you hit anything besides the old woman?"

Del shrugged out of his web gear. "Course not."

With the three of them too pooped to grumble, we had a quiet meal prepared by Mama-san. When we finished she gathered our homemade cups and filled them to the brim with the horrible tea. Faced with the impossible task of drinking it, we settled back to consider ingenious ways to dispose of the liquid under her nose. When she turned her back for an instant, I dumped mine over my shoulder, to the others' envy. As she chattered to Jerry in unintelligible gibberish, Del poured his into the top of his unlaced boot and grinned triumphantly. Jerry laughed and when Mama-san looked at him, Bernie reached over and dumped his into Del's other boot. When Mama-san turned to stare at me in confusion as I cackled, Jerry saw his opening and deftly poured his into a stunned Del's empty cup. We kept our cans well out of his reach as Mama-san settled down across from him and began humming her song in the gathering dusk. He sighed and bravely swallowed the sour liquid in measured gulps, finishing with a twitch at the corners of his mouth. Laughing, we bid Mama-san good night and drifted back to our positions.

I dreamed of burning helicopters and broken bodies, one of which kept trying to jump on my back and choke me. I awoke in a cold sweat and pulled guard the remainder of the night for an unknowing but grateful Del.

———

I spent three long, exasperating days recuperating from my injuries assigned to the inferior mobile reserve force, where I pulled guard duty while the combat platoons were out in the bush, a miserable existence considered below the dignity of true warriors.

On the fourth day, I slunk over to Doc. "You've got to return me to duty."

He probed my injuries as I pretended indifference. "A couple more days should do it."

"Today, Doc," I begged. "I can't take any more of this REMF shit."

"Maybe if you carried only your own gear," he agreed reluctantly.

"Thanks, Doc!"

During my absence the platoon pulled an uneventful patrol, fought an extended engagement against an estimated platoon sized enemy force during an air assault, which resulted in three confirmed enemy kills and one of our own wounded, and had just completed a night ambush without contact. After breakfast and a short rest, the platoon assembled before Deputy Dog and Black for a briefing on the day's mission, a blocking force around a village sheltering a VC tax committee. Third platoon would conduct the search. We moved to the waiting aircraft and departed in a whirl of flying debris as I settled down to worrying about minefields and hot LZs, paying scant attention to the country below. Soon the choppers dipped to the ground as the gunships streaked overhead. I searched the shrubbery for trouble as we bounced to the ground and raced for the tree line to fall into prone positions.

As the noise of the departing choppers faded away, I experienced troubling pangs as I watched the empty expanse of silent jungle. The distant crackle of Deputy Dog's radio confirmed we were down and LZ cold. In the static of third platoon's reply, I heard cheering in the background for our good fortune as they prepared to join us. My unease increased when Lunas stood and swept his hand forward. Silverstein clambered up under his awkward load and moved in the indicated direction as I fell in behind him, with Del and the rest of the squad following me as the other three squads broke off in different directions. When parts of the hamlet appeared through the heavy brush, we made a sharp turn and trotted parallel to the cluster of hooches, seeing no movement as we flanked the area. The absence of people means trouble, I reminded myself, the foreboding becoming more pronounced as Lunas dropped us off into single man positions at thirty-yard intervals. I knelt beside a tree, weapon pointing inward, part of a long line facing the deserted village fifty yards away.

A VC carbine popped from the far side of the village. I crouched as the chatter of rotor blades announced the imminent arrival of third platoon. Several rapid shots cracked from the same general area as before, the carbine again. Third squad sent back a thunderous response, and we dove into prone positions as their bullets whined into our ranks. When their firing tapered off, silence again surrounded us. The choppers touched down to our right and departed. Voices denoted third platoon beginning their sweep through the village with us sealing the box and trapping the enemy.

"Be alert. Watch for—" Lunas began.

"Look out!" Silverstein yelped as a VC carbine spoke sharply before us.

"Here they come!" Johnson shouted as he fired a rapid burst.

I fired at a flash of black silk and an AK-47 automatic rifle peppered my position as I scrounged for cover with the rounds barking all around me. Two more carbines popped along with the AK and second squad on our left erupted en masse, sending a furious swarm of hornets through us as I hugged the ground. The AK and two carbines chattered wildly as the black shirts passed through us like a blur heading for deeper brush. In the melee, Johnson turned to fire at the vanishing figures. I dug for another magazine as he sagged against a tree and lowered his muzzle before collapsing onto his knees.

"Cease fire!" Sergeant Lunas yelled. "Goddamn it, hold your fire!"

When the second squad stopped firing into us, I ran in a crouch to the sagging Johnson, now clutching his side with both hands as blood seeped through his fingers from a spreading stain on his fatigue jacket.

"Medic! Medic!" I yelled as I settled him back into a sitting position against a tree, unbuckled his web gear, and peeled it off his shoulders as he grunted.

Sergeant Lunas trotted up with Silverstein close on his heels. "Bad?"

"Better get Doc," I advised as he leaned down to see for himself.

"Peel a packet!" I ordered Silverstein as Lunas raced off. I unbuttoned Johnson's shirt and lifted his hands away from his side to reveal a small, ugly blue hole oozing blood. I pulled him forward and lifted his shirt, finding no exit wound in his back, indicating the bullet was still inside him. I leaned him back against the tree as Silverstein thrust his first aid packet at me.

"Took ... my breath," Johnson whispered.

"Easy now," I soothed as I pressed the white gauze against his wound.

"Water ..." Johnson begged.

"Easy, Doc's on the way," I consoled him, ignoring his request, knowing water could not be given to lower intestines wounds.

"Got ... one ... there," Johnson pointed a bloody, trembling finger to the bushes where the VC had fled as Doc and Lunas scrambled through the trees.

"I'll take him now," Doc said as he knelt and unsnapped his kit. "Somebody tell the Lieutenant to call a dustoff."

"I'll do it," Harley called and sprinted away.

"Get ... him," Johnson urged.

I eased into the brush to our rear as Silverstein flanked me with raised weapon.

"Where are you going?" Lunas panted.

"Johnson thinks he got one of them," I called over my shoulder.

"Spread out," Lunas ordered as he and Del joined us on line.

"Dung lai! *Freeze*," Silverstein shouted after twenty yards and braced with rifle at shoulder level pointed into a thick mass of bushes near him. "Careful, he's alive!" he cautioned as we closed in on the position.

A black clad figure lay on his side partly concealed by jumbled vegetation drawing short, painful breaths. Blood covered his lower body, saturating his clothing in a sticky mass. Del snatched a carbine off the ground as the VC grimaced and glanced in the direction his buddies had fled.

"Patch him up," Lunas ordered. "The rest of you cover the rear."

I slung my rifle over my shoulder and knelt to pat him down, finding one full magazine of ammo and one empty, along with a government issued identification card with his picture on it. I handed the items to Lunas and pulled the wounded man into a sitting position as he shuddered in pain, raised his shirt, and found a small entrance hole in his back near the waist. A jagged tear near his midsection where the bullet exited seeped blood mixed with greenish brown matter around his protruding intestines. I grimaced at the ugly mess as I pulled my first-aid packet from its pouch, stripped the cover, and pressed the pad against the ripped flesh in front. Lunas handed me his packet and I fastened it to the wound in back, pulled one of the VC's arms over my shoulder, and lifted him to his feet. He panted in suppressed pain as I carried him to the LZ and placed him next to Johnson.

"Good job," Doc acknowledged as he inspected my bandages and then dug in his bag for a morphine packet to administer to the VC.

I knelt next to Johnson with his glazed eyes. "How you feeling, man?"

"How ... you think ... white-boy ... I been shot," he replied, his voice slurred from the morphine. He turned his head to VC next to us. "That ... the one ... I got?"

"You half-assed did the job," I replied. "He'll be back shooting at us in a month."

He grimaced. "Should have ... finished the job for me ... white boy ... I done killed all I want to ... know what I mean?"

"You're going home for some sham time," I assured him as the sound of an approaching helicopter filled the air. "See you."

"Yeah ... be careful ... white boy," he replied. "Tell Barney I said ... kiss my black ass."

The chopper settled on the grass with a bounce. The stretcher teams rushed to the wide doors carrying the two men whose war had just ended. Doc followed and tossed Johnson's rifle and web gear aboard. Seconds later the bird was streaking back to the field hospital.

"Hell of a good man, Doc," I observed as the bird disappeared. "Will he make it?"

"Be chasing nurses in a month," Doc assured me as he stooped to gather his bag.

We remained for another hour while third platoon continued their detailed search of the village, and then flew back to the firebase to congregate at the platoon CP for the debriefing.

"You dumb shits damned near wiped yourselves out when those bastards charged through our line." Black chewed on the end of his cigar for a thoughtful minute as he glared at us. "I've told you a thousand times not to blast away indiscriminately. When are you silly shits going to get that through your thick skulls? You've got to exercise fire control. Goddamn it, if we kill one of our own through stupidity the operation is a failure no matter what the final count." He viewed our bowed heads in satisfaction. "Our little encounter netted eight mortar rounds, seven grenades, two M-1 carbines, one AK-47 automatic rifle, two confirmed kills, one wounded, two VC suspects, and recovered eighteen bags of harvested rice collected by the VC tax agents. Johnson was our only casualty, inflicted by our own friendly fire. You shits get back to your positions now."

We four gathered in front of Mama-san's hooch to clean our rifles. Afterwards, we stripped off pants, shirts, and boots and sprawled in the sun in our underwear to allow the soothing rays to ease tired muscles, dry small sores, soothe raw shoulders and hips worn thin by web gear, air out swollen feet, raw underarms, and crotches. Unaccustomed to this luxury, our battered bodies that had not received baths in over a week or clean clothes for days languished through the afternoon in contented bliss.

———

Mama-san woke us in late afternoon with cups of steaming tea, ignoring our partially nude bodies, and we made an honest attempt to drink the brew for once.

Jerry sighed. "Think of the round eyed women waiting for us back in the real world."

Del yawned. "And ice cold beer."

"How about showers and real sit down food," Bernie dreamed.

"I just want to get back to base camp," I groaned.

"I'm going to win a Silver Star before I go back," Jerry bragged. "I'll need a stick to beat all the chicks off me."

"More than likely the Army will issue you a nice black body bag to wear that medal on," Bernie sniffed.

"I'm going to get a million dollar wound," Del promised. "You know, one in the fleshy part of my leg. When you guys get back, I'll have everything set up and waiting for you in Chicago, girls, booze, the whole works."

Bernie scooped a pebble off the ground and scored a perfect strike on a distant tree. "I'm going back to the Angels."

"I'm going to win a battlefield commission," I dreamed. "And go to flight school and fly helicopters."

This provoked a united attack of scorn from my compatriots, who accused me of being a 'lifer,' and I thus sank into sullen silence as we settled into drowsy lassitude. Mama-san collected our C-rations as we filled our steel pots with water and bathed from head to toe. We then donned our cleanest set of dirty fatigues and settled onto the straw mats inside the hooch before bowls of rice mixed with different kinds of meat from our C-rations, small green onions, and bits of fried egg topped with reddish brown sauce. She also prepared canteen cups of hot chocolate and coffee syrupy with packets of powdered cream and sugar. We feasted like kings and then lay back in contentment listening to Mama-san hum her haunting lullaby.

As the dark settled, the shadows seemed less menacing as parachute flares lit the night in smoking spirals under their silk tops, drifting lazily as the artillery boomed outward in grumbling intimidation. The guns and flares added a depth to the night with its full moon and millions of stars overhead, leaving me feeling lost and insignificant as gripping homesickness clutched at me. Wordlessly, we returned to our positions for our routine with rifles by our side.

The days in the firebase stretched into weeks, with the action gradually tapering off as our saturation patrolling began to have its planned effect. Our platoon in particular seemed to lead a charmed existence. Other platoons occasionally hit snipers and squad sized enemy elements, with little damage to either side. Bravo Company hit a VC company and fought a hell of a battle for most of one day before Charlie Company teamed up with them to put the enemy in retreat. Charlie Company wandered into a minefield that cost them six wounded and sprung an ambush that killed nine VC. One of our Alpha Company platoons recovered an arms cache on an airmobile assault, and the other jumped on top of an enemy squad scattering them in all directions amid a lively running battle. But as time moved along our platoon encountered no enemy action and took no losses from mines or booby traps. Dry ambushes, cold LZs, and empty sweeps were our lot, and we weren't complaining.

As we patrolled through the happy little rice harvesters, we gained a feeling of accomplishment in the war effort. Black worked us hard and assured us we were reaping the benefits every time we left the firebase and returned without encountering the enemy. The miles and heat were all worthwhile when we entered villages to find swarms of happy children rushing to hold our hands and smiling old men and women in place of the sullen suspicion we encountered upon our arrival. Now every village we entered had a group of old people and young babies for Doc to administer to as best he could with his limited medical training orientated primarily to the treatment of war wounds. With our streak of luck, we sagely agreed we had become a known entity to the VC, who obviously feared and avoided us at all costs.

After several days of the good life, we completed a large battalion sized operation late one afternoon where our Alpha and Bravo Company provided blocking forces for Charlie Company's sweep through a string of hamlets. We flushed out no Cong during the operation, and detained only a small number of VC suspects in the boring venture. With our mission complete, we waited for the choppers to return us to the firebase.

During this period, our platoon loitered in a large grove of fruit trees, where we helped ourselves to the bountiful fruit in generous amounts. With our full stomachs growling and churning from the unaccustomed rich harvest, we soon learned choppers were unavailable to extract us due to a priority mission. Our battalion commander decided this presented no great problem, we could just walk back to the firebase instead of the more reasonable alternative of sitting down in our present location until the Department of the Army provided us with transportation. Walking back in the hot afternoon sun was nothing short of inhumane, we figured, and with such a prized force as ourselves, they would surely send somebody out to get us if we exhibited a little patience. Deputy Dog agreed but said we would walk back anyway. As I was leaning on my rifle explaining to Del, Bernie, and Jerry how simple it was to be an officer and make these kinds of heavy decisions, Sergeant Lunas told me to get my ass out on point.

I moved my grumbling stomach out across the paddies, hugging the tree line when possible, as Del plodded along behind me followed by the rest of the squad, the platoon, the company, and the battalion. Looking over my shoulder, I could see over a mile of pissed off Wolfhounds on my heels following where I led, thinking this heady stuff, being point man for the mightiest force in Vietnam. Imagine me, spearhead for this battle hardened, combat tested unit. If only my dad could see me now. Obviously, no VC in his right mind would attack such a force, so all I had to worry about was mines and booby traps. This was right where I belonged, I reflected with pride, wondering if old 'Sky-Eye' knew who was leading him home. He might even have asked for me himself. After all, he wouldn't trust just anybody to be point for his whole battalion, would he? No sir, the fact was that out of four hundred troops, I'd been singled out. I could imagine Jerry eating his heart out behind me as I continued to ignore the ominous rumbling in my stomach.

As pressure built inside my gut, I considered stepping off to the side and relieving myself. Del could take the point for a while and then I could hurry back to the front. But the thought of sharing the prestige with anyone else was unbearable ... I could hold it until we reached the firebase. Ten minutes later, I figured I'd made a bad decision because I was about to explode. I squeezed my buttocks tightly together to keep from messing my pants, figuring my worst mistake was in finding myself in the middle of a large, open rice paddy with the nearest bush two hundred yards away on the opposite side. Desperation set in as sweat beaded my forehead and my mind became fuzzy. I concentrated on those bushes along the hedgerow to my front drawing slowly closer as my trembling legs jittered along under my tightly puckered ass. I was in a tunnel watching those bushes at the far end of my vision, and began to breathe in short gasps as a cold, clammy feeling encased me. I took short, prissy little steps to keep my bowels in check, my feverish mind locked on those bushes. I wanted to run but was afraid to take bigger steps. I pranced along in my odd gait, drawing nearer to my goal, holding my breath, urging myself to hold on just a minute longer, praying I didn't stumble, my whole focus on those bushes, the growing pressure becoming unbearable as I gritted my teeth. Five steps out I unfastened my web gear, at two steps my pants, at one step my arm flashed up in the halt signal and I charged through the bushes not really giving a damn what was in there. I slung my web gear to the ground, propped my weapon against a tree, jerked my pants down, and squatted in the same instant that I exploded in gratification. Never had I felt such physical relief. The fever and dizziness dissipated with the gushing as my vision cleared and my heart slowed to a comfortable thumping. This was better than sex, or even nickel beer, I reflected in wonder as I emptied almost pure liquid from my guts.

"Hey, Jay, what's going on?" Del called from the opposite side of the bushes.

"I'm taking a shit. Be a minute." Calmly, I searched for my roll of C-ration toilet paper in my shirt pocket as I heard the *second* most awful sound in the world.

"Mustang Six wants to know what's the holdup?" a voice called from where the battalion had come to a jolting halt behind me in the open rice paddy bunched up like an accordion.

"Jay's taking a shit," Del replied.

The *first* most awful sound in the world followed the second back—loud, cackling laughter, growing in volume and intensity, all the way down that long line through the heart of the mighty Wolfhound Battalion, man to man, through the squads, platoons, companies, and right back to old Mustang Six himself in the rear with Charlie Company.

"Pass it on, Sharpe's taking a shit."

"Sharpe's taking a shit, pass it back."

I wanted to die. I hitched up my pants, gathered my gear, and stepped through the bushes with arm raised to motion the column forward and was greeted with thunderous applause and cheers amidst peals of laughter and cries of *"Encore! Encore!"*

I glared at an ashen faced Del. "Thanks, asshole!" With as much dignity as I could muster, I spun on my heel and stomped back through the hedgerow with the rest following in a whooping column.

I was a long time living the event down. Back in the firebase I faced unmerciful kidding, even from a grinning Deputy Dog and Black. Days later, out of the blue someone would lean over to the man next to him and shout, "Sharpe's taking a shit—pass it on!" and everyone would break up into screaming fits of silliness.

I never did fully appreciate the humor of it all.

CHAPTER 14

An instinct for the day's hot commodity and luck of the draw made men rich overnight in our capitalistic free trade system.

The biggest asset in dealing in such a volatile market as the 'C-Ration Exchange' was to keep others guessing as to one's actual desires. The sky was the limit on those meals known to tickle the palate of an individual and our favorites were among our most closely guarded secrets. Some items were ridiculously high anyway, such as pound cake, and bartering reserved to three to one strict offerings. Others, such as ham and lima beans, were on the opposite end of the scale and held little worth. The rest of the selections were somewhere in between and operated under wildly fluctuating values on a day-by-day basis. A can of beans and franks could go for an even swap of beefsteak and two packs of cocoa in the morning, and by evening command a price of one sliced ham, three cocoas, a can of peaches, and a lid of jam, or just as easily drop to one beefsteak and one cocoa.

The luck of the draw was a daily bid for the jackpot after one man placed a case of C-rations containing twelve individual meals upside down on the ground in front of three other men. The three drew one meal apiece three times around, leaving three for the man who placed them. From that moment on the market was open with the haggling occurring off and on through patrol and firefight as offer and counteroffer were made. Inevitably, brokers, men who excelled at the craft of trading and developed uncanny instincts as to what the market would bear for a given item on a given day, evolved to dominate the process.

Our foursome fared better than most because Jerry became the best victuals trader in the battalion, if not Nam itself. His miraculous manipulations kept us in luxuries, and his skill was a constant source of inspiration. He departed on one occasion flipping a paltry tin of cheese in his palm, and returned an hour later after a dozen different trades carrying a can of beans and franks, a can of fruit cocktail, and two packages of cocoa. In the fifteenth century, a man would burn at the stake for such witchcraft.

Over the weeks, we built up a tidy little stockpile of goodies in one corner of Mama-san's hooch, which she guarded zealously. While we were in the firebase, a steady trickle of men beat a path to the door to dicker for goods as Jerry sat cross-legged on a mat and performed his magic. Bernie kept a running inventory of stocks on hand, Del kept the cans sorted and stacked, and I fetched this and that from the back as each artful customer stated his preference. This usually resulted in several trips per man as each pretended to deal for one item with the full intention of trading for another once he wore our broker down. During one afternoon of heavy trading, I was hustling back and forth for cans of C-rations as Jerry alternated between indignation and sublime acceptance as he worked the crowd around him.

Del grabbed my arm as I passed. "Look at Mama-san."

I glanced over my shoulder as I juggled cans to see Mama-san standing erect in her paddy with head back and hands pressed in the small of her back. After a moment of concentration, she sagged, collected her basket, and plodded towards the hooch with her head down.

"What do you make of that?"

I shrugged. "Tired, I guess."

"Jay! Need a can of turkey loaf and a beefsteak," Jerry called. "Where's that fruit cocktail?"

"Coming, coming," I called irritably.

"I've never seen her quit in the afternoon," Del persisted as I hustled out with the order.

"Here, stack these." I dumped a load of cans in his arms when I returned.

"Hey, she's going into her bunker," Del exclaimed as she descended into the dark underground opening just inside the door of her hooch. "Why would she do that?"

"Damn, you can ask some dumb assed questions," I scolded.

"Jay?" Jerry called impatiently.

"All right, all right, hold your horses," I growled as I rushed off to fill the latest order.

With the ongoing wheeling dealing, Mama-san's unusual actions were soon forgotten. By late afternoon,

Jerry had fleeced all the customers available and we lay on our mats in the sun soaking up the remaining rays before the coming night's ambush. Mama-san climbed out of her bunker, limped over to the well beside her hooch, and drew water from the hole with a rusty bucket attached to a small rope.

"What's wrong with Mama-san?" Bernie asked.

"She quit early today," Del vouched.

"Pulling rice is hard work," I replied lazily.

Jerry rose on his elbow to study her. "Something's different."

"I've never seen her quit before evening," Del insisted.

I watched in silence trying to put the oddity in focus as she hauled the cans of water from the well, pulled the elastic band away from her waist, and dumped the contents down the front of her stomach. "She's just taking a bath."

"She looks funny," Bernie mused. "Hey, her *stomach's* gone!"

Del frowned. "Gone?"

"It is!" Jerry exclaimed as she descended back into the black opening of her underground bunker. "She's skinny now!"

"How can it be gone?" Del demanded. "She's been here the whole time. Can't be gone!"

I scrambled to my feet. "We better check it out."

We grabbed our rifles and converged on the opening to peer into the gloom below, where the glow of a flickering candle portrayed a frail shadow on the wall at the bottom of the narrow earthen steps. As we stared into the pit, a faint wail floated up to us.

"What was that?" Del whispered as we drew back in surprise.

"A b-b-baby?" Jerry stuttered.

Bernie stared in wonder. "*Nah* ... couldn't be!"

"Was too!" Jerry insisted.

"Hey, uh, Mama-san?" I called into the hole.

"*Waaaaa!*" a weak wail answered.

"Oh shit! Get Doc! Hurry!" I ordered as a stronger cry drifted up to us, insistent and angry. "*Move it!*" Del and Bernie attempted to go in different directions and collided, nearly knocking Jerry headfirst into the hole as he stooped to look inside. "*Damn!*" I swore, pulling him back from the brink as he teetered with arms wind milling for balance.

"*Ouch!*" Bernie groaned as Del's rifle poked him in the eye.

"Let *go!*" Del insisted, jerking to free his rifle entangled with Bernie's.

"*Whaaaaaa!*"

"*Get Doc!*" I screamed in exasperation at the two tussling figures.

"*Medic! Medic!* We need a medic!" Del shouted as he ran off.

"Doc? Hey, Doc! Somebody get Doc over here!" Bernie yelled as he raced off.

Troops sprang up from positions of slumber as the frantic shouts ruptured the afternoon lull, with some jumping into foxholes and drawing rifles and web gear close as they anxiously looked in our direction. Deputy Dog, wearing only pants and flip-flops, rounded the corner of the hooch at a dead run, with Black, bareheaded and one flip-flop missing, sprinting after him. Sergeant Lunas, fully dressed to include web gear but barefoot, closed in from the opposite direction chasing a screaming Del, who had made a half-circle and was running back to us. Doc, clutching his kit bag in one hand and his trousers in the other, rounded the corner with Deputy Dog's RTO scrambling behind him trying to slip the heavy radio onto his bare back.

"Snake bite?" Doc shouted as he diverted his direction to intercept Del.

"No, here, back here, Doc!" I shouted.

Doc slid to a stop as the RTO stumbled and fell in a heap of dust, his radio skidding along in front of his prostrate form.

"What is it? What is it?" Deputy Dog shouted.

"Watch the goddamn front!" Black yelled at the troops staring fearfully in our direction.

They swung about and poked their rifles out across the empty paddies as Jerry grasped Doc's arm and tried to stuff him in the hole. "Down there, Doc, hurry!"

"What is it?" Deputy Dog pleaded as Bernie and Del closed in on us.

A loud wail stopped everyone in mid-stride. Mouths flew open in the dead silence. We edged closer to the bunker opening as a second robust cry echoed from the depths.

"A *baby*?" Doc exclaimed.

"Huh?" Deputy Dog peered down into the hole skeptically.

"Yeah, in there, hurry," Jerry insisted, trying to push Doc into the black hole.

"Baby?" Deputy Dog asked as his RTO scrambled up on all fours and retrieved his radio.

Doc shook off Jerry and pulled on his trousers. We gathered around the opening elbowing to get to the front as he eased down the steep steps and breathlessly watched his shadow merge with Mama-san's as another broken cry echoed from the cavern.

"Get me a couple of flashlights," Doc called from below.

Sergeant Lunas snatched his light off his web gear and tossed it to me. I juggled it before handing it to Jerry. The RTO pulled his light off his radio and handed it to me. I passed it to Jerry as he thrust the first at Black. Black snatched both lights and descended into the darkness as we crowded around again.

"And get me some hot water," Doc called.

"Get some canteens," Deputy Dog shouted.

"And bring some cups," Jerry added.

"Get your block of C-4," I commanded, pushing Del towards our position.

We filled canteen cups with water, placed them on the blazing chunks of explosives to boil, and then passed the hot containers from man to man in a chain down to Black at the bottom of the steps. A short time later he and Doc emerged.

"It's a girl," Doc announced.

"Hey, Doc, can we see her?" Silverstein begged as we cheered.

"Okay, but no one closer than five feet." Doc turned to the bunker as we backed away from the opening and jockeyed for position in the half-circle. He reemerged followed by a nervous Mama-san cradling a tiny figure wrapped in rags. We watched in wonder as Doc pulled the rag coverings back to expose a head full of black hair topping the ugliest little red, wrinkled face in the world, its eyes squeezed shut, little fists waving in the air, and swooned when the infant emitted a weak cry such as a kitten might make.

Even Black and Barney grinned as Mama-san clucked her tongue and rocked the baby in her arms. Doc offered her a steadying hand as she reentered the bunker.

"Aw man, she's beautiful," Harley whispered.

Silverstein beamed. "Did you see all that hair?"

"I can't believe she did that without even a hospital or a doctor," Del exclaimed. "Can you believe she did that all by herself?"

"Sheeeeettt," Barney offered as he rolled his cud of tobacco. "Cows do it all thuh time."

"Well, she ain't no goddamn cow," Silverstein blustered. "*We* helped her."

"How'd we help, fool?" Harley scoffed. "She already done it when we got here."

"Didn't we help, Doc, with the water and all?" Silverstein pleaded.

"Every man here contributed," Doc assured us.

Silverstein thrust his chin forward. "See, asshole!"

"Hey, let's adopt her," Jerry shouted. "You know … the whole Platoon … sort of like a mascot?" he finished weakly as we tapered into silence.

"Why not?" Bernie offered. "Mama-san doesn't seem to have a husband."

"Sheeeeetttt!" Barney spat a stream of tobacco juice for emphasis. "She's got one all right—probably a Sergeant in thuh local VC."

"Man, you really *are* an ass," Silverstein glowered. "Besides, she can't help what her father is. Can she?" he asked doubtfully.

"Come on, let's do it," Del urged. "What do you say?"

"Yeah, what the hell," Harley seconded.

"Sir?" I turned to the lieutenant.

Deputy Dog looked thoughtful as we waited. "Well ..." He tugged at his earlobe. "We might be able to do it informal like, I suppose." He looked at Black for approval, who didn't change expression in the heavy silence. "Just make sure she has food and everything ... as long as we're here anyway," he continued to Black, sounding as hopeful as the rest of us.

Black looked out across the paddies with no comment, intent on letting the lieutenant dig his own hole, so to speak.

"And have Doc look after her," Jerry added. "Sometimes ... when he's not doing anything else," he amended as Black scowled at him.

Barney spat in the dust at his feet. "Sheeeettt."

"What Doc does with his own time and what you morons do with your own rations is no concern of mine," Black growled.

"All right," Jerry shouted, the matter officially settled.

"What'll we name her?" Del questioned.

"Mary!" "Debbie!" voices offered, obviously the girlfriends of the donors.

"I rather think that's up to Mama-san," Black observed coldly.

"Let's give her our stock of rations." Bernie nodded at the stack of cans in the back corner of Mama-san's hooch.

"Done!" Jerry agreed. "The rest of you guys bring your extra C-rats to Jay and Del."

"Okay!" "Will do!" "I've got some now," voices offered.

"Get organized," Black ordered. "We move out in an hour."

During the next hour, a large pile of C-rations accumulated next to our position. Jerry and Bernie cooked for us as Del and I sorted the cans into meats, fruits, and cakes before stacking them in neat rows against the rear wall of the hooch on the dirt floor.

———

The night ambush was uneventful, and we returned the following morning in a high state of excitement at the prospect of seeing our adopted daughter again. As we crossed the paddy, we were alarmed to see Mama-san standing knee-deep in the water pulling rice stalks. She stared in bewilderment as we urged her to return to the hooch and insistently carried her reed basket and tools ourselves. At the hooch, she stood in front of us in puzzlement, and then descended into the bunker to return with the bundle to show us the baby, becoming further confused as we maintained the five-foot distance prescribed by Doc each time she attempted to approach one of us. Doc elbowed his way through and pulled the rags aside to inspect the child. A healthy cry greeted him as we strained to see around his bulk. Satisfied all was well, we drifted back to our positions, where a pile of C-rations rapidly grew beside Del and me. Black even wandered over with a can of peaches, his absolute favorite, which he'd been known to trade a whole meal for in the past.

———

In the next week, we alternated patrols, ambushes, and air assaults as the stack of C-rations grew in the back of Mama-san's hooch. Donations poured in from the rest of the company, some even reaching us from our sister companies and the artillery positions within the perimeter. By the end of the week, over five hundred cans of assorted foodstuffs were stacked in neat rows almost to the ceiling. At least four C-ration boxes of cocoa, coffee, sugar, and cream joined another box of chocolate candy. We became selective in items we kept, which produced a richer offering from those anxious to receive acceptance from our committee. Volunteers from within the platoon worked the rice paddy under Bernie's careful guidance, where a two-hour stint was enough to fell even the strongest man as legs, backs, and arms gave out under the grueling labor. Mama-san held court with the baby on a straw mat laid on the bare floor, feeding the infant openly from her sagging breasts, as a continuous group of men lingered at the front of the hooch cooing at the baby and imagining she recognized them from previous visits.

One afternoon Mama-san placed the baby in Jerry's startled arms and produced an old, rusted can. From this she emptied the last shreds of green tea leaves into a pot to brew us a cup of tea. In shame, realizing it was her last, we sipped at it and promptly dumped it when she turned her back. Over Black's mutterings, we took up a collection within the platoon and requested our supply courier provide us with four large cans of green tea, baby blankets and clothes, a couple sets of black silk pajama type women's clothes, and any available toys he could find. Our astounded supply sergeant purchased the items on the economy and brought them forward in person on the daily resupply run to see what the hell was going on. Mama-san was ecstatic over the cans of tea and clothes for herself, but wailed and hugged each of us as we stood in stiff embarrassment when presented with the blankets and toys for the baby, obviously never having dreamed of such riches for her child. The old cranky supply sergeant, touched by her gratitude, sent out two air mattresses and silk poncho liners the following day.

––––––

Persistent rumors circulated that we were going home. Our operation had extended into almost six weeks. We were dirty, tattered, bone weary, and longed for civilization and cold beer. Cu Chi seemed years away, its primitive structures viewed as elaborate havens of comfort. Showers and sit down, kitchen prepared meals were but a faint memory. The constant patrolling had wrecked us physically and mentally. Feet were raw and blistered, hands calloused, hair long and matted, bodies covered with scrapes, cuts, bruises, bites, stings, and welts. Deeply tanned, with eyes sunk back into gaunt faces over hollow cheeks, we wore threadbare uniforms shining with grease and dirt around the multiple rips and tears. Patrols produced almost no contact with the enemy now. Even the mines and booby traps had all but disappeared as we chased the VC into other, more productive areas. A good number of them were pushing up daisies. It was time to go home. Black assured us it would be soon but grew gruff if pressed for an exact date. Our grumbling grew louder and tempers shorter until one morning Deputy Dog assembled us.

"Men, it's been a long, hard mission," he began as my heart pounded and hope lined the faces around me. "But we're finally going home. Unfortunately, the plan calls for our withdrawal to be conducted in three stages," he continued, cutting our jubilation short. "Phase one will begin tomorrow morning when Bravo Company will be lifted by chopper to conduct a sweep operation. From there they will move into a blocking position. Our Alpha Company will fall back and prepare new fighting positions inside our current perimeter. We will then conduct a sweep from our reduced firebase here to Bravo's blocking force as the artillery and most of the support units move back to our base camp at Cu Chi. Bravo Company will airlift back to Cu Chi when we reach them, and we will remain in the field to conduct a night ambush. Phase two will begin the morning of the second day. We will conduct a search and destroy mission back here to the firebase as Charlie

Company and the remaining support forces airlift back to Cu Chi. We will remain here overnight. Phase three on the morning of the third day will see us lifted back to Cu Chi, thus ending this operation." Total silence ensued as Black released us.

"Why are *we* the *last* to go home?" Del moaned as we trudged back to our position.

"Why should *we* dig somebody else's fighting position?" I fumed.

"Why do *we* have to *walk* while everyone else gets to *fly*?" Bernie groaned.

"Why do *we* have to pull *another* night ambush?" Jerry whined.

"Candy ass Bravo *always* gets the breaks," Silverstein swore.

"I bet their commander is some dandy *general's* son," Harley insisted.

"Shhheeetttt, more'n likely a *senator's* nephew," Barney spat.

We complained bitterly about the heat, each other's disgusting personal habits, and life in general as Mama-san attempted to cheer us up with cups of the vile tea, to our utter despair. We spent a long, hard day in the sun searching for and finding nothing, curt and cutting in our responses to each other throughout, and returned to the firebase a foul tempered little group wallowing in self pity. We cooked our meal in Mama-san's hooch and ate in strained silence, then returned to our foxholes, unable to bear the sight of one another any longer. We passed a mean night of harsh artillery fires and blinding parachute flares watching the shadows in annoyance.

Del woke me three minutes early for one of my shifts and I offered to kick his ass. Thereafter he was always at least five minutes beyond his watch when we switched. We greeted the dawn with snarls as those behind us prepared to depart for home. Mama-san was disturbed by our bad tempers and bickering at breakfast, which preceded the dismantling of our fighting positions by ripping the sandbags apart to refill our foxholes. We packed our personal gear in waterproof bags and sent them to the LZ for pickup, and then, under Sergeant Lunas' authoritarian guidance, collected the trip flares and rolled the concertina wire before shifting back fifty yards to establish a new, smaller perimeter in the vast clearing to our rear.

Del and I scraped out a half hearted shallow pit, and then dug it waist deep after Sergeant Lunas came around and raised hell. Then we dug it shoulder deep after Black came around and raised hell, grumbling and cursing throughout since we would not even use it ourselves and some dumb REMF would probably sleep like a log the whole night through thanks to our labors. When we finished, I sat in disgust on the side of the hole peeling raw skin from my blistered hands and surveyed the area once again crawling with men and equipment.

Bunkers came down one sandbag at a time as men ripped the canvas bags open and dumped the dirt into the holes. Trash burned in heaps at scattered locations. Trucks lumbered along with men standing in the rear clinging to the rails. Aircraft rotors swirled loose objects around the area as they landed and departed in successive waves with lines of men rushing to clamber aboard.

High radio antennas melted into the ground with men clinging to the guy-wires on each side dismantling and packing them joint by joint. Details of men rolled strands of communication wire onto large doughnut shaped spools. Others prepared giant artillery pieces for movement as their enclosures faded away around them and trucks backed up to attach themselves to the tow bars. The whole area was one of intense activity and confusion as men darted everywhere spurred by their desire to get home. The two days we ourselves had left seemed like months.

"*Wimps!*" I shouted, drawing startled glances from those close enough to hear, and then proceeded to curse them in high fashion.

Soon Black got our disgruntled platoon formed and moving through the paddy area as Mama-san stood watching after us until we were out of sight on the far side. The only foe encountered was the blinding sun and energy draining heat as we left the open rice fields and entered a dry, sparsely vegetated area of randomly spaced hooches and thick hedgerows. We switched to a horseshoe formation with second and third squads on line, and first and fourth squads in file on each flank, wherein Lunas directed me fifty yards out on flank security.

The heat seemed unbearable as I wiped streaming rivulets of sweat from my face with my grimy towel. White half-moons of salt stains formed under my arms as my drenched shirt stuck to my body and grated against my grubby skin. My shoulders and hips were constant points of pain from the chafing web gear as I listened to the platoon blow two booby traps, the cries of *"Fire in the hole!"* preceding the dull explosions. I scanned my path with greater care as we moved again trying to pick out the deadly thin wires stretched across openings in the tangled brush, avoiding trails and footpaths. An hour later the platoon ground to a halt for the noon break and I sank down with a sigh, stripped off web gear and shirt, and dropped my steel pot to the ground beside me, relishing the cool air circulating through my wet, matted hair. In the deep shade of some bushes I dug out a can of peaches and propped my canteen beside my leg as I ate, feeling the fatigue settle into my bones as I stared out across a small field in front of me surrounded by thick hedgerows. A half burned hooch sagged in disrepair to my right front beside a small pagoda, abandoned to the elements, its tile roof broken and scattered about its chipped stone sides. Grass grew wild at the base of eight or ten stone grave markers clustered around the ruins.

As I tipped my head back to drain the juice from my can of peaches a flicker on the far side of the field caught my eye. I watched the area for several minutes, saw nothing alarming, and decided it had been a bird or my imagination. Settling back into the shade, I reached for my canteen. A flash of metal glinted near the same area. I eased my hand around to grab my rifle propped against the tree beside me and sat very still, eyes glued to the spot, seeing nothing. I rose to a crouch and slipped through the bushes to pause behind the small graveyard. Two Vietnamese men crossed an open space in the hedgerow to my front a little ahead of my position fifty yards away. I lurched behind one of the gravestones.

Both were looking to my left towards the platoon. Both carried rifles. Stunned, I watched them creep forward, experiencing a moment of panic as I realized I had left my web gear and shirt draped across a bush. If either of them looked to their left ... I opened my mouth to shout a warning to the platoon but closed it, realizing it would also alert the VC. With a trembling hand, I inserted a finger into the trigger guard and clicked my safety off, flinching at the metallic pop. From a prone position, I eased around the headstone and sighted on the lead man. A cold calm washed over me as the metal tip of my front sight lined up and framed his head in the oval of the rear sight. I drew a shallow breath and held it.

The sudden slap of my rifle against my shoulder took me by surprise as the sharp *crack* reverberated across the still pasture. The lead man lifted sideways in the air and dropped with his arms flopping away from his body. The second man crouched for an instant and then darted to his fallen comrade. I fired twice. Bark flew from a tree near his head and a bush shuddered by his side as he grabbed the first man's rifle. I tracked him as he raced back down the hedgerow, shooting blindly through the bushes at his fleeing figure. He spun into the field and collapsed near the edge. I trained my sights on him, breathing heavily as sweat clung to my eyelashes.

The platoon was in an uproar. Sporadic shots intermingled with Black's shouts of '*Cease fire!*' as men scrambled for cover and retrieved rifles and gear laid about carelessly in the tranquility of moments before. The second man rolled over on his stomach and crawled towards the bushes. I sighted a foot in front of his head and squeezed the trigger, throwing dirt in his face as the bullet whined off into the bushes. He froze and looked back over his shoulder at me. I sighted again, this time on him, and waited. He laid his head in the dirt and made no further attempt to move. A crashing of bushes and thudding of running boots announced the arrival of Black, Lunas, and three others.

Black crouched beside a tree behind me. "VC?"

"Yeah," I panted, my nerves going haywire. "This one's wounded. Don't know about the other one. He's off to the left there. I-I saw him go down."

"Lunas, take these men to the right for security," Black ordered. "I'll bring a team down the hedgerow across the field. Sharpe, you keep that one pinned down. Let's move!"

Sergeant Lunas led his group off to the right behind me as Black headed back to the platoon at a gallop. Two minutes later, he led a group down the wood line across the field. When they approached the spot where I had fired on the first man, they circled around a clump of bushes with rifles pointed downward. Black edged forward, knelt to examine something, and then dropped one man off while he and the rest continued on to the man I was still covering. Two men approach the fallen VC from different directions and the remainder sidled on past to the end of the hedgerow. Silverstein eased forward, collected the two enemy weapons, and backed away as the man raised his head to watch him. Barney placed his foot under him and rolled him over as he kept his rifle trained on the man's head before kneeling to search him. I used the edge of the tombstone to pull myself up onto rubbery legs, breathing in deep, measured pulls to control my hypertension. I stumbled back to my equipment, brushed the dirt and sand off my sweat-drenched body, and donned my shirt and web gear as Deputy Dog brought the rest of the platoon forward and emplaced them around the field. I picked up my rifle and experienced a momentary faintness when I saw the bolt locked to the rear on the empty magazine and realized I had been out of ammo as I guarded the VC. I reloaded and eased across the clearing to where Doc was now working on the wounded man, as Barney and Silverstein dragged the first man through the bushes by his arms towards us.

Black indicated the two weapons at his feet. "An AK and a carbine."

"Good shootin'," Barney complimented as they dropped the corpse next to the wounded man.

I looked at the other one, who was grimacing as Doc probed his hip area.

Barney chuckled and wiped tobacco juice from his chin with the back of his hand. "You almost got that one in thuh ass."

My stomach soured at the smell of burnt powder and scorched oil from my rifle. *I had killed a man.* It seemed like a dream as I stared at the dead man unable to take my eyes from the horror. A small blue hole was on the left side of his head. Half his skull was missing on the right side with one eye pulled back into the skull leaving a gaping socket. The other eye stared at a sharp angle at his nose as if crossed. Pink foam frothed chunks of gray matter clung to the jagged tear. I placed my rifle on the ground, gripped the muzzle to steady my trembling, and looked at the second man. Red syrupy blood stained the sand in pools by his side. He whimpered as Doc shifted him to place a bandage over a blood soaked piece of bone protruding through the flesh in the hole below his hip. I sank down next to a tree, my stomach queasy. Barney edged over to me absorbed with cutting a fresh plug of tobacco from his chunk. He placed it in his mouth, settled it in the bulge of his cheek, and wiped his lips on his sleeve.

"Felt thuh same way thuh furst time," he offered cautiously. "Cept I weren't as cool bout it. Ain't sure I'd be now either." He stared off into the trees. "Lucky you was out there. Could of been one of us lyin' back there."

Lunas appeared in front of me. "Not bad, two out of two for the First of the First."

I scowled, realizing I still didn't like the man.

Deputy Dog and Black appeared next to him. "A chopper's inbound to pick up the POW," Deputy Dog said, without mentioning the dead man. "How would you like a nice cool ride back to the firebase?"

"No, Sir," I croaked. "I'm fine, thanks."

"What the Lieutenant means is, Intelligence will probably want to talk to you and all," Black said. "Besides, we've got to provide a guard for the prisoner until he's turned over to the proper authorities, and I can't think of anybody better suited for that job than you."

I looked from one of them to the other, everything seeming to revolve in slow circles as my dull mind tried to analyze things.

"Sheeetttt, all we gonna do is swat skeeters all night," Barney drawled. "If it was me, I'd get my ass on that dad-dam' bird. Ain't no way I'd turn down a good night's sleep."

I climbed to my feet as the thumping chopper grew near. "Thanks, Barney." I locked eyes with him in a meaningful way for his encouraging words.

He scowled and shifted his gaze away. "Go on an get outta here."

"Keep an eye on Del for me," I implored as I gathered my gear.

"Shheeettt, don't spect much of me, do you?" he grumbled with a skewed grin.

Del slapped my shoulder as I passed him on the way to the LZ, beaming with pride. Jerry waved from across the field and flashed a victory sign. Someone had wrapped the VC body in a poncho, I saw with relief. The other one was propped on his elbows smoking one of Doc's cigarettes. I stood as far away from them as I could and watched the chopper descend down to the smoke grenade Black threw to mark the LZ, and then ran in a stoop to climb aboard as it touched down. Two men tossed the VC body on the floor at my feet as another laid the enemy weapons beside it. Doc and another helped the wounded man aboard, who looked wide eyed around the interior of the helicopter before shrinking fearfully away from me. I ignored him, watching the ground flash under us as we lifted off, thinking that from up here the area below did not seem nearly as fraught with danger and discomfort.

The chopper landed in the field on the outside of our new tiny perimeter at the firebase and a group of men rushed forward with bowed heads in the swirling grass as the skids bounced onto the ground. Two men took the body and dumped it into a jeep trailer, and two others placed the wounded man on a stretcher and carried him into the only remaining command bunker, as another questioned him in Vietnamese. A captain spoke to me, determined I had nothing of value to offer, and hurried into the bunker after the others carrying the two enemy weapons. I limped over and reported to the Field First Sergeant, who informed me I was to stay at the CP for the night. I sank down beside the bunker, and under tactful questioning, gave an account of the engagement to the Field First and the RTOs. The commander came out of the bunker to shake my hand and offer his congratulations as the others looked on in admiration.

I felt better now that my two victims were out of my sight and slept an uninterrupted deep sleep the whole night through.

CHAPTER 15

I awoke early the next morning refreshed and guilt ridden because the platoon had a long day ahead of them walking back to the firebase. I lay around in the morning sun trying to recall the events of the day before, but a large part of me refused to dwell on it.

The same chaos existed around me now, but half the actors were missing, as a bevy of sweating, shirtless men ripped the remaining command bunker apart and filled the hole while others lined the last of the equipment up for the convoy back. Making an educated guess that a private standing around with his hands in his pockets would soon bring ill tidings, I slipped off to the tree line and Mama-san's hooch. She smiled with genuine pleasure around her blackish, beetle nut stained teeth and looked expectantly beyond me for the other three.

"Out there, Mama-san." I waved at the misted paddies, eliciting her tongue clucking concern, and playfully stroked a beaming Baby-san's dark curls. Mama-san prepared cans of C-rations for us before cradling the child to suckle at her breast while we ate in the majestic golden sunrise reflecting from the shimmering paddies. Afterwards she collected her tools and left Baby-san on a straw mat in the open door of the hooch as she set out for her rice patch. I stripped to my shorts and placed one of the mats in the sun to begin my day of leisure. Mama-san returned every few hours to feed the baby and at noon prepared us tea, which I drank, convinced I was cultivating a taste for the horrid stuff. With Mama-san back in her paddy, I stretched out in the sun again, turning often to toast different parts of my wrecked body. Baby-san woke for brief periods to smile and coo as she clutched my finger in her tiny fist. In late afternoon the platoon plodded across the rice paddies at a slow, methodical pace with a jabbering Mama-san following.

"Beginning to think I'd have to come fetch you guys," I growled.

"Some of us have a war to fight," Jerry countered as he cast a disdainful glance at my underwear-clad body before bending down to goo-goo at Baby-san.

Others crowded around until a grumpy Black chased them on to the clearing, where the last of the support troops were departing. We four lingered until Lunas came back a second time to yell about us lollygagging around and then fell in on the tail to follow the rest back to our new perimeter. With the last of the support troops gone, our company, looking small and vulnerable, grouped together in a rough circle near the middle of the once mighty firebase and began digging in amongst the forlorn refuge of those who had departed. Del and I needed no encouragement to dig our foxhole as the shadows gathered about us. Jerry and Bernie fin-

ished their position and drifted over to give us unsolic-
ited advice on how to best finish ours. As they stoically
absorbed our less than grateful verbal responses, Barney
slouched over.

"Looks like your Mama-san's ol' man's back." He
inclined his head to her hooch, now a hundred yards
to our front and partially hidden by the intervening bushes, where Mama-san squatted before a man in
the fading light with Baby-san clutched to her breast.
Barney spat a stream of tobacco juice. "Don't look too
friendly like either."

"She looks scared," Bernie speculated.

"Maybe we should go check it out," Jerry suggested.

Mama-san stood and hurried our way when the man
moved beyond her hooch.

"What the shit's going on here?" Black growled as he
and Deputy Dog joined us.

"We're not sure, Sarge," Jerry replied as Mama-san
paused in front of us and waved in the direction of her
hooch while chattering excitedly. "There was a man at
her hooch a few moments ago and she's acting all weird
now."

"Dad-dam' VC," Barney spat as Lunas joined us.

"Something's sure as hell making her all crazy," I
agreed. "We should check it out."

"It's too risky," Black objected. "It'll be full dark
soon."

"We goin' tu get our ass kicked tu night fur sure,"
Barney warned ominously.

"We could be out and back in ten minutes," Jerry
pleaded.

"We don't have time to alert the perimeter," Black replied firmly.

"What about her?" Lunas asked as Mama-san stood silently trembling before us.

"Send her back to her hooch," Black ordered impatiently. "This ain't no by god hospitality center, it's a goddamned fighting position."

"What's the problem here, Lieutenant?" an authoritative voice demanded, startling us.

"This lady was visited by an unknown man a few minutes ago and seems upset, Sir," Deputy Dog replied to our commander as Mama-san began jabbering again.

"Let's get control of the situation, Lieutenant," the Old Man ordered before turning back to his CP in the center of the perimeter.

"Get her on out of here, she's jeopardizing our position," Black ordered.

"Go away. *Ditty mau.*" Lunas pushed at Mama-san's arm and then turned to Jerry in exasperation when she began wailing. "Shit! *You* make her leave."

"But what if that really was a VC out there, Sir?" Jerry asked, turning to Deputy Dog.

"*Shhheeeettt!*" Barney sneered.

Deputy Dog shifted hesitantly. "Well ... she can't stay here ..."

"Sir, couldn't we just make a quick check of things?" Jerry pleaded.

"Have you *lost* your goddamn mind?" Black raged. "Are you *deaf*? What the *shit* did *I* just *say*?"

"No, uh, I don't think so," Deputy Dog interjected, casting a sidelong glance at Black. "If that *was* the enemy scouting our position she'll be safer in her bunker if we get attacked."

A strong sense of impending danger settled over me as Mama-san watched with fearful eyes as we debated her fate. When Jerry reluctantly pointed to her hooch and gently urged her to return, she tearfully offered the child to him.

"No, no, Mama-san," Jerry refused, backing away from her outstretched arms. "No can do, *boom-boom-boom* here tonight, maybe. You go, you keep Baby-san."

Mama-san turned to Bernie and again offered the bundle.

"No, Mama-san, no can do," he said sadly.

She offered the baby to Del, to me, and to Barney as we shook our heads, and then looked past us to Lunas, Black, and Deputy Dog. When their dark outlines remained immobile, she turned to her hooch weeping and cradling the baby in her arms.

"Sure'n shit gonna get hit tu night," Barney predicted in the silence as the sad little creature shuffled off into the gathering darkness.

"There's something not quite right about all this," Black agreed as he and Deputy Dog turned back to the platoon CP. "Lunas, get your men settled in deep and tight."

"Sure'n shit, Sir Charles' gonna be half steppin' all round us tu night," Barney spat.

"Isn't that the plan?" Bernie demanded. "Aren't we *supposed* to be bait out here?"

A fluid hiss produced a fresh stream of tobacco juice at our feet as Barney chuckled and ambled off. "You heroes be careful now, you hear?"

Bernie and Jerry returned to their position next to us, becoming blurred outlines, as Del and I strung our claymores to the front and arranged our gear to each side before settling in for the long night. Del stretched out on the ground beside our foxhole as I took first shift watching flares drift earthward far off on the horizon making the dark, sinister area to our front more foreboding. I hunched forward wishing our commander would fire flares for us while idly wondering if we really were bait left behind. I shivered, sensing not all was well.

"Jay?" Del whispered.

"Yeah?" I answered, trying to steady my taut nerves.

"You did good yesterday. You know, with the two VC."

"Get some sleep, dumb shit."

"I heard Black say you were sergeant material."

"What's *he* know?" I retorted, seeing again the shattered head and crooked eye.

"Deputy Dog said he was recommending you for a medal."

"Bullshit ... for what?"

"I'm glad it was you," Del vowed. "I'd have screwed it up for sure and got an ass chewing instead of a medal."

"Would you cap it?" I hissed, wishing I had been as cool as everybody seemed to think.

"If you make sergeant someday, can I be in your squad?"

"You asshole," I whispered in exasperation. "I ain't even made *PFC* yet, remember?"

"Did it bother you? You know ... *doing* them?"

"Would you go to sleep damn it, I ain't pulling guard all night!"

How *did* I feel? Mostly I didn't. Not yet anyway.

Del shifted and within minutes was snoring as I strained to hear the small sounds of approaching death, electing not to make him turn over for fear he would resume conversation. I stared into the inky void, my ears picking apart and analyzing each sound before discarding it. I let my mind wander, seeing blue water, green trees, and my high school chums drinking bootleg beer. I longed to be back with them and dreamed of my red and white '56 Ford, hearing the gutsy roar of the twin glass pack exhausts from the Thunderbird engine. I thought of B.J., to whom I had not written for several weeks. Nor had she written me. I would write her when we returned to base camp, I decided. She would understand since I was in a war zone. Maybe she wouldn't. To hell with it. I checked my watch to find it ten minutes beyond my shift and elected to let Del sleep. I imagined being a sergeant and retraced my time in the army analyzing each leader I had known. I would be like the old black airborne sergeant back in the Replacement Depot, or like Sergeant First Class Black, or maybe a combination of the two—strong, wise, and in total command. I grabbed my rifle in panic with my finger digging for the trigger well as a stooped form loomed out of the darkness.

"*Lunas, coming in!*"

"*Christ*, you trying to get your shit blown away?" I snarled, my nerves frazzled as I swung my rifle back to the front and drew a ragged breath.

He knelt beside me standing in my hole, his rifle cradled across his knees, its muzzle level with my eyes. "What do you make of it?"

I cocked my head and concentrated on a faint metallic clatter across the distance, sounds I had tuned out in my half daze of moments before. "*Cans! Coming from Mama-san's hooch!*" I guessed, pinpointing the direction.

"*Shhhhhh!* Damn, hold it down," Lunas grated. "Keep your eyes peeled. I'll notify Black." He glided off to my rear.

I grabbed Del's shoulder. "Noise to the front," I hissed as he lifted his head. "Sounds like it's coming from Mama-san's hooch."

He tensed as the dull clump of metal reached us and then slid into the hole beside me feeling for his weapon in the darkness.

"*Pssssst! Pssssst!* Jay? Coming in," Jerry's strained warning floated across to us.

"*Clear,*" I acknowledged.

His shadow emerged from the blackness to squat beside us. "Can you make it out?"

"Sounds like cans to me," I whispered, straining to catch the faint sounds as my heart thudded. "Lots of them."

"Yeah, that's it," he reasoned. "*The dirty bastards are robbing Mama-san's C-rations!*"

"*Coming in,*" Lunas whispered from behind us as three shadows crept up to our position. "What are *you* doing here?" he hissed at Jerry. "Get your ass back where you belong!"

"*Shhhhh! Listen,* damn it!" Black's voice stilled us as a loud, audible clunk drifted across to us, the sound a sack of cans might make if bumped against something solid.

"I'll ask Alpha Six for some illumination," Deputy Dog whispered as he slipped away.

"*You* get back to your position, and *you* alert the rest of the Platoon," Black directed to Jerry and Lunas.

For several minutes, we heard nothing except our own shallow breathing and the buzzing of mosquitoes. I swallowed with a dry throat, squinting as I tried to pick up anything unnatural. Suddenly a frightened voice pleading in Vietnamese preceded a shriek ending in mid-pitch, which made the hair on the back of my neck rise.

"You guys hear that?" Jerry's low voice carried across to us.

"*Quiet*, damn it!" Black snapped back.

The sound of wood hammering on wood drifted out to us, followed by a pause and then a slightly different beat with more blows. Silence followed.

"What the shit?" Del began.

"*Shhhhh!*" Black cut him off.

A loud swish streaked overhead ending with a hollow pop. We hunkered down as Black stretched out on the ground beside us. Deputy Dog lumbered up and threw himself flat behind us as the night sprang into a yellow glow with the flare spiraling under its crooked trail of smoke. Deep shadows raced across the ground as the bushes and trees wavered in the artificial light. Deputy Dog propped up on his elbows as Mama-san's hooch danced into view standing lonely in the contrasting shadows.

WRAPPPPPPPPPPP! The roar of an AK-47 split the air. Immediately other automatic rifles opened up intermingling with softer snaps of carbines sending hornets swarming around us as we gaped in surprise. An M-14 cracked from within our perimeter, followed by an M-60 machine gun's thumping support. In an instant, our entire line exploded into a crushing crescendo of sprouting light and thunder as our rifles, machine guns, and M-79 grenade launchers answered in growing anger. Geysers of sand erupted from the ground like heavy rain on a still lake. Hot flashes of light billowed from the M-79 grenades as their lethal circles of razor sharp shrapnel sliced bushes in half. Streams of red M-60 tracers walked through the shrubbery, hosing down the area as their whining ricochets darted about.

The enemy fire intensified, tearing up chunks of dirt around us, the angry whines penetrating the roar of our return fire. A row of bullets riveted the earth across my front, filling the air with dust. A broken line of green tracers from an enemy machine gun stitched the air a foot above my head and then lowered, chewing the soil around me. I ducked into our hole as Black and Deputy Dog clung to the ground in their exposed positions beside me. One of our machine guns picked out the enemy gun and engaged it as I popped my head back up. The enemy tracers switched from us to suppress our gun head on. The two fought a brief, bitter duel within the larger battle, where red tracers met, crossed, and interlaced with the green stream, each line clawing at the other without mercy. I cheered while firing madly as the green stream ended and the red line continued to dance on the now silent point.

Yellow explosions ripped the night as our commander walked artillery into the trees, the dull B-B-B-BOOMS! throwing up mounds of dirt and leaves. The enemy fire slackened in the onslaught of our cannons but increased again between the salvos and to each side, signaling they were dug in and ducking our artillery to reappear and pour deadly fire back into us from all directions. The intensity of the struggle took on new meaning, both frightening and exhilarating, as toe to toe we fought with everything we had in the savage encounter. After weeks of hit and run tactics the bastards were standing and fighting, something they only did when prepared.

CR-*ABOOM*! CR-*ABOOM*! CR-*ABOOM*! I ducked as harsh explosions from screaming mortars blinded me with flashes of light and cringed as dirt and debris cascaded down around me in mind numbing jars.

"*Move over!*" Black commanded as he squirmed into our hole headfirst. I rose up firing madly, the discharge of my bucking rifle lost in the deafening rumble, the orange flash of the muzzle joining others in a winking line of searching death. Numerous flares floated overhead bathing the area in yellow flickering light. Another intense wave of screaming mortars rolled over us rupturing the air with angry whines and jaw clenching explosions, forcing me to tuck my head below ground level to avoid decapitation.

"*Gimme room!*" Deputy Dog screamed.

I popped up and began firing again as Deputy Dog clawed head first into our foxhole, jamming Del and me against the front while shoving Black into the bottom, all two hundred pounds of him determined to avoid the certain death of remaining above ground.

"There's no room!" Del shouted, trying to reload as we jostled about in a gaggle.

CR-*ABOOM*! CR-*ABOOM*! CR-*ABOOM*!

I hugged the ground grimly as mortars dropped straight out of the sky sending red-hot shrapnel screaming by my ears.

"Uugh ugurrumph," Black's strangled voice protested as he thrashed about under us. "I can't—uggghhh—bre-athe—uggghhh!"

CR-*ABOOM*! CR-*ABOOM*! CR-*ABOOM*!

The explosions dulled my senses and rattled my teeth as a piece of sizzling metal ripped into my web gear with terrific force, the concussion sending my helmet rolling out in front of me. In my cramped position, I couldn't retrieve it. In fact, I couldn't move at all because I was wedged solidly against the front of the hole by Deputy Dog's thrashing body to my rear. I hugged the ground as more explosions walked over us, with Del pinned beside me in the same wide eyed predicament. I kicked and squirmed to disentangle myself from Black below and Deputy Dog in the rear, and with a mighty effort, planted my feet into a soft, yielding mass under me and lunged forward to grab my web gear. Deputy Dog slid deeper into the hole making it impossible for me to get back in myself. I hunkered down on his back and wiggled as low as I could get as more explosions picked through us, jerked at my ammo pouches to reload in my exposed position without even my steel pot for protection, and began firing as fast as I could pull the trigger.

The VC matched us round for round in the gripping struggle, our artillery and their mortars shattering bodies as bullets tore from both directions in murderous torrents, and lines of tracers forked back and forth. Dirt flew in showering spurts as a heavy mist of dust and burnt powder dimmed the light from the flares. Through the inferno, I saw red and green airplane lights blinking overhead and hoped the morbid fool was having a hell of a good time watching this madness below. *This is serious*, I thought in fleeting panic. We're outnumbered and surrounded. The enemy fire is growing in intensity. Sweat beaded my forehead as chills crept through me. *If we're the bait, where the shit is the trap?*

BBBBBBBBBBBBRRRRRRRRRRRRRUUUUUUUU-UUUUUURRRRRRRRR!

The roar dwarfed all other noise and devoured the night. The ground shook under my feet as I cringed and waited for the earth to crack and suck me down into hell. A wide river of red thick enough to walk on streamed from the sky above to the ground below. The trees to our front wilted, sagged, and snapped in half as a heavy rain of hot lead swept through the vegetation engulfing everything before it. I imagined bodies fluttering, arms separating, and heads splitting open as chunks of flesh flew. The very earth seemed to convulse as the giant miniguns spewed their liquid death in utter destruction and all sound ended except for the mighty, mind bending, uninterrupted BBBBBBBBBBRRRRRRRRRRRRRRRRU-UUUUUUUUURRRRRRRRR!

The bird of death took sole possession of the battle, swinging its ugly snout at will, unchallenged, total master of our destiny. The artillery stopped. The mortars stopped. All rifles and machine guns stopped. *No infantry should be subjected to this—VC or otherwise*, I thought in stunned fascination as I watched the fabled *Puff the Magic Dragon* with its three miniguns work overhead. I recalled hearing that a three second burst from one gun of this machine would place a round every three inches over a hundred square yards. Now we were getting almost a minute's worth from all three guns. Or rather the enemy was. The roar stopped suddenly, leaving fading echoes and the crackle of burning vegetation as Puff's tracers glowered here and there and then winked out, leaving brush and leaves smoldering as smoke hung over us in a heavy pall. Trees sagged and slipped to the ground. Flares sizzled overhead mixing with the droning of the plane in the dark sky. I looked up at the angry predator and saw its lights winking as it circled waiting to strike again, praying it knew we were the good guys.

"Medic! We need a medic over here," a voice carried across the stillness.

"Here! We need a medic here, too!"

"Doc!"

"Oh god, somebody give me a hand! Medic!"

My shock wore off as cries rang from within the perimeter calling for help, wailing in frustration, calling thankful greetings to friends found safe. I had a gripping urge to laugh, to throw back my head and howl with glee. We had won. Hadn't we?

"*Ugheeee! I-can't-breathe!*" Black's muffled, desperate voice begged from below.

"*Can't—move!*" Deputy Dog's garbled voice advised in anguish from my rear.

I squirmed around trying to free myself as Deputy Dog's legs kicked in the air above his head and shoulders buried in the hole and realized I was standing in Black's face and chest, my efforts only succeeding in lodging Deputy Dog deeper into the space behind me.

"I think I'm standing in Sarge's nuts," Del grunted as he twisted and turned.

"*Umph-greeewwwoooo!*" Black acknowledged from below.

"*Help!*" I panted. "Jerry? Bernie, give us a hand!"

"On the way!" Jerry scrambled over with Bernie in tow.

"Get him out!" I urged, indicating the gyrating legs behind me.

They each grabbed one of the flailing limbs and tugged in earnest to work Deputy Dog out of the pit, finally popping him out with a hard jerk that sent them sprawling backward with the lieutenant thumping after them.

I scrambled out of one side of the hole as Del leapt out of the other. Black pulled himself over the rim and rolled out behind us, his face covered with dirt and his nose bleeding. He looked around, wild and unseeing, before slumping forward in a choking heap. Jerry knelt and pounded his back as Bernie helped a shaky Deputy Dog into a sitting position.

"You okay, Sarge?" Jerry asked.

"*Ack*-you-ass-holes-almost-stomped-me-to-death," he sputtered between sucking lips covered with foam and grit.

Lunas hurried over and ordered Jerry and Bernie back to their position before draping one of Black's arms over his shoulder and pulling him to his feet to stumble back to the platoon CP. Deputy Dog collected their weapons and limped along behind them. I retrieved my helmet and darted back to the CP to replenish our ammo. Doc treated several of the wounded there as our commander attempted to get dustoff helicopters for them, and then cursed vehemently when informed they deemed conditions too risky.

In the light of the flares, I lit a cigarette and settled down with Del in watchful vigilance with no thought of sleep as we surveyed the confused mass of broken trees and smoking shrubbery to our front. As we waited for dawn to put an end to this nightmare, I prayed Mama-san and Baby-san were deep in their underground bunker and that we had killed the bastards who were stealing her C-rations.

The night slipped away amidst sporadic shots fired chasing shadows. No enemy fire was returned. I squeezed off a few rounds to calm my nerves and let the little shits know we were still full of piss and vinegar if they wanted more. With Puff gnashing its teeth overhead, they didn't.

Dawn brought Lunas trotting by our position. "Prepare for a coordinated attack!"

As I shrugged into my gear, I found one of my canteens had a jagged rip in it with the piece of shrapnel inside rattling against the plastic sides. Deputy Dog and his RTO kneeled behind us, the radio against his ear. Black moved to the center of our line and raised his arm high. We tensed. The radio crackled. Deputy Dog nodded. Black's arm swept forward.

"*Cover me!*" I yelled as I scrambled out with butterflies in my stomach and charged.

The thud of feet and clanking of equipment were the only sounds in the still morning air as I swept forward with others in a ragged line. After thirty yards our line fell prone with our rifles trained on the woods. The second wave leapt up and sped past us to fall prone on the edge of the trees. Our line rose as one and sprang forward. As we came abreast of Del's line and entered the trees, a rifle boomed off to my left. Other shots fired from our line as frayed nerves snapped. All the shooting was our own. I threw myself down at the rear corner of Mama-san's hooch hoping she would stay put a few moments longer, concerned that some fool might mistake her in the dim light. Jerry, on the opposite corner of the hooch, flashed a brave grin. Hell, this was just like in the movies, I thought, grinning back. Del galloped by, equipment jangling around him like wares in a peddler's wagon, rounded the front corner of the hooch, and lurched to a halt as the men in his wave continued past and fell prone on the edge of the paddy. Del stood frozen in place, his features drawn in twisted horror. I rushed past his immobile figure to the front of the hooch and stopped before two blobs in the smoky half-light. I staggered back in terror as ice water coursed through my veins and my stomach twisted in horror. My mind reeled and my gut convulsed in painful spasms as I focused on the two grisly heads, one large and one small, suspended from stakes driven in the ground.

"*Ohooo nooooo ...*" Jerry moaned as he sank to the ground before the bloody stumps.

Bernie stood behind him, his features twisted in a grimace of revulsion. Del slipped to all fours and threw up as he gasped and sobbed. I lurched on wooden legs to the two stakes driven into the ground with the tops waist high. Mama-san's matted, blood encrusted hair stuck out in frozen strands ghoulishly framing eyes rolled back so that only the whites showed above the jagged flesh of her neck. The tiny head suspended next to her had blood-streaked cheeks framing half-slit milky eyes above its shredded neck.

"Awaaoooohh, god nooooo!" Jerry cried as he slumped in anguished.

Bernie stumbled to the edge of the rice paddy and sank down on the trunk of a small tree disgorged by artillery fire, dropped his helmet between his feet, leaned forward, and placed his head on his crossed arms as his shoulders shook in grief. Del struggled to his feet and stumbled over to Bernie to stare out across the paddies.

"*Jesus H. Christ!*" Sergeant Lunas gasped as he rounded the corner. Black and Deputy Dog stopped in disbelief behind him.

I pulled Jerry to his feet, led him over to Bernie and Del, pushed him down, backed up to a tree, and slid to the ground, my body flushed with heat, a hard lump in the pit of my stomach as tears trickled down my cheeks, my throat so tight I feared suffocation. Other members of the platoon gathered in front of the hooch in shocked silence.

"*You dad-dam' did that!*" Barney's rage filled voice cut like a knife as he snatched off his helmet and threw it in our direction, where it bounced and lodged in a bush. He stomped over with tobacco juice streaming from the corners of his mouth. "*It was thuh dad-dam' C-rations! They made an example out of 'em! Cause of you stupid dad-dam' sons of bitches! You killed 'em!*"

None of us moved as his words clubbed us. Silverstein grabbed his arm and tried to pull him away, but he jerked free and pointed a finger at our bowed heads. "*You all responsible, you hear! You oughta be charged with murder, you dad-dam' son of bitchin' do-gooders!*"

"You barnyard shit!" Bernie screamed as he leapt up and charged at him. "You buck-toothed hypocrite! *You're* the one that said she was a *VC*, you rotten bastard!" He swung and caught Barney a glancing blow as Silverstein tried to restrain him.

Sergeant Black interjected himself between them in a blur. Bernie's head snapped back and his body stumbled after it on awkward legs with arms flailing for balance and collapsed onto his butt. Black spun and slapped Barney across the face, the impact sending out a spray of brown juice as Barney sagged in Silverstein's arms and stared open mouthed.

"Now, goddamn it, you shits wanna fight, I'm your man," Black challenged, coiled like a snake. When Barney lowered his head, Black turned to glare at Bernie, who dropped his eyes as the fire drained out of him. Black punched his finger in Barney's chest. "I never want to hear that shit out of you again! Understand?"

Barney nodded dumbly as Silverstein released his grip on him. Black glared at the other members of the platoon, eyes blazing pure fire and lips pencil thin. They wordlessly shuffled back into position facing out across the paddies.

"You four, get off your ass and come with me!" Black directed as he stalked off towards the perimeter. He paused on the edge of the tree line as we grouped around him. "I want every hole filled in our platoon sector, and make damn sure nothing is left behind that can be used." He elbowed his way through us back to the hooch as we stumbled out into the perimeter.

Members of the platoon searched the wood line picking up discarded enemy equipment. Occasional shouts reached us as enemy bodies were located among the many blood trails leading through the brush. Two men dug holes at the rear of the hooch, one large, one small, as we worked through the platoon position refusing to think or communicate. After we filled all the holes, we rejoined the platoon gathered around the two fresh graves behind the hooch. Doc removed his helmet and cleared his throat. We removed our helmets and bowed our heads as he recited the Twenty-third Psalm. I paid scant attention to the words as I analyzed the bitterness inside me. The other platoon members drifted away, leaving the four of us and Barney and Silverstein standing before the graves.

"I didn't really mean all that shit back there," Barney said after a silence. "You know?"

"Friggin' forget it," Del said bitterly.

"It's partly true," Jerry insisted grimly.

"I never realized you cared so much," Bernie replied.

"Don't pay to over here." Barney put his helmet on and moved off digging for his plug.

"He really means it," Silverstein vowed as he turned to follow Barney.

"Did we really kill them?" Bernie asked.

"What the hell do you think?" Jerry demanded.

I turned away wracked with guilt as Black called for a platoon formation.

"We recovered eighteen bodies, with numerous blood trails indicating the actual count is extensive," Deputy Dog informed us in a subdued voice filled with fatigue. "We recovered six weapons and untold miscellaneous equipment and ordnance. On our side, we have five dead and seventeen wounded. Sergeant Black, let's get organized for our flight home."

Under Lunas' guidance our squad soon rushed to the doors of the aircraft as other platoons secured the LZ. As we lifted off, I looked out at the area below filled with overwhelming sadness. In the last six weeks everything here had changed—the area, the people, and us. Yet nothing had changed. I tried to close my mind to the troubling thoughts out of control in my head as I looked out at the sunlight reflecting off the paddy water below, letting the cool air whip through my unkempt hair. I forced myself to visualize Cu Chi base camp with its cold beer, showers, real food, and haircuts. In minutes we would be back, be safe. In a few short months, we would return home, to our real home, the world. America.

I looked back at the top of Mama-san's hooch still visible through the shattered narrow strip of woods growing smaller in the distance. I did not feel very *diplomatic* and wondered if I ever would again. We had lost. After weeks of mud, heat, booby traps, and snipers, we had lost. In the end, they showed us. They showed all the villagers around us. They were still in control. If we physically stood on a piece of land, it was ours. If not, it was theirs. With our departure they would tax, recruit, and rebuild their infrastructure. A month from now any unit entering this area would never know we had just sacrificed so much to *pacify* it. They would zero out the casualties we had taken and the pain we had suffered.

My frustration grew as I realized we were helpless. What were we doing over here? What were we supposed to accomplish? I watched the workers in the fields shade their eyes as they tracked our flying machines and tried to imagine how we must appear to them in their world without electricity, radio, TV, or movies—a world devoid of fast food joints and different styles of clothes to wear. I thought of them sleeping on straw mats placed on the earth floors of their crude little one room mud and thatch huts, of them eating rice 365 days a year, when they were lucky enough to have even that. I imagined them having children without hospitals and living without doctors or dentists, pain and disease a fact of their pitiful little lives. They were merely peasants with no education, no hope of a better life for their children, with each family's survival tied to one small rice paddy and vegetable garden, living with no running water or bathrooms, their claim to middle income tied to one water buffalo to till the soil and pull their cart to market.

Take that existence and turn loose a war on them. Have their fellow countrymen talk about Ho Chi Minh, who they did not know, and the glories of communism, which they did not understand. Let these men demand large portions of their meager rice crop in the name of the revolution. Demand sons to fill their ranks and daughters to fill their beds and carry ammunition over countless miles of trackless jungle, both possibly never to return. Let these men press rusty rifles and a dozen corroded bullets into the hands of the remaining old men. Tell them they must fight the American imperialists who have come—come to take their sons and daughters and rice. And if they don't use those weapons, or don't resist the foreign American dogs, let these men come in the dead of night to sever heads and place them on stakes in front of their grim little hovels to serve as a reminder to the others.

I sighed despondently. Both sides fought this bloody war for the hearts and minds of a people who undeniably paid a higher price than either side. All these people wanted in life was to grow their rice and have healthy sons and daughters to pass their small patches of mud to through the generations. But first, they must embrace this thing called communism or die.

And if they *do* embrace communism, *I* will kill them, I concluded soberly. I will fire artillery into their ranks, bomb and napalm their villages with jets, rocket their bunkers with gunships, and shoot down their sons and daughters with my rifle in the name of freedom, which they understand as much as communism. What was it

Barney said? *If you overanalyze this place, you'll get flaky between the ears,* or some such as that.

I directed my attention back to the front as our aircraft descended down to the acres of olive drab tents and bunkers stretching before me. I was home safe. For now anyway.

Thank you, God, for allowing me another day.

CHAPTER 16

I experienced a surge of appreciation I would never have thought possible three months previously.

Cu Chi still looked like a primitive Dog Patch, but now our home base represented all the luxury we craved. We scrambled aboard trucks at the LZ shouting like kids let out of nursery school, and heckled REMFs along the way as they stared at our ragged, longhaired appearance and grime encrusted uniforms, sniffing with distaste our overriding stink after six weeks without baths. I scrambled to clean my rifle before charging the shower point to join a crowd of grinning, naked bodies washing the layers of scum off our half-decomposed bodies. A group ganged up on Harley determined to scrub him *clean*, but with black soapy skin gleaming, he fought them to a draw in the cheering chaos. I discarded my filthy, worn out jungle fatigues and boots behind the supply room for the animals to burn and paraded in naked to draw a new set from the crusty old supply sergeant. Next, the mess hall treated us to a superb sit down meal, wherein we entertained ourselves by snatching portions from unwary trays to toss at others across the room, proper etiquette long forgotten. Our unwieldy mob then stormed the Wolf's Den for our first beer determined to make up for lost time, where we discovered they had added a long room in our absence to house us privates. We clambered on top of the tables in our rush to get at the bar and began our serious march into oblivion as local REMFs scrambled out of our way.

Jerry punctured the top of a can of beer with his survival knife and lifted the spewing foam to his mouth, sucked it down, and belched as he focused on a neatly coiffed battalion clerk at the next table. "That phony assed little jackass galls the hell out of me."

Barney pulled a long swig from his can and swiped at his chin as he focused his skewed eyes on the man in tailored jungle fatigues wearing a flamboyant bush hat with a feather in the hatband and an eleven inch Bowie knife strapped to his thigh. "Little dad-dam' REMF bastard."

"Nine out of ten troops in Nam are in a support role," Bernie advised indifferently.

Barney spat on the floor. "Shit sits on his ass all day doin' *nuthin'*!"

I shrugged. "Somebody's got to keep us warrior types in beans and bullets."

"Thinks he's a dad-dam' *commando or somthin'*," Barney persisted. "It pisses me off just lookin' at 'em!"

"He seems harmless enough," I soothed.

"Thuh only thin worse'n a REMF is a *commando*," Barney swore.

Bernie chuckled. "I'd say he's definitely prepared if a VC jumps him here in base camp."

"Thuh presumptuous little shit thinks he's a badass," Barney insisted. "Well, he's just a little dad-dam' *pussy* is all he is!"

As the party progressed, the REMFs listened spellbound to the gory details of our battle the night before, with some claimed it involved over a thousand VC. The body count reached astronomical proportions as we poured beer down our throats, on each other's heads, and slung the cans off the walls. Brief fights erupted amongst us, quickly broken up by others and accompanied by great shows of friendship amid renewed arguments between the combatants as to who was going to buy the next round. At some point in the evening one of our guys vomited on one of the REMFs, who foolishly took offense, therefore a fight ensued with much cheering and making of side bets. When our guy passed out while sitting on the REMF's chest, it necessitated several additional scuffles to determine the winner. When the defeated REMF protested our collective judgment, a couple of our guys beat the crap out of him, after which Bernie and I felt obliged to drag him out and toss his tattered self in the urine saturated ditch beside the club. As we were admiring our handiwork, Silverstein hastened up.

"Jay, you better get back inside quick! Barney and Del jumped on that silly commando with the Bowie knife!"

When I weeded my way through the packed crowd, Del had the commando pinned over a table with his drawers pulled down around his ankles and a grinning Barney stood with the man's gleaming knife in hand poised inches away from the poor man's bare genitals. Since no one else seemed interested in stopping them, I took it upon myself to reason with the rascals.

"Damn, Barney, that's a mighty fine knife you got there," I observed as I eased over to them.

Barney leered. "Ain't *my* 'nife, it's thuh 'lil' *pussy's* 'nife!"

I nodded. "Oh, okay, so, um, why do you feel the need to whack his balls off with it?"

Barney glared down at the terrified man. "Som bitch was makin' fun of Del fur cryin' over Mom-sun an baby-sun, that's why!"

"*Please, Sergeant, help me!*" the commando begged as tears glistened down his cheeks.

"Jay ain't no dad-dam' sergeant, you dad-dam' ass 'ole, he's jus *Jay*!" Barney corrected nastily.

"Were you making fun of my buddy?" I ask sternly.

"*Man, I'm sorry!*" the man begged. "*Please!* I-I didn't understand the situation!"

"Okay, that settles it," I replied pleasantly and threw my arm around Barney's shoulders to guide him to the bar as the others made an opening for us. "Let the little pussy go, Del, and I'll buy you guys a beer."

Barney frowned indecisively as I led him away. "You shore bout this, Jay?"

"Sure I'm sure," I reasoned. "He apologized, didn't he? Hey, let me see that pig sticker you got there. Sure is a pretty thing." I eased the knife from his hand and propped him against the bar as I slid it into the waist of my pants. "Del, you coming?"

When Del released the commando and staggered after us, the man didn't even bother to pull his trousers up or ask for his knife back as he hobbled frantically for the door.

With the two of them in tow, Bernie and I bought a case of beer and began a search for Jerry, finally locating him outside the club lying on the edge of the drainage ditch with his pecker hanging out of his pants, evidently having passed out after stepping out to take a piss. Bernie and Del dragged him back to the hooch by his arms, where he eventually came around and helped us consume the beer until the world disappeared.

———

I was convinced a tank had run over me and drained its crankcase in my mouth as I wobbled up to survey the interior of the hooch in wonder, which appeared as if a giant had strolled in during the night and tossed men and equipment about in a rampage, leaving the place in shambles. Bodies were heaped everywhere with heads thrown back, mouths open, arms and legs draped in haphazard fashion as snores rasped from dry throats amid overturned bunks, scattered beer cans, and discarded clothing littering the floor amongst puddles of stale beer.

I tried to focus on the far end of the hooch where three blurry figures sat side by side on a bunk and nearly fell on my face as I clutched for support. "Woo—ugh, ack—who the hell'er you?" I moaned as I attempted to swallow the accumulated dust lodged in my throat clinging to all the little green hairs, noticing the foot of my bunk had collapsed causing the steep angle of the mattress I was fighting to stay on. "Ohooooo," I groaned and flopped back on the high end clutching my head to slow the pounding as the ceiling rotated in slow circles.

One of the three stood. "We've been assigned to the First Platoon."

"We were on the bunker line yesterday when you came back," a second man offered.

I sat up, determined to live, my head reeling from the effort. "You goddamn newbies?"

The three exchanged glances. "We've been here ten days," the third man defended.

"Water?" I whined. "Got a canteen or something?"

"I'll get you some." The one on the end rushed out, sending convulsions of pain through my head as the door slammed shut behind him.

The other two picked their way through the litter to the foot of my bunk. "You okay?"

"Shit no," I moaned. "I'm dying."

The third man raced back through the door, paralyzing me anew with the crash, and thrust a canteen cup in my face. I spilt most of it down my chin while shuddering with pleasure as the coolness washed down my parched throat to my sour stomach.

"I'm Private Renfro," the tall, scrawny one offered. "Most folks call me Reno for short."

I collapsed back on my bunk. "Jay."

"Bob," chimed the nondescript average everything second one.

"Phil," greeted the third, a short, barrel-chested individual with a sloping forehead and bushy eyebrows that made him look like a dwarf ape.

I looked at Jerry's legs sticking out from under his collapsed bunk. "What happened?"

Reno grinned. "You guys got in a fight."

I searched for a scrap of memory. "A fight with who?"

"Each other," Bob answered.

"Two sergeants came over to break it up, but another one about five feet tall told them to stay out of it," Reno added. "After that they just stood outside with us and watched."

"Black?" I asked. "The little runt sergeant, was his name Black?"

"Dunno. He just stood there with his cigar in his mouth laughing like hell."

"The bastard," I growled, fingering my swollen lip. "Who won?"

"He was the last one standing." Bob pointed at Bernie, snoring with his arms folded across his chest and a leg sprawled over each side of his bunk with one boot on and one off, his helmet on his head with the chinstrap cinched tight under his jaw.

"He's the one that knocked you out," Phil added.

"Bernie hit me?"

"Near as I could tell, you and that one," he nodded at Del lying on the floor with his mattress pulled over the top of him, "were going to kill that one over there." He pointed at a member of second squad lying on the floor a couple of bunks away.

"What'd he do?" I asked, baffled.

"Punched that one." Reno pointed at Harley, naked except for his boots, lying on top of his collapsed bunk.

"Why'd he punch Harley?" I asked, bewildered.

"Because he hit both of them," Bob indicated two sprawled figures on Jerry and Bernie's side of the hooch.

"Shit, First Squad fought Second Squad?" I mused. "What started it?"

"Somebody on your side said somebody on that side was chicken shit because he didn't fire his weapon. That one punched him." He pointed at Jerry's partly visible body.

I grimaced. "What squad are you guys going to?"

"We're First Squad, he's Second." Reno pointed at Bob.

"Well, Reno, Phil, welcome to the First of the First. Why don't you two beat the shit out of Bob here so we can claim the victory?"

They looked at me uneasily as I rummaged for my toilet kit and stumbled out of the wrecked hooch. I returned from the shower point and awoke Jerry, Bernie, and Del before departing for the mess hall, pulling the door to its limit and allowing the spring to snap it closed behind me with a resounding *WHACK!*, turning the slobs inside into a shrieking mass of pain as they groped for their ears with trembling hands.

Reno rushed to join me, and after seating myself behind a heaping platter of bacon and eggs, I studied his six foot, three inch skinny frame with his coal black hair combed straight back above casual, heavy lidded eyes ... until one looked closer and saw the cold, calculating gleam. A schemer, I decided, a man who played the odds. "Where you from, Reno?"

"Tennessee. And you?"

"Texas."

"Heard them say last night you got a confirmed kill," he gushed. "I've been going crazy back here sitting on my ass on that damned bunker line! I didn't join this man's army to fight rats and cut weeds. Know what I mean?"

I buttered my toast, secretly confirming he was an idiot.

"I mean, I'm here to fight, so let's get it on, right?"

I forked a mouthful of eggs, labeling him crazy to boot.

"I guess I sound stupid to somebody like you, huh?"

I paused to stare at him. "Somebody like me?"

"You know, a proven veteran and all, somebody that's been there."

"Oh," I replied, realizing I was now indeed a veteran, somebody who had *been there*, becoming self-conscious of my stringy hair, scab infested arms, and sun darkened skin. "Your time will come."

"I wanna *kill* something." He flushed as I stared at him. "I-I mean ..."

"Yeah," I replied, finding my eggs suddenly distasteful.

He leaned forward eagerly. "Can I be your buddy?"

"My buddy?" I drew back, half expecting him to reach for my hand.

"Your partner—you won't be sorry if you take me on."

I looked around to see who might be listening. "What the shit are you talking about?"

"They told us in Basic we had to rely on the buddy system over here. You know, two men looking after each other, knowing everything about one another, sharing the same position."

I stared at him in surprise. He was right. Del and I were always together, night and day, as were Bernie and Jerry, Silverstein and Harley, Barney and Lunas. The whole platoon was paired off. No one ever said anything, we just automatically went together, always. And I did know everything about Del, his every weakness and strength, when I could count on him and when I knew I had to cover his ass.

"The little sergeant last night said if we were smart we'd team up with you and Barney. Phil and I flipped a coin and I got you."

"Oh," I said. "Was that a win or a loss?"

"Are you shitting me? After you got all those gooks in one operation, a KIA, a WIA, and a POW? That's some record!" I squelched an urge to laugh as he beamed at me. "You can count on me not letting you down. We'll rack up a body count nobody can touch. How about it?"

He's *serious*, I realized, the thought of taking a newbie under my wing leaving a disagreeable effect within me. "Look, uh, the thing is, I've already *got* a buddy." I grabbed my tray and headed for the door to get away from him.

Back in the hooch, I straightened out my area and repaired my bunk. Soon Jerry, Bernie, and Del joined me, all well along the road to recovery. We set out for the division service area, a large cluster of buildings a few blocks from our unit where they trucked in Vietnamese civilians to operate concession stands for the base camp. There we pampered ourselves with haircuts, steam baths, and a massage. Feeling almost human again, we returned in late afternoon to replace worn items in our gear before striking out for the Wolf's Den, where, upon discovering it closed for repairs, we grabbed some beer from the PX and went to the movies instead.

———

Over the next couple of weeks, Reno and Phil slipped into a natural team. With Reno tall and lanky, Phil short and stocky, Reno impulsive and aggressive, Phil easygoing and thoughtful, the two argued constantly, but in the end always seemed to do the right thing. We worked hard to keep them out of harm's way as much as possible by ensuring the more experienced among us handled the tricky situations we faced on day to day operations. Though we fought occasional sharp actions with snipers and constantly found mines and booby traps, we thankfully took no casualties while finding only indifferent old men and women and eager young children in the villages we searched. Two weeks of the good life slipped by and restored us to our former heights of physical and mental prowess as we became impatient for action, finding base camp offered no excitement beyond the grueling bunker line and dull routine patrols.

———

The night evil crept amongst us we were sleeping off the latest drunk. Harsh lights snapped on as Sergeant

Lunas strode down the aisle yelling for us to get our gear together on the double. Through slits in my eyelids, I saw it was near 0230 in the morning, an ungodly hour to get up after a hard night of boozing. Under Lunas' snapping commands, we tumbled out of the hooch in a gaggle rubbing red eyes and belching stale beer to mingle with loud suggestions as to what the whole Army could do in relation to our dragging posteriors.

"You shits get your heads straight," Black instructed as he and Deputy Dog trotted up. "We've got trouble!"

"Thuh dad-dam' 9th!" Barney swore.

"Knock off the shit!" Black turned to the lieutenant. "Sir?"

"Our Third Platoon got hit half an hour ago," Deputy Dog advised grimly. "All contact with them has been lost. Gunships flying over the area report scattered fighting but are unable to assist because they can't determine friend from foe. The Platoon Leader got off only one desperate call—a fire for effect on their position."

"Thuh dad-dam' 9th," Barney swore again as others murmured fearfully.

"Knock the shit off," Black snapped, stifling the clamor as I experienced a pulsating urge to write a letter home.

"Reaction forces are en route to the location on foot," Deputy Dog continued. "More are on standby at the Division LZ awaiting first light to air assault into the area. The Old Man feels we can reach them faster with assistance from the 5th Mechanized Infantry."

Minutes later a column of five tracked Armored Personnel Carriers lurched to a halt on the road beside our company in a roar of diesel engines. Black quickly organized us into fire teams and we scrambled up into the rear of the APCs. The giant steel doors clanked up behind us and we rumbled to the gate in front of Charlie Company's sector. We lined the sides of the track with all but our heads protected by the reinforced steel sides, with the driver's head sticking out of the left front of the vehicle, and the Track Commander encased in his steel cubicle in the center hanging on to a nasty looking .50 caliber machine gun. We paused briefly while the TC communicated with the other tracks through his radio mounted in his helmet, and then our hearts beat a frantic tempo as we roared through the fifth wire and out into the rubber plantation crashing through small trees and bushes in a headlong plunge. Twenty minutes later, we cleared the rubber plantation and emerged onto the grass plains of the Golf Course, a feat that normally took several hours on foot.

I looked around at Del, Reno, Phil, Harley, and Silverstein, who had accompanied me in the wild scramble to board, as we clanked to a stop fifty yards into the moonlit terrain. A quarter mile to our front gunships circled high in the dark sky, their blades slapping the air above two flares trailing smoke as they spiraled to the ground. The radios hissed in the crew's headsets, the voices lost to me as I waited for some sign of activity, imagining myself part of that force out there now shot to pieces and praying for help.

"Shit, let's go, man, move out!" Silverstein pleaded with the track commander.

The TC lifted one side of his helmet and leaned down. "What's that?"

"What's the goddamned hold up?" Harley snapped. "Let's move it!"

"We're separated from two of our tracks and trying to confirm their location," the TC shouted to us. "You guys keep your eyes peeled. We may be moving into an ambush ourselves."

"Screw the ambush," Reno growled. "Let's *do* something!"

"Knock it off!" I silenced the growing dissension, feeling as though we should be doing *something* besides just sitting on our asses. A flurry of shots drew our attention to our right front in the far tree line. "Hey, that was one of our M-14's!" I called up to the TC. "Screw the other tracks, we've got to go help them!"

We rumbled towards the trees with the other two tracks flanking us. An illumination round burst overhead and three more M-14 shots rang out over the noise of the track as we plowed through the brush.

"*Hey, here!*" a voice hailed, all but lost in the crashing brush and diesel engine's throb. Our track stopped as the other two lumbered to a halt beside us. "*We're American! Hey, don't shoot, American!*" the voice pleaded from the darkness. "I've got one wounded with me! We're coming out!" Two figures stumbled forward in the flickering light of the flares, one half carrying the other and dragging a rifle in his free hand, both hatless and without web gear.

"Let's give them a hand!" I yelled and scrambled over the side into the entanglement of crushed vines as

Del thrashed about on the other side. I rushed towards the two men and then leapt for safety as bullets threw bark in my face. I hugged the ground grimly as sharp cracks stung my ears and bullets ricocheted off the steel side of the APC to my rear in a barrage of automatic rifle fire. The tracks opened up with their thumping .50 cals as our men in back raked the area to our front with rifle fire, trapping us between the two opposing forces. I raised my head in the lull of enemy fire as the big 50s worked the area over and saw one man crawling on his belly dragging the other behind him.

"Cover me!" I yelled, wondering if I had lost my mind, and sprinted forward to grab one arm of the wounded man. "Let's go!" The other man grasped the other arm and we ran for our lives, dragging the wounded man between us as two of the tracks crashed through the brush on each side to flank the enemy and cover our retreat. Del stood as we passed and back peddled while firing into the trees. Bullets careened off the side of the APC as we pulled the wounded man through the tangled brush and collapsed in exhaustion behind the protection of the track.

Del dove around the opposite side and craw fished back against the steel door. "You son of a bitch, you almost got us friggin' killed!" he gasped.

"Heads up!" Reno shouted. "We're dropping the ramp!"

We dragged the wounded man with us as we rolled away from the back, and when the big door groaned down, scrambled up into the rear. The TC lifted the door back into place and we lurched forward to join the running battle with the other two tracks, the only firing our own now as the VC vanished into the night.

"You okay?" I shouted to the man we rescued.

"Yea, but Randy's hit bad," he shouted back.

The tearing brush subsided as we reentered the field. I tugged at the TC's legs and he ducked down through his hole. "We need light," I yelled.

He slid back up into his hole and a dim red glow illuminated the interior. I helped shift the unconscious man on the floor and stretch him out as best we could in the cramped interior. The other man began patching his several wounds as I opened field dressings for him.

We lurched to a halt and the TC ducked down to us. "Who's in charge?"

"He is!" Del pointed at me.

"We're at the ambush site. Another platoon is already here. Your Alpha One is enroute and wants you to dismount and help secure the area. We'll cover you from here."

"Yeah, okay," I shouted back and turned to the others leaning down to hear the exchange. "You heard the man. Keep it spread out when we get out there. Let's go." The giant door groaned downward. "You stay with your buddy," I directed the man from third platoon.

We spread out on each side of the track and moved forward with rifles poised under the wavering light of the flares, which backlit five other APCs and a platoon of infantry securing the area as gunships circled overhead.

I approached the third platoon position, or what had once been their position, observing bodies strung everywhere with assorted pieces of gear dotting the scene. Dreading each step, I looked closely at the immobile figures, grimacing at the mutilation they suffered, noting eyes gouged out, lips sliced off, fingers chopped off, and several with their genitals ripped from between their legs and stuffed in their mouths in grotesque insult, along with ears hacked from several of the heads. In the center of the massacre site, a stick jammed in the ground held a black and white picture of a smirking woman pinned to the top that appeared to be in her mid-twenties, with short black hair, wearing tiger striped jungle fatigues. A dozen Vietnamese men and women surrounded her with rifles raised in sardonic salute as they stared at the camera.

I stood mesmerized by the photo in the rough circle of butchered bodies, my jaw set, the grisly site too horrible to make me sick, too tragic to make me cry, a raging desire for revenge rising within me. No force on earth could have induced me to take an enemy prisoner at that moment. I wanted to kill for the sake of killing, to get my hands on the filthy bitch in the picture with the contemptuous smile and rip her guts out with my hands while she screamed for mercy. Like the corpse at my feet sliced from the bottom of his rib cage to his groin with his insides spilled out onto the ground. In death, he clutched his entrails with both hands in a gruesome attempt to hold them in, his eyes begging for mercy. Cold fear chilled the marrow of my bones as the others stood listlessly about with their heads hung in shame.

"Fan out and provide security," I ordered gruffly as our two missing tracks lumbered across the field to us.

They shifted about on stiff legs as I stumbled to the edge of the site tuning out the scene behind me. When the tracks lurched to a halt, Black trotted around from the rear of one and Deputy Dog from the other.

"It's bad," I whispered as they stopped in front of me.

They moved beyond me in slow, measured steps as I followed. On the opposite side of the ambush site, Deputy Dog motioned for his RTO as tears glistened in his eyes.

"Alpha Six, Alpha One, over," he croaked.

"Alpha One, Alpha Six, go."

"Alpha Six, request you rendezvous with my element and bring Mustang Six, over."

"Roger, One, estimated time of arrival first light, over."

"Roger, understand ETA first light. One, out."

Black organized us into a defensive perimeter with the other tracks and platoon that had arrived on site before us. Deputy Dog and the TC brewed coffee on a small stove inside his track and passed us cups of the strong brew as the flares wavered overhead. Scattered men from third platoon, attracted by the flares, were directed back to our small perimeter by the growing circle of troops around us, about half of who stumbled in injured. All were in shock. A few had lost their weapons and most were without their web gear. Deputy Dog and Black questioned them in an effort to piece together the tragic event, which came out in sobs and half whispers as I listened in sorrowful fury.

I discerned third platoon spent the day sweeping through the Golf Course area, where they found several mines and booby traps but encountered no direct enemy action. They established a defensive position at dusk to await full darkness, and then set out for the present site, stopping once to set up a hasty ambush when rear security reported movement behind them. When nothing materialized, they continued on, reaching this position before midnight. Several times after they set up they spotted movement in the starlight scopes, but each time were unsure of what they had seen. Two hours after reaching this location, the enemy was suddenly all over them. The platoon leader yelled for them to disperse, most likely coinciding with his attempt to call in artillery on their own position. Since his was one of the mutilated bodies, no one would ever know for sure. From that point, the platoon fought running battles and hid as best they could to get out of the trap. Estimates of the enemy force ranged from platoon to company strength.

With the gray of dawn, a chopper descended to land just outside our perimeter. Our company and battalion commanders joined Deputy Dog and the track lieutenant to walk the site. They paused in front of the stake with the picture on it to stare at the grinning woman. Mustang Six removed the picture and pressed it into his map case.

Black gathered us around him and Deputy Dog. "There were thirty eight men in the platoon," the lieutenant reported, his voice filled with grief. "Counting the ones who straggled back in to us during the night, the dead here, and the two we rescued, we still have seven men missing. We will continue with the tracks and conduct a search in our assigned sector for our missing men. Others will move by foot and air to canvas their assigned sectors. What you have seen here is now classified and not to be discussed with anyone outside of this immediate platoon. Is this understood? Sergeant Black, form them into teams."

As we moved to out assigned tracks, the other platoon began moving among the dead and shoveling the gruesome remains into body bags.

———

During the morning, we rumbled through the countryside in search of our missing men as choppers flew high overhead and others tramped through thick vegetation in a huge, coordinated effort saturating the area with troops as more units joined the search pattern. We were gruff and impatient in our attempts to question the peasants we encountered, and called for interrogators flying in the choppers overhead if any seemed to have anything to say, or seemed overly scared, or we just didn't like their attitude. By noon, various units recovered five of the missing men, two of them dead, one wounded, with the remaining two in shock but otherwise okay. They found the two dead suspended upside down in a tree and tortured, as evidenced by their stomachs slit open to spill their guts out, along with their eyes gouged out and tongues cut off. Both undoubtedly welcomed death.

My anger mounted as we searched the remainder of the day without finding a trace of the last two men. The interrogation teams kept busy with peasants from scattered locations reporting VC passage with American prisoners, which accounted for at least six men. We knew most were false but treated all as if true. Air assault teams rushed into the suspected areas in an attempt to cut off avenues of escape without producing results. Casualties were taken from booby traps and mines and a firefight developed between one of Bravo Company's platoons and a couple of VC snipers who hadn't gotten the word. Within minutes of their first salvo, they found themselves swamped with gunships, APCs, and running troops, all thinking we had located our missing men, and unfortunately exterminating the hapless chaps before we could capture them for questioning. By the end of the day, over five thousand troops were involved in the manhunt.

We spent the night in the field, the various units formed into widely spaced strong points, with our own perimeter strung around the tracks in a wooded area. C-rations and water were flown in, and we spent an uneventful night watching flares and listening to other, less heavily defended locations beating off sporadic attacks from local VC forces. The morning of the second day, the search continued and spread into ever widening circles. The VC, now better organized, reacted to our wide-ranging invasion of their domain with numerous firefights resulting in massive counterattacks from us in hopes we had stumbled onto the main force. Nine enemy were killed, three wounded, and six taken prisoner, but our MIAs were not located. Throughout the search mission we lost several more men to booby traps and mines.

By the third day, we were discouraged but continued the search with a vengeance, encountering no opposition as the tattered remains of the guerrillas fled before our determined advance. We spent an exhausted night in our crude perimeter, and on the morning of the fourth day, Deputy Dog informed us we were returning to base camp. We lined the sides of the APCs with heavy hearts for the long trek back as choppers lifted troops out from far-flung locations around us. We found the villages we rolled through deserted now as the local populace fled at our approach, and we brazenly crossed danger areas inviting attack, but nothing took the bait.

The Mech dropped us off in frustrated defeat and we slunk into our company area as if whipped puppies, guilt ridden and sullen, covered with grime, our bodies battered from the constant jostling with the iron sides of the bucking tracks. Black and a limping Deputy Dog drew up in front of us as we straggled into a sloppy formation. Black called us to attention. We more or less stood straight. Deputy Dog told us to stand at ease. We more or less slouched.

"Men, I think you're pretty well read in on the situation, so I'll cut this short," Deputy Dog said grimly. "We have two men missing in action, presumed to be prisoners of war. I want each of us to observe a quiet moment." We hung our heads as some spoke prayers and others vowed revenge. "We did everything possible to find them," he continued. "We will never stop looking for them. We will follow every lead, every clue, until we recover them." Muttered agreement drifted from sullen lips. "This unit has suffered a major setback with the attack on our Third

Platoon. A lot of good men were lost. The Platoon Leader was my best friend. The ones that survived did so by the grace of God. Sergeant Black, take charge!"

Black called us to attention. This time we put a little snap into it as the two of them exchanged salutes and the lieutenant limped off by himself. Black watched us from under his bushy eyebrows as he pulled a soggy cigar from his pocket and jammed it into his mouth.

"Rest. Smoke if you've got them," he growled around the stub.

We collapsed onto the ground at his feet digging for crumpled packs of cigarettes or bumming from those who had them as he waited for us to settle in. "The Lieutenant's right. We did everything we could do. Now, I'm not going to Monday morning quarterback this thing, because a lot of things took place that we'll never know about. But one thing I will say is, mistakes were made along the way. Mistakes *this* platoon has made from time to time. You see the results. But I want you shits to understand one thing. That will *never* happen to *this* platoon. *Never!* I'll shoot your sorry ass myself before I let you get as sloppy. You can count on me to stand dead in your shit when I see any member of this platoon let down, even for a minute. Now, goddamn it, you shits pick your chins up off the ground and get the hell out of my sight. I'm tired of looking at you. Dismissed!" He stomped off chewing on his cigar, head held high.

I watched his departure knowing he was right—he *would* kick the shit out of us before he let us get killed through carelessness.

Jerry grinned. "That old fart."

"He'd have to stand on a bucket to kick *my* ass," Reno allowed.

"I'd sure as hell be happy to fetch him that bucket!" Phil teased.

"Wonder what makes the little bastard so mean?" Silverstein quipped.

"Sheeeet, he's jus a lifer," Barney drawled as he shifted his plug. "Lifers think they own thuh whole dad-dam' Army."

"Careful man, you're talking about Jay's daddy," Del cackled. "He's a lifer too."

"Kiss my ass, jerk," I retorted as others laughed.

"Dad-damn, I'm dry," Barney swore as we began filtering into the hooches. "Whose got thurty cents for some beer?"

"Fifty back?" Silverstein challenged.

"Dad-dam Jew shark!" Barney howled.

"For you, fifty-five, *Bucky*!" Silverstein insisted, knowing Barney would talk him out of it interest free but determined to make him work for it.

We cleaned our weapons and straightened our gear before spending a slow evening at the Wolf's Den talking about everything but the recent operation, none of us managing to get drunk, and all turning in early, where I grimly devoted one long private moment for our lost men before slipping into slumber.

———

We resumed our normal schedule of bunker, ambush, and patrols. Several days after the tragedy our commander held a memorial service. Rifles were stuck muzzle down in the ground by the points of their bayonets and a steel helmet hung from the upturned butt of each weapon with a pair of empty boots at the bottom. In front of this solemn row, two weapons were stuck into the ground minus the helmet and boots to symbolize the two MIAs. A chaplain conducted a brief ceremony for the dead and led us in prayer for the missing. Our commander then informed us the facts indicated the woman in the picture, called *Tiger Woman* by the intelligence teams, commanded a reinforced company of guerrillas and was rumored to be the mistress of the Viet Cong Southern District Commander.

When dismissed, we wandered off with hardening hearts vowing that one day we would have another opportunity to face Tiger Woman and her band of thugs, and that on that day we would show her as much chivalry as she had shown us.

CHAPTER 17

Something was up, something big and sinister.

I lay on my bunk after an uneventful ambush patrol, too tired to be awake and too hot to sleep, with my hazy mind focused on the promise of a cool evening and a cold beer, and dully tuned in to a convoy of jeeps pulling up to the commander's hooch to deposit a gaggle of officers. My interest intensified when the executive officer gathered our NCOs out under the rubber trees. Shortly after that, word circulated that our commander cancelled second platoon's ambush and replaced our newly reconstructed third platoon on the bunker line with members of the animal platoon. I joined others to watch from a distance as our platoon leaders hurried inside the officers' hooch with our commander and lowered the bamboo mats on the sides for privacy.

I methodically cleaned my spotless weapon, checked my flawless gear, and then restlessly gathered with others in hushed groups to watch the ominous proceedings. Each new arrival and departure at the officers' hooch brought fresh speculations.

We drifted to the mess hall for a silent meal before returning to our vigil, all eyes on the shuttered windows of the officers' hooch. Phil and Reno volunteered to make a beer run, and we sat on the sandbagged walls around our hooch quietly sipping amid glowing cigarette butts in the suspenseful darkness as men scurried from one group to another spreading the latest rumors.

"Intelligence has located Tiger Woman," one proclaimed. "We're going after her."

"*Tell* me it's *so*," Jerry begged.

"Sheeeeettt," Barney spat contemptuously.

"That bitch, she gonna die *hard*," Harley vowed.

Barney spewed a stream of tobacco. "Sheeeett, got tu be thuh dad-dam' 9th!"

"Man, you're really hung up on those friggin' Ghost Regiment dudes," Del snapped.

"Sheeeeeetttt." Barney smirked as he dug for his pouch to replenish his cud. "Dad-dam' pays tu be, sonny boy, dad-dam' pays tu be."

"It's *got* to be Tiger Woman," Jerry insisted.

"Dad-dam' 9th," Barney repeated.

At midnight, we slipped to our bunks to rest for what was to come and nervously catnapped the night away. The next morning, half-mad with anticipation, our platoon sergeants at last summoned us before our commander as the battalion commander stood in the background.

The Old Man looked across our eager faces as we sat cross-legged on the ground in a large horseshoe around him. "Gentlemen, we have been selected for the most important mission thus far in the war." He paused at

our buzz of anticipation. "This was not an indiscrimi-
nate choice. We were chosen because of our proven
record." He hesitated again while we murmured. "And
because we have a *personal* interest in the outcome." *It is
Tiger Woman,* those around me hissed anxiously. "At this
point, it is important for you to know that if we are successful, our nation will praise our accomplishment." A
low roar swept us. "If we fail, our nation will bear the
shame." *No way,* an angry growl murmured. "Our mission is sensitive to those involved in its final objective.
Our mission is secret. Only volunteers will participate."
He waited for this to sink in as we sat before him with
gaping mouths. "Let each man understand, this mission
is dangerous. Each man must make his own individual
choice." He drew a line in the dirt before us with a stick.
"If you wish to accept a role in this mission, remain
in place. If you decline, please step over this line." We
looked at each other uneasily. "No one will think less of
any man who declines to participate in this mission. No
one will discriminate against you in any way. I personally
guarantee that you will rejoin the Company upon com-
pletion of this mission with every privilege accumulated
to this point. I ask you now to make your choice."

I blinked as our commander stood silent before us
and my skin grew cold. I swallowed as his gaze swept over
me and looked him straight in the eye as his brief glance
passed, deciding I would be a part of this, whatever it
was. I watched in disbelief as Sergeant First Class Black
stood, walked up to the line, and paused to look back
at us, lowering my eyes in shame as others sneered. He
looked down at the line in the dirt, lifted his foot, placed

it on the mark, and dragged it from one end to the other. The company broke into thunderous applause as he returned to his place. I felt a surge of pride. His simple gesture spoke for us all. The commander stared at the battalion commander with a wide grin. The two exchanged nods and he turned back to us.

"Beginning now, you are restricted to the unit area. Today and tomorrow, you will practice certain drills. You will be told only what you are required to do. You will not discuss your particular mission with anyone else. Tomorrow afternoon those of you who have satisfactorily completed the training will reassemble here. At that time, I will brief you on the full mission. The following day, God willing, you will execute that mission to perfection. Platoon Leaders, take charge!"

We leapt to attention.

We marched off in different directions. Black halted us inside the rubber trees behind the bunker line, where he and Deputy Dog held a brief conference before breaking us up into four individual teams. Lunas took charge of our team and marched us off to where a strange officer stood beside a large board covered with canvas with hands on hips watching our approach. On the opposite side of him was a stack of green tubes four feet long. Coils of wire and small handheld detonators clustered in front of the tubes. I settled on the ground in front of the little captain as he glared at us through horn-rimmed glasses and studied his short, slim frame as his piercing brown eyes squinted at us, judging him a REMF.

"Good morning, gentlemen," he began. "I am Captain Davis of the Combat Engineers. I will command your team for the next three days."

I squirmed, thinking this must be big for a captain to command such a small team—or he wasn't worth a damn.

"Your mission is the most critical. If you fail, the other teams will fail. I will mold you into a team of split second precision. Every man here must know every other man's job. You will be the first wave in. You will be the first to engage the enemy. You will be the first to suffer casualties."

I sat frozen as Barney spat a stream of tobacco. "Zackly what's it we're supposed tu do?" he questioned, deliberately omitting the "Sir."

The captain stepped over to the board and flipped the canvas aside to reveal scrawled drawings depicting a rectangle with numerous black squares and a series of slanted lines outlining the whole group. "This schematic portrays a village. The rectangle represents a hedgerow. The black squares are buildings inside the hedgerow. These slanted lines are representative of a minefield that encircles the village. Your mission is to breach this minefield. The follow on forces will move through that breach and accomplish their mission. You will assume a secondary mission of providing security outside this hedgerow while they are inside." He waited for us to absorb the picture.

Reno raised his hand. "Sir, what is their mission, the, uh, follow on forces?"

"That is not relevant at this time," the captain snapped.

"Sir, how are we going to breach that minefield?" Del wondered.

The captain stooped and picked up one of the tubes on the ground. "With Bangalore torpedoes—these little devices right here." He hefted one of the two-inch round, four-foot-long pipes over his head for emphasis. "This cylinder is a training device. The real ones contain TNT. Each end is designed to fit into the rear of the next making a string as long as you need. The last piece is fitted with an electrical blasting cap and wired to a plunger." He lifted one of the firing devices in his other palm. "The charge is blown by depressing the triggering device. After lacing the ends together, you will push this tube across the minefield. On order, they will be blown and blast a two foot path on each side. One man from each team will then cross the cleared zone while laying a strip of white tape for the follow on forces. Questions?"

I sat in uneasy silence absorbing this troubling information.

Barney spat, and looked at the captain with his crooked, askew style. "You say these here Bangalore things are filled with explosives? Well, seems tu me if we was tu hit one of those mines pushin' it across, it'd just blow us clean tu hell cause we'd be holdin' thuh other end."

The captain nodded. "That is correct, if you hit a mine, they will blow."

"That line still there?" Silverstein asked as we chuckled nervously.

"'An, uh,'" Barney paused for effect watching the captain slyly from the corner of his corkscrewed eyes. "Where'll *you* be, since you'll be *commandin'* our team?"

Every man waited as the two stared at each other.

"I will be pushing the first Bangalore torpedo across," he replied firmly. "The rest of you will be guiding on me. Are there any other questions?"

We formed into teams to practice assembling the tubes and placing the blasting caps into the ends and connecting them to the plunger device. It was good the equipment was for training because half of us would have blown ourselves up as we consistently missed steps in the sequence. Captain Davis constantly switched us about until each man knew every function. We broke for the noon meal and spent the afternoon practicing running forward, assembling the tubes, and pushing them across an imaginary minefield. Captain Davis led one team made up of members from another squad, Lunas led a second with Barney, Silverstein, and Harley, and I led the third, with Del, Reno, and Phil.

The plan called for me to rush forward, kneel behind a small dirt berm, and push the first tube out. Reno would race forward, connect the end of his tube to mine and withdraw to provide covering fire as I again pushed the two sections across. Phil would then come forward and perform the same function. If I were still alive, Del would then connect his fourth section, which would have the blasting cap attached to the end. As I pushed it out, Phil would attach the wires to the plunger device. We would then all fall back fifteen yards and assume a prone position. On Captain Davis' command, we would detonate the devices. Reno would then grab a roll of white cloth and run across the cleared trench unraveling the strip behind him. The rest of us would charge in behind him to take up positions in the hedge-row and cover the follow-on forces as they raced inside to accomplish their mission. The plan was simple to execute, and we ran through the drill several times refining the procedures before Captain Davis released us for the day.

We were a silent group sprawled on our bunks that night. Unable to discuss any part of our mission, we talked in aimless spurts. I reviewed the operation in my mind as I stared up at the sagging ceiling, figuring I had one chance of glory and four chances to get my ass blown away with each section of pipe I pushed out into the minefield. I began my last letter home.

Following breakfast, we again assembled into our teams at the isolated locations to practice getting on and off imaginary helicopters in the correct order, and ran through the drills repeatedly under Captain Davis' unmerciful demands for perfection. Beginning with three minutes and eleven seconds from touchdown to explosion, he honed us down to thirty-five seconds. Still dissatisfied, he hammered at us demanding more and raising hell at every little flaw, until we were con-vinced we could execute the mission blindfolded. He set off simulated artillery devices next to us creating large flashes and harmless ear splitting explosions to check if we hesitated or even flinched. Assuming the team next to us had just tripped one of the mines and got its shit blown away, we were to ignore that minor detail and keep plugging and pushing as the brains and guts flew around our heads. He fired small arms blanks near our ears and demanded that we keep plugging and pushing while ignoring the enemy fire directed at us. In the middle of practice runs he would reach out and grab a man or two from a team and shove them down to simulate casualties. The rest of the team would fulfill the missing man's function and keep plugging and pushing. On our noon break, we agreed he was demented, but figured it would be better to push the tubes across the minefield rather than piss him off and suffer the consequences. In late afternoon, staggering under the heat, we hit twenty-eight seconds three times in succession—artillery simulators, missing men, small arms fire, and all. Wiping sweat from his brow, he assembled our exhausted group before him.

"All right," he panted as he removed his glasses and polished them. "Twenty-eight seconds will have to do. You'll get the lead out when the bullets zip by your ears. Sergeant Lunas, give them ten minutes and move them back for the briefing."

"Arse'hole," Barney mouthed sideways, his face streaming sweat, as Captain Davis hurried off.

"That little candy assed REMF," Silverstein growled from my other side. "What's *he* know about bullets zipping by anyone's ears? He can go build a bridge across a mud hole somewhere for all I care."

Fifteen minutes later Lunas had us seated with the rest of the company in cross-legged rows on the ground before our commander. A large board with an improved version of Captain Davis' sketch map stood to his side.

Our buzzing excitement faded as our commander stepped forward.

"Men, I have been apprised of your dedication and skill in the training just completed. The Battalion Commander and I bet a fifth of bourbon yesterday that every man here would volunteer." He held up his palms as we applauded. "Today, we bet a *case* of bourbon that every man would qualify for the mission. Unfortunately ..." he looked at our eager faces as our spirits sank. "You have cost Mustang Six a great deal of bourbon and I intend to see every man here gets a sip!" We cheered as the battalion commander smiled in the background. "Now, to the *mission*." Total silence gripped us as we leaned forward in anticipation. "Tomorrow morning, we will board aircraft at 0330 hours and depart during darkness. We will land at 0515 hours and refuel. We will depart at 0600 hours and at 0645 hours, one minute after sunrise, touch down in the objective area." We held our collective breath, the suspense growing as he swept us with narrowed eyes. "Our objective will be a North Vietnamese Headquarters. We will burst through their defenses and *free eleven American prisoners of war!*" For two full seconds not a soul moved. Then we went wild. Eventually the commander's shouts penetrated our tumultuous roar.

"Gentlemen, this mission is the first of its kind in this theater of war. Within hours of the launch of this operation the news will flash around the world." We dwindled into complete silence. "But that is insignificant. What is important, what is essential, is that every man execute his part of the mission flawlessly. The freedom of *eleven* of our countrymen depends on it. Now, I ask you, are you *ready*?" he screamed with clenched fist. We erupted into complete bedlam, with men jumping to their feet and dancing as others yelped and threw head-gear in the air.

"We'll beat *fifteen* seconds," Silverstein yelled in my ear.

I nodded as I applauded and whistled in the excite-ment.

"I want you to understand we will be counting pri-marily on surprise to overcome the enemy fortifica-tions," the commander continued as I listened with care, determined that *my* part would be perfect. "*Violent execution* is the order of the day. Our first wave will land simultaneously next to the compound on three differ-ent sides, breach the minefields, race across and mark the cleared paths, and secure the hedgerow. The second wave will follow the first wave through and nullify hard points of resistance within the enemy compound. The third wave will follow them through, go straight to the POW enclosure, and lead the freed men back to waiting Chinook helicopters. The fourth wave will secure the LZ. The second wave will then render the area combat ineffective and withdraw to the aircraft landing behind the departing POWs. The first wave will withdraw on the next lift, and lastly, the fourth wave. Tactical Air Groups will strafe, bomb, and napalm the area to cover our exit. The entire operation, from first bird down to last bird off, will take twelve minutes. Expected opposition is an estimated fifty enemy soldiers. You will carry nothing of a personal nature such as pictures, letters, addresses, unit identification, or anything else that will identify you beyond name, rank, and serial number."

With this, I knew we were going into Cambodia to get our two MIAs and nine others. We were going in to get our own in the very enemy sanctuaries that were off limits to us. The price was right and I was more than willing to pay it.

———

False dawn found us rising above the intermediate refueling point in a damp, gray mist as red lights blinked in revolving orbs from the top of each aircraft hypnotizing our senses. Navigation lights, steady red and green smaller blotches, marked the side of each airship adding contrasting hues to the murky haze. Whispery tendrils of ground fog wafted below us. The floor of the chopper vibrated in perfect rhythm with the muted percussion of the blades slapping against the morning air. I leaned forward to look back at the mass of rising and falling lights strung out far to my rear, seemingly disorganized and perilously close to one another, comforted by the fact our follow on forces were following on. Gunships prowled our flanks and two heavy lift Chinooks brought up the rear.

By design, we would touch down forty seconds in front of the second wave, enough time to blow the mine-field without endangering the other aircraft with flying debris. The second, third, and fourth waves would have fifteen-second separations. The Chinooks would follow and remain on the ground until the third wave with the POWs boarded and then depart. The second lift would return from their orbit overhead to extract their wave, followed by the first and fourth. The empty aircraft of third lift would provide transport for any aircraft lost from the other lifts. The gunships would pick off targets of opportunity in the surrounding area and prevent any reinforcement of the defenders. The plan involved one minute and twenty-five seconds for the insertion, two minutes even for the extraction, and eight minutes and thirty-five seconds of *violent execution*. Perfect, down to the unit chosen to carry it out.

The rotating beacons switched off in succession, followed by the small running lights as the aircraft faded into misty black hulks. A hand clutched my shoulder and I looked back to see Captain Davis hold up his palm with all fingers extended as he mouthed *five minutes* over the roar. I adjusted the strap of my rifle slung over my shoulder and grasped my Bangalore torpedo. Forward, the dull red ball of the sun crept over the horizon fighting its way through the haze. My stomach grew queasy as we swooped down, leveled off just above the ground, and streaked through the morning stillness, lifting and descending in stomach-gripping undulations. We flashed across trees and isolated hooches, sending panicked water buffalo stampeding as the hammering blades set our pulses racing in anticipation. The pace became frantic as bushes zipped by at eye level in smoky blurs. A hand shook my shoulder. My heart pounded as Captain Davis held one finger aloft. I looked back to the front and saw the bottom edge of the dull-red ball clear the horizon right on schedule. A hooch flashed by at eye level. We jumped a row of trees and dropped down on the opposite side in a rush. The nose of the aircraft pitched up as the blades clawed at the air and our forward speed diminished. The chopper fishtailed to the ground, bounced hard, and slid forward.

"*Go-go-go!*" Captain Davis pounded my back.

I leapt as others tumbled out on my heels and surged toward the hedgerow, flung myself down behind the last berm just as the second lift cleared the trees and charged down on the LZ as the first lift wobbled into the air. The second lift attempted to slow down to keep from overrunning the first lift still on the ground, and in a terrorizing split second the whole LZ became a tangle of gyrating aircraft fighting to avoid collision. I shoved my pipe of explosives into the field as Reno rushed up and locked his tube into the rear. Phil was on top of him attempting to fit his into the wavering end of Reno's.

"Give us some room," I yelled at Phil as Reno and I maneuvered the pipes into a straight line to lock them together. When we made the connection, Reno ran to the rear as Phil again thrust his at the end of the line I was pushing forward. Del was already connecting his to the end of Phil's even before Phil had his locked into Reno's, completely out of sequence as practiced.

"*Damn,*" I screamed at their impatience. A loud explosion erupted from my right front on the other side of the hedgerow. A helmet and fragments lifted into the air above a mass of smoke and I realized second platoon had hit a mine. I felt my nerve slip away and froze as I stared in terror at the tip of my tube lying in the middle of the minefield. Phil and Del linked their tubes together and jammed it into the rear of Reno's.

"*We got it, let's go!*" Del screamed at my immobile form as Phil connected the wires to the plunger. "*Get it across!*"

I whimpered and shoved as hard as I could in a desperate attempt to get the pole across before I turned to jelly. To my relief it skidded straight into the field and cleared the end of the berm. I stumbled to the rear on quaking legs and grabbed the plunger from Phil as he completed the connection, turned to Captain Davis' team and, seeing we were the first team to complete the task, waited for his and Lunas' teams to scramble back with us.

"*Fire in the hole, fire in the hole!*" Captain Davis screamed as he ran. Everyone covered their faces and wallowed deeper into the ground as I pulled the plunger to the top.

"Ready?" Captain Davis scanned us. "*Fire!*"

I rammed the plunger downward.

BOOM! B-BOOM! B-B-BOOM!

The ground tilted and jarred as dust and debris showered down over me. I heard the metal reel unraveling as Reno charged across the gouged, smoking path and raced behind him staying on the white line of tape spilling from his side. The others followed us through the smoke as burnt powder stung my eyes and clogged my nostrils. We spread out along the heavy shrubbery as Reno anchored the end of the ribbon to a small tree. The second wave scrambled out of their choppers on the far side of the LZ, where they had found a place to land amidst the confusion, but the third lift was attempting to land between them and us, causing more havoc. In horror I watched the fourth lift clear the trees to their rear and desperately attempt to check their speed as they sailed over the third lift.

"*Shit*! *Friggin' aviators*," Del screamed in disgust as the LZ turned into a boiling drama of flashing blades, wobbling aircraft, and running, ducking men. The fourth lift hovered high in the air over the disaster below trying to find a place to land. The third lift careened around trying to empty out panicky troops as the second lift sought a clear patch of sky to climb into. Two aircraft collided, sending troops spinning out of their sides and chunks of broken fuselage flying as others bobbled trying to avoid them in the madness.

Pop! *Zing*!

I ducked as bullets clipped the branches overhead.

"Shoot only at known targets!" Captain Davis screamed. "We've got friendlies in there!"

I couldn't see through the thick bushes to my front and was unwilling to fire blind for fear of hitting the prisoners trapped in their cages.

"*Inside*! *Move inside*!" Lunas yelled as he charged into the hedgerow.

I plowed into the maze and clawed my way free of the entangling briars to stumble into the clearing on the opposite side. A crashing to my right produced a helmet skidding past. An instant later Del scrambled through on all fours and thrust it on his head backwards. Others broke free and knelt in a line as bullets hummed through the air. Three loud explosions shook the ground under billowing dust clouds across from us indicating third platoon had blown their paths. Three Vietnamese men near the end of the village fired into the air at the aircraft to our rear. Our line turned as one and fired in unison crumpling all three in a shower of bullets. Another man ran from one of the hooches to our front. Del hit him in mid-stride with a burst of fire. The man's rifle spun end over end as he slammed backwards. Another explosion shook the compound to our right as second platoon blew one of their paths.

"Hold your fire! Hold your fire!" Captain Davis yelled as men from the third platoon's second wave swarmed through the compound across from us. "Select your targets!" Another blast shook us from second platoon's direction as they blew their third and last charge. The men from third platoon raced through the area searching the hooches and shoving half-clad figures in front of them with their hands clasped on top of their heads.

"Clear those hooches!" Lunas ordered, indicating the three hooches to our front.

Del, Reno, and I ran to the nearest one as Lunas and the others descended on the other two. Reno entered first and fired two shots as Del and I lunged in behind him. A man sank to the ground against the rear wall. I trained my rifle on two people in the center of the hooch hugging each other in terror as a bullet whined through the thatched side of the hooch throwing wisps of straw in the air.

"Lai dai! Lai dai!" I yelled at the two cowering forms before me. A woman and a young girl of five or six years crawled to me on hands and knees. Del squatted beside the bunker with his rifle trained into the dark interior. "Cover them!" I snapped at Reno as the woman at my feet clutched the little girl to her bosom and wailed in terror. I hurried over to Del. "Lai dai! Lai dai!" I yelled into the gloom below. "Hey, Mama-san! Hey!" I gestured to the crying woman as she rocked her child and shielded her from us. Reno grabbed a handful of her hair and forced her head around. "VC down there? VC?" I demanded as she rolled her eyes and wailed louder.

Jerry rushed into the hooch with Bernie in tow.

I grinned. "Welcome to the war, assholes."

"Goddamned pilots," Jerry sputtered as he eyed the two wailing Vietnamese at his feet. "Bastards almost killed us." He looked at Reno still holding the woman's hair to force her to look at me. "What's her problem?"

"She thinks she's next." I indicated the dead man at the rear of the hooch.

"Let her go," Bernie ordered.

Reno raised his eyebrows. I nodded. He released his grip and the woman collapsed on the floor and pulled her child under her protectively.

Jerry edged over to the bunker. "What've we got here?"

"We're trying to find out if anybody's down there," I advised. "The bitch ain't saying."

Reno unsnapped a grenade from his belt. "Well, let's find out!"

"Wait, give them a chance to surrender," Bernie demanded.

I sighed. "We already *did*, damn it!"

"Let *me* try," he pleaded.

I grimaced. "So *do* it!"

Bernie stooped and called into the bunker several times, to no avail.

"Blow it!" I ordered.

"Stand back," Reno advised as he pulled the pin and released the handle, hesitated for three seconds, and flipped the grenade inside the bunker. We crouched holding our ears as a muffled explosion shook the ground and smoke billowed out of the opening. The woman and child screamed louder as Captain Davis and Lunas entered the hooch.

"What's going on here?" Lunas shouted over the woman's howling.

"Clearing a bunker," Del replied, fanning smoke from his face.

Captain Davis strode to the rear and knelt over the dead man.

"I got that one," Reno reported.

"Where's his weapon?" Captain Davis asked.

"Hell, the bastard's VC, ain't he?" Reno protested under his cold stare. "I didn't have to see no goddamned weapon to know that."

"Is this what you're looking for?" Jerry called from the opposite side of the hooch as he hefted a Chinese assault rifle.

"Yeah," Captain Davis sneered. "He must have dropped it over there when you shot him, right?" When he received no answer from the sullen Reno, he hurried out of the hooch.

"You, take the woman and her child to the center of the village where they're setting up a holding area," Lunas ordered Bernie. "The rest of you come with me."

"Suck-ass officers," Reno spat in rage as he trailed us out of the hooch.

Occasional shots rang out as men moved through the area. Women and children huddled together in the center of the village. Guards pushed men into squatting lines with their hands clasped over their heads. Others dragged bodies to the side of the compound. More men were sorting items from the hooches into piles. The gunships prowled to our flanks and the Chinook helicopters still sat on the ground with blades turning near the two wrecked aircraft as Lunas led us to the edge of the compound near the hedgerow we had busted through earlier.

"Form a square and guard the VC prisoners as we round them up."

As other men brought the prisoners to us, we searched them and forced them to squat before us with their hands clasped behind their head, assembling some sixty men between fifteen and fifty years of age, a third of them wounded in various degrees. Two of our medics treated their wounds as two other medics treated the women and children in a second holding area near us. A group of approximately twenty ARVN prisoners we had freed approached our group and spat on our huddled charges while launching into loud singsong tirades of abuse as the VC cowered on the ground before them.

"Keep them separated," Captain Davis ordered, which we did with some reluctance.

———

Our twelve minutes on the ground turned into almost two hours. The Chinook aircraft used long slings to lift out the two helicopters that collided with each other in the LZ. Teams carted two American bodies wrapped in ponchos out to the LZ, along with three of our wounded and the freed ARVN POWs as word spread that they found no American POWs. Vietnamese interpreters singled out prisoners from our group to question, as American Intelligence Officers picked through the heaped equipment in search of usable information. Nineteen VC bodies lay in a row near us and the interpreters led some of our prisoners over to identify them. Men heaped food, clothing, and other staples in a pile, soaked them in gasoline, and set the piles ablaze. Others loaded weapons, ammo, and papers aboard outbound aircraft. The interrogators began questioning our prisoners in earnest, kicking and beating them until they got responses that satisfied them. One Vietnamese produced a long bamboo switch and lashed at the huddled men leaving angry welts on their backs and across their faces in thin bloody lines as they groveled on the ground.

"Stop it!" Bernie yelled at the Vietnamese man as an American major moved to block his path. "Sir, tell them to knock that shit off!"

"Stay out of it, Private," the major ordered coldly.

"They can't do that shit," Bernie insisted. "It's illegal."

"For us, not them," the major replied.

"Sir, I'm warning you!" Bernie threatened as Jerry turned and hurried away.

"You're *warning* me?" the major bristled. "And just *what* are *you* warning *me* about, *Private*?"

"Y-You'd better stop them—" Bernie insisted.

I grabbed his elbow, but he shook me off as the major braced him.

"Hold on there," our commander called as he hurried over with Jerry in tow. "Get back to your position," he ordered Bernie.

"Not so fast, *Captain!*" the major ordered. "This *Private* was in the act of *warning* me about something, so I want to *hear* what he has to *say!*"

"Get back to your position," the commander repeated to Bernie.

"*Stay where you are!*" the major countermanded.

Jerry took Bernie by the elbow and deliberately turned away.

"I *said* stay where you *are!*" the major screamed at Bernie. "Do *you* want me to file charges against *you* as well as this insubordinate *Private* here, *Captain*?" the major demanded as he stabbed his finger in our commander's chest.

Jerry turned back with Reno hurrying after him and the major paused in open-mouthed surprise as the two converged on him with fixed concentration.

"Hold it!" our commander ordered as he blocked Jerry.

The major placed his hand on his holstered pistol and Reno clicked off his safety as his rifle drifted up to the major's midsection. The major licked his lips and froze.

"Get back," Lunas ordered as he rushed up and pushed Jerry back.

Jerry withdrew a few paces and watched menacingly as our commander pulled the major aside and talked to him in an urgent, subdued voice while glancing at us over his shoulder. Our commander then turned and strode off to the far end of the village. The major stared hard at us and then turned to the interpreters now standing mute and spoke to them in Vietnamese before storming off. There were no more beatings.

Two more Chinook helicopters landed in the LZ and guards herded the male prisoners into the back. Other men forced the women and children away from the village and then set fire to the hooches. Under Lunas' direction, we hurried to a line of aircraft as great columns of smoke rose into the air. The gunships darted into the holocaust, spitting tongues of red and trailing strips of smoke as their rockets streaked downward. I sagged against the side of the aircraft and dully watched as the village erupted into exploding flame.

———

I dismounted from the last truckload of troops and straggled into the group of red-rimmed eyes and dirty faces clustered around our grim commander in the company street as he cleared his throat and all became still.

"I share your disappointment. Do not let the results cloud the fact that you performed magnificently. There were no American prisoners of war, but this mission was not a failure. Do not let faulty intelligence detract from your accomplishment. If there had been any of our men there, they would be free now. Apparently, the NVA cadre pulled out one day ago with our POWs and selected ARVN prisoners, leaving behind the local Vietcong and the Vietnamese POWs we rescued. This was a failure of intelligence, not of execution. I am proud of each of you, and I promised each of you a sip of Mustang Six's private stock of sipping whiskey. By god, let's have it. First Sergeant!"

Two of the animals brought a table and a case of bourbon forward as Top passed out small paper cups. The commander poured several ounces into each cup as we filed by before lifting his cup in salute.

"Gentlemen, to your victory!" He tossed half of his drink back as the rest of us murmured and sipped amongst a chorus of coughs from the unaccustomed harsh liquid.

"I commend you for your loyalty to me, for your duty to your country, and for the professionalism you displayed today. In the confusion of the LZ you reacted admirably by executing missions assigned to others as the situation dictated. You remained cool and organized when all about you was chaos. Your discipline and good judgment carried the day. I am proud to command the finest company of infantry in the world!" He raised his cup again. "*To the Wolfhounds!*" He tossed the remainder of his whiskey down and crumpled the cup as we broke into a thunderous roar of *First Wolfhounds!*

The heat from the whiskey rose in my stomach to flush my face as tears sprang into my eyes from pride, and the despair slipped away as I cheered.

After stowing our gear we continued the celebration at the Wolf's Den into the small hours of the morning, partying hard to make up for the one thing we were missing ... moral satisfaction.

———

Black called us to formation, a rare event signifying some special occasion.

The commander approached and exchanged salutes as we stood at attention. The executive officer called several names, including Del, Bernie's, and mine and we formed a line in front of our commander, who then worked his way along the row promoting individuals. I stood stiffly, reveling in the tugging at my sleeves as they affixed the yellow stripes to each arm and removed me for the second time from the hated rank of private.

The commander leaned close with a gleam of amusement in his eyes. "Congratulations, Private First Class Sharpe. I recommend you do not celebrate in such a high fashion this time."

"Yes Sir," I choked in embarrassment as he chuckled and moved on.

We moved back into the platoon ranks, and our commander again called us to attention as the battalion commander and a captain marched to the front of the formation. The two commanders exchanged salutes. The captain read names from a list as each man double-timed to the front before them. I was so surprised when he called Del's name, Harley had to nudge me when they called mine, and I hurried to fall in next to Del. The two commanders moved down the line, paused in front of each man as the captain read a long citation, and pinned a medal on the man's chest.

"By order of the Secretary of the Army," the captain read as they drew up in front of Del. "Private First Class Delarosa is awarded the Army Commendation Medal for valorous actions against a hostile force." He continued a dissertation that sounded like Del single-handedly fought the Ghost Regiment, and won, with a lot of 'disregarding personal safeties' and 'in the face of fierce enemy oppositions' thrown in. With pounding heart, I realized this was for the help we rendered to the two men from our third platoon when Tiger Woman wiped their ambush out. From the corner of my eye I watched them pin the medal to Del's chest and shake his hand, each leaning forward to speak to him in low tones.

Both faced right and moved in front of me, executed a left face, and stood at attention as the captain read again. I half-listened to virtually the same citation, this time with my name inserted, and felt the tugging at my left breast pocket. The captain again read from his script. I listened to the words 'is awarded the Bronze Star for valorous actions against a hostile force' and realized this medal was for the two VC I shot when we were at the firebase, the weight of the two medals hanging on my chest frightening as I fought to maintain my composure.

"Congratulations, Soldier," the battalion commander intoned as he took my hand and looked me in the eye. "Your valorous actions speak for your dedication to duty and service to your country. You have brought a measure of honor to the entire Wolfhound Battalion. I am proud to serve as your Commander."

I could only nod as he stepped back and my company commander stepped forward and grasped my hand. "I share the Commander's regards. Your unselfish actions and willingness to expose yourself to danger for the benefit of others is the highest praise a soldier can receive. This entire Company shares the glory of your moment of triumph. I thank you for the distinction and honor you have brought us through your individual performance of duty."

I worked my tightly constricted throat as he stepped back and thought of my dad's Bronze Star and Purple Heart in the cedar chest back home. "*Dad, I have proven myself worthy,*" I whispered as tears formed in my eyes.

With the battalion commander's departure, our company commander then made a long speech in which he mentioned each of us by name and reminded us that as soldiers our actions spoke for our nation. He then called my name for yet a third line of men to form in front of him.

"The following individuals have earned the *highest* award an infantryman can receive, the badge that *only* an infantryman is qualified to wear, the *Combat Infantry Badge!*"

I closed my eyes in gratitude, relishing the moment. No single award in the Army was worn above the silver wreath around the silver rifle on the baby blue background, a broadcast to the world that we alone, as infantrymen, had stood on the field of battle and met the enemy face to face, and fought him with skill, pride, and courage. This was our nation's recognition of the hardships and discomfort suffered, for the dedication given in defense of the people we represented, and the nation we served. In less than thirty minutes, I was promoted in rank, twice decorated for valor, and awarded the mystical CIB. The emotion of the moment was overwhelming.

When the commander released us, I squirmed in embarrassment as everyone crowded around to shake my hand and marvel over my medals, knowing I hadn't been nearly as heroic as the citations made me out to be.

Del leaned over to whisper in my ear. "Anytime you want to get me half-friggin' killed again, it's okay with me!"

Afterwards I hurried to the division service area to have the PFC stripes sewn on my sleeves—after losing them the last time before I even had a chance to wear them, and in my present mood to celebrate—I was determined to wear them *once* anyway. Del and I then descended on the Wolf's Den where our fellow Wolfhounds bought us bona fide heroes round after round.

The following morning Black informed us the unit had a large quota of Rest and Recuperation passes for those qualified. Del, Bernie, Jerry, and I were, and after hassling with the unit clerk, we got four spaces to Taipei, Taiwan, wherever that was. None of us really cared, as long as it was out of Vietnam and we could go together.

We spent the next two days having our class A uniforms cleaned and pressed, boots shined, hair cut, hands manicured, bodies steamed and massaged—and persuading Barney, Silverstein, Harley, Phil, and Reno to loan us most of their month's pay ...

CHAPTER 18

I was tail end Charlie as we enlisted filled two thirds of the seats in the rear of the plane.

I ended up in a window seat overflowing into the officers' section as Jerry, Bernie, and Del settled in behind me, deciding I just couldn't win as I viewed the two empty seats beside me and the ones before me as the NCOs settled in across the aisle and forward. Maybe the two officers assigned to the seats would be Infantry and with luck I might survive the ordeal.

The plane was an oven and we were soon drenched in sweat as we waited. At last, buses pulled up beside us and discharged the officers to straggle down the aisle in search of their seats. Two nurses wearing the silver bars of first lieutenant approached, checked the seat number, and stuffed their hats and purses in the over-head rack. I flashed an evil grin over my shoulder at the three disgruntled faces behind me watching their every move and smirked as they rolled their eyes in envy. The tall, slim brunette with a heart-shaped face and friendly eyes smiled as she settled in beside me. The other, *my heart stuttered*, was the most beautiful woman I had ever seen with a petite, perfect figure wrapped in skin tanned a deep bronze highlighting the bluest eyes in the world framed by silky white hair above soft, sensuous lips. I closed my unhinged jaw as the goddess looked directly into my eyes and quickly turned away, unable to sustain her inquisitive glance. In the reflection from the window, I watched the angel of my dreams slip into the seat on the aisle as the flight attendant worked her way down checking seatbelts. When the big jet engines whined and the air conditioning came on, I directed the overhead nozzle full into my face, self-conscious of the half moons of perspiration under my arms.

"Hi," the brunette greeted as we streaked down the runway.

"Hi, er, Ma'am," I replied stiffly after the initial alarm of being addressed by an officer.

"I'm Gail, this is Sandy." She indicated the gorgeous creature beside her, who nodded.

"Private First Class Sharpe, Ma'am," I choked out, feeling foolish and wondering why.

"What is your given name?" she inquired.

"Everyone calls me Jay, Ma'am," I replied, ignoring Jerry's kick on the back of my seat.

"Is this your first R&R, Jay?" she asked.

"Yes Ma'am." I peeked at Sandy, which set my senses reeling.

"Hey, you can drop the *Ma'am* shit," she commanded. "Otherwise this is going to be a long flight. Call me Gail."

I eyed her nervously thinking she should know enlisted did not call officers by their first name. Or even their last name. They were *Sir*, or in this case, *Ma'am*. Period. Still, when an officer gave you an order, you obeyed. This was awkward.

"Where are you from?" she asked as Sandy opened a book and adjusted her overhead light.

"Uh, *Texas*," I fumbled as Jerry kicked the bottom of my seat insistently.

"In Vietnam, I mean," she corrected.

"Oh, the Wolfhounds," I groped, stealing another glance at Sandy deep in her book.

She frowned. "The Wolfhounds?"

"The 1st of the 27th Infantry, 25th Infantry Division."

"Oh!" she exclaimed. "We've got us a real *warrior* here, Sandy."

Sandy glanced at me curiously, which sent a flash of heat streaking though me.

"He's got medals, too," Jerry smoothed his way in as he draped himself over the back of my seat.

I considered punching him as Gail turned to look up at him. "Medals? What kind?"

"The Bronze Star and Army Commendation for valor," Jerry supplied, looking deep into her almond eyes. "He's a real terror in combat."

"Really?" Gail cooed, meeting his direct gaze as I looked out the window in disgust.

"I'm Jerry, by the way." He offered his hand.

She smiled. "I'm Gail, this is Sandy." Sandy nodded and went back to her book.

"He's a paratrooper too," Del chimed in, materializing out of thin air over the back of Gail's seat. "I got my medal backing him up when he took on a whole gang of VC all by himself." He pointed his stubby finger at the ribbon on his chest as I grimaced in mortification.

She graced him with a smile. "That sounds very heroic of you both."

"They charged through intense enemy crossfire to save two of our men," Bernie joined in, aggravating Sandy as his head blocked her beam of light when he appeared over her seat.

"He got the other medal for taking on a VC sniper team all by himself," Jerry continued, drawing Gail's attention back as he flashed a look of annoyance at his two competitors.

"And wiped them out," Bernie added, refusing to withdraw.

"He's cool as ice in a firefight," Del struggled as I shook my head in disgust.

"And he once captured a Viet Cong while we were on a night ambush," Bernie allowed with a smirk at Del. *"Weren't you backing him up on that one too?"*

"Remember when he gave his foxhole to Deputy Dog and Black?" Jerry jumped back in.

"Yeah, right in the middle of a VC Battalion attack," Bernie exclaimed.

"I was with him that time too." Del sighed and shook his head despondently. "I spend an *awful* lot of time getting him out of trouble."

"Who are Deputy Dog and Black?" Gail quizzed.

"Our Lieutenant and Platoon Sergeant," Bernie interjected, stealing the initiative. "Mortars and bullets were flying everywhere and he gives them his foxhole because they were trapped out in the open." Sandy shifted in annoyance, trying to reclaim part of her light from his hulking form as he offered his hand to Gail. "Hi, I'm Bernie."

"Hi, I'm Gail," Gail said, grasping Bernie's hand.

"You're blocking my light," Sandy fussed.

"Oh, sorry," Bernie apologized and shifted out of her beam.

"We don't see many women where we come from," I apologized, and received a slight smile from Sandy before she returned to her book.

"Where are you from?" Jerry inquired.

"The hospital in Saigon," Gail replied.

I released my seat into the recline position forcing Jerry into a cramped crouch and closed my eyes. Sometime later I was shaken as the flight attendant served trays of food and found Gail and Jerry now in the aisle seats and Sandy beside me. From the unhappy looks on Bernie and Del's faces, they had given up the struggle, and Jerry was making the most of his victory immersed in some outlandish lie to Gail with his arms spread wide in exaggeration as she listened intently.

I eased my chair into an upright position and took my tray as Sandy closed her book and took hers. Though I made a conscious effort not to gobble my food, I was still finished before she even had her bread buttered.

"May I have your cream?" she murmured when she observed me drinking my coffee black. I handed it to her without comment, the brief touch of her fingers leaving me shaky. She smiled *thank you* and opened her book again. I reclined my chair and closed my eyes.

"Jay?" her soft voice aroused me.

"Huh? Yes Ma'am?" I sat up.

"Do you want a cocktail?"

"Cocktail?"

"Would you like to order, Sir?" the stewardess inquired.

"Oh, no thanks," I replied amid grand visions of impressing Sandy with my piousness.

"I'd like a scotch on the rocks," Sandy ordered.

"Uh, Ma'am, me too," I pleaded amid visions of impressing Sandy with my debonair, aristocratic nature while wondering what scotch tasted like.

I gagged and almost choked to death on the first swallow, amid visions of impressing Sandy with my imminent death, as I coughed and searched through the tears for the nearest escape hatch to fling myself out of, wondering if I had been served kerosene by mistake.

She smiled and handed me her napkin. "You cultivate a taste for it."

"It's *awful*," I protested, giving up on impressing her with anything but me being an idiot.

She laughed in a soft musical tone, which left me faint with gratitude for the pleasure I brought her with my near strangulation. "Here, I'll take it. Perhaps you'd prefer beer?" She drained my drink into her glass with one exquisite finger on the rim to contain the ice before turning to the stewardess serving the three ruffians behind us and ordering me a beer.

"Your friend is quite the charmer," she observed, glancing at Jerry and Gail.

"He's just full of himself," I retorted, inhaling her lingering fragrance, her whole effect leaving me breathless as her eyes searched mine and sent my heart hammering. I turned to the window to subtly study her image and imagine the taste of her soft, inviting lips as I suffered the pain of something that could never be.

"How old are you, Jay?" she asked.

I turned and lost myself again in her eyes. "Nineteen." I fudged, calculating she was twenty-three or four. "Be twenty soon," I stretched it further for no reason I could fathom.

"So young," she observed sadly.

"For what?" I challenged.

"For such ... heroics ..." she replied tentatively.

"Most of that was pure crap," I retorted. "Those fools would say *anything* to talk to you."

"But you *do* have the hero medals," she chided. "Aren't you just being modest?"

My face flushed from her mocking tone. "Look, I'm not modest, and I'm no hero." I turned to the window in frustration wishing I had never worn the stupid things.

"I didn't mean to offend you." She smiled at my reflection in the window. "Forgive me?"

I turned back. "What I meant was, it just wasn't the way they said ... it was really nothing heroic at all ..." I choked, as I got lost in her blue eyes again.

"Want to tell me how it really was?" she offered.

I hesitated, recalling the gut clenching fear when I first spotted the two enemy snipers. The utter revulsion of seeing the one dead with his eyes crossed and half his head missing, the other awash in his own blood with his hip bone protruding, and my overzealous stupidity in rushing out to help the men from third platoon that got Del and me pinned between the two forces. "Uh, no, not really ..."

"Okay," she snipped, somewhat miffed, and opened her book.

I cursed myself for not having the words to explain what combat was like to someone who had never been there and lowered my seat back in despair as we roared through the sky.

———

We landed at Taipei in the afternoon and formed into lines as we cleared customs and changed our money into Chinese currency. Sandy and Gail went with the officers in one direction as a Naval officer assembled us enlisted types in a large room for a quick briefing on things to do if we got into trouble and things to do to stay out of trouble in the first place, none of which sounded very interesting. He finished with a list of hotel prices and bus numbers in relation to our choice. We chose the cheapest one available and scrambled aboard for a short ride to the Dragon Hotel, where a wave of bowing bellhops greeted us. My room was clean compared to the standards I had grown accustomed to in Vietnam, but I wouldn't have recommended it to my mother. I showered, basking under the streams of hot water, changed into my new civilian clothes, and gathered in the lobby with the others to conquer the city.

A hundred horns blew and tires squealed in all directions. Heavy trucks and chugging buses wallowed in the chaos that served as a street amongst throngs of milling people darting about everywhere. A group of drivers standing beside tiny red taxis drawn up at the curb, each capable of hauling only two passengers assaulted us, assuring us in Pidgin English they knew exactly where we wanted to go. We agreed that was more than we knew, selected two of the more promising looking of them, and paired off, with Jerry and me in the lead, Bernie and Del at drag. Off we roared, to exactly where we wanted to go, charging through the crowded streets with horns blowing and tires screeching as our drivers attempted to run over everything that got in our way. We lurched about in the back clinging to the sides of the little car as we took corners on two wheels, darted in front of and across the paths of trucks and buses, brushed stampeding pedestrians crossing at intersections, and passed slower vehicles on the right, left, and sidewalks. I was never as scared even in combat as when we slid to a halt fifteen minutes later in front of the *Fabulous Meteor Lounge*. At least that's what the green neon sign proclaimed, underlined by a red streaking meteor.

I shifted my feet from the two indentures in the floor and pried my fingers away from the little impressions etched into the back of the front seat where I had hung on in white knuckled terror, deciding the driver was little more than a frustrated kamikaze pilot. I fell out of the death trap and clung to the door for support with my ears still ringing from the shouts and curses that had rained along our zooming path, figuring I needed a double beer badly. Jerry and I split the bill, leaving a large tip in gratitude for our lives, and stumbled back to Del and Bernie as the taxis streaked off into the gathering dusk.

Del shook his head. "Whew, how about that friggin' shit?"

"I'm *walking* back," I declared.

"Nothing to it, just close your eyes," Jerry assured us with a weak grin.

"Where the hell are we?" Bernie demanded.

We stared at the blinking neon sign reflecting ghostly pools of light on the rather seedy street as several rough looking Chinese men lounging near the mouth of an alley watched us with narrow, hungry eyes. I instinctively figured this the type of place where you wanted to keep one eye on the exit and one hand on your wallet, preferably while backed up against a wall, as one of the men in the alley started our way.

"Uh, I think we better get inside," I urged as another fell in behind the first.

"Is this place off limits?" Bernie demanded as we hurried to the door in a tight pack.

"If it's not, it ought to be," I vouched as I scooted in front of Del through the door.

Inside the pit we halted in a cluster to adjust to the deep gloom. A single naked green bulb of low wattage lit the bar in a sea of flashing black lights illuminating streaking meteors randomly spaced along the velvet black walls. Pressed tight together, we moved to the bar and selected seats as I sensed furry little creatures scurrying from our path in the darkness. I noticed the opposite wall lined with small tables, each holding a single Chinese woman eyeing us in a brazen fashion as loud rock music blared from unseen speakers. Three Americans on the opposite end of the bar studied us with casual interest.

"Four beers," Jerry shouted as the bartender approached.

"Is anybody watching the rear?" Del joked.

I laughed and then looked over my shoulder at the pitch-black darkness. Even the door was gone. I half turned on my bar stool so I could see in both directions. "I've got rear security."

"Man, I ain't seen a snakier looking place than this in all of friggin' Nam," Del swore.

Jerry clutched his beer and slid off the stool. "You guys cover me, I'll see what gives." He approached the three Americans, leaned close to shout over the music and introduced himself. We relaxed when they shook hands and sipped our beer as they talked. When he returned we eagerly clustered around him. "Those guys are sailors," he shouted to us. We waved at the trio and they waved back. "They're stationed here. This is a good bar. All the women have health cards that guarantee they don't have any disease. Ten dollars buys one of the girls for twenty-four hours. You sign a contract with the bartender. They're guaranteed by the Meteor Lounge, which means they won't roll you or take your money or anything. The swabbies say they can be trusted after you've bought one and to give her money to pay for things so you don't get ripped off. You sit at a table and order a drink for them. If you like them, you order a second drink and the bartender brings a contract. If you don't, you move on to the next one." We turned to look at the girls strung out along the wall smiling provocatively at us.

"Let's do it," Del chortled, grinning foolishly as he and Bernie made for the tables.

Jerry clutched my arm. "Jay, are you willing to bet a bird in hand for two in a bush?"

"What the hell are you talking about?" I demanded as I watched Del slip down at the table of the little lovely I'd been eyeing.

"Gail mentioned she and Sandy were going to a place called The Oasis, which is an American hang out with a live band. What have we got to lose, we can always come back here if things don't work out?"

I shrugged as butterflies fluttered through my stomach at the thought of seeing Sandy again. "I'm game."

When Del and Bernie made their selections and signed contracts, we waved them off as they headed back to the hotel in separate taxis. Jerry and I selected another and requested The Oasis. The ride was even wilder than before, with the taxi racing through the narrow streets as we ducked and prayed. I arrived in need of a calming tonic for my frayed nerves, but somewhat relieved that we seemed to be in a better class of neighborhood with streets well lit and filled with people strolling at a leisurely pace. Even The Oasis looked serene and orderly. Inside we found small lights overhead and flickering candles on every table. White coated waiters served drinks to a moderate crowd of mostly Americans as a Chinese band played popular American songs at a moderate decibel level. After scoping the place out and finding no trace of Gail or Sandy, we ordered beers and settled back in the cozy atmosphere to wait.

After an hour of moody music making us homesick, a happy voice chirped. "Well, look who's here!"

"Well, hello!" Jerry jumped to his feet as I stood, heart pounding, and met Sandy's blue eyes. "Sit down!" Jerry pulled out a chair.

"Sandy?" Gail questioned as Sandy's eyes seared my soul.

"Just for a moment," she decided.

I tripped over my feet pulling out a chair for her, thinking *this can't be happening!*

"I thought you guys would be mauling some poor little whore by now," Gail teased.

"Naw, that's not our scene, right, Jay?" Jerry purred.

I almost choked on my beer. "Uh, right."

"How presumptuous of me," Gail giggled. "So what are you going to do with yourselves for the next seven glorious days?"

I squirmed. "Whatever, drink a little beer, sight see, visit a museum or two, you know."

Gail smirked. "Uh huh, we know."

I gazed like a lovesick fawn at Sandy. "And you?"

"About the same, drink a little scotch, sight see—"

"Visit a museum or two—you know!" Jerry and Gail finished for her, laughing.

The waiter hovered and I looked at Sandy. "Scotch?"

She glanced at Gail as I hung by a thread. "We're just on our way to dinner ..."

Gail played eye games with Sandy. "There's a fabulous rooftop restaurant a couple of blocks from here …"

I bit my tongue to keep from telling them that if their *fabulous rooftop restaurant* was anything like our *Fabulous Meteor Lounge* they'd need an armed escort.

"Have you had dinner?" Sandy asked.

"We were just talking about grabbing a bite …" I held my breath.

"Great, let's go together," Gail invited.

"Bottoms up!" Jerry drained his glass.

We walked the two blocks with Jerry and Gail leading the way, the two talking and laughing as Sandy and I followed in easy silence. We discovered they were staying at the Taipei Hotel across the street from The Oasis, had been in Vietnam about three months, and both had attended the Army Nursing School together. I stole quick glances at Sandy as we strolled along, approving of the blue dress clinging invitingly to her pleasing figure and enjoying her laughter at Jerry and Gail's teasing monologue. After entering a tall building and taking a long elevator ride, we emerged into a swank looking place, which immediately sent fear darting through me as I estimated how much cash I had left. A Maitre d' in a tuxedo escorted us to a corner of the glass walled interior where the city lights spread below us dancing in an inky void. Jerry and Gail ordered wine from a small menu as Sandy and I shared a larger one translated into English. We settled on lobster and sat sipping our wine and enjoying the view. Jerry and Gail kept us entertained throughout the meal with their silly antics, which Sandy seemed to be enjoying, so I didn't push too hard to be talkative or witty.

At their insistence, we split a pleasantly small tab between the four of us and stepped out to the patio where a soft wind bathed us in warm air as oriental music floated from the background and mingled with the crowded city far below. Exotic aromas filled the air and the view was spectacular with a carpet of lights stretching to the far mountains rising in black outline to crop the star-studded skyline. We selected a table on the very edge of the towering structure and ordered fresh drinks in the romantic ambiance.

"I can't believe we're here," Jerry murmured.

"Why can't you believe it?" Gail shot back.

Jerry sipped his drink. "It's hard to explain."

Sandy looked at me. "Is it really that bad?"

"Not really," I groped. "It's just ..." I looked at Jerry.

"Dirty, rotten, miserable, grinding, day in day out," he supplied.

"It's hard to believe places like this exist," I tried again. "In the jungle you sort of forget and fall into a primitive pattern. I don't know how to explain it."

"Is the combat part bad?" Sandy pressed.

"Well, it sort of ends the monotony," I explained cautiously. "I mean, you spend days and days searching for the enemy and then it happens and is all over before you know it. Then you go back to days and days of searching again. The combat part isn't as bad as the boredom."

"What's it like to be shot at, to have people trying to kill you?" Sandy asked as she gazed out across the city.

I sensed a deeper meaning to her question and searched for an honest answer. "It's not really scary or anything—well, it is later, but at the time it's kind of exciting."

"It scares the hell out of me *all* the time," Jerry joked.

"Yeah, but at the time, you know what I mean, you just think about what needs doing," I insisted. "Later you get scared."

"Now you know why the fool has two medals," Jerry quipped, refusing to cooperate.

Sandy ignored Jerry. "Did you ask to be in the infantry?"

I was aghast. "Of course."

"Why?" she persisted.

"Because that's what being a soldier is all about," I stumbled. "I mean, who wants to be a REMF? Why not be where the fighting is?"

"Is being a *REMF* so bad?" she demanded. "Where would you *heroes* be without *us*?"

"I-It's not so bad if you're a *girl,* I guess," I mumbled, thinking *damn, she's tough,* as I wiped my forehead with my napkin. "Or one of the guys who aren't *fit* to—um ..."

"*Fight*?" she offered. "Don't you think there's more to war than killing?"

"No, uh, yes, uh, you've got me confused!" I swiped at my forehead again.

"Sounds like you've got *yourself* confused," she replied. "Do you *want* to kill?"

I realized I was in deeper than I wanted to be. "Well, no, not the way you mean, but to meet an enemy in combat is not like murder. It has honor, a certain pride—"

"That's the dumbest thing I've ever heard," she sniffed.

How could I explain something like that to a woman, especially one of the most sensuous creatures on earth? "Look, I didn't start this stupid war, and I don't really want to kill anybody, I just do what I have to do."

"In the name of democracy?" she challenged.

"Americans always fight for liberty, even for other people," I explained. "Honestly, most of the VC I've seen don't know a democrat from a card carrying commie, and don't care either. He's shooting at us because somebody's going to burn his hooch down if he doesn't. It's the hardcore mothers who cause all the trouble."

Her features hardened. "And what are you going to do if he *does* shoot at you?" she chided. "Kill him *and* burn his hooch down? I'm missing your point here."

How could you explain combat to a REMF? "My point is that somebody has to fight," I argued. "This thing is bigger than me and an ignorant VC out there chasing each other around in the bush. This thing is all about aggression, somebody trying to take something away from someone else. In this case, their right to make decisions on what they want to do with their lives, their freedom of *choice*. We're just giving them a helping hand and buying time until the big guys get it all sorted out."

"But *you* are doing all the suffering and dying, not the *big guys!*"

"Of course, that's why they have to make the whole thing honorable by giving out medals and such," I bristled. "Otherwise us little dumb shits wouldn't have any part of it."

She shook her head in disbelief. "I guess it's good our country has men like you."

"Sandy, I don't have all the answers," I admitted despondently. "But I *am* a damned good soldier who *will* fight for my country. All I can do is hope our people in power make the right decision on when to fight. If they do their part, I'll do mine."

"What if they're wrong—do you have so much faith in them?"

"Do you have so little?" I challenged.

Her lips drew a slow, sad, smile. "It's not that easy, Jay."

Gail turned to Jerry. "How did it feel when you first killed somebody?"

"Don't know as I have," he replied. "When all the crap starts flying everything gets pretty confused. You just shoot at bushes and things where you think they are, but you never see them."

She was incredulous. "You mean you've *never* seen the men you're fighting?"

Jerry squirmed. "Sure, I've *seen* them, but not any that I know I've *killed*. Sometimes it's dark, or the jungle is thick, stuff like that. When the shooting starts, everybody gets their head down. Hell, ask *him*, he's the one with notches on his gun."

"Well?" Gail redirected to me.

"Well ... you, uh ..." I stumbled, annoyed, still waiting for a feeling myself as I recalled the surprise of that moment. "I felt ... the recoil of my rifle against my shoulder ..."

"You ass!" Gail giggled as Jerry laughed with her.

Sandy stared at me as I shifted uncomfortably. "That is the coldest, most impersonal statement of death I have ever heard."

I seethed inside as I glared at her. "How would you *prefer* it to be, lady?"

Gail clapped her hands in the strained silence. "Hey, this is getting heavy, folks. What do you say we smoke a joint?"

Sandy shifted away from our locked gaze. "Not here."

"Let's go back to the hotel then," Gail insisted. "If I don't get high soon I'm going to lose my mind."

Jerry and I looked at each other. Neither of us smoked dope of course. The dope heads were all rear echelon types, not men who faced the enemy. None of us would tolerate a man with a cloudy mind when our lives depended on him.

Gail tuned in to our silence. "Hey, you guys aren't puritans or something, are you?"

Jerry cleared his throat. "No, uh, you see, back in the bush, we don't use the stuff."

"We depend on each other," I explained.

"Well, you're not back in the *bush* now, so what's the big deal?" Gail demanded. "Besides, you both drink like fish. What are you, hypocrites?"

"Okay, so you smoke, we'll drink," Jerry offered. "You do your thing, we'll do ours."

"Damn, you're probably not the promiscuous type either, are you?" Gail quipped.

"Got a Health Card?" Jerry snipped back.

Gail giggled. "Could you read it if I did?"

"Doesn't it have your picture on it?" Jerry demanded, breaking us up into laughter.

Gail feigned horror. "God, you got us into this, Sandy!"

CHAPTER 19

I walked back to their hotel in a pensive mood and paused in the lobby to purchase beer. When we entered their suite, I was dumbstruck. Opulence was an understatement, I thought as I stood at the entrance of the large, central room containing wall-to-wall white shag carpet, a small kitchen, and a built-in bar. Two overstuffed couches faced each other on opposite sides of a low table with two large easy chairs flanking the ends. The solid glass outside wall provided a picturesque view of the glimmering city twenty stories below with a small private balcony. Doors on each side of the center room opened into separate bedrooms with private baths. Soft lighting provided an intimate atmosphere in spite of the room's size and low, enchanting music piped out of hidden speakers. I felt as though I should remove my shoes before entering. Hell, I needed a bath.

Jerry whistled in wonder. "Fantastic. Is this how Officers live?"

"Sandy's treat," Gail replied.

"My brother's," Sandy corrected with a touch of sadness in her tone.

"Now don't start," Gail warned and turned to Jerry. "Come, my Prince, let me show you my boudoir." She pulled him into the bedroom on the left.

"Sit down, please," Sandy offered.

I settled down in one of the massive chairs as a giggling Gail returned to the main room dragging a reluctant Jerry behind her. Sandy prepared herself a scotch at the bar and opened me a beer as Jerry and Gail flopped down on one of the couches together. Gail dug into her purse and produced a fat, lumpy cigarette, struck a match to it, and sank back closing her eyes as she inhaled deeply. Sandy handed me my beer before seating herself on the chair across from me and raised her glass in salute. I acknowledged with my bottle of beer and we drank as her eyes studied me, making me uncomfortable. Gail drew another lungful of the sweet smoke and held it as she handed the butt to Sandy. Jerry went to the bar, opened himself a beer, and returned to sit beside Gail as Sandy repeated the inhaling act and passed it back to Gail.

We sat for a time trading small talk and silly jokes, drinking as the two of them shared a second joint. I opened a second beer and splashed some more scotch into Sandy's glass as Gail snuggled in closer to Jerry. When he tilted her chin up and kissed her, Sandy stood abruptly and walked out to the balcony. I followed and sat at a small table as she crossed her arms on the rail and rested her chin on her forearms looking out across the beautiful city ablaze in multicolored lights far below.

"Thank you for not being pushy, Jay," she said softly.

"Thank you for sharing your evening with me."

"That's not a lot," she murmured.

"It is to me."

She sighed. "I'm just going through a bad time right now ... my world is all screwed up."

"What's the problem?"

She turned to me in the half-light. "It's complicated."

"I've got nothing but time."

"I'm ... looking for answers that don't exist."

I shrugged. "Okay."

"Do you always talk so much?"

I laughed. "Not always. Pretty girls make me gabby. Look, I don't know what your questions are, and I'm sure I wouldn't have the answers if I did, but I do know some things just aren't meant to be."

"How do you know what isn't meant to be?"

"You just feel it."

"That's not very definite," she insisted. "Give me an example."

"Well, like meeting you on the plane, I knew we weren't meant to be."

"How could you know we weren't meant to be?"

"For starters, you're an officer and I'm enlisted. Also, you're beautiful and rich."

"I'll get us fresh drinks." She returned with my beer, stirred the ice in her glass with her finger, and licked the end. "You've lost your friend."

I glanced over my shoulder at the empty couch and Gail's closed bedroom door. "Mine can take care of himself, it's yours you need to be concerned about."

"She's a barracuda," she asserted.

"He hasn't seen a woman in months," I warned.

"All the easier to tame," she teased. "So why are you here tonight, Jay, if we aren't meant to be?"

"I don't know yet. Do you?"

"Maybe," she replied sadly. "Have you ever lost someone you loved?"

"Yes," I replied, wondering to what degree of *lost* and *loved* she meant.

"What did you do?" she asked, near tears now.

"I grieved at first. Now I try to remember the good times and be thankful I had that much." I wished she would get to the point.

"I think you're wrong, Jay. For some strange reason, I think we *were* meant to be," she said softly. "But things could get complicated ... so we probably need an understanding before we get ... foolish ..."

My heart stuttered in my chest. "Okay."

"As for being an officer, I'm in the Medical Corps, which is not like your real army. It's like a pay grade for my skills."

"Unfortunately, in my world, it's still fraternization and a court martial offense," I replied.

She shrugged. "We're on R&R and in civilian clothes."

I grinned. "Works for me."

"I'm not rich, and beauty is in the eye of the beholder," she continued. "And although you didn't mention it, the age thing doesn't bother me."

"What does bother you?"

"Your girlfriend waiting back home. I know you have one."

"There ... was one. We dated through high school. We haven't written in over a month."

"Do you love her?"

"I thought I did. She wanted to get married. I wanted to ... see the world ..."

"Did you plan to get a whore while you were here?"

"Yes."

"If we were to be together tonight how would you feel about it tomorrow?"

"Where I'm going back to, there are no tomorrows," I answered.

She watched me, her eyes lost in the shadow. "I like the way you put things in perspective and keep it simple and uncomplicated."

"I've never felt so complicated in my whole life as I have since I met you."

She sat for a moment. "How do I complicate things for you?"

I shrugged. "I've never met anyone like you. You scare me. When you look at me I can't think straight. I say stupid things and have silly thoughts, like how I want to touch you and get lost in your smell. The sound you make when you laugh makes me want to laugh with you ..."

"That's ... that's ... what do you expect from me, Jay?"

"I expect nothing from you—but I *want* everything."

"If we stay the night together what will come of it?"

"It will make things simple again."

She glided into my lap. "I desperately want things simple again."

Light danced from the center of her eyes as her lips softened into a teasing smile and her arms lifted to encircle my neck. I wasn't that much of a fool. I kissed her. She responded, soft and sensuous. My pulse surged and a roaring filled my ears as her moist lips bruised mine in delicious swirls, sending tingling sensations helter-skelter through my body.

"Is that simple enough?" she whispered.

"It's a good start," I vowed, trembling with desire.

She studied me with half lidded eyes. "If I let you pretend I'm your whore tonight, will you let me pretend I'm in love with you?"

"Yes," I said and meant it.

"And we will make no promises so there will be no tomorrows, right?"

"Right," I lied.

She pulled my head down, her lips tantalizing, sending my senses reeling as my dizzy brain insisted this couldn't be happening, but it was a dream I never wanted to end. She slid out of my lap and pulled me to my feet. "Come. I'm not an exhibitionist."

I followed her into her bedroom and sat on the edge of the bed as she peeled off her clothes and turned off the light. Her white halo of hair moved to me in the darkened room and paused in front of me. "I love you, Jay," she whispered as I pulled her down into my arms. "For tonight, anyway."

———

Something thrust itself across my body in the black pit. I lurched in panic and searched for my rifle before freezing in bewilderment as I stared at the silky hair covering my chest in the eerie glow of morning filtering through hazy curtains. She shifted, sending painful tingles through my arm as circulation was restored. I lay absorbing her beauty as my sensibilities stabilized and touched my fingers to her bronze face as I recalled her animalism of the night before. She stretched and kissed the tip of my chin without opening her eyes.

"Good morning, hero," she murmured. "I'm putting you in for another medal."

I kissed the top of her head and winced as her fingers explored my tender groin. "Make it a Purple Heart. I'm wounded."

She caressed my lips with hers, yielding and gentle. This time the tempo was slow, searching, giving and deliberate. Afterwards we lay entwined.

"Jay, will you let me pretend to love you another day?"

"Yes," I murmured happily.

She snuggled in close and hugged me. "Then I'll love you today with all my heart since you have no tomorrows."

We showered together with her laughing at my new arousal as I soaped and teased her hardened nipples. A knock shook the bathroom door.

"Are you two alive in there?" Gail called. "Breakfast is served!"

Sandy squeezed me playfully. "You save that for later, hero."

We dressed and joined Gail and Jerry on the patio for a huge breakfast and feasted like starved kings in the scintillating morning air, savoring the moment. Over coffee, Gail called the lobby to arrange a tour and we departed for a day of beautiful flower gardens, ancient palaces, and scenic mountain waterfalls. I spent the time marveling that Sandy was mine, for today anyway. In sunshine and laughter, we shared a warm companionship while holding hands and sneaking kisses. Gail and Jerry alternately clowned, fussed, pouted, and lovingly made up, their escapades keeping us in near hysterics. We had a wild lunch at some out of the way place where we ate dishes none of us could guess the contents of, or dared to. We returned in late afternoon filled with happiness and, after a brief discussion, agreed Jerry and I should move in with them. They escorted us down and waved us off as we selected one of the manpowered two-wheeled buggies instead of the careening cabs.

Jerry sighed as the rickshaw glided through the traffic. "Am I dreaming?"

"If you are, don't wake me up," I threatened.

"You reckon we stepped on a land mine and got killed?"

"It sure feels like heaven," I agreed. "But how did *you* get up here with me?"

He elbowed me stiffly, laughing. "How was Sandy?"

"Nice," I replied happily.

"Gail, too."

"She's pretending she's in love with me," I vowed.

"Gail is?" he demanded.

"No, fool, Sandy."

"Oh, us too."

I glowered. "Sandy?"

"No, fool, Gail!"

We howled in glee, our hearts aglow. At the hotel, we located a worried Bernie and Del, who had notified the Naval Shore Patrol that we were missing in action. Thankfully, we were able to straighten the situation out on the phone with the Department of the Navy, who could get indignant as hell, but were no match for a good old-fashioned ass chewing Sergeant First Class Black style. We checked out of the hotel amid hurried explanations and assurances that we would link up with them at the airport in six days—with both of them doubting every word we said. In our haste to get back, we took the dreaded taxis, the unspoken anxiety heavy on us that the girls might have changed their minds in our absence. The door flung open on the first knock and a relieved Gail rushed into Jerry's arms and then started raising hell with him for taking so long.

"I'm back," I whispered foolishly, as Sandy floated into my arms.

"I missed you, hero," she whispered as her lips closed over mine.

We had dinner sent up that night, roast something under glass, with wine and a new supply of beer. Later a soft knock at the door produced several more joints for the girls from a nervous bellhop. The evening was perfect as we sat drinking, smoking, laughing, lost in our own world. Jerry and Gail retired at midnight. Sandy and I pulled all the cushions off the two sofas, along with the pillows and blankets from the bed, and made a pallet on the outside patio high over the city. There we allowed the mystic Orient to flow around us from the hidden speakers inside and the million stars overhead as we meshed in perfect harmony.

Incessant pounding on the door by the maid in midmorning sent us scurrying to the shower while she tidied up the place. We curled up on the couch across from a drowsy Jerry and Gail to sleep the afternoon away in bliss. Roused at last, Gail arranged tickets for a dinner theater and dispatched Jerry and me to the hotel tailor shop to rent tuxedos for the evening. Later, formally dressed, I drifted into the main room for a drink and stood in awe as Jerry slipped out of his room. Gone was the dirty, rangy, untrimmed soldier criss-crossed with bandoleers of ammo and grenades I had come to know so well. Before me stood a distinguished man of the world, handsome, polished ... and digging in irritation at his collar with a wry grin.

"This monkey suit is itching me to death," he groaned. "How did you manage to get such a perfect fit?"

I laughed and saluted him with my beer. "My crotch is so tight I'm afraid to sit down."

Sandy twirled into the room a golden enchantress in a low cut, snow white evening dress with eyes sparkling like twin emeralds as she spun to me in delight. "Isn't it gorgeous?"

"*Sensational*," I croaked. "Let's stay here tonight!" She shrieked and retreated behind the couch as I clutched at her.

"*Beast!* Unhand that Maiden!" Gail chastised as she swept into the room wearing a shimmering red-sequined gown. Jerry gulped and charged.

We eventually talked the girls out of Gail's barricaded bedroom and descended to the street where the hotel limousine waited with opened door and bowed driver. We were escorted to a private balcony at the theater and enjoyed an eight-course meal during the performance of an enchanting Chinese play, where to our sorrow the hero died at the feet of the stricken heroine, though we couldn't understand a word. After the meal, Jerry and I were served brandy and cigars, and then beer, to the maitre'd's raised eyebrows, which I'm positive he had to send out for. Our chauffeur met us at the entrance and delivered us back to the hotel with the same flourish. We were minus bowties and collars by the time we reached the top floor and had our coats off at the front door. We prepared drinks and paired off into separate bedrooms without delay. Sandy filled the tub with hot water and we lay soaking with no desire to end the magic of the evening. Using our toes to adjust the water taps to keep the temperature perfect, we soaped each other down, building the languishing pleasure to unbearable, alternately giving and taking. Later, appetites sated, we sat naked in the easy chairs in the dark before the large window holding hands with the city spread before us.

"Jay?"

"Mmm?"

"Promise me something."

"I promise."

"Wake up."

"I'm listening."

"Jay, please never come to me in pieces."

"Huh?"

"I never want to see you shot up and wasted."

"I'm too much of a coward to get shot," I scoffed, yawning.

"I see so many," she whispered bitterly. "I never want to see you that way."

"Hey, I'm not going to get shot," I insisted, alarmed by the tears glistening in her eyes.

"Promise me!" she sobbed.

I reached for her and she jerked away. "Sandy, people get hurt in war. Some get killed. I can't change that."

"You don't see them begging for help," she gasped. "You don't see their eyes pleading for me to do something. *I* can't put legs and arms back on. I can't do *anything* for them!"

Her near hysteria cut me deeply. "They know that," I soothed, picturing a long ward full of shattered men with her standing in the middle of them, imagining how her beauty must reflect their loss and wound them as deeply as the enemy's bullets. If my number ever came up I wanted an ugly nurse with warts on her nose. "Sandy, no one expects more than you can give. They reach out to you because you're there and they can't do anything else."

She calmed and wiped her eyes. "Why do you men do this to one another?"

"I guess because we believe."

"What do you believe in that would make you want to kill and maim each other in such a vicious fashion?"

"I don't know if *what* we believe is all that important, only that we *do* believe."

"It must be important if you're willing to die for your beliefs."

"I believe enough to fight for my beliefs, but I don't ever think I'm actually going to die. If I did I probably wouldn't go out there. But I know there's always a chance of dying. And I know others *will* die. But I believe enough to take the risk that it won't be me."

"Promise me," she demanded.

"I will never come to you in pieces," I vowed with as much sincerity as I could muster.

She curled into my lap and laid her head on my shoulder as she hugged her bare breasts. "I never want to see you again when we leave here."

"Okay," I said, understanding her meaning.

"Do you know how priceless that makes the next four days?" she murmured.

"More than you could ever imagine," I whispered as heavy green brush flashed through my mind, and shadows dancing in the night with explosions sending pieces of flesh rising in the air. I heard the indistinct echo of angry carbines and saw the flash of mortars and artillery mixing with the heated drum of fire and counter-fire, saw helicopters burning surrounded by smoldering bodies sprawled about. I sensed the slap of my rifle's recoil and saw again the shattered head with the crossed eyes and pink foam. I crushed her to me wanting to remember the feel of her naked flesh, the softness of her voice, and her fragrance on dark nights ahead. For the first time, I felt vulnerable. I *could* be killed. What if I had never known her? What a waste my life would have been. She shifted and I realized I was crushing her to me in near desperation and fought to regain my perspective.

She cupped my face in her palms. "I'm so sorry." She kissed my eyes. "How could I forget you *do* see it? And *live* it every day," she whispered. "I love you."

I laughed, pressing my emotions back into their depths. "That's important ... for tonight anyway."

"Make love to me," she pleaded.

"You're a nymphomaniac," I teased as she pulled me down on the carpet.

She giggled and bit my ear. "Maybe you just have so little to offer I need a lot to make it worthwhile ..."

Hours later the cold of the early morning forced us back to bed, where we clung together under the sheets. My last conscious thought was that war did not stop on the front line. Its ugliness reached us all in its own way, tearing at souls and ripping minds along with bodies, driving us all to madness with its horror. With Sandy molded to me, I promised myself I wouldn't be so hard on REMFs in the future. They had their own private hell along with the rest of us. In fact, maybe our piece of hell was better. At least we could see the enemy on occasion and strike back ... could *close with and destroy*.

———

I showered and dressed at noon before awakening a sleepy Sandy and launching her to the shower with a slap on the bottom. I then joined Gail and Jerry on the patio for brunch high above the teeming city.

"Thank you," Gail said.

"You're welcome," Jerry answered.

"Not you, horse's ass," she snipped.

"Me?" I asked. "For what?"

"For helping Sandy. This was her idea." Gail swept her arm around our palace. "And you were the final decoration."

"That sounds deliberate," Jerry appraised.

Gail shrugged. "You don't think I would subject myself to your abuse for nothing, do you?"

Jerry grimaced. "Thanks, prune face."

"She's been good for me," I said.

"You've been good for her. She thinks you're very special."

"I think I'm going to be *especially sick* ..." Jerry threatened.

"You already are, so buzz off," Gail offered.

Jerry smacked his lips at her. "You're so sweet."

"She's very sensitive about her work," I observed.

"She has good reason," Gail defended. "She works in the bits and pieces ward."

Jerry stiffened. "Bits and pieces?"

"Traumatic Amputees," Gail explained. "All of her cases involve men with missing parts and gross disfigurements."

He shrank back. "Where do *you* work?"

"Gunshot, Lower Anatomies."

He grimaced. "Sounds morbid."

"It is," she snapped. "You little boys make a hell of a mess with your sport."

"Couldn't Sandy get into another ward?" I asked. "Maybe one with less serious injuries?"

"She has special training to do that kind of work."

"But if it's driving her crazy?" I argued.

"Oh, it gets to you after a while. It would anybody. But that's not her real problem."

"Her *real* problem?" Jerry pried shamelessly.

"Her brother spent four days on her ward last month."

"*What*?" I gasped.

"He was an infantryman, too." Gail's eyes filled with pain. "A handsome young man."

"What, uh ..." I fumbled.

"What did he lose?" Gail lowered her eyes. "His life ultimately, after losing both legs. She can't accept the fact he died so horribly for reasons she can't understand."

I experienced a jumble of emotions as I recalled our conversations and reviewed my answers. "How did it happen?"

"Land mine," Gail replied.

Jerry frowned. "And she thought we could give her the answer?"

"She thought Jay could. Her brother was a hero, too," Gail retorted, making me wince. "I didn't mean that the way it sounded. I mean, he volunteered for the infantry even though he had a safe job in the rear as a mechanic."

"What was his unit?" Jerry asked.

"Screaming Eagles," she answered.

My pulse missed a beat. A paratrooper? I searched my mind for the name to see if we had trained together, but came up empty.

"All this luxury we're enjoying is from his G.I. Insurance," Gail continued. "He named her the sole beneficiary and made her promise to use it for a good time in memory of him."

"Now I really *do* feel sick," Jerry groped, his features chiseled stone as he looked uneasily around at the luxury surrounding us, avoiding my eyes.

"You jerk!" Gail stormed. "Do you think she's celebrating? She picked Jay so she could try to understand. She's been crazy with grief."

A surge of guilt swept over me. "So that's why I'm here—to give her answers?"

"I hope something's left for me." Sandy chirped happily as she joined us, and then paused as Gail smiled grimly and Jerry and I hung our heads, her smile fading as she looked from one of us to another. "You blew it, Gail!"

"Sorry," Gail mumbled.

Sandy reached for my hand. "Jay?"

"Sandy?" I looked into her eyes and then turned to stare over the city, pulling my hand away. Jerry pulled Gail to her feet and the two disappeared into the main room.

"Jay? Look at me," she commanded. I couldn't. "Jay, it's not the way it seems. I was confused—about Andy."

"No sweat," I said numbly. "You don't need to explain. We've had a hell of a good time for Andy. Maybe I can be as generous if my number comes up."

"You bastard!" She turned to the rail in suppressed rage. "Listen to me, Jay, you owe me that."

"*Owe?*" I asked her rigid back. "How the *hell* do you figure I *owe* you the opportunity to fulfill an oath to a dying man and live like a queen on his insurance with *me* as your toy?"

"It's not like that!" she sobbed.

"Isn't it?"

"*No!*" she yelled.

I sighed. "Sandy, I'm sorry as hell about Andy, and I truly admire his style, may he rest in peace, but I wish you had told me how things were up front because I sure as hell don't feel real good about celebrating his death in this fashion."

"That's not fair, Jay!"

"Look, I just want to make this easy on the both of us," I replied, aching in every part of me. "I don't want to hurt you. But I don't want you to hurt me, either."

"Jay, please!" She turned to me with tearful eyes, melting my heart with her misery. "This wasn't about you. This was about Andy and me ... I needed to understand. I needed to forgive him for dying when he didn't have to. You've given me that. Don't you understand?"

"I'm not sure I understand what you expect from me now," I said.

"Three more days," she whispered, eyes brimming. "I want nothing more than that, with no tomorrows and no commitments."

"For Andy?" I longed for her, for what was slipping away.

"For *me*," she insisted as I stared at her, wanting to believe. "Don't end it yet," she pleaded as I hung my head. "Jay, I admit I used you in the beginning. I just wanted to talk to you, to understand." She wiped at her eyes. "But *this* is for me. *Just* me! You touched something in me, helped me."

"Sandy—"

"Let me finish," she demanded. "I want to be with you, if you'll let me. I didn't mean for it to go this far, for it to get *personal*. But it did."

"It won't bring Andy back," I argued.

"He was a lot like you."

"*No!*" I begged.

"*Yes.* He even won a *medal!*"

"Sandy, he was *himself* and I'm *me*. I didn't win a medal. I told you, it just happened. Andy was probably brave. I'm sure as hell not. He was a soldier and a paratrooper. That's the only thing we had in common."

"I couldn't do anything for him!" She sagged in grief. "Just like the others. Maybe like *you* someday!" I pulled her to me as her wracking sobs tore at my heart. She fought to regain control as she snatched a napkin from the table and moved to the banister. "Jay, we have something good," she whispered. "We have something unexpected. I started it wrong, but it's not wrong now, is it?"

Was I losing my mind? I *loved* this woman. And I was acting like some selfish, immature oaf. Who cared what fickle fate of fortune sent her my way? Or why on God's green earth she wanted *me* to stay? I reached out to touch her arm, fighting my tightly constricted throat as my heart swelled. "No, it's not wrong now, Sandy." I pulled her around to face me. "And I really don't give a damn what your reasons are as long as you are here with me now."

"Please hold me, Jay!" She melted into my arms.

Something inside me was complete again, leaving me trembling with the realization that I had come close to destroying the only sane thing I had found in this crazy war. I breathed her tantalizing perfume, kissed her hair and lips, tasted the salt on her cheeks and eyes, and squeezed her until she cried out.

"I love you so much, Jay."

"I love you too, Sandy."

That was important for us ... for today anyway.

———

The days flew by, each special and unique. We were filled with the wonder of each other and the world around us and talked late into the night hours with Vietnam never entering our discussions, nor war or death. Jerry and Gail quarreled and loved. Sandy and I immersed in each other. We were quiet, loud, solemn, and hysterical together as our world revolved, never ending and dream filled. I treasured each moment, especially the ones deep in the darkness of the nights, while savoring the softness of her body, the tenderness of her touch, the way she clung to me, the way I clung back. I loved her and she loved me—for those moments.

On the plane back Sandy and I sat together, flanked by Del, with Jerry, Gail, and Bernie behind us. With the blanket covering us we held hands, kissed, and touched until desperation overcame us. I slipped to the restroom while the others slept, and she followed. There, in the tiny confines of the lavatory at 32,000 feet as our plane roared across the South China Sea, we made love for the last time, giving with all our hearts. Nothing else mattered.

————

As our chopper descended into Cu Chi base camp, I recalled the painful parting. Neither of us had asked for the other's address. Neither dared ask for more than we received. I dreamed again of the light blue eyes and saw the bronze skin, the halo of silk in the night. I ached with the memory of her soft, husky voice, the chimes of her laughter, knowing I would love her forever.

I looked across at Jerry as the aircraft flared above the division helipad.

"*Was* it a dream?" he asked.

"Yes, and we've got to wake up now," I advised sadly.

He smiled sadly and reached across Bernie and Del to grip hands with me Indian fashion, thumbs interlocked, as the skids bounced onto the raw, sun scorched tarmac of hell.

CHAPTER 20

We discovered Tiger Woman was still loose in the chill of night.

In our absence she ambushed a platoon from our sister company, Bravo, and another from one of the battalions across the perimeter, each time with the same paralyzing results. The atrocities swept through the division like wildfire, instilling fear and hatred while focusing us on one objective: get the bitch. The days saw us romping like wild beasts searching high and low for something that did not exist. Night ambush patrols became ordeals of paranoia as we skulked along terror-ized by our own shadows. She hid by day, we by night, each seeking a tactical advantage and waiting for an opportunity, each fearing the other with the rising and setting sun as the pendulum of power swung to and fro.

As we grimly settled into our routine of bunker line, patrol, and ambush, the mosquitoes welcomed us back, rating our fresh blood supply five star, while circling in droves awaiting an opening. The mines and booby traps still awaited our unwary boots and the snipers were as ambitious as ever, though they still hadn't learned to shoot worth a damn. Sandy dominated my mind as I set-tled back into the daily grind, her memory too much a part of me to share, though at times Jerry and I locked pain-filled eyes of mutual empathy.

———

I was somewhat dismayed when we turned in our M-14 rifles and drew M-16s in exchange. All were iden-tical with not a single mark or color to distinguish one from another. I toured the rows of black plastic and steel touching, hefting, sighting, searching for the right feel. None had it. Ultimately, I picked one at random, ago-nizing over the loss of character of my former unique weapon. This new one seemed cold and impersonal, an object designed solely for destruction, a kill machine with no personality.

However, the publicity campaign was effective. The ugly little weapon was touted as weighing only half that of an M-14, and supposedly could spit streams of lead out like a garden hose with little vibration and no kick. The bullet tumbled in flight, and was capable of striking an arm or leg and exiting through a man's chest, with an effective range of four hundred yards.

We quickly learned the bullet was so light it would annoy more than harm at four hundred yards, but it *did* tumble, especially in thick brush where a twig could send the round anywhere but where aimed. We also found that twenty bullets in the magazine increased the spring pressure to the point where rounds jammed at the top, thereby forcing us to reduce the load to eighteen.

Most disillusioning of all however, was discovering that when a round did chamber the bolt often stripped the end off the cartridge in the extraction phase and left the expended shell locked into the chamber with a live round jammed into its rear.

Engagements became comical. When hit, we would unleash a resounding volley of return fire, which fizzled within seconds into isolated pops as we hugged the ground cursing our jammed weapons. We then locked the bolt to the rear, removed the magazine, cleared the jammed live bullet in the chamber, rammed a cleaning rod down the barrel to dislodge the stripped expended bullet, rein-serted the magazine, released the bolt to chamber a new round, raised up and fired once more, which almost always jammed yet again. Then we repeated the whole process while feeling like Daniel Boone in the wilderness.

As our confidence quickly eroded, we begged for our M-14s back. Expert non-infantry types told us our weapons had to be clean—this to those whose lives depended on their equipment. They informed us we had to use a special type of oil on the weapons. We got the lubricant and it didn't help. They briefed us that the experts had discovered a few bugs in the operating mechanisms and modifications would soon be available to correct the problem. No modifications came our way. A congressional representative flew over to study the situation, but couldn't see the problem from his hotel suite in Saigon, where all demonstrations by the REMF headquarters worked fine.

In self-preservation, we learned to carry cleaning rods strapped to the side of the barrel for convenience and speed, which was cumbersome in heavy brush and required constant checking to ensure it was still in place. We offered high prices for the few M-79 grenade launchers and M-60 machine guns, which no one previously wanted due to their weight before modern technology caught up with us. Army .45 caliber pistols became a hot black market commodity. Hand grenades saw a revival in popularity, though reducing our effective range to less than thirty yards. Some, in desperation, ordered pistols from home against Army Regulations and the Geneva Convention. Morale sagged as gunships and artillery became our saviors with their two-hundred dollar cannon shells and rockets taking the place of two-cent bullets.

———

"Shhooooorrrrrttttt!"

I rolled off my bunk and hugged the floor with heart pounding among thuds of others scrambling for their lives with me. I looked across the aisle at Jerry lying on the floor blinking in confusion as Del peeped at me from under his bunk with sleep-crusted eyes.

"Shhhooorrrtttttt!"

I flinched as the piercing scream slammed against my eardrums and raised my head to stare down the row of cots at Barney standing in the middle of his bunk, fists clenched above his head, grinning like a mad man. I scrambled up and eased down the aisle as Harley crept up on him from the other side.

"Shhhhooooooooooorrrrrrrrrrrrrrrrtttttttt!" Barney bellowed as heads popped up between the cots to stare at the lunatic standing in the middle of his bed.

"What's wrong with you, man?" Harley demanded as he eased towards Barney with his arms spread wide to grab him.

Barney grinned down at him with gleaming eyes as Harley and I exchanged quick glances. "Goooooodd mornin', Harley! How thuh hell are you?"

"Take it easy now, you hear?" Harley soothed. "Everything's gonna be just fine."

"What thuh shit you talkin' bout, black man? Ever thin's *great*! I'm shhoooo—"

I lunged and grabbed him around the legs, toppling him over his bunk onto the floor.

"Lemme go!" Barney screamed, fighting like a wild man as Harley pounced on his chest. "What you assholes thin' you doin'? Lemme go, dad-dam' you!"

"*Ouch!*" I moaned as Harley caught me in the mouth with his elbow.

"Grab his feet—*ooowweeee!*"!" Harley panted as Barney kicked him in the crotch.

"*Lemme go, dad-dam' you!*" Barney screamed.

"*Ahwaaa!*" Harley yelled. "*He's biting my arm! Ahwaaa!*"

"Not *me*, fool, *him!*" I pleaded as Harley swung at Barney and caught me a glancing blow alongside my jaw.

"*Heelllppp!*" Barney yelled.

Others rushed to help pin him to the floor as I sat back and nursed my bleeding lip.

"Somebody get Doc!" Harley shouted as he wrestled with Barney.

"*Lemme go, dad-dam' you!*" Barney screamed, foaming at the mouth.

"Easy, man, everything's gonna be okay," Reno soothed from one leg.

"*Arss holes!*" Barney raved. "*Have you lost your dad-dam' minds? Lemme go, dad-dam' you!*"

Black rushed through the door wearing his boxer shorts and flip-flops and quickly took in the scene. "He gone loony?"

"Yeah, Sarge, all of a sudden like!" Harley panted as he fought to stay astride Barney's bucking chest.

"*Loony my arse!*" Barney screamed. "I'm sane as you crazy mothers. Lemme go dad-dam' you!"

Black knelt to prop open one eyelid as Barney snapped at him with his teeth. "What's wrong with you?"

"Hell, I'm short's all," Barney gritted.

"Short?"

"I only got thurty days left in this dad-dam' shit hole. Now lemme go, dad-dam' it!"

"Let him go," Black ordered.

"Dad-dam' animals," Barney spat as he sat up. "Oughta be in a dad-dam' cage!"

"Attention!" Black snapped as Deputy Dog loped in, shrugging into his shirt.

"*Carry on,* uh, *At Ease!*" Deputy Dog stammered as he took in the overturned bunks and Barney sitting on the floor in our circle. "What's going on, Sergeant Black?"

"Barney's short, Sir," Black replied. "Says he's only got thirty days left."

Deputy Dog peered at Barney as if he was contagious. "Goodness, has Doc looked at him yet?"

A brief epidemic of laughter broke out, silenced by Black's scowl. "Uh, Sir, he's only got thirty days left in *Nam*."

"Oh, in Nam," Deputy Dog replied perplexed. "Well, um, you handle it, Sergeant." He padded out of the hooch, no doubt composing his report on the ruckus to the Old Man.

Black growled at us and we began straightening the hooch as Barney assured us we had 29 days left to the biggest party in Nam. We began practicing that night.

A few days later we learned Deputy Dog and our commander would be reassigned to Division Headquarters at the end of the month as part of the normal officer rotation of six months in the field and six months in a staff assignment. Then the harshest blow of all landed. Our first sergeant was rotating back to the states within six weeks and Black would replace him as the company top sergeant. This was unbearable. Black was our soul. Going beyond the fifth wire without him at the helm was unthinkable. Four other men within the platoon were due to rotate with Barney. The looming loss of key personnel shook us to the core because we were but a reflection of their leadership.

Tiger Woman picked her next victim from our sister battalion, the 2nd of the 27th Infantry, the scene almost identical to the other three disasters, except she took no prisoners this time. Only six men survived her assault, with the rest mutilated in the same gruesome fashion.

The shock of this fourth tragedy snapped us out of our despair and sent a lust for vengeance coursing through our veins. A week later, the 2nd of the 14th Infantry found her on a dark night. One man survived by crawling under a bush. Unfounded rumors circulated they had to place him in a mental ward after he witnessed her drinking blood from the bodies.

We were awestricken with this maniac. How could she move with such impunity picking and choosing her victims at will? What kind of force did she lead that could walk over us with such destructive ease and then disappear? We became obsessed. Pride demanded we redeem these defeats. Terror demanded we search out and destroy this deadly menace from our sector. Circulating among us were rumors of rewards for her—dead or alive—laced with mystical stories of her invincibility. We dreamed of pinning her down with artillery and gunships and finishing off the remains with rifle and bayonet, willing to suffer any hardship to meet her in combat—while living in constant fear that we would—at night, on her terms.

Every ambush patrol became an ordeal of terror as we clung to the ground in cold sweat, on 100 percent alert. By day we reigned supreme. By night, we slunk about with our tails between our legs cowering at every suspicious sight and sound. Our point man stumbled onto a half burned stump one night and mistook the form for a VC. With a fearful yelp, he ripped off half a magazine on full automatic and we engaged in the dandiest firefight with the bushes around us I'd ever seen. I personally tallied three rubber trees before my weapon jammed and followed this up with two shredded bushes from grenades before Black got us calmed down, but by that time gunships were enroute and the 5th Mechanized Ready Reaction Force was streaking to our rescue. We felt more than a bit foolish afterwards.

We searched in vain and became scornful of the local VC we encountered, dealing with them in disdain and treating them as little more than nuisances in our quest for Tiger Woman. Our intelligence developed a lead on her base camp, and we cheered when the brass chose our unit to smoke her out. The plan called for an extended operation in an area known as The Iron Triangle, one of the roughest zones in our entire core of control. Our company would air assault into the area to conduct day sweeps in platoon operations. Bravo Company would provide blocking forces to cut off avenues of escape. Charlie Company would be on strip alert to spring on top of us once we located our victim. The Wolfhounds were always a brotherhood, but never as tight as the day we departed with each man, squad, platoon, and company filled with a single purpose: *Find Tiger Woman—close with and destroy*.

———

Our choppers dipped to the ground as gunships flashed past spewing tracers through the dirty explosions as smoke and dust boiled on each side of the narrow LZ. I viewed the inhospitable, thick brush dotting the vast expanse of foliage below me thinking it a perfect lair for a vixen. The aircraft flared and I leapt with the others to charge full tilt for the protective cover of the brush line through waist deep grass thick as a carpet, twisting through the maze to force openings as the aircraft chattered into the air. I flopped down on the edge of the dark green patch of snarled vines breathing hard, my face streaming sweat as I searched the heavy undergrowth bordering the now eerily quiet LZ where not a bird, animal, nor blade of grass stirred. I shivered in the bright sunlight making the dark interior before me sinister by comparison and inhaled the pungent, rotting dampness, feeling hostile eyes upon me. I fought an urge to stand to reassure myself the rest of the platoon was here with me and caught the reassuring sound of Deputy Dog's radio crackling as his muted voice reported the platoon down, LZ cold. My nostrils twitched from the acrid burnt powder hanging in the air from the gunships. I licked droplets of salty moisture from the corners of my mouth as I tuned in to the familiar vibrations signaling this was a bad assed place, wishing I had brought a wooden stake to drive into the heart of the vampire lurking within. A rustle set my heart pounding, and I tracked the sound with my rifle as it traveled through the coarse jungle in front of me. I clicked my safety off when a subdued pop sounded off to my right, recognizing it as one of our M-16s. A loud swishing brought Lunas to my side with rivulets of sweat running down his face.

He knelt and brushed his forehead with his sleeve. "Where did that come from?"

"Farther off to the right," I advised. The sea of gray swallowed him, leaving me isolated again. Angry voices, all but lost in the stifling weeds, reached me.

"… when you have target damn it!" Lunas, yelling.

"But … thought …" Reno, sullen.

"Do … say … god … it!" Lunas, still yelling.

I sympathized with Reno, relieved I had held my own fire when the noise startled me. Thudding rotor blades filled the air announcing our second platoon inbound. I crawled forward to get a clear field of fire as Lunas hurried to the center of the squad. The choppers fishtailed in behind us and the clamor of disembarking troops thrashing through the grass followed. The birds rose into the air and circled away without incident as a man off to my left collapsed into the weeds, gasping for breath. A radio crackled nearby. Deputy Dog answered on his radio. Second platoon would now secure the LZ.

"Sharpe?" Lunas called.

"Yo?" I answered.

"Take point, straight ahead!"

I climbed to my feet and shifted my heavy load as Del fell in on my heels followed by Reno, Phil, Lunas, Harley, Silverstein, and Barney, with second, third, and fourth squads trailing after them. I made slow headway as brambles snatched at me, stealing strips of skin as I twisted to free myself from their clutch. Sweat stung my eyes and drenched my uniform as I fought my way through the dense brush with gnats swarming around my head and waves of mosquitoes rising from the soggy ground at my feet. I halted on the edge of a small field to survey the far tree line as Del and Reno moved up to cover me, sucked in my breath, strode boldly out into the open, and hesitated, testing the air with my senses as my nerves tingled. I moved swiftly across, my rifle poised, my eyes flickering along the edge of the jungle to my front, and surged the last few steps to kneel in the bushes. I searched thirty yards to each side before motioning the platoon across and pushed on as choppers bearing third platoon drew near, the aircraft lost from sight in the suffocating interior of the jungle.

My skin crawled as shivers of fearful anticipation ran up my spine. *Something was not right.* I tested the air with my radar trying to pick out the specific area sending out vibrations as the platoon faded into kneeling positions behind me. I eased forward again as the pulsating signals grew stronger making the hairs on the back of my neck tingle. *Damn, still nothing*! *What is it*? I held one finger aloft. Del moved close behind, eyes wide. I brushed small limbs aside and eased forward in hesitant steps, the danger signals pulsating in waves now, and almost touched it before I saw it, a thick matted bulk five feet in front of me. I studied it intently as Del followed my gaze, frowned, and then beamed recognition as the all but hidden outline evolved into a camouflaged hooch. I raised my clenched fist, pumped it twice, and swung it left and right to deploy the squad to each side of me. I edged forward again, as they shadowed my movements, observing the surrounding area cleverly cleared with just enough shrubbery to hide the paths until we were standing on them. The hooch showed signs of recent occupancy by a discarded piece of material near the door and fresh scuff marks visible on the earth floor. I gauged the area now deserted, but from minutes to an hour ago, it held people who felt it necessary to hide their existence. With the danger signals humming now, I picked out two other outlines nearby and then a fourth. Two steps later, I halted with my heart in my throat and lowered my eyes to my thigh where a strand of wire no thicker than a thread indented my leg six inches above my knee.

"*Freeze!*" I yelped. The others paused in mid-stride. "Booby trap! Wire! I'm against it!" I breathed, my eyes glued to the almost invisible strand. I looked to the right following the copper thread to the spot where it tied off against a small bush. Rotating my head to the left, ensuring no part of my body moved, I saw an American C-ration can wired to the side of a tree beside me, knee high, covered by leaves. Sweat beaded my forehead. Another inch forward would certainly blow me to hell, but releasing the pressure could also trigger it if I backed away. *Oh shit!* Cold chills gripped me. "Move back. Take cover," I gasped.

"Jay?" Del questioned.

"Damn it, man, move your ass," I ordered as the tension mounted, knowing my nerves would not hold much longer. As the others scrambled away, I pictured myself torn and bloody, legs mangled and a foot missing. I steeled myself as uncontrollable trembling shook me to the core, fearful the jerking would set the thing off. "*Thanks, God,*" I groaned. "*Uh, I didn't mean that the way it sounded, honest, God,*" I corrected as the others squatted behind trees or lay prone. I took a deep breath. I had two options, the first to ease back and hope the released pressure did not blow me to smithereens, or the other to *jump for my life*! As I sailed back a blinding flash enveloped me with crushing force in a smashing roar. Something punched me hard in my lower abdomen as I hit the ground with ears ringing and bits of leaves and bark flying around my head.

"*Medic!*" Del screamed.

Good old Del, I thought as Sandy's face hovered above me. I lay on my back feeling pain near the center of my spine and a dull throbbing in my stomach. When I shifted, pieces of bone grated through the prickling flesh in my lower back. *I won't die*, I swore to myself, realizing the shrapnel had entered my stomach and exited near my spine.

"Jay?" Del's frightened face hovered above me in the swirling smoke.

"It only hurts a little," I gasped.

"Stay put!" Lunas yelled as he hurried up. "Nobody move! This way, Doc!"

"Don't move, Jay," Del pleaded as I tried to shift away from the burning pain sweeping my lower back. "Doc's on the way."

Doc swung his bag to the ground and pushed Del back. "Easy now, where are you hit?"

"I-I can feel my ribs sticking out of my back and it burns," I apprised as he unbuckled my web gear, proud of my calmness, even if I was scared shitless.

"What was it?" Lunas questioned as Doc ran his hands down my legs.

"C-rat can," I reported. "Knee high, placed against a tree, wire detonated."

"I'm going to roll you over now," Doc advised, placing one hand on my shoulder and another near my waist. "Ready?"

"I-I guess," I agreed bravely, hoping my intestines didn't pour out of the opening in my stomach as he rolled me over and lifted my shirt. I lay quietly, praying the jagged holes were something he could handle.

"He'll never make it, Sarge," Doc reported to Lunas as my heart raced and my vision blurred. Del giggled and I lifted my head to stare at the idiot.

"Shouldn't we put a tourniquet around his neck?" Lunas asked.

"Maybe I should just shoot the poor bastard and save him the suffering," Reno proposed.

I ran my fingers over the solid skin of my back and then my belly where only sweaty skin found my fingers. Doc waved a thorn-studded limb in front of my eyes.

"Shit! How'd I know?" I demanded as they howled in glee.

Black crept forward as I sat up, snatched my rifle, and dusted it off. "You bastards are all shell shocked anyway," I cursed as they squealed in laughter amid the somewhat distorted report working its way back through the platoon, filling the jungle with yowling hyenas. I checked my web gear and found a gash in one of my ammo pouches in front where shrapnel had penetrated the fabric and ripped open two of the magazines inside.

"Alright, let's get organized and get this place cleared," Black ordered.

"We could save time by having Sharpe stick his fingers in his ears and stomp around the area for us," Lunas suggested as he tossed out a hook tied to the end of a rope and drew it back.

I had nothing worthwhile to say to him as he detonated two more booby traps without injury. When the clearing operation was complete, we conducted a thorough search, finding nothing of importance beyond numerous signs of recent occupancy. We set the structures on fire and I again took point, glad to put the grins of the platoon behind me. I followed a well-worn trail leading in the general direction we wished to go keeping to the brush ten yards to the side of its meandering course in hopes of finding another way station, preferably one with Tiger Woman sitting on her ass eating a bowl of rice. After an hour of tiresome movement, the distant sound of gunfire and Deputy Dog's radio informed us third platoon was engaged in a firefight with a small VC element. We halted for a C-ration lunch and listened to the battle rage, joined now by gunships and artillery. Minutes later the dispute ended as quickly as it began and we learned from Deputy Dog's radio that third platoon found a hideaway like ours and was now searching it, reporting three pools of blood. We moved on down our trail envious of their success. Within an hour, second platoon was trading blows with another small enemy element, confirming we were definitely in Apache country. As I continued with one ear cocked to the fierce fight behind us, I began picking up vibrations again as my antenna hummed and searched the wall of green with care. Five hundred yards farther along a flicker of movement caught my eye. I scanned the jungle inch by inch but found nothing. I eased forward again and halted as the hairs on the back of my neck rose, lifted my arm and fanned it left and right signaling the squad to take up protective positions. Still nothing.

Lunas crawled up beside me and wiped his glistening face. "What you got?"

"Movement."

"Where?"

I pointed to the jungle. "There."

He searched the dense foliage. "You sure?"

"Damn right," I snapped. "Cloth or something."

"Okay, we'll maneuver in a skirmish line." We moved in short rushes, one fire team covering the other's advance. A hundred yards later, we discovered only that it was damn awkward running through thick jungle in 110-degree temperature. *Was the movement just my imagination, an overreaction to the danger signals I was experiencing,* I wondered as I lay panting? The rest of the platoon joined us and I led them out again in our original trail formation. A hundred yards farther along, I again saw something. Lunas deployed the squad and we conducted another empty charge through the tangled thorns, for which I received hostile stares from the exhausted men around me.

Lunas stomped over as the platoon moved forward. "Barney's on point," he gasped, face red from heat, his shirt soaked white with salt.

"I *saw* something!" I wheezed back.

"You're tired. You been busting trail all morning."

"Barney's too short for point," I argued.

"You take tail," he replied.

I glared at him. He ignored me. Barney spat a stream of tobacco juice at his feet and grinned as he slipped into the jumbled growth with the rest of the squad falling in behind him. Del and I slunk in at the end, followed by the rest of the platoon.

"I thought I saw something too," Del patronized over his shoulder.

"Stow it!" I hissed, so pissed my ears burned.

He released a limb that smacked me soundly across the chops and left a stinging welt across the bridge of my nose. "Oops, sorry," he apologized snidely.

"Shithead!" I raged as I staggered back half blinded.

An instant later an AK-47 spat angrily, clipping leaves around us as we dove for cover.

"First Squad, on line!" Lunas yelled as two of our M-16s answered.

"*Medic! Medic!*" Silverstein screamed through the firing, striking fear in my heart.

Del and I circled on line with five enemy weapons firing on us now. I squeezed off four rounds before my rifle jammed. Swearing, I snatched my cleaning rod and rammed it down the barrel, conscious of the rest of the squad sputtering also and unable to put out effective fire as weapons jammed to the accompaniment of profuse cursing.

"Let's move!" Lunas yelled from the center of the squad.

"Cover me," I shouted as Del worked to clear his own jammed rifle, and raced forward only to trip and sprawl head first into the growth. I heaved myself up to rejoin the ragged line of attacking men and fired two rounds from the hip before experiencing another jam. I knelt beside a tree and ran my cleaning rod down the muzzle as Del ricocheted by twisting through the encircling briars. I fired two quick rounds before my rifle jammed again and our assault faltered as every man in the squad worked to clear his weapon. Second squad crashed through on our left and third squad on our right as the VC faded into the jungle under covering fire.

I stumbled to Doc bent over a white-faced Barney as Silverstein and Black looked on.

"Get back to your position," Black ordered grimly.

I returned to Del guilt ridden. But for my stupidity, I would have been on point. I knew the bastards were out there. I could feel them. Hell, I had *seen* them twice. Now Barney, our stalwart barnyard philosopher, was near death with less than two weeks left in-country and four days remaining in the field. I cursed in a blue torrent as Del shied away from me. God, I wanted to *hurt* something, *anything* with slanted eyes.

We secured a small LZ for the dustoff, and the last I ever saw of our lovable hardcore veteran was a poncho rushing by with his arms flopping lifeless over the sides and his eyes rolled back above a blood soaked bandage covering his naked chest. Someone tossed his rifle, web gear, and steel pot in after him and the chopper leapt into the air racing against time for the nearest field hospital as I dismally watched it out of sight. We formed into a tight perimeter for the night and a resupply bird flew in our day's rations and water. Del and I dug a shallow hole, strung out our claymores and trip flares, and tied empty cans with small pebbles inside to bushes before cooking a gloomy meal over balls of C-4. The night crept over as we began our long vigil to thwart enemy probes.

The VC never developed an attack as we exchanged sniper fire and grenades in the darkness. We suffered no casualties, and as far as we could tell, inflicted none.

We greeted a dreary daybreak with bleary-eyed relief, dismantled our perimeter, and resumed the offensive. With second squad leading, Jerry on point, we spent a long, hot, frustrating day tramping through the jungle facing delay after delay as we searched for our elusive prey. Jerry located mines in two of the grassy fields and others found numerous booby traps in the vegetation as we fought three brief, ineffective firefights with snipers. Our high point involved the destruction of two more of the deserted enemy camps, both showing signs of recent activity but providing no usable intelligence. Another day followed, hot, tiring, and empty as we fought engagements against bushes and snapping carbines without seeing the enemy. The point man from third squad tripped a booby trap and was medevacked out. Someone found his boot with bloody stump inside after the aircraft departed and Black had it buried in the jungle. The fourth day was another grind of heat and fruitless engagements where we accomplished nothing tangible. Exhausted, we slumped into our night defensive perimeter to turn over the next phase to the enemy, feeling impotent because of our constantly jammed rifles.

"Where the hell *is* that bitch?" Reno demanded.

"This mission is friggin' crazy," Del moaned. "We've got to be some kind of dumb asses to let her lead us around by the nose like this."

"She knows our every move," Silverstein agreed. "She knows where we are even when *we* don't know where the shit we are and she runs along in front of us laughing her ass off while stringing booby traps and ambushes for us to blunder into."

"I'm gonna *get* that bitch," Reno swore.

"Well hop to it, shitface!" Silverstein snarled. "Go on out there and *get* her!"

"Get off my back, you Jew bastard!" Reno growled.

"*Or?*" Silverstein challenged.

"Knock off the shit!" I scolded as they blustered.

"I'm hurting, man." Del rubbed his toes to restore circulation as flakes of skin fell away.

I stared out into the tangle imagining Tiger Woman skipping along in front of us, clearing all the camps, darting at us and striking at will before fading happily away again as we cowered on the rotten jungle floor with useless rifles. We were fooling ourselves to think she would stand and fight. Why would she when she could pick us apart at leisure choosing her time and place.

I began cleaning my worthless rifle while sharing my cleaning rod with Del since he had lost his somewhere in the bush and was now virtually defenseless without it unless he was near one of us who had one. I glanced over at Jerry busily cleaning his own weapon as Bernie cooked a meal for them. Bernie's rifle was always clean of course since he never fired it. Here he was cooking chow while the rest of us were raging over the pieces of shit the Army gave us. *He* didn't care since it didn't matter if his worked or not. The injustice of the situation seared through me as I passed my rod to Del, reassembled my rifle, and clumped over to their position.

"Hey, Jay," Jerry greeted, his grungy face filled with fatigue as he squinted down the barrel of his rifle.

I stood over Bernie squatting at his C-ration stove. "Give me your damn cleaning rod."

Bernie half smiled up at me. "What? Why?"

"*Just give me the goddamned rod!*" I shouted.

Jerry rose to his feet as Bernie gaped up at me. "Jay?"

"Stay out of this," I insisted.

Jerry edged closer. "Stay out of what?"

"Del lost his rod today so I'm taking Bernie's," I explained.

Jerry's eyes narrowed. "Taking?"

I held out my palm. "Hand it over."

"Bernie may need it himself," Jerry argued cautiously.

"*May?*" I bellowed. "He *may* need it? *Bullshit!* Del *does* need it *now!*"

Del moved up behind me. "Hey, I don't want to take—"

"Shut up, Del!" I snapped. "Give me the rod, Bernie!"

Jerry shifted in front of me. "Jay, you ain't taking his rod."

Bernie stood up behind him ashen faced.

"Your ears full of shit?" I growled. "I *told* you to stay out of this! Del can't fight with a jammed weapon, and Bernie doesn't need one because *he* doesn't *fight* anyway!"

"Okay, asshole!" Jerry placed his hand on my chest and shoved. "*Get out of here!*"

I caught him a solid blow on his jaw. He came back around swinging and his knuckles glanced off my head. We grappled as Del jumped on my back and Bernie grabbed Jerry.

"*Enough!*" Black commanded. We untangled ourselves and stood before him as he glared, fists balled on his narrow waist. "What the shit do you morons think you're doing?"

"My fault," I mumbled as Lunas hurried up.

"No, mine," Jerry insisted.

"You're both right," Black retorted, and punched me right between the eyes.

I sailed backwards and an instant later Jerry landed beside me in a tangle of brush.

Black stood over us. "If you two start feeling frisky again, look me up." He turned on his heel and marched back to the platoon CP as Bernie and Del leapt out of his way.

Jerry climbed to his feet and offered me a hand up.

"You can have my rod," Bernie offered sheepishly, extending it to Del.

"No, that's not right," I argued awkwardly. "He can share mine."

"Take it," Jerry urged Del.

"No, really," Del insisted.

"Jay's right," Bernie insisted. "I don't need it."

"You might," I encouraged.

"Bernie can share mine," Jerry promised.

"No," I insisted. "It's his by right."

"You guys are real dumb shits, you know that?" Lunas grated. "Here, you take mine." He shoved his rod into Del's hands. "And I'll take yours—until you need it." He snatched Bernie's rod. "Now, get back to your positions." He stomped off talking to himself.

"I'm sorry, guys," I mumbled. "Don't know what got into me."

Jerry dusted himself off. "Forget it, man, that's what friends are for, to knock hell out of when nothing else is available to vent your frustrations on—like an evil eyed bitch dressed in tiger stripes."

"Bernie, if you want to take a swing at me?" I offered.

He grinned. "I'll take a rain check for some time when Black's not around."

I offered my hand. "Sorry, man, honest. I was a bit loony, you know?"

He grasped it and shook. "I know."

Del and I returned to our position to prepare a hurried meal. Later Jerry and Bernie drifted over to share a quick cup of coffee before darkness. No further mention was made of my insanity as my right eye swelled and blackened and Jerry's cheek grew a large knot along the jawbone.

———

We spent another sleepless watch trading punches with Charlie. Del and I threw half a dozen grenades and received two back in return, one close enough to leave our ears ringing. The VC sent random rounds into our perimeter but we held our own fire unwilling to pinpoint our position with the muzzle flash. The night urchins gave special attention to the few that did fire back by bombarding them with grenades from the darkness and leaving the area around their position pocketed with ragged patches of torn earth with them sitting frazzled in the middle. Morning found us with raw nerves, red-rimmed eyes, and bodies aching with fatigue. Third squad led us on another endless day of heat and frustration, where we found a minefield and several booby traps, all of which we bypassed successfully. We fought two brief firefights and found one large pool of blood in the damp underbrush. Morale lifted—we had finally hit *something*.

Several men were without cleaning rods now, which rendered them ineffective after the first volley of counter fire as they crawled about borrowing rods to clear their weapons. Spirits sagged into hopelessness as we found ourselves outgunned, outmaneuvered, and outsmarted. We sulked along feeling sorry for ourselves and pissed off at the world. The mere mention of Tiger Woman evoked tirades of abuse from our parched throats and frayed minds, with only our chain of command eliciting a more resounding string of oaths from us for sticking us poor fools out here under these circumstances. We decided if we had our Brass on one side and Tiger Woman on the other, we would attack in both directions and take no prisoners on either side.

When we settled into our perimeter for the night, I elected to set our trip flare wires straight out in front of us instead of in the customary horizontal line, aware that not once had the sappers tripped one of them on our whole perimeter, yet continued to crawl all over us in the darkness. I figured I had nothing to lose, except my ass if Black found out about it. An hour after sunset a snap and fizzle lit the area revealing a startled man in black pajama shorts twenty feet in front of us. I was so shocked I let him run about three steps before I remembered I was supposed to kill the bastard and almost knocked Del other over in my excitement as I let loose a short blast that spun him around before my weapon jammed. The price for my small victory was a hazardous night of thumps and ear splitting *BOOMS*! as the SOB's pals bombarded us with grenades in revenge. By morning I was sorry I had been so innovative and more than eager to share my formula for success with the others in order to divert some of the animosity, as the VC obviously had little use for Yankee ingenuity.

At dawn, we searched through the smoky, crater-filled area. The VC body was gone, but enough blood was left on the ground to ensure he had not crawled off under his own power. A happy Black gave me credit for a kill and instructed the platoon that hereafter we would place our trip flare wires alternately horizontally and vertically. A resupply ship brought us extra cleaning rods, which further raised our spirits, and we began a new day with increased hope. I again took point, and by noon had found four booby traps and located another of the small VC camps, which we burned without incident before settling down amid the wafting smoke for a meal of unheated C-rations. Rumor circulated we had covered our entire sector and would be returning to Cu Chi in the next day or two. Things were looking up.

After lunch, I struggled along on point under my load, my mind numb and body stiff jointed and sore, the week in this thick entangling hell having extracted its toll. I longed for base camp and cold beer, hope having faded with my strength of pinning Tiger Woman against our blocking forces and knowing ten times our number could not bring her to bay in this terrain. I had no doubt she would stand against us again, at night in a place and time of her own choosing when her forces had us outnumbered and outflanked, the bitter knowledge bile in my stomach.

Through my stupor, I sensed the vibrant danger signals return and pulled myself to full alert, taking greater pains to search danger areas. I became more hesitant with each step and halted the platoon twice within fifty yards to conduct long searches before moving again. Five minutes later, I again called a halt to scan the area to my front, testing the air, trying to pick out something to justify my growing chill.

Lunas lumbered up in irritation. "What now?"

"I feel something."

"I'm putting Harley on point."

"No."

"Look, we ain't getting anywhere at this pace. You're having a bad day of nerves."

"Something's out there."

"What? Where?"

"I can't tell. But I know."

"I'm getting damned tired of your hunches," he growled.

"I've been right more than wrong," I challenged.

"Move out or drop back to the rear," he snapped.

I picked my way faster than my feelings told me I should, thrashing through the jungle amid strong tingles coursing through my body, a growing knot of fear forming in my stomach, breathing heavily as my eyes searched everywhere at once. I halted on the edge of a field covered with short grass, my legs refusing to move, wanting to crawl in a hole and hide.

Lunas stomped up. "What now? Did you see something?"

"No, but they're out there."

"Shit!"

"Believe me this time, Sarge," I warned.

He searched the far side of the field. "I'll talk to Black." He moved back down the line of kneeling, sweating men behind me.

Black returned with him and knelt to look hard at the other side. "I don't see anything."

"They're there," I insisted.

He studied me. "You're spooky, kid. Okay, I'll put the platoon on line."

He moved back down the line growling about us not reaching our objective until midnight at this pace. To my astonishment, I heard Lunas defending me and decided I couldn't figure either of them out. The knot of fear in my stomach dissipated somewhat as the platoon formed on line, knowing it would take a sizable force to stand against us fully deployed.

Deputy Dog, Doc, and the RTO placed themselves at our rear and centered. Black looked left and right at the kneeling men and nodded his head at me. I shifted my load as the rest of the platoon surged up, eyes to the front, face set, and waded through the remaining bushes shrugging the branches aside. I flipped off my safety, my muzzle trained on the tree line fifty yards distant as I studied the dark interior. My heart beat rapidly as the pressure grew in my chest. *Any minute now.* I shook my head to clear the sweat clinging to my eyes as the platoon burst through the fringes of the jungle in measured steps to my rear. At the halfway point, I figured I was wrong; if there were anything in front of us, they would have jumped us by now. I ignored the chill growing in me as my eyes flickered from the tree line to the ground, back to the tree line and back to the ground. I froze and threw up my hand to halt the platoon as I tried to decipher the latest warning flashing through my overloaded senses. I scanned the tree line, then the ground. Three feet in front of me a small piece of bamboo stuck up two inches from the ground—*sticks did not grow in fields with the tops cut off.*

"*Minefield!*" I shouted over my shoulder. "Watch your feet!"

"*Move back!*" Black ordered as the platoon turned with care back to the tree line. "Walk in the same—"

WWHHHAAAAPPPPP! I ducked as the noise of a stuttering AK-47 followed the angry buzz of bullets slicing the air. I knew I had no chance of making the trees with the others as the air sang with whining lead amid a chorus of popping carbines joining the AK. In near hysteria, I stepped sideways to avoid the mine and flung myself to the ground as the platoon scrambled for cover behind me. A man from third squad spun and stumbled in shock as a bullet pierced his lower back. Another man ran after him calling his name as gunfire streamed into us from the opposite side, answered by our own broken response from behind me. As I hugged the ground, a geyser of dirt and flame sent the second man running after the first flopping into a heap on the ground amidst drifting smoke.

"*Get down!*" I screamed as the first man, disoriented by panic and pain, stumbled toward me, and rose to my

knees to tackle him. A crushing force knocked me backwards and enveloped the man in fire lifting him high
into the air with his rifle and helmet separating from
his form. I was unable to make my limbs function as
the man's body thumped down beside me, his head two
feet from my own, his charred face looking directly into
mine as his jaw unhinged and a pink tongue slid out,
quivering as life drained away. The lower part of his
body was jagged flesh without legs and his entrails strung
out below him in green strands with one arm missing
at the elbow, the other a bloody stump at the wrist with
blood pumping from the stump at my face as the arm
twitched.

I heard screaming. I had to get away, had to run, but
no part of me worked as the field spun slowly around
me. I was conscious of firing on both sides of me, of
voices yelling, some calling my name, telling me to get
down. I sprawled about in crooked, staggering jerks as
bullets whined by me. The voice was still screaming and
I wished it would stop as my mind drifted in and out of
focus and fought to shake off the dullness as I lurched
along on all fours. *Which way was I supposed to go?* Through
the reeling images, I saw another of the bamboo stakes,
then lost it and turned in an indecisive circle. Nothing
was right. I had no control over anything. I wished the
voice would stop screaming. I collapsed in anguish, my
fingers digging into the soft grass as dirt sprayed across
my face, and realized I wasn't breathing. My chest was
heaving, but no air was coming in. I listened to the
screams die out as darkness settled around me, and knew
the screaming was my own. I tried to beg for help, but

managed only a moan. I saw one of my detached legs lying nearby in a scorched, bloody lump and saw my mother crying and my dad holding his bowed head in his hands as I floated over them under a brilliant white parachute with no wind and no noise.

No! I thrashed about and felt the ground jar as explosions crumpled dully. *Artillery*! I felt giddy, and then the color began to fade into blackness. *My eyes are closed. Open them*! my mind commanded. Grass swam into focus inches from my nose. I lifted my head. Men were kneeling along the tree line firing across the top of me. Another man was walking out to me with his eyes glued to the ground in front of him. He carried no weapon and placed each foot with care. I tried to remember his name. *Where is his weapon? Why is he moving so slowly?* There were men behind him … *Bernie and Del. Bernie is firing*! *That's Jerry coming to get me. I'm in a minefield,* I remembered in anguish. *And I'm dying.* I tried to struggle to my knees as Jerry reached me, tried to tell him Bernie was firing, but only guttural sounds emerged as he pulled me to my feet and dipped under me. The world spun again as I looked down at his heels flashing in and out of my vision. The sunlight grew dimmer. I was staring up at the tops of trees turning in slow circles below the blue sky above them. I turned my head to stare at Jerry beside me, propped on his elbows, gasping for air, his chest heaving, drenched in sweat. *That's odd, I'm freezing and he's sweating.* He laid his head on the ground and coughed.

"I-I …" My mind couldn't seem to work my mouth and everything seemed in slow motion.

Doc looked down at me. Above and behind him two helicopters slipped through the air pointing downward. Furls of smoke poured out of the pods on their side as yellow flames charged to the ground. Vaguely, I heard the *crump's* of their impact. My face stung. I blinked and saw Doc's arm flash and heard the meaty impact of his palm against my cheek. *Why is he hitting me?* I tried to sit up and he pressed me back against the ground.

"*Can-you-hear-me*?" his voice called from a distance, sounding like an echo, stilted and unnatural, drifting in and out of my head. I tried to focus on him, to say *yes*. Jerry's terrified face appeared near his shoulder. I tried to smile at him, hoping he wasn't going to hit me again, feeling numb all over and unsure of where I hurt, but knowing I must hurt somewhere. Black's face appeared over Doc's other shoulder.

"Dustoff's on the way," he panted as he peered down at me.

"He's in shock. Somebody prop his feet up," Doc directed.

Somebody outside my vision lifted my feet into the air. I remembered the torn and bloody leg. *I still have feet?* My head began clearing.

"We're moving a hundred yards to the south to a small LZ," Black advised.

"I'll need a litter," Doc answered.

I tried to sit up and the area began to rotate as Doc held me propped against his arm. "The concussion knocked you senseless. You've got a flesh wound on your arm and chest, but nothing to worry about. Can you hear me? Talk to me, damn it!"

"I-I'm ... numb ..." I gasped, my voice sounding strange to my ears, my head seemingly disconnected from my shoulders.

"Roll over onto this." Doc guided me onto a poncho litter.

The sky continued to revolve as the litter lifted me into the air. Del's upside down face stared at me, spinning with the trees. I closed my eyes as we jolted along, conscious of vines scraping at my arms as the world spun faster. When the bouncing stopped, two more poncho litters appeared beside me holding the two men who had stepped on the mines, each body wrapped tightly in ponchos now. Doc stuck a needle in my arm and the world turned faster as blackness closed in. I tried to concentrate on the point of light above me, opening my eyes wider as it grew smaller, and then let go and spiraled downward into blackness.

CHAPTER 21

I was suffocating in a yellow fog.

I realized I had been wallowing in it for some time and concentrated on breathing. A light bulb with a white reflective cover swam into view. I turned my head and my body tilted and then righted as a long room came into focus lined on each side by beds with white sheets and bandaged men. I swung my legs over the bedside and clutched at the sheets as my limp body folded into a heap on the floor. I lay with my cheek against the cool tile as my vision grew fuzzy and my head pounded. Footsteps brought a pair of jungle boots in front of my nose.

"Let me help you," a female voice soothed. Hands propped me back onto the bed. A pretty face hovered above me, a sting punctured my arm, and blackness took me again.

My head ached and my mouth seemed full of cotton. I opened my eyes. I was still in the cold room with the lines of beds and bandaged men. A woman wearing jungle fatigues sat at a desk at the far end of the room writing on a clipboard. I was wearing a blue gown with my bare backside hanging out.

"Help ..." I moaned.

The woman hurried to me. "Welcome back."

I clenched my jaw as waves of nauseous pain gripped me. "My head ..."

"You need rest. I'll get you something for the pain." She turned away.

"Please don't ... stick me ... again," I begged.

"Try these." She extended a small paper cup with pills in the bottom.

I washed them down with a glass of water she held for me, lay back, and closed my eyes to lessen the pounding in my head.

Someone shook my arm. A different nurse stood beside me with a bored looking man in a white jacket reading a clipboard. "Wake up now. The doctor needs to check you."

He moved around the nurse as she stepped back. "How do you feel?"

"Like shit," I replied, hoping he wouldn't put me to sleep again.

He propped my eyelid open with his thumb to shine a small penlight in my eye and repeated the examination on the other before holding up his hand. "How many fingers?"

I grimaced through the swimming spots. "Two."

"Do you have any pain?"

"Yeah, I've got to pee bad," I groaned.

The nurse helped me to my feet and steadied me as she walked me back to the rear of the ward to the latrine door. Using the wall for support, I shuffled back to a stall and sank down in gratitude. She was waiting to help me back and the doctor watched as I wobbled along. Once I was back in bed, he wrote on his clipboard, assured me I would be fine, and charged off in search of someone more in need of his time. The nurse made me stand while she changed my sheets, gave me two more pills, helped me back into bed, and went back to her desk after informing me I would change my own linen hereafter. On her next visit to take my pulse and temperature, I learned I had been here three days and would probably be here three or four more. She changed the small bandages on my right forearm and left chest, and I spent the day napping and staring at the ceiling. I ate every morsel of food served on the dinner tray and asked for seconds, but got only an apple instead. The next afternoon I showered and changed my gown. When I returned from the latrine, Del, Jerry, and Bernie were waiting beside my bed.

"Hey, guys!" I called as they swarmed around me.

"How much longer you planning on shamming in here?" Jerry demanded.

Del eyed the nurse watching us in cold disapproval from her desk. "I knew you'd get a ward with the prettiest nurse."

"Where have you guys been?" I demanded.

"Chasing Tiger Woman and her merry band of faggots all over the jungle while you laze around here on your ass being pampered to death by round eyes," Bernie exclaimed.

"Did you find the bitch?" I asked eagerly.

"Hell no," Del complained.

"Amateurs," I sniffed.

"You don't see *us* wearing no silly nightgown with our ass hanging out," Jerry countered.

I flopped onto the bed. "What the hell happened out there, anyway?"

"Some damn fool led us into the biggest minefield in all of Nam," Jerry retorted.

"And an ambush, to boot," Del added.

"Kiss my ass," I offered scornfully.

"You're lucky you've got enough ass *left* to kiss," Bernie ribbed.

"Hey, I saw you shoot, Bernie. Didn't I? I *know* I did."

"Well, damn, with you crawling around on your hands and knees screeching like a little girl and this fool running out after you," he nodded at Jerry, "I didn't have much choice."

"Thanks, man," I said to Jerry, who shrugged and studied the floor.

"Your friends are going to have to leave now," a tart voice intruded.

"I'm going with them," I replied struggling to my feet.

"*You're* going to get your ass back in bed," she informed me as they howled in glee.

"I'm being starved to death in here," I yelled as she herded them out. "Bring food!"

"Catch you later!" Jerry called as the nurse closed the door in his face.

The next day the commanding general came through the ward with half a dozen officers in tow and pinned Purple Hearts to our pajama tops. He made a short speech about us afterwards, but I was so groggy from the pills I'd just swallowed I couldn't follow most of it. The doctor released me the following day with the stipulation that I would be on bed rest back at the hooch and under the Battalion Aid Station's care for the two small punctures in my chest and arm.

The whole platoon gathered around to welcome me back, and I learned Deputy Dog put Jerry in for a Silver Star for his actions in rescuing me from the minefield. In my opinion, none deserved it more, and we celebrated with one hell of a party that night. The next day I got a letter from home:

"Dear Jay,

It's been almost a year since you enlisted and I have seen you for less than three weeks during these many months. At the time, I thought my love for you was strong enough to endure your foolish venture, but your letters are so infrequent and say so little time has proven me wrong. I guess there is no good way to say this. I have met someone. Please don't think badly of me. I hope you find what you are searching for since it wasn't me, and wish you every happiness.

BJ"

I wasn't devastated. I had met someone too. I spent the next five days lying around drinking beer in a brooding funk until boredom overcame me. After hassling Lunas, who sought guidance from Doc, who cleared it with the Battalion Aid Station, I rejoined the platoon and slipped back into the routine of hunting Tiger Woman by day as she stalked us by night. Nothing had changed.

Bernie the pacifist evolved into Bernie the fanatic. The change was so remarkable it left me uneasy. He now fired without hesitation, took unnecessary risks to maneuver close to snipers, volunteered for point, and even talked of joining the Long Range Recon Platoon, notably one of the most dangerous assignments in Nam.

After one engagement, we found a blood trail in the bushes and he became enraged when Battalion refused to give us a confirmed kill, swearing he had seen the man fall after he hit him with a burst of fire. In another instance, he raced recklessly along our flank to rout a sniper with a roaring burst of counter fire, stunning us with the amount of shooting he did on full automatic without a single stoppage while the rest of us squirmed on the ground trying to un-jam our weapons. Black was furious with his antics, but the rest of us damned curious.

Back in the base camp, Jerry, Del, and I cornered him.

"How did you do that?" Jerry demanded.

"Do what?" he inquired innocently.

"You put out more firepower than the whole friggin' platoon!" Del accused.

He grinned. "Simple, I modified my weapon."

"Modified it how?" I demanded.

He took his rifle from the wall and stripped it down. "When I started shooting this damned thing, I got as frustrated as the rest of you," he explained. "So I went to the zero range to run some tests and checked each stoppage until I understood the problem. You see, the chamber here is perfectly milled. When a bullet is fired the cartridge expands from the heat. Powder residue from spent cartridges or even a grain of sand in the chamber further aggravates the situation and wedges the shell casing tightly into the chamber. The bolt then strips off the rim as it attempts to extract the cartridge and chamber another round, causing a double jam. Based on this, I took a very fine grade of sandpaper, wrapped it around a chamber brush, and sanded the inside of the chamber to make it larger. You saw the results out there today."

We fell over each other grabbing sandpaper, chamber brushes, and weapons, practically running to the zero range. Under his tutelage, we test fired and sanded away. In less than an hour every one of us was firing fully automatic without a stoppage. We passed the secret along to the others, with dramatic results as the remedy swept through the company, battalion, and division.

We were back in business and staggered the enemy back on his heels under our sudden wall of fire as our aggressive spirit returned. Within a week, our platoon racked up eleven VC confirmed kills compared to almost none the previous month, and even Deputy Dog and Black's weapons no longer jammed.

―――――

We warily waited for Tiger Woman to reappear following our operation against her base camp, with some speculating we killed her during one of our many skirmishes with her force. Others thought she was merely regrouping. Like the passing of a fearsome plague, her influence began to wane and we talked of her as one might a ghost, assuring ourselves we had nothing to fear as we looked over our shoulders for confirmation.

We were on ambush when she chose her next victim. One minute we were lying in our position fighting sleep. The next the night split asunder with the viciousness of her attack against a platoon less than a mile away. With the opening fire a voice within our platoon perimeter cried *"Tiger Woman!"*

The declaration struck fear in my heart and my first thought was gratitude—*it's not us*!

Even as the unfortunate platoon met her attack with return fire, we scrambled to recover our claymores and pull on our web gear. No order was necessary to form us into a travel formation as the desperate voice of their platoon leader calling for artillery and reinforcements came over Deputy Dog's radio. With no commands spoken and no strategy devised, we shifted from a fast stride to a grim trot as we closed the distance like crazed animals, clear in our own minds of what we needed to do—*close with and destroy*. We could not, must not let her escape again. Self-preservation demanded she die.

As we raced to the distant flares and thunderous noise intent on reaching the victims before she could butcher them, I jogged along on point ignoring the pains tearing at my heaving chest and unmindful of the danger areas we passed without pause, reminded of a story in Basic of a farm boy in World War II. During a major attack on our lines by the Germans, this simple lad took refuge in an abandoned farmhouse. When the attacking Germans surrounded the house, he retreated to the second floor where he fought them until he ran out of ammo. There five of the enemy cornered him against a wall giving him no chance of escape, no place left to retreat, and no hope of survival. Days later, our forces recaptured the area and found the dead farm boy at the house. Around him were the bodies of the five enemy soldiers he attacked and killed with his bayonet. The moral of the story was that any man faced with certain destruction is capable of inhuman actions—*never leave an enemy with no alternative other than death.*

I grimly realized this was what Tiger Woman had instilled in us. With her unrelenting success and mocking butchery after defeat, any force attacked by her counted itself as dead. Thus, with nothing left to lose, the besieged platoon before us changed character and became savages bent on counter destruction, the tone of the battle foretelling the grim struggle. From the roaring fire of the first attack, to the now dwindling scattered fights between determined pockets of resistance, they were dying like avengers from hell, asking no quarter and giving none, having conquered fear itself.

Gunships thundered overhead and hurled their rockets and miniguns into the melee below. Far off to our right a methodical roar announced the 5th Mech charging through the rubber trees in their iron monsters to join the battle raging a quarter of a mile in front of us now. In a mob, we raced through the rubber trees separating us from the grim massacre as flares filled the forest with dancing shadows and bewildering half-light.

Suddenly men running in the opposite direction from our own determined advance intermingled with us in the pulsating darkness creating instant chaos as our two forces swirled into each other. My first thought was elements of one of the reaction forces had blundered into us. Then I heard a startled cry in Vietnamese and knew instantly that Tiger Woman had decided the reinforcements pouring in coupled with the determined stand of the gallant men of the attacked platoon was too much and elected to break contact, thereby causing our charging platoon to run pell-mell into her retreating company amid the rubber trees.

Pandemonium broke out as friend and foe alike filled the night with death as we collided, groped, shouted, lunged, and fought in a mad frenzy of shock and terror. Every rifle and machine gun spit flames in every direction as our two entangled forces degenerated into snarling pits of individual animals fighting to survive the fiasco.

Deputy Dog screamed into his radio as Black yelled for us to pull back amid Vietnamese voices crying out in bewilderment. Anything that stood drew instant fire, as muzzle flashes bloomed from every quadrant and tracers skipped across the ground amongst grenades exploding in blinding light while bullets whined through the swirls of arid smoke in the mind-jarring roar.

A flare opened overhead outlining targets on both sides. I emptied two magazines on full automatic and decided to get the hell out of the inferno. I crawled as fast as I could to the fringes of the madness where I rolled into a small depression and reloaded. A man crawled by in the darkness, but I was afraid to shoot because he might be a friend, and afraid to call out because he might not. Lying flat on my back, I raised my rifle above my stomach and sprayed the area all around me, flinching as the hot cartridges fell back onto my face in scorching ripples. I pulled the pin on a grenade and heaved it into the darkness, and threw a second in the opposite direction. As the explosions tore at me, I reloaded while dirt and leaves showered down around me. A pajama-clad shadow ran by and then crumpled to the ground. Two more rushed to him, grabbed him by the arms, and began dragging him away. I sprayed all three of them and flopped back into my shallow hole to reload.

An American voice screamed for M-60 ammo. I tore my box off my shoulder and shouted to him. When he answered, I jumped and ran at his voice. Something slammed my left shoulder and spun me half around. I staggered forward, tripped over a soft lump, and sprawled face first into the leaves as my rifle skidded away.

"*Ammo! Ammo!*" the voice at my feet pleaded through the uproar.

I shoved the box into his greedy hands, rummaged through the leaves for my rifle, and wiggled to the opposite side of his tree as he loaded the belt in the mechanism in the faint light. A VC ran by us and disappeared before I could swing and fire on him. The gunner crumpled over his gun and gurgled as blood spurted from his throat. I pushed him aside, crawled behind the machine gun, pointed it into the thick of the fighting, and squeezed the trigger, sending a red roar of death out as the jangling belt unraveled beside me. When it emptied, I shoved the smoking barrel away, grabbed my rifle again, and continued to fire at flashes of orange.

I knew I would not survive this fiasco, which filled me with consuming rage at the injustice of dying here and now. I waited for death as I ripped magazines out and reloaded, the heat from my barrel scorching my hands. I considered running as I reloaded, and screamed curses as I squeezed the trigger in violent jabs. A terrifying rumble filled the darkness and the ground quivered as the 5th Mech roared into our ranks with bullets dancing off their sides in showers of sparks. Red tracers sprouted from their tops as machine guns lashed out on all sides as they churned among us chewing up bushes and small trees. I clawed into the ground seeking cover from the impartial onslaught in an attempt to survive, as the embattled VC fled in all directions, one even leaping over the fallen gunner and me to disappear into the trees. I hugged the backside of the tree grimly as one of the Mech gunners threw a stream of tracers so close I could feel the heat as they sizzled past.

In an instant it was over. The growling tracks ground to a halt as scattered shots replaced the previous roar. I raised my head. Heavy smoke hung over the twisted and torn trees. Bodies lay sprawled and flung about. Small crackling fires flared and smoldered in isolated patches. The throbbing diesel engines idled in the pall hanging over the battle area as if to underscore their victory. No one stood before them. Their headlights blinked on like two benevolent eyes high on each side of their steel frames lighting the area in harsh brightness. Fresh flares popped overhead sending distorted shafts through the drifting haze.

God, I'm alive! I thought wondrously as a voice screamed for a medic. I pulled myself up on trembling legs and stumbled into the light so the languishing beasts could identify me in the wasteland of drifting smoke, splintered limbs, and leaning trees. I knelt beside the unconscious gunner and applied pressure to his throat while yelling for a medic. When one of the medics from the Mech appeared and placed a battle dressing over the oozing wound, I helped carry him to one of the tracks. I stumbled out into the center of the area covered with bodies as men dismounted from the APCs with raised rifles to check the dead and wounded.

"*Jerry*?" I called anxiously into the carnage. "*Del*? *Bernie*?"

"Jay, over here," Bernie answered.

I found him sitting against a tree staring at the destruction. "You okay?"

"Think so," he replied dully.

"Jay, I'm hit!" Del called from a pile of crushed bushes.

I rushed over, stomped out a small fire, and pulled him from the tangle. He held the upper part of his left thigh with blood covered hands. I pulled my knife from its holster and slit his trousers to reveal an ugly hole in the fleshy part of his calf. "Don't think it hit a bone," I advised as I tore open one of his battle dressings.

"Holy shit, Jay, how did we survive that?" he moaned. "I almost got run over by the friggin' Mech. I *did* get run over by one of the friggin' Gooks. Bastard stepped right in my stomach as he ran off."

"We must have lost half the platoon," I appraised as I tied his bandage off.

"What did we hit?" he asked.

I stood and grasped my rifle. "Tiger Woman, I think. You stay here. I'll get a medic over to you as soon as I can." I checked the men I came across, most gathering into broken little groups now as Lunas tried to organize security teams to the flanks. I found Phil, hit by half a dozen rounds that left jagged holes in his uniform, his unseeing eyes staring blankly. Reno was near him with an ugly gash across his forehead streaming blood down his nose and cheeks. I bandaged his head turban-style as Silverstein stumbled up to me, hatless and missing his rifle, dripping blood from both arms. I used his battle dressings to patch both limbs, one a neat hole near the biceps and the other an angry gouge in the forearm. I found Doc shot through the chest and head, disentangled his bloody medical bag and hurried over to Black kneeling beside Deputy Dog, who was clutching his stomach and grimacing as slimy blood seeped through his fingers. His RTO lay dead beside him, his shattered radio still strapped to his back. Black snatched the medical bag and I stumbled off in search of Jerry.

A man I had never seen before approached. "Hey, you're wounded. Let me look at you."

"Are you a medic?"

"No, but we've got one somewhere around here."

"Get him over there to my Lieutenant quick!" I ordered. "He's hit bad and needs help!"

"Yeah, okay." He rushed off into the smoky light.

I placed my rifle in my numb left hand and reached back with my right to explore my left shoulder, my fingers coming away sticky red as I became conscious of a throbbing ache. I stepped over a wounded Vietnamese moaning on the ground and finally spotted Jerry in the eerie light piling captured enemy weapons against a tree as men from the tracks dragged the enemy dead and wounded into the light provided by the vehicles. Others helped wounded members of our platoon into a central location as a medic worked over them. Guards stood over several VC prisoners as they cowered before them with their hands behind their head. As I moved along the line, one of the prisoners clutched at my leg pleading in a singsong whine and held up two fingers, begging for a cigarette. The mutilated corpses of our third platoon flashed through my numb mind, and I kicked him in the face.

The man guarding him chuckled. "Remember the Geneva Conventions, man."

"You should see their leavings," I retorted.

"I have—three times!" He shoved the muzzle of his rifle into the man's mouth splitting his lips. "Ain't that right, Slope, you *bic*?" he demanded as the VC's eyes rolled back in his head and he fainted, or had a heart attack. I hurried on to Jerry, not caring which.

"Jay! I've been looking everywhere—you're wounded!"

I grinned, wanting to hug him. "Yeah, no shit. You okay?"

He pressed me down. "Damn, let me look at you."

"I think it's just a scratch." I assured him as he unbuckled my web gear and peeled it off my shoulders.

"Del's hit in the leg, but he'll be okay. Bernie made it through unharmed. You two must have crawled into the same damned deep hole. Reno has a gash across his forehead. Deputy Dog's gut shot and it looks bad. Silverstein got it in both arms. Phil and Doc and the RTO are dead. I haven't seen Harley, but Lunas and Black are okay."

"And now you again, you silly bastard," he fussed as he pulled my sticky shirt from my back to examine my shoulder. "Have I got to mother you our whole damn tour? And you're damned right I crawled in a hole. A man could have got his balls shot off out there. Later on, a dink crawled in with me. I didn't even bother to shoot him until it was all over. The bastard had been eating rotten fish. You ever tried to share a hole with someone with fish breath?"

"I can't imagine," I sympathized. "I thought I had it bad out here in the open with a hundred gooks and the tracks running around shooting up the world." I jerked away as he pressed my shoulder. "Damn, you trying to finish me off? Cut me some slack, asshole, you don't have a license to practice medicine."

"I'm on the job training. It's just a little hole, but the bullet is still in there."

"It's getting all tingly now," I complained.

"Learn to keep your head down, dumb ass," he consoled.

I grinned. "I can't help myself, I like nurses."

"Introducing yourself works a hell of a lot better than your current system."

I grimaced as he bound my shoulder. "I'll try that next time. Thank God for Bernie. Can you imagine tonight with our weapons jamming?"

He surveyed the destruction. "We'd have been slaughtered."

"Hey, Lieutenant, over here, Sir!" an eager voice called from the darkness.

Several of the Mech guys rushed over as their platoon leader joined them. "It's Tiger Woman!" someone yelped as others cheered.

Jerry and I joined the growing mob and elbowed our way to the front to stare down at our nemesis, a plain looking oriental woman about twenty-five or thirty years old with short hair wearing a tiger striped camouflaged uniform. Shot in the chest and stomach, her evil eyes were mere slits staring dully up at us now. I felt no empathy for the monster that had haunted us over the weeks, the stalker who turned every shadow into a cunning adversary and showed no mercy for the vanquished or decency for the dead. I had visions of the captives she ripped to shreds as they screamed to die, of the corpses she sent home in caskets that loved ones could never open. Hate surged through me as a man spat in her face and another kicked her in the side, splintering her ribs. Another kicked her in her crotch. Another stripped her tiger fatigues off, leaving her frail, nude body shamed before us in the light of the flares. A man with a bowie knife knelt, stabbed her in both breasts, and then tried to scalp her as a sergeant wrapped commo wire around her feet and attached it to the back of an APC. He then drove around in circles dragging the body through the brush behind him as others cheered. When the APC stopped, another crowd of men rushed forward to kick and stab the corpse in fury before stumbling away, their vengeance sated.

Black placed us wounded in three of the APCs and we rumbled back to Cu Chi while the other tracks remained with our platoon to guard the enemy prisoners. At the field hospital, a corpsman separated us into groups, with some rushed on stretchers straight into the operating rooms, Deputy Dog among them. Del was the first of our group called into the emergency room. Silverstein and I followed a few minutes later. A surgeon looked at my wound as a nurse washed it out with a strong smelling liquid. With my attention diverted, another nurse jabbed a needle in my right arm. As I turned to protest, the other nurse stabbed my left arm.

"*Damn*! This is worse than the firefight," I groaned as blunt instruments dug into my flesh behind me without warning. An instant later, he held a bloody piece of misshapen lead before my eyes.

"Want a souvenir?"

"Sure." I replied, recognizing it as one of our own M-16 rounds.

"The nurse will clean it up for you." The doctor dropped the lump of metal into a small pan with a clatter and issued rapid instructions to one of the nurses before turning to the next table. After my shoulder received another cleaning, the doctor returned to stitch the skin together and the nurse handed me a swab of cotton with the bullet inside. Within five minutes of entering the operating room, a corpsman pushed me down a narrow corridor in a wheelchair and deposited me in one of the long wards. There, a nurse assisted me into one of the silly gowns before popping two pills in my mouth and steering me to a bed. As the pills took effect, I was vaguely aware of a corpsman depositing Del into the bed next to me.

———

Reno happily left us two days later for the less formal surroundings of the Wolf's Den. Jerry and Bernie visited us every day with glowing descriptions of the celebration we were missing. On each visit, they smuggled in a beer for us, which we hid out in the latrine to drink. From them we learned we annihilated Tiger Woman and twenty-one members of her band that night, in addition to taking thirteen prisoners. Her force killed six of our own and wounded fifteen. Three of the wounded, Deputy Dog among them, were being shipped stateside. The platoon she originally attacked lost nine men killed and seventeen wounded. They also informed us the Mech dragged Tiger Woman's body behind one of their APCs back to the base camp and hung her up by her heels from one of the rubber trees outside the fifth wire to rot.

Silverstein and I hobbled down to Deputy Dog's ward pushing Del in a wheelchair and stood around his bed as he labored to breathe. When his ward nurse ran us off, we returned to our beds to lay in silent grief during the hour the battalion conducted a memorial service for our KIAs back in the unit area.

Later in the day, our commander appeared to pin Purple Hearts to our gowns and say his goodbyes following his change of command ceremony. Each of us fumbled for words to convey what he had meant to us over the months, but none did an eloquent job of it. As we shook hands, he extracted promises to support our new captain as we had him, and made us swear we would visit him at Division Headquarters. All knew we never would since privates did not wander those hallowed halls, but we felt he would welcome us if we did.

Late that afternoon Jerry charmed his way past our evil nurse and hurried to me grinning in anticipation. "Come, fool, we gotta talk." He led me to the end of the ward. "I ain't got a lot of time because we're departing on an extended operation for a week, but before I go, what would you like most in the world?"

I swooned. "I'm going home?"

He frowned. "No, dumb ass, better than that."

I shrugged. "What then?"

His eyes sparkled. "A letter, maybe?"

"From Betty Jean?"

He scowled. "Who the hell is Betty Jean?"

"Who then?"

He smirked. "I wrote Gail."

My heart skipped a beat. "Sandy?"

My stomach did flip-flops as he handed it over. I took it with trembling fingers, read my name and hers in neat, looping letters, and then held it to my nose to savor her faint fragrance.

"Well, read the damn thing," he demanded. "I ain't got all day!"

"Now?" I looked over my shoulder as Del and the nurse watched us suspiciously.

"Come on, I gotta know if she mentions Gail," he pleaded.

I peeled the flap open and read the handwritten words as heat rose within me.

Jerry quivered at my side. "Well?"

"She said Gail was writing you now. Yours will probably be here tomorrow."

"I'll be in the *field* tomorrow," he groaned. "What else did she say?"

"None of your damn business!"

"But she *did* say Gail was writing? Let me see," he begged, snatching at the letter.

"She said they heard about our fight with Tiger Woman all the way in Saigon."

He made another grab at the letter. "What else? What did they hear?"

"They're just worried about us. Read your own, damn it."

"I *can't*, it ain't *here* yet, dumb ass! But I'll let you read it if I can read yours now."

I laughed as the nurse glared at us. "No way."

"I love her," he swore.

I frowned. "Sandy?"

"No, fool, Gail."

"Oh, me too."

He grinned. "Gail?"

"No, fool, Sandy!"

We howled raucously, overcome with excitement, which got Jerry ejected on his ear by the stern nurse and allowed me to settle down on my bed to reread the letter, lingering over every word as I inhaled her aroma through the pages and conjured images of her impossible blue eyes and silky halo of hair.

"What are you smiling at?" Del demanded with a lecherous grin. "Jumping out of airplanes?"

I held my middle finger aloft for his inspection as haunting memories swept through me. A postscript mentioned she had a friend recently assigned to the 25th and that if I was ever near the hospital I was to look her up and say hello for her. I approached the night nurse to inquire about the name mentioned, was informed she worked two wards down, and received permission to carry a message to her. When I first entered the ward, the nurse demanded to know why I was roaming the corridors. After showing her Sandy's letter and explaining she asked me to look her up, she insisted I come back at 2300 hours when she had all of her patients bedded down for the night so we could talk more, and even accompanied me back to my ward to clear the visit with my own headmaster. At eleven on the dot, I slipped out of my sleeping ward and returned to hers. She seated me in a chair and poured us a cup of coffee as we chatted about her and Sandy for half an hour. The field phone rang, she answered, smiled, and extended the object to me.

"It's for you," she said, and walked of to the end of the ward.

I lifted the set to my ear. "Hello?"

"Jay?"

Chills washed over me from the whispery voice filling my ear. "Sandy?"

"Jay, you've been hurt again!"

"It's nothing. Just a scratch."

She sighed. "Oh, Jay! Jerry wrote Gail and told her about the minefield so I wrote to check on you."

"Yeah, I got your letter today."

"Barb called earlier. She thought you and I might like to talk."

"She's a super lady. She never even told me."

"How badly are you hurt, Jay?"

"It's nothing, just a small hole in the shoulder. I'll be out of here in a couple of days."

"I wish I could see you."

"If only there was a way," I whispered, yearning for her touch.

"I wish you could come to Saigon on R and R, or that we could go to Vung Tau together."

"I'd love that."

"I miss you, Jay."

"God, I miss you too, Sandy."

"Please be careful."

"Always," I assured her. I held the phone a minute longer, unable to find adequate words to express the emptiness and longing I felt.

"Bye, Jay. Take care of yourself."

"I will."

The click on the end of the line was louder than any bullet I ever faced. I wanted to shout into the phone, to pull her voice back. Why hadn't I told her I loved her, I flailed myself in remorse. Sandy's friend approached and I nodded my thanks, too emotional to speak.

She hugged me. "Damn, an infantryman." She shook her head. "I always gave her credit for having better sense."

I grinned. "We're not so bad."

She hugged me again. "I suppose not, once you've had a bath. But you're all crazy and not worth one moment's heartache. Now get off my ward."

"Yes, Ma'am, and ... someday I'll find a way to thank you for that."

"You just make my friend happy."

"Count on it."

She smiled. "Get!"

My spirit soared as I returned to my ward amid dreams of Sandy and those bittersweet days in Taipei, Taiwan.

CHAPTER 22

Living this life of luxurious nothingness while my buddies were in the boonies eating cold C-rations coated with grease, smelling of unwashed bodies, mosquito repellent, and dung-infested mud, was driving me crazy.

I envisioned them easing down some shadowy trail, eyes narrowed in concentration as they searched for the invisible wire that waited to steal a foot from the unwary, ears strained for the inaudible rustle of the top of a spider hole lifting a few inches to slip the muzzle of a rifle through. In resignation, I searched out my favorite model in the much passed around copy of *GOOD HOUSE-KEEPING*, who had a slight resemblance to Sandy, at least close enough to stir vague recollections, and discovered some jerk had drooled on her face.

In despair, I laced my hands behind my head and stared at the ceiling letting the air stream out in a long drawn out sigh of boredom. It seemed unreal that in the middle of a war zone one could pick up a phone and call another person in another theater of war. Of course, it had been an official Army phone connecting all the hospitals together, but who could question it hadn't been official since it helped speed a first rate, top notch, hard nosed infantryman along the road to recovery and return him to the war effort days ahead of schedule. Hell, I'd gladly go back into combat this very day for another one of those short calls.

As I daydreamed, I tuned in to the steady thumping of rotor blades arriving and departing from the hospital helipad. Though they flew in at all hours of the day and night with their grisly cargos, today they had a different beat, coming in faster, one behind the other, and hardly pausing on the pads to discharge their load before rising again. My curiosity piqued when the nurses and orderlies disappeared from the ward.

With our gatekeepers gone, I couldn't resist the opportunity. "Let's see what gives."

"I'm game," Silverstein agreed.

"We're restricted to the ward," Del reminded us lazily.

I indicated the empty nurses' station. "Who's to stop us?"

Del yawned. "I'll pass."

I grabbed a wheelchair. "We need you as a decoy."

"No way," he protested as I pressed him into the chair and pushed him out, where a prune faced nurse immediately accosted us in the corridor.

"Where do you think you're going?"

Silverstein hesitated. "Uh, to the, um ..."

"X-ray," I injected. "We were told to take him to x-ray."

"You're going in the wrong direction," she snapped impatiently as she turned down the corridor in the opposite direction. "Follow me!"

"*No way!*" Del protested as I wheeled him around to follow her.

"*Quiet,*" I shushed. "I *could've* told her we're taking you to surgery to have your gangrenous leg removed!"

She turned us over to the technician there, and we patiently waited for Del to get x-rayed.

"Take me back to the friggin' ward!" Del insisted as I wheeled him back down the corridor. "I ain't by god undergoing no more friggin' examinations!"

Using an alternate route, we arrived in the emergency waiting room to find forty or more men lying on stretchers or sitting with heads lowered, each covered with dirty, blood-soaked bandages, their faces drawn beneath bloodshot eyes staring into space.

"Hey," I greeted three men sitting together.

Their dull eyes took in our robes and bandages. "Hey," one with a grimy bandage covering an area that had once held his ear responded.

"What happened?"

"Got our ass kicked."

"Where?"

"Boi Loi Woods."

"Nasty place," I observed.

"No shit. How about you guys?"

"Got our ass kicked out in the Rubber Plantation," I said.

The second man, wearing a bandage over one eye and another on his arm, looked up. "You guys them Wolfhounds?"

"Yep."

"No shit? Hear tell you doggies got the *bitch*."

"More or less," I affirmed. "Truth be told, a lot of *getting* was done on both sides."

"Hey, Al, Ben, these guys got Tiger Woman!"

"Way to go!" "All right!" his pals greeted us.

"What did you guys hit, an NVA Army?"

"Worse," he responded. "The damned Ghost Regiment."

"The 9th, the *real* 9th?" Del asked in awe.

"The one and only," he affirmed. "Bad assed dudes, let me tell you."

"So I hear," I replied. "They ambushed our unit a few months back and we've been looking to settle the score ever since."

"Us Golden Dragons aim to have another go at the bastards ourselves," he vowed. "They caught us by surprise this time."

"Hear tell that's the way they operate," Del stated. "They ain't never where you expect them to be, and always where you'd least friggin' expect them to be."

"There it is," the man agreed.

"See you around," I called as I wheeled Del around and pushed him back to our ward.

"In twenty years they've never been defeated," I mused as we lay on our beds visualizing the battle with the famed 9th NVA Regiment. "They're damned good."

"The ARVNs won't even fight them," Silverstein swore.

Del shrugged. "Tough bastards."

"One day we'll pin them," I promised.

"Can you imagine fighting a real hard core unit just like ours instead of the VC?" Silverstein exclaimed, eyes gleaming in anticipation.

"You guys are truly nuts," Del swore.

"Toe to toe," I agreed with Silverstein. "With none of the sneaky VC shit, just us slugging it out man-o, man-o."

"And may the best man win," Silverstein approved.

"If the bastards would fight an honorable fight we'd be home in a month," I vowed.

"They're damned near our equals," Silverstein praised.

"The best the enemy has," I agreed, wondering if we'd ever have our chance at them.

―――――

Due to a shortage of beds with the influx of casualties, they released the three of us early to return to our unit on an outpatient status under the care of our Battalion Aid Station. We scrambled to change into new jungle fatigues after the nurse put fresh bandages on us and issued Del a crutch, and hurried to the front of the hospital to await transport as directed. After an hour, we decided we could just as well walk back and be drinking beer by the time the bureaucracy got us there. We set an easy pace for Del on his crutch, enjoying the sunshine after the frigid ward. We turned onto the main road dissecting the division area and ambled along beside trucks parked bumper to bumper on the opposite side with the drivers gathered in groups laughing and talking.

"Those convoys keep us in the war," Silverstein appraised. "I've always admired the truckers who make those insane weekly runs."

"You got that right," I replied comfortably, recalling the splendor of our run into Cu Chi long ago and the raw power the convoy portrayed on the move, imagining myself steering one of those five ton monsters all out down a narrow danger-infested ribbon of asphalt.

"Hey, Airborne! Hey, Jay-Jay!" a big black man called from one of the groups.

I hurried to meet him in joyous surprise. "Sammy? Son of a bitch! How the hell are you?"

He clasped my arms and danced a jig sending pains through my shoulder. "I'm fine, dude, just fine, how bout you?"

I pulled him over to Del and Silverstein. "Guys, this is the craziest bastard in the whole world. I haven't seen him since he got drunk and broke his leg trying to do a PLF off the second story of our barracks back at Gordon."

"Hi." Silverstein offered his hand. "What's a PLF?"

Sammy laughed in delight. "A Parachute Landing Fall, and I broke my wrist too."

"Everything would've worked out fine if he'd landed on his head, the fool," I joked.

Del shook hands. "Are you airborne?"

"Naw, the ol' leg ain't been much good since then, so they done made a teamster outta me now." He punched my sore shoulder. "Dude, it's good to see you again! Hey, ol' Roberts and me was in the hospital together."

"Aw man, he was solid gold." I shook my head sadly. "We three were a *team*."

"Bastard's out now, you know that?" Sammy replied. "I ain't lying! Dude got a medical discharge and is just sittin' on his butt drinking beer all day and waiting on those government checks to roll in."

"That's Roberts," I agreed, laughing. "If there was a way to beat the system he'd find it."

"What'd he break?" Del asked.

"His back when he walked us over a cliff on the night land navigation course," Sammy answered. "Hey, did Jay-Jay ever tell you dudes about the fight ol' Roberts got us in over some little ol' gal down in Augusta? Cost us a hundred dollars in damages. I ain't lying!"

I laughed. "Roberts asked her to dance and her asshole boyfriend punched him. I was going to kill the son of a bitch, but Sammy wouldn't let me."

Sammy grinned like a mule chewing briars. "*Kill* him? That dude was sittin' on your chest playing basketball with your head 'til I up and clobbered him one with my chair!"

"Who was the girl?" Silverstein asked.

"Don't know," I answered, remembering the slim little brunette playing eye games with us that far off night in some dingy bar. "She was pretty, though. After four beers Roberts thought he was bigger than the man she was with."

"Those were good times," Sammy said as I eyed his monster truck towering over us, a half baked plan taking shape.

"So now you're running supplies to Cu Chi?"

Sammy nodded. "Yeah, from Long Binh twice a week for the whole two months I been in-country. It's not a bad gig."

"And you still form up at Ton Son Nhut for the run here?"

"That's right," he affirmed. "We hav'ta hook up with the transports from the airbase."

My mind raced. "When you coming back this way?"

"Four days from now."

"How close is the hospital in Saigon to Ton Son Nhut?"

"Bout two blocks outside the main gate," he replied, eyes narrowing. "Now why you askin' that, fool? You up to no good?"

I grabbed his arms. "Can you give me a lift to Ton Son Nhut?"

"You got a pass?" he hedged.

"What do you think?"

"I think you talkin' AWOL," he cautioned.

"Only if I get caught."

He grimaced. "Man, you crazy! MP's everywhere down there—big, mean assed dudes. They'd get you fore you got a block down the street!"

"I ain't going down the street, Sammy, I'm going to the hospital."

"Not legal like, you ain't," he reasoned.

"Are you saying no?"

"Ain't sayin' yes, that's for sure, think too much of you to see you go to the stockade."

"I'd do it for you and you know that for a fact," I insisted.

"Jay-Jay, please. You don't know what it's like down there."

"I'm going, Sammy, even if I have to go to the stockade for it."

"Man, what you done got down there you gotta get at so bad?" He studied me, and then grinned. "A split tail! I do believe you got a woman there!"

"Sammy, I've *got* to go, so *you've* got to help me!"

"You won't be on the streets? You already got a place to go?"

"Of course," I lied.

"Now wait a minute, Jay, you can't go AWOL," Del protested. "This is crazy!"

"Our unit's in the field for a week, right?" I reasoned. "I'll be back in four days, so who's going to know?"

"What if you get caught?"

"What are they going to do to me, Del? Send me to Nam? Make an infantryman out of me? Bust me to private? Shoot me? Goddamn it, anything they can do has already *been* done, and they can do it all again for four days with ..."

"Now lookey here, Jay-Jay, I might can get you to Ton Son Nhut alright," Sammy cautioned. "And I might can pick you up there next Thursday, but you *still* gotta get those two blocks to the hospital and back, and they've got guards on *both* ends."

"Sammy, all I ask is that you get me to Ton Son Nhut and back here next Thursday."

"You always was a crazy bastard," he swore. "You get caught, it ain't on my head."

"Then I'm going too," Del insisted.

"Bullshit!" I retorted. "I've got enough worries without *you* hanging around my neck! Besides, you're crippled."

"I'm going with you, Jay," he insisted.

"You fools make up your minds," Sammy ordered as the drivers swung into their cabs. "Cause this here ol' train's gonna roll in about two minutes."

I glared at Del. "You're *not* going!"

"Yes I *am*, Jay, somebody's got to look after you."

"Look after *me*? You asshole, *I've* been taking care of *you* since the day we *got* here!"

"I'm *going*!" he shouted back.

"Well, I know I am!" Sammy turned to his truck. "All 'board that's comin' 'board."

"Shit! Silverstein, cover for us!" I called as I hurried after Sammy.

"You guys are nuts," Silverstein shouted as Del hobbled after me.

Sammy unlatched the double doors on the back of his frozen food trailer and shoved us up into the arctic interior, where the hollow clang of their closing encased us in total darkness as we groped to settle down on some crates, shivering in the frigid air. We lurched about in our surreal void as the column crawled through the main gate and then gained momentum in the open country as the hammering diesel propelled us rapidly forward while we clung to anything we could find for support, prisoners of our own making.

I realized this was insane and prayed we wouldn't be ambushed or blown to smithereens by one of the mines the VC frequently planted in the road, but visions of Sandy softened the lunacy, leaving only a smattering of guilt for having drawn Del into this dilemma with me. I laughed in the darkness. *The dumb shit, always following me around like a little puppy, actually thinking he was looking out for me. If the truth be known, I spend so much time looking after him I barely have time to see to myself. God only knows where he'd be if it weren't for me.*

"You're friggin' nuts, Jay!" Del shouted angrily over the roaring clamor. "*I can't believe I let you get us in such a stupid friggin' predicament!*"

Two hours later we were subjected to a period of swaying turns and pressing stops accompanied by lurching starts before hissing air brakes brought us to a prolonged halt. A moment later the rear doors swung open and intense sunlight blinded us. Sammy helped us down into the sizzling heat, which was a comfort after the refrigerated interior of the trailer.

"Good luck, dude." Sammy slapped my back as I surveyed the line of warehouses with not another person visible. "I gotta roll. Meet me right here Thursday at 1100 hours, and *don't* be late cause I *can't* wait on you." With a big grin and a wave of his arm, he double clutched and shifted gears as smoke boiled from his stack in rolling black clouds mixing with the dust curling up behind him as he departed in a growling rumble. Without a word, I turned and trudged down the dusty road absorbed by the enormity of being AWOL and lost in a strange world with no clue of my next move. The squishing of Del's rubber tipped crutch in the powdery dust punctuated my despair as he limped along behind me in despair.

A three-quarter ton truck chugged down the road, lurched to a halt beside us, and a tanned face peered out curiously. "You guys lost?"

"Sort of, we're looking for the hospital," I replied cautiously.

"Need a lift?"

"Sure!" I scrambled into the small cab and Del crawled in beside me holding his crutch out the window with the tip resting on the running board.

The driver shifted gears around my knees and rattled off. "Hot, ain't it? Which infirmary you looking for?"

"The hospital in Saigon," I replied.

"Oh, well, I can drop you near the gate, okay?"

"Appreciate it," I said.

A few minutes later, he pointed down a narrow street. "That's the main gate there."

"Thanks," I called as we climbed out and he clattered away.

I eased down the street and paused fifty yards short of the rolls of concertina wire with the sandbagged guardhouse planted in the middle of the road as Del hobbled after me.

"What now?" he demanded as I watched the MPs checking the vehicles and passengers entering and leaving.

I shrugged. "Let's get in the shade over there and study the situation."

Del limped over and sank down wearily beside me as I observed the operation, noting the MPs were all business in checking each man for his pass and searching each vehicle for contraband. It looked hopeless, but with Sandy only two blocks away, I took a deep breath and started for the checkpoint. "Come on. Act dumb and let me do the talking."

"What do you have in mind?" Del asked as he stumbled after me.

"I've a mind to go to the hospital even if I have to get shot again to do it," I replied grimly. "You just keep your trap closed and let me handle things. Understand?"

I paused in front of a barrel-chested MP watching us with hooded eyed interest. "Hi, can you point us in the direction of the hospital?"

He glanced down the street. "Two blocks down on the right."

I edged to the side to pass. "Thanks."

He stepped in front of me. "Got a pass?"

Someone must have tried that maneuver before, I thought bleakly as I summoned my ultra innocent voice. "Do we need a pass to go to the hospital?"

"Either that or an appointment slip," he replied.

"We're just going to visit a friend," I bluffed, thinking *tough bastard*.

He held out his palm. "Then I assume you have got a pass."

"Where do you get a pass from?" Del inquired.

I sighed in dismay as the MP's eyes narrowed. "Where are you from?"

"Cu Chi," Del replied as I grimaced.

"You AWOL?" the MP asked.

I knew the game was over and considered running, but reluctantly gave up the thought with Del's bum leg. "Look, we just wanted to visit one of our buddies. Forget it, okay?"

"Not so fast, hot shot," he growled as his huge paw latched onto my left shoulder and jerked me around. "We ain't finished yet."

I yelped and stumbled onto one knee, milking the pain for all it was worth and hoping like hell Del would hobble off with the big man distracted.

The MP released me, alarmed. "What's wrong with you?"

"My shoulder," I whined.

"He got shot a few days ago," Del scolded as he hobbled over to me.

"Shot? Why ain't he in the hospital then?"

Del propped the crutch under his arm and helped me up. "We were until this morning."

"You been shot too?"

"No, I was born with a crutch under my arm," Del snapped as he pulled the top of my shirt back to examine my shoulder. "You're bleeding."

The MP eyed us anxiously. "Bleeding? You guys better come inside."

I played the pain to the hilt in hopes of coming out of this alive as Del helped me inside to a chair and took a closer look at my shoulder. "I think you ripped his stitches out," he accused, turning to glare at the MP. "*Now* can we go to the friggin' hospital to get him looked at? All we wanted was to visit a friend who's being medevacked back to The World in a few days. We don't know about passes and shit because we've never been here before."

The MP licked his lips and shifted nervously. "How did you get here from Cu Chi?"

"We flew down with our First Sergeant this morning and are supposed to meet him back at the helipad at 1800 hours," Del lied smoothly.

"Why didn't he give you a pass?"

"Hell, *he* didn't know we had to have a friggin' pass to go to the friggin' hospital either," Del chided as I held my breath, my admiration growing as he manipulated the big man. "That's some crazy shit!"

"Well, I guess I can see how you guys out in the boonies wouldn't know that," the MP mused hesitantly. "Tell you what, I'll give you a pass until 1800 hours and run you down to the hospital myself. I won't be on shift then, so you'll have to make it back on your own."

"Hell, it's *only* two blocks," I scoffed, grimacing for effect as my heart raced.

He scribbled on some paper as Del and I rolled our eyes at each other, spoke to the guard on the opposite side of the little room, rushed out to a shiny jeep with whip antennas on the back, and lurched alongside for us to scramble aboard. In a neck snapping surge, we leapt into the heavy traffic outside the gate and charged down the street. Two blocks later, we swerved through a concertina and sandbagged gate, sped by the MPs there without slowing down, and skidded to a stop before the main entrance of the massive hospital building.

"Sorry about the shoulder," the MP apologized as we scrambled out. "Get it looked at, okay? Hope your buddy makes it home safe. Good luck to you guys!" He charged off in a shower of gravel as we stood looking after him in shock.

"*Hot damn, we made it!*" I shouted.

Del scowled. "Yeah, so *now* what?"

I turned to the double doors. "Would you stop that shit, for Christ's sake? How the hell do I know? Just follow my lead."

We approached a large counter with an efficient looking nurse working behind it.

"Yes?" she inquired without looking up.

"Ma'am, can you tell us how to get to the, uh, bits and pieces ward?" I asked.

She looked up. "Bits and pieces?"

"Yes, Ma'am," I confirmed.

"Who are you looking for, young man?"

"A friend."

"His name?"

"We don't know his name," Del replied as I hesitated.

She frowned. "How's that?"

"We know what he looks like," Del said. "He saved our life and we want to thank him."

"Well, you can't go around looking at everyone in the hospital. How was he wounded?"

"Both legs were blown off," I supplied.

"Oh my, that would be the Traumatic Amputee ward," she decided, and gave us directions.

We departed the main building and turned right through rows of smaller ones as directed until we arrived at one in the rear. I paused in front of the double doors and licked my lips, suddenly feeling foolish.

"Well?" Del demanded.

"Maybe we should wait out here until she comes out," I suggested.

"*What*?" he shouted. "I don't friggin' *believe* you! You browbeat a friend into smuggling us halfway across Vietnam, go AWOL in the process, bluff your way through *two* MP check points and a head nurse to get here, and now you want to *chicken shit* out?" He hobbled over to the steps, sank down in disgust, and rubbed his injured leg as he muttered to himself.

I sighed. "Okay, we'll go in."

He placed the crutch under his arm, opened the door, and grandly swept his arm forward. I elbowed my way past into the cool, subdued interior and paused at a nurse's station as I studied the rows of beds occupied by bandage encased men beyond her, my senses assaulted by the heavy smell of disinfectant.

A nurse seated behind the low counter looked up. "Yes?"

"Ma'am, we're looking for, uh ..." I groped.

"Sandy," Del supplied as he squeaked up behind me.

"Wait in there, please." She indicated a small room across from her.

Del flopped into a chair and picked up a magazine as I paced near the window seriously considering darting out before it was too late, the foolishness of my actions astounding me. How could I have been so dumb? Sandy would not appreciate my intrusion into her work place, or her life, in such a callous manner. Crepe soled shoes approached the door. With heart pounding and blood rushing to my face, I stood frozen as she entered the room and stared at us in shock.

Her features softened. "*Jay!*" Her arms encircled me as her fragrance engulfed me.

I squeezed her tight to my chest. "I-I didn't have any way to warn you ..."

Del cleared his throat. "Hi, I'm Del, remember?"

"Yes, I remember," she acknowledged. "How did you two get here?"

Del smirked. "In the back of a refrigerated produce truck."

"A *what*?"

"We're AWOL," Del added as I glared at him. "No passes."

Sandy's eyes widened. "AWOL?"

"We're supposed to be in the hospital," I explained. "They had to release us early on out patient status because they needed the beds. We hitched a ride here with a friend."

"And we can't hitch a ride back with him until Thursday," Del replied, standing with difficulty. "We need a place to hide out until then."

Sandy exploded in her unique laughter. "We'll work on that," she assured us, wiping her eyes. "Technically, you're still under medical authority in a medical facility." She slid into my arms and smiled up at me. "And you obviously need special care and attention. I think we can arrange something, but it's going to cost you!" She checked her watch. "*You* can stay with me, hero, and I'll figure out something for your mouthpiece here. Go to the cafeteria two buildings down and wait for me." She kissed me, her lips sending hot thrills speeding through me.

With cups of coffee before us, surrounded by doctors and nurses in white uniforms and patients in striped robes, Del laughed and shook his head. "You're incredible."

I grinned. "Remember that when they offer us the blindfolds."

He frowned. "Jay, I'm sorry I tagged along. I guess I am a rock around your neck. I didn't know what you were getting yourself into, you know?"

"You're my cross to bear for all my past sins."

"Look, I never thought about this being awkward."

"Del, you're the biggest pain in the ass in the world. But I've never had a more loyal or trusted friend, nor one I would rather have around when I don't want anyone around."

"Thanks. So why don't I just sky out and meet you on Thursday?"

"Where do you think you'd go, dummy? These passes expire at 1800 hours. Let's see what Sandy has in mind. If she can't work something out, we'll both leave."

"You'd do that for me?"

"I'd have to. You couldn't make it without me."

"I couldn't live with myself if I messed this up for you," he vowed.

"You won't have to—I'll kill you myself," I assured him.

"God, she's beautiful."

"She's one special lady," I agreed.

"Is she in love with you?"

I shrugged. "It's hard to explain."

"But you're in love with her, right?"

I sighed. "It's sort of a day to day thing with us."

"You're a dope." He brightened. "Hey, maybe she can hide me in one of the wards here as one of the wounded."

"Yeah, Gail works in gunshot, lower anatomy," I agreed.

Sandy hurried into the cafeteria followed by a petite brunette. "This is Pat. Pat, this is Del and Jay," she introduced as Del and Pat eyed each other. "Pat's roommate is on R&R so she has an extra bunk only two doors down from us."

Del shrank back in alarm. "Hey, I can't—"

"It's *done*!" Sandy insisted. "Pat will behave herself. Won't you, Pat?"

"Scout's honor," she promised as Del blushed.

"I've arranged to be off duty until Thursday," Sandy continued. "I pulled some strings and you two are officially logged in here for specialized treatment now, so the AWOL problem is solved. Let's grab a quick bite to eat before we smuggle you up to our quarters."

We dined in the cafeteria, with Pat carrying Del's portions on her tray as he hobbled along beside her. By the end of the meal, they were laughing and talking as if they'd known each other for years. Afterwards, we tiptoed down the hall of the nurse's quarters with the girls scouting to the front and rear and encountered a brief scare on the second floor when we were forced to hide in a mop closet for a few nerve wracking moments while Pat conversed with her supervisor inches away on the opposite side of the door. Jammed together inside, I stood on Del's foot and he bit my shoulder to squelch the laughter brought on by our predicament. When the woman moved on we scampered safely up to the third floor, where Del hurried into Pat's room as I slid in behind Sandy to hers.

I appraised the high-ceilinged, old-fashioned dormitory space from the French colonial days, complete with moldy walls and peeling strips of paint, and the large, outdated bathroom situated just inside the door. One small window centered on the rear wall held an air conditioner jammed into the lower half. A table with a two-burner hot plate and stacks of canned goods separated two army beds and another held an expensive stereo.

"That's Gail's bunk," she said as she slid into my arms. "She's staying with a friend to give us some privacy, though I expect we'll see her tomorrow since she's dying to hear about Jerry. I can't believe you're really here."

"It all happened so fast I can't believe it myself."

"I'm so glad you are," she whispered as her lips sought mine. "Now hurry up and get in the tub, hero. You smell like cabbages and rotten oranges." She shoved me through the door of the bathroom, where I stripped off my soiled clothes as she ran the water.

I soaked in the warmth, taking extra care with the wound, which she dressed and bandaged with supplies from a small kit, complaining that I was a big baby because I flinched a little and cried out as she applied the antiseptic. With that ordeal finished, I borrowed one of Gail's robes and a spare toothbrush. While she bathed, I settled in on her bunk listening to moody music and watching the flickering candle she lit, wondering what such a beautiful girl saw in a downtrodden grunt like me. I became morose as I thought of the platoon lying in some jungle watching the shadows while I enjoyed the pleasures of Saigon and Sandy, and then chased away the guilt with humorous visions of Del holed up down the hall with Pat. When Sandy emerged from the bathroom wearing a silk robe with a towel wrapped around her damp hair I pulled her down beside me.

"I missed you," I whispered, enjoying the sensation of just holding her again. Nothing seemed more natural. I dozed in contentment wrapped in her warm embrace as the strain of the long day eased away. Somewhere in my numb twilight, the pain and ugliness of war departed and a deep serenity settled over me that left nothing desired.

"Hey, soldier boy." She kissed me awake. "You're not getting free room and board, you know."

"What did you have in mind, pretty lady?" I teased amid warm stirrings of desire.

She peeled my robe away and slid over me, all fire. "I have it in mind to exploit your weakened condition."

"Anything for a lady in distress," I breathed as ripples of passion raced through me.

"You're so gallant and generous and kind," she teased in rhythm to her hips bringing pleasure, as she stared down at me with half lidded eyes, driving me deep into a fog-shrouded valley of sensuous heat and primitive fulfillment that turned my mind inside out and back again in eddies of swirling ecstasy.

———

I awoke to hot coffee and a radiantly beautiful woman smiling down at me.

"Morning, hero."

I stretched. "Have I died and gone to heaven?"

"I think I like you better all shot up," she teased as she nibbled my ear. "Have you heard from your girl back home?"

"Yes, she met someone."

"I'm sorry."

"I met you, so I have no reason to complain."

She snuggled in against me. "At least now I don't have to feel guilty about being the jaded woman in your life."

"I've never known anyone like you before."

"You're still young. You'll go home soon and forget about me."

"What if I don't want to forget about you?"

"We have no tomorrows, remember?"

"What if I want tomorrows?"

She tightened. "Where are you going with this, Jay?"

"I want more of you than just today, Sandy."

She shifted. "Jay, please don't do this to me. I can't bear the thought of something happening to you ... of giving you my heart and ... let's just take it one day at a time, okay?"

"Can we still pretend to be in love?"

"My hero," she whispered, her lips searching for mine.

"My jaded lady," I whispered back, filled with wonder.

Later we sat in our robes sipping coffee as I stared into her eyes, memorizing every detail for the looming time when memories would be all that remained of her.

In early afternoon a tapping at the door produced Gail carrying loaves of bread, bottles of wine, slices of cheese, and cold cuts. We invited Del and Pat over for the feast, with Del looking as silly as me wrapped in one of Pat's flowery silk robes. A Polaroid recorded the event as I prayed none of our buddies would ever get a glimpse of the snapshot. It was apparent Del and Pat had established a relationship beyond that of mere roommates, with him adoring her with his mooneyes while she fussed over him, propping his leg on a pillow and keeping his wine glass full, playing with his dark curls, listening attentively to every word he uttered. I smiled, thinking no one ever listened to anything Del had to say, and that Pat's attention was going to his head more strongly than the wine. He was in heaven talking nonstop about our unit and the men we served with. I sat quietly throughout while the girls plied the idiot with questions, only bothering to correct some of his grosser exaggerations. I let him have his day talking his fool head off with his very own private audience, his bubbly personality keeping us entertained throughout the afternoon.

Gail was heartsick that Jerry was not with us, but relieved to know he was well. Her eyes glowed with pride when Del related how Jerry earned the Silver Star for rescuing me from the minefield, and I was eternally grateful when his description turned the event into almost a comedy rather than the horrific hell it had been. They dispersed in late evening with each of us feeling a closeness that belied the short time we had known one another.

Sandy and I sat wrapped in each other's arms finishing off the wine and dreaming as we verbalized our images of a perfect life shared on a warm deserted island where we had everything all our own way. Together we built flowing waterfalls above lazy pools of clear spring water surrounded by trees heavily laden with fruit and beaches of fine white sand. Although we elected to have nothing of civilization, we did include one stereo and half a dozen carefully chosen albums for our one room thatched hut, and speared fish in the shallow rock strewn surf. Thinking we would in time become lonely, we included Jerry and Gail. Crowded, and craving exclusive attention from one another, we moved to the opposite side of our island to regain our privacy. Caught up in our dreams, we made love on the floor in a bed of strewn blankets and pillows listening to Rod McKuen recite: *"It doesn't matter who you love or how you love, but that you love."*

The night was ours. "This is perfect, Sandy," I breathed against her ear.

"It's not real, but I want it to be, Jay," she whispered back. "I want it to last for eternity."

"Someday, when I'm old and withered and sitting in my rocking chair on the porch of the Old Soldier's Home, I'll think of this night and cry," I promised as I held her close.

"Can I still be your nurse?"

"You will always be my nurse. Can I still be your hero?"

"You will always be my hero," she whispered as tears gathered in her eyes.

———

The next afternoon Del and I got our freshly laundered fatigues back and the four of us slipped out to the rear of the compound to picnic in the warm shade under the towering palm trees. After sating our hunger, we dozed as we listened to the Armed Forces Radio Network play the newest tunes from back in The World, resenting the swiftly passing time, our eminent departure weighing heavy on our mood. Safely back in our room, sluggish from the heat and sun, we made love, each demanding and desperate to satisfy a need far beyond the physical one. Exhausted, we slept with our sweaty bodies meshed together, our hair matted to our foreheads. I awoke in the deep of night with Sandy clinging to me.

"Don't go back," she begged.

"I have to," I whispered.

"Oh please, Jay! You'll be killed. I know it!"

"I *will* come back."

"I'm sorry. I didn't mean that."

"I know."

"I already miss you," she whimpered.

"I'll carry a part of you with me every minute I'm away to marvel at on dark nights."

"Get out of the infantry."

"No."

"Why?"

"That's what I am."

"You don't have to be," she insisted.

"You don't understand."

"I'm sorry."

"I need you so much." I squeezed her to me.

"Show me, Jay, show me!"

We made love again, emotion alone driving our need, and then lay wrapped in one another content that we were as close physically as we were spiritually. A growing hollowness built within me as the hours slipped away, locking me in the depths of desperation as I half slept clinging to her.

The following morning we bathed together and made love in languid, sensuous gasps, fearing the moment to be our last. We parted bravely, each leaving part of our heart with the other, each promising to write. Then we rushed back together throwing bravery to the wind, me clutching her grimly, she clinging in quivering tears, our lips grinding against each other attempting to sate our appetites for a lifetime. At the last possible moment, Del and I climbed into the back of the army ambulance Sandy had arranged to sneak us back onto Ton Son Nhut and crowded the tiny windows on the back doors for a last glimpse as we turned through the gate and roared through the crowded streets. Only then did we collapse back to stare at one another.

"Thanks, Jay."

"This is private," I cautioned, aware of his tendency to brag.

He shrugged. "I know. Nobody would believe me anyway."

"True," I agreed. "I don't believe it myself."

He grinned. "Me, either." His eyes filled with hope. "Will we come back, Jay?"

"We'll have to take it one day at a time and see, I guess."

"They'll be long days, Jay."

"Not as long as the nights," I warned, recalling the pain of long hours of stressful vigilance with nothing to occupy my mind but memories of something that tore my heart out.

———

The ambulance dropped us off inside Ton Son Nhut near the line of warehouses and we strolled down the road holding the gathering column of vehicles until we spotted a relieved Sammy. He issued us flak vests, rifles, and steel pots after informing us we would ride shotgun back, with Del in the truck behind us.

"Was it worth it, Jay?" Sammy questioned.

"Sammy, if there is ever anything in this world you need, I mean *anything*!"

He grinned. "It was worth it."

"There is one more thing you can do for me, though."

"Name it, Jay, you know it's yours."

"I want to drive this beast back to Cu Chi."

"*What?* Now, now, you just wait a minute here, Jay-Jay!"

"Come on, Sammy. This is the only chance I may ever get."

"Jay, this bitch has twenty-eight forward gears and weighs twice as many tons. I went to school for months to learn how to handle it. You can't just climb aboard and *drive* it!"

"Shit, Sammy, I don't care how many gears it has. You just tell me when to push in the clutch and *you* can shift. I just want to steer the mother down the road. How difficult is *that*?"

"Oh man, you gotta be crazy! There's *no* way!"

But of course Sammy could never turn me down. Hell of a good man. Within the hour, I was thundering down the winding ribbon of asphalt in a column that stretched for a mile through hostile country with Sammy yelling in my ear to do this and do that, gears grinding and double clutching as we churned through the countryside boiling smoke and trailing clouds of dust. That monster truck could flat out get down the highway. The thrill of the invincible convoy gripped me again and I lived another of my wildest fantasies as we flashed through the villages and along the fields of rice with children crowding along our path waving and cheering. The hammering diesel engine captured my soul, filling me with an exhilarating freedom. I yelled and waved my clenched fist as we rumbled along in our numbing charge, my voice lost to the wind. Tired, hot, covered with dust and sweat, we parted company with Sammy at the entrance to the battalion area, where we hugged like long lost brothers as we exchanged sad farewells.

Del and I watched as he rumbled off in hissing air and bellowing smoke, his arm raised out the window in a farewell salute. I said a silent prayer to see him through the months of ambushes and land mines he still had to face. Somehow, I was sure he would make it ... but a month later I learned he didn't, bless his beautiful soul.

CHAPTER 23

The next morning I reported to Top as directed somewhat worried that he had discovered I had gone AWOL, but relieved that Del wasn't summoned with me. Top motioned to a chair beside his desk.

"How was Saigon?" he asked without preamble.

"What do you mean?" I evaded uneasily.

"I understand you and Delarosa had to have some sort of special treatment there. Is all well with you now?"

"Couldn't be better, Top," I gushed, somewhat relieved, but unsure of exactly what Sandy had reported back to our field hospital in Cu Chi. "I should get the stitches out in a couple of days and be fit as a fiddle again."

"Great." He fixed me with a bland stare. "So where do you want to be reassigned?"

I stared at him, stunned. "I-I ... don't want to be reassigned anywhere."

"You want to stay here in the animal platoon?" he demanded.

I fought back a surge of panic. "*I'm* not going to the *animal platoon*!"

"Have you got any skills?"

"S-Skills?" I choked.

"Can you type or anything?"

"Type? W-What are you talking about?"

"You're being reassigned to rear duty."

I gulped. "I-I'm *what*? Rear duty? *Bullshit*! I'm not a goddamned *REMF*!"

"Division policy—two wounds and you're out of combat—Commanding General's directive."

"Well, he's full of *shit*!" I argued in alarm. "I'm staying *right here*! I'm an *infantryman*, not some *jerk-clerk*!" I glowered over my shoulder at the two clerks, who ducked their heads and busied themselves at their desks.

Top half smiled. "Black said you would probably say something like that."

"What's *he* know?" I scoffed, fighting through my distress. "But I'm staying *here* all the same anyway!"

"Okay, sign here." He slid a sheet of paper in front of me. "I'll have to get it approved, but it shouldn't be too much of a problem."

I took the sheet of paper. "What's this?"

"A request for a waiver of the two wound policy," he explained. "Once it's been approved it's irreversible, so be sure about it."

I signed my name and lurched for the door as waves of relief swept through me.

"Oh, by the way," he called after me. "Sergeant Black seems to think you've also got the makings of a noncommissioned officer. Based on his recommendation, I'm requesting a waiver of your time in grade.

Congratulations—you'll soon be the Army's newest Corporal."

———

The company returned from the boonies two days later and as the wild beer bust and barbecue rolled along I tucked a six-pack under my arm and led Jerry away to the quiet of the rubber trees to tell him of my trip to Saigon. He was envious beyond consolation and made me repeat every word Gail uttered. I even made up a few as he sat with eyes closed dreaming of the lost opportunity.

When we rejoined the others, I listened to glowing accounts of the Ghost Regiment which our company had chased since their clash with the Golden Dragons. They fought elements of the withdrawing enemy force off and on for a week before they slipped back across the border into their Cambodian sanctuaries to regroup. From all accounts, the famed enemy regiment fought well. All deemed their discipline and conduct worthy of respect and I was secretly pleased they had slipped away so I could have the opportunity to go against them myself someday and match steel and nerve, courage and resolve, in a pitched battle of maneuver instead of the agonizing hit and run brushes with the local VC.

The next day Black stepped up to the First Sergeant's job. In his farewell address, he insisted he had nursed us enough to last him a lifetime and swore we were the sorriest excuse for soldiers he had ever led, but the tears trickling down his cheeks said otherwise. Afterwards he got drunk as a skunk and made a complete ass of himself hugging and slobbering over us, and we loved him the more for it.

After Black passed out we journeyed to the Wolf's Den where our company of happy, drunk Wolfhounds soon turned things to chaos until four NCOs appeared to help maintain order. With our fun spoiled, we grabbed extra beer and headed to the hooch to close out the night, where I found a huge black man lying squarely in the middle of my bunk with his hands clasped behind his head. I looked incredulously at my gear stacked in a neat pile on top of my footlocker in the middle of the aisle as the rest of the hooch members scrambled for choice positions.

"*Hey, you!*" I shouted at him. "That's *my* bunk!"

His eyes fluttered as he gazed up at the canvas ceiling.

I kicked the railing. "What I'm *saying* here is, get your fat ass off *my* bunk!"

He graced me with a brief, contemptuous glance.

I looked back at the grinning faces as money passed hands and odds were called out, pleased with the points given in my favor. "Hey, asshole, are you deaf as well as dumb?"

The man sat up and swung his legs over the edge of the bed.

"I told you, goddamn it, you're—" I was suddenly standing with my head tilted back looking up into his frowning face and realizing he almost had to stoop to stand in the hooch. *Oh shit.* I blinked as he squinted at me with nostrils flaring and in the background heard new odds called out at a frantic pace. "You, uh, you're, uh, on my, uh—"

Bloop! My feet lifted off the floor desperately trying to follow my body sailing backwards across the hooch. I landed on Jerry and Bernie in a tangle of arms and legs, shook my head to clear the fog as my ears rang, and focused on the black mountain standing across the aisle staring with disinterest at a half-pint Del crouched in front of him.

Bloop! Del arched across his bunk and landed on Silverstein sitting on his bunk on the other side, upturning both. Jerry and Bernie braced on each side of the giant eyeing him as I scrambled to my feet and spit blood from my split lips.

Bloop! *Bloop*! A right and a left followed each other in quick succession. I gulped as the placid eyes settled back on me even as my two buddies skidded down the aisle in different directions and backed up a step contemplating the feasibility of jumping through the screen side of the hooch if the beast came after me. Reno backed down the aisle as the man turned to him and dropped the short club he held as Harley scurried to help Jerry. I eased over to Bernie slumped against the wall, eyes glazed, nose gushing blood, as every eye in the hooch looked elsewhere when the *man-ster* stared at each in turn. Sighing in satisfaction, he walked over to *his* bunk, lay down, and laced his fingers behind his head as he stared up at the ceiling.

Seething with rage, I wiped my bloody chin and edged over to my footlocker as the others watched apprehensively. I hefted a grenade, looked at the man lying on *my* bunk, smiled at him through my bloody mouth, hooked a finger through the ring, and pulled the pin, keeping the handle depressed.

"Holy shit!"

"Ohhhh, hell!"

"Let me out of here!"

"That mother's crazy!"

"Outta my way!"

In the blink of an eye the black man and I had the place to ourselves as stampeding bodies crashed through the doors on each end. The Goliath watched as I walked over with blood trickling down my chin. His paws eased from behind his head and his eyes narrowed as I sat on the edge of the bunk next to him and held the grenade up for his inspection.

"Tell you what, pal," I sputtered. "We'll play a little game. When I release this handle, this thing will explode in precisely four and a half seconds. The last man sitting here gets the bunk. Fair enough? We'll count together. You *can* count, can't you?"

His eyes widened as I lifted my little finger away from the charging handle. He sat upright as I lifted my ring finger away. As my middle finger lifted away he scrambled off the end of the bunk insuring he didn't bump against me.

I gave him my most malicious grin while holding the grenade suspended by thumb and forefinger. "Hold on, pal, I haven't started counting yet—I have to release the handle first."

He turned and busted through the screen door in a shower of splinters, leaving the hinges in place, and tossed the warped frame aside as he leapt over the top of the sandbag wall. His head reappeared at the end of a line of equally astounded faces watching me. The row of heads sank lower in unison as I walked to the shattered door.

"You don't want to play the game?" I asked as I scooped the discarded pin off the floor, reinserted it into the slot, and tossed it onto *my* bunk. I piled his junk on his footlocker, shoved it into the middle of the aisle, and pulled my own back into place as the others trickled back into the hooch. I rearranged my gear into its rightful place as Jerry, Bernie, and Del gathered their battered mugs around to slap my back and others paid off their wagers.

The big man entered last, paused inside the door to stare at me, and then walked to the center of the hooch, stooped to lift Phil's empty bunk into the air intact, turned, and walked back up the aisle as men on each side ducked. He snaked his foot out to kick Del's bunk against Silverstein's and placed his new bunk in the now empty spot beside me, pulled his locker to him, and sat down.

"No hard feelings?" I asked as Del and Silverstein moved their bunks down a space while scowling at his back.

He flashed a gold tooth centered amid his upper molars in the dim light at me.

"Name's Jay." I offered my hand as Jerry, Bernie, and Del watched in cold reserve. He crushed my hand in his mammoth fist and I shook the lifeless stump to restore circulation. "Don't you talk?"

He shrugged.

"Okay, I'll call you *Bloop* then, how's that?"

He grinned, his gold tooth sparkling.

———

A week later following a brief ceremony where I received my promotion to corporal, Sergeant Lunas took me to the NCO side of the Wolf's Den and bought me a bourbon and Coke.

"You're my assistant squad leader now," he said lifting his glass to me. "Welcome to the Noncommissioned Officer Corps. Normally, they reassign you when first promoted to NCO status, but I requested you stay with us and Sergeant Black agreed. You'll feel a little awkward at first when the men start treating you differently, but that'll pass soon enough."

"I don't feel any different," I replied.

"You will. The men will turn to you with their problems and expect you to know the answers. They'll look to you for direction when the shit hits the fan, but only follow you if they trust where you lead. I expect you to set the example by never asking them to do anything you're unwilling to do yourself, and to always put their best interest ahead your own. You tend to do that naturally, so it shouldn't be a problem."

"What are my duties as your assistant squad leader?"

"Take charge when I'm not around and follow orders given when I am."

The whole squad treated me to a roaring promotion party that evening in the hooch since I could no longer accompany them to the enlisted side of the Wolf's Den, nor invite them into the NCO side. Though we partied hard and long into the night, I sensed a growing distance between us that had not been there before.

Sadly, the two hash marks on my sleeves alienated me from their easygoing world and I was no longer one of them. I was in a leadership role now and deftly treated accordingly by men I once knew as brothers.

The day after, Lunas formed us into a platoon formation for our new platoon sergeant.

"At ease, smoke if you've got them," he commanded, and waited patiently as we shuffled around and lit up. "I'm Sergeant Baker. I understand from Sergeant Black I've inherited a mighty fine platoon. Prior to deploying over here, I was an instructor in the Noncommissioned Officer's Academy. I like to do things by the book. This is my first combat assignment, and I appreciate the fact that most of you are veterans with combat experience. As such, I will rely heavily on each of you until I learn the ropes. I look forward to serving as your Platoon Sergeant." He turned and walked away.

After a startled moment, Sergeant Lunas released us and hurried after him.

"What do you make of that?" Silverstein mused in the silence.

"Well, he didn't threaten us or call us dumb shits," Bernie observed hesitantly.

"He seems indecisive as hell," Jerry judged.

"*He's* going to lead *us* into friggin' *combat*?" Del demanded contemptuously. "Hell's bells, I always feared Black more than the friggin' VC."

"Lunas will help him get his shit together," I offered lamely.

The next morning Sergeant B called us to attention as a second lieutenant about twenty years old, but looking fifteen, approached and exchanged salutes with him.

"Stand at ... *EASE!*" the butter bar barked.

We shuffled about, eyeing him skeptically as I fought an impulse to raise my hand and ask him if he had a note from his mother granting him permission to be here.

"I am Lieutenant Kelly, your new Platoon Leader," he announced primly. "I understand this platoon has a good record thus far, but I want each of you to understand that in my book *good* is not enough. I want this platoon to be the *best* platoon in this Division!"

I groaned inwardly with this bit of enlightenment, thinking him high strung and ambitious—the type that wanted to be a general someday and viewed us as his ticket to the top.

"I will settle for nothing less," he continued. "In the two weeks I've been in-country, I'm somewhat dismayed at the slackness I've seen over here. This platoon is no exception. From this moment forward, you will *dress* and *act* like disciplined soldiers. You will be aggressive in your spirit and your actions as we face the enemy and defeat him in battle. Sergeant Baker, *take charge!*"

I sighed as they exchanged salutes and he did a precise about face and marched off. He'd been in-country two weeks and never heard a shot fired in anger. Training this jackass fresh out of Officer Candidate School was going to be an ordeal for us. Staying alive long enough to appreciate the accomplishment was going to be even more of a challenge. When Sergeant B released us, we clustered together in an apprehensive pack.

"Who died and made that friggin' little ninety-day wonder emperor?" Del grossed. "He's going to get us all killed!"

"He looks like Bat Man's pal Robin, the *Boy Wonder*," Bernie fussed.

"With Black to check his foolishness he might make a decent officer," Jerry allowed sourly. "But under Sergeant B, he's going to be downright dangerous. We need to watch the little bastard close so he doesn't get us *decisively engaged*, *surrounded*, and out of *ideas*."

We stood a full stateside inspection the next morning, a trying ordeal where he was upset to find none of us carried bayonets, as we each preferred the more practical survival knife. We immediately drew bayonets under Sergeant B's placid stare. Then we withstood a two hour practical exercise under Sergeant Lunas on how to put them on our stubby little M-16s and use them.

Harley drew first blood when he nicked Silverstein in the buttocks during a *long thrust and hold* maneuver, which caused quite a commotion as Silverstein proceeded to chase Harley through the rubber trees with every intention of jabbing him in the ass in retaliation. The scene was right out of the Keystone Cops, with Harley streaking along yelling for his life and Silverstein hot on his heels cursing him for every kind of mother as the rest of us ran in circles chasing first one and then the other, with Silverstein turning to chase after us on occasion. Fortunately Harley managed to escape and hide out until we could subdue the enraged Silverstein and get him drunk enough to laugh at the incident.

The rest of the company gave us hell for the bayonet practice, which resulted in a number of additional scuffles. We attempted to shrug off our new lieutenant's idiosyncrasies by assuring ourselves that once we got our new little *Boy Wonder* out in the bush he would see the pig stickers weren't necessary since we couldn't *find* the enemy half the time much less get close enough to *cut* them with a *knife*.

"*He'll learn*," became our byword.

———

Boy Wonder and Sergeant B's shakedown cruise with us occurred on a routine patrol to Nightmare Village, which we prepared for as if we were setting out to engage the 9th NVA Regiment. We stood a platoon inspection and full scale briefing for a mission we performed every third day or so in which we by now knew every tree, punji pit, and villager from the fifth wire to the hamlet, as well as the snipers we encountered, each identifiable by the well known sound of their individual weapons. We essentially considered them our allies since they had never hit any of us in the many months we had patrolled their area and actually were a little concerned that if we fooled around and accidentally killed one of them the hardcore VC might replace them with someone who could shoot. As things were, we dutifully searched their area and they obediently sniped at us. Everybody was happy. Why tamper with success? Leave the war to the outlying areas. Hell, this was our backyard. The last thing we wanted was to piss them off. When these facts were mentioned halfway through the briefing, the lieutenant spent twenty minutes telling us he didn't give a damn what we had done in the past, it was all a new game now. We were going to do things *his* way—the *right* way.

We moved meekly up to the bunker line glaring at the rest of the company watching our procession with glee, as each of us had our chinstrap fastened under our jaw and sported brand new camouflage covers with no personal markings, products of our lieutenant's new creed. We crossed the fifth wire and a thin lipped Lunas, who had gotten his ass chewed numerous times over the last couple of days trying to square away our two new nerds, ordered me to take point. Bloop fell in behind me after staring Del down and the rest of the platoon straggled into line behind them as we set out to conquer friendly, hospitable Nightmare Village for the hundredth time. I snickered when Lunas had to remind Boy Wonder to call the platoon clear of the fifth wire, which he did while trying to mask his embarrassment for having forgotten. Legally in enemy territory now, I approached the first danger area and halted the platoon as usual in order to check it out before the crossing, wherein Boy Wonder and his RTO thrashed up.

"What have you got?" he demanded.

I masked my despair. We were all of two hundred yards from the fifth wire with the bunker line still visible to our rear and *he* thought we had already found the enemy. I fought an impulse to tell him to get his silly ass back into the platoon where he belonged.

"Just checking the area," I advised, unable to keep the surliness out of my tone.

"Why? Do you *feel* something, Corporal?"

"No," I snapped.

"Sir!" he corrected.

"No, *Sir*," I replied.

"Sergeant Black says you're something of a medium and can feel the enemy."

"Well, I don't *feel* anything right now, *Sir*!" I replied irately, thinking, *except aggravated as hell that you're up here under my ass.*

"I'll cover you."

I indicated Bloop to my rear. "He does that, *Sir*."

"I'll go with you then."

Why not, I thought, maybe the bastard will fall in a punji pit. "Yes, *Sir*."

"Follow me!" he ordered as he snaked forward looking like a man sneaking up on a camp of Apaches as his RTO brushed by struggling to keep up with his erratic lieutenant.

I threw a frustrated glare at Lunas, who pointedly ignored me, and followed feeling somewhat silly. We searched the danger area without incident and he crept back to the edge of the clearing, crouched in the bushes in a heroic stance, and motioned the platoon forward. We repeated this procedure at every danger area, although he did learn to leave his RTO back with the platoon since the poor man was half-dead from trying to keep up while lugging his cumbersome radio around.

We approached the large paddy separating the rubber trees from the hedgerows a hundred yards away and I halted. Boy Wonder came hustling up the line to me and I grinned over his shoulder at Lunas and winked. Three out of five times, we got sniped at as we crossed the open space. We had grown to expect half a dozen rounds widely spaced and very high. We had searched the area a hundred times and never found anything.

The VC on the other side dutifully fired his ration of ammo and then happily went back to working his paddy as we moved through the area. I hoped the guy was alert today and not off to market or anything.

The lieutenant and I separated with fifteen yards between us and moved forward. Twenty steps into the open field three rounds streaked overhead, their pop sharp in the midmorning air. Boy Wonder flung himself to the ground on the dusty edge of the paddy as I squatted, counting the rounds, thinking, okay, that was three right off, which meant he had three more, four at the most, although one day he fired a total of ten. Boy Wonder fired a burst of six rounds before his unmodified M-16 jammed and he looked wild-eyed back at me with my rifle cradled in my arms.

"Get down!" he yelled.

I stretched out on the ground picking a grassy spot so I wouldn't get dirt on my sweaty uniform, carefully assumed a proper textbook prone firing position, and watched with interest as Boy Wonder tried to clear his weapon. He had no cleaning rod, of course—how long would it take him to figure it out?

"Cover me!" he yelled back at me, even though everything was so quiet you could hear the birds chirping.

I thumbed my safety off and spent a few rounds at a disfigured tree across the paddy to see how close I could get at this distance, pleased with my marksmanship when bark flew off the base. I looked to the lieutenant for approval, who had given up on his jammed rifle and was crawling back to the tree line now on his elbows, rifle cradled commando style in the crook of each arm. Two more carbine rounds whined overhead and he paused to duck assuming he was the target. I stood and walked in behind him dusting myself off as Boy Wonder frantically issued orders. The platoon slouched up on line under his rapid directions as the squad leaders, bypassed when the lieutenant took charge personally, looked on in puzzlement. With the platoon spaced out on each side of him, every head turned to him in open curiosity, he crouched.

"*Fix bayonets!*" he ordered.

"Do what?"

"Bayonets?"

"Huh?"

"Us?"

He glared left and right. I unfastened my bayonet along with the others and locked it in place on the tip of my muzzle, and looked back at him, thinking *this is getting interesting*.

He stared hard across the hundred yards of mud and water, steeled his nerves, raised his right arm, and charged forward yelling in a shrill voice "*Follow me!*"

All heads rotated as we watched him. Sergeant B and the RTO dashed out into the paddy behind him as two more rounds whizzed overhead adding a spot of color to the debacle.

What should we do now? I wondered. Seriously, a fixed bayonet charge by a platoon against one lone sniper who was already out of ammo and packing up to go home—did he *really* expect us to run a hundred yards across knee deep mud and water in this heat when we could walk across on the berms without getting our feet wet? The three-man attack petered out after about thirty yards as they wallowed in the mud and water behind a berm and looked back over their shoulders at us, expressions baleful.

"*Shit!*" Lunas stomped about in a fury foaming at the mouth amid a scattering of laughter rippling along the line. "*Goddamn it!* Move out! Come on, guys, *please*," he pleaded as the volume of mirth grew.

Stifling grins, we sauntered out behind him to wade into the mud and water on line holding our bayoneted rifles in the classic thrust stance. I splashed by between Boy Wonder and Sergeant B following a sloshing Lunas as he ranted and raved. In laughter, with some trumpeting the bugle charge through their throats, we assaulted the hedgerow in a derisive stroll, with Boy Wonder, Sergeant B, and the RTO dripping along behind us. Not one fired a shot during the heroic attack. Our only casualty was Silverstein, who slipped when he stepped over one of the intervening berms and sprawled headlong into the mud on the opposite side as we courageously pressed onward, not a man hesitating other than Silverstein, who sputtered around searching for his rifle in the murky water. Minutes later, dripping and howling with laughter, we clambered onto the high ground, our objective seized and victory complete.

Boy Wonder stood off to the side as Lunas directed our search of Nightmare Village, where we of course found nothing as usual, and we began our trip back without incident. Boy Wonder did not come forward to help search the danger areas on the return trip, and when we assembled in the debriefing area behind the bunker line, he stormed through our sprawled forms without a glance.

We watched his grim faced, mud encrusted figure disappear down the trail with his haggard RTO attempting to keep up as Sergeant B drew up in front of us, panting.

"You, uh, you men did fine today," he sputtered. His face turned ashen as we roared in laughter. "Dismissed!"

He limped down the trail a defeated man as Lunas stood and our laughter faded. "No part of today will ever be discussed outside this platoon. Understood?"

He and the other squad leaders hurried down the trail in a huddle talking in low voices.

Jerry sighed. "What an experience."

I grinned. "That poor old papa-san VC probably thought we were making fun of him."

Del chuckled. "I hope we didn't look as dumb as I felt."

Bernie shrugged. "Aw hell, he'll learn."

"If the bastard don't get us killed first," Reno growled.

"Ump!" Bloop agreed. Or disagreed. It was hard to tell with him.

"I'm sure as hell glad we had Lunas out there today," Jerry swore.

"The old boy's made a decent sergeant," I agreed. "Remember how he was in the beginning? I guess there's always hope."

"To hell with it," Del snorted. "Let's grab a friggin' beer."

We fell in behind him, leaving the incident forever behind us in the rubber trees.

———

A sullen Boy Wonder stood before us as a downcast Sergeant B sulked off to the side. "Today we will conduct a far ranging patrol in the Golf Course area. At dusk we will set up in an intermediary position until full darkness and then move to a crossroads for a night ambush."

When he finished briefing the radio frequencies and formations, I sat against a tree and lit a cigarette, thinking with Tiger Woman gone things were not so grim, but night ambushes were still not my most beloved duty, especially under our current leadership.

Boy Wonder stayed in his place within the platoon as we spent a long day patrolling throughout the area. We took sniper fire on two occasions and routed the enemy in both instances with artillery fire with neither side suffering any casualties during the brief encounters. The whole operation was a routine day of heat, grind, empty hooches, and old men and women tending rice paddies. The platoon seemed disjointed as we struggled along with a sense of dread waiting for something to happen. Lunas more or less ran the patrol, receiving quiet instructions only when he asked for them. Everybody felt rotten. Dusk found us sprawled around a small cluster of abandoned hooches eating a silent meal of cold C-rations.

As I scowled at the unappetizing contents of my can, Lunas squatted down in front of Del, Bloop, and me. "We got company."

I reached for my rifle. "Where?"

"Real easy like, look over my right shoulder to the left of the burned out hooch," he directed.

I focused on the broken outline of a squatting man in the thick bushes almost invisible in the gathering dusk. "Got him! I can drop him from here."

"No. Get him alive if you can." He moved to another group without glancing in the hidden figure's direction.

"You come with me, Del," I ordered as I stood and stretched. Carrying only my rifle, I started for the bushes behind me and unzipped my pants as if I were going to take a leak. A minute later Del slipped up beside me and we hurried around the perimeter keeping well inside the bushes and ensuring we approached the man from behind. Del took up a covering position behind a tree and drew a bead on him as I covered the last twenty feet one step at a time with rifle poised, and paused five feet from the man with my sights in the middle of his back.

"*Dung lai*," I called.

The man spun in disbelief and looked down the barrel of my rifle. His eyes flickered from side to side. I had seen that look before, and when he lunged I stepped forward and butt-stroked him in the gut with my rifle, slamming him into the vines with a painful gasp.

I pressed the tip of my muzzle to his temple as he withered on the ground. "*Dung lai*, mother. *You bic?*"

He bicked. His eyes rolled sideways to stare up at me as I pressed his cheek into the leaves with the business end of my rifle while Del rushed up to run his fingers along his body searching for weapons. Others joined us as Del extracted a battered wallet from our captive and passed it to Lunas. The man rolled over on his back to look up at our circle, every rifle of our Polish firing squad trained dead on him, and began pleading and pointing to the left.

"What's he saying?" Silverstein asked.

I shrugged. "Who knows, but he sure is excited about something."

The man rose to a kneeling position jabbering and still pointing to our left.

"He's trying to tell us something," Lunas guessed.

"He wants us to go where he's pointing," Del suggested.

"Probably got a nice big ambush waiting for us," Jerry ventured.

"Do you think he's Vietcong?" Boy Wonder asked.

"Shit, yes," Del scoffed.

"Probably so, Sir," Lunas advised. "He was spying on us."

The man grew silent as we mulled the situation over, and then tugged at my pants leg, jabbering again and extending his hand in the same direction.

"He's definitely trying to tell us something," I observed.

"Should we go have a look?" Boy Wonder asked.

"It's getting dark, Sir," Lunas advised, trying to guide the lieutenant to the right decision.

"Let's go see what he wants," I suggested, curiosity getting the better of my judgment.

"Okay," Lunas snapped, glaring at me. "Pick a couple of men to go with you. The rest of us will follow fifty yards back in case it's an ambush."

"Oh, thanks a hell of a lot," I whined.

Lunas smiled sweetly. "*You're* the one who wants to *go see*, Corporal."

"I changed my mind."

"I didn't. Move out."

"Shit. Del, Reno, Bloop, get your gear."

"*I* didn't wanna go see," Del fussed.

"Shut up, asshole," I grumbled. "Let's get a move on before it gets dark."

The platoon saddled up as Boy Wonder called in our intentions to the battalion, and we moved out behind the Vietnamese with the rest of the platoon following at a safe distance. I had to slow the impatient man as he hurried through the growing darkness, with us watching him and the area around us as with care. He paused once to indicate a bare patch of ground. I saw nothing but left Bloop behind as a precaution to guide the platoon around the spot as we hurried on. A hundred yards farther along, he indicated for us to be quiet. I sensed danger and debated with Del and Reno as to whether we should wait for the platoon. The impatience of the man convinced us to move on without them, at least close enough to find out what we were facing. With greater care, we crept forward, keeping away from the trail, and halted on the edge of a small clearing containing a single thatched hut with a well-tilled rice paddy on the opposite side. Crawling now on our elbows, we circled to the front of the dwelling and peeped through the bushes. Five men squatted near the entrance to the hooch, each holding a bowl. I counted three rifles propped against the mud wall near them and placed my lips against Del's ear.

"Tell Lunas to bring the platoon up on the left. We'll cover the front."

Del slid back and disappeared to the rear as Reno and I trained our rifles on the group, hearts hammering in anticipation. The man beside us whimpered as a sixth man emerged from the dark interior of the hooch dragging a disheveled woman behind him. The man who led us here laid his head on the ground, his eyes filled with pain, as the sixth man laughed and jerked the woman up beside him while speaking rapidly to the others. They joined in his laughter, and one of them grabbed the woman by her arm as she stood in passive submission before them. He ran his hand inside the elastic waist of her pajama pants as she tried to shrink away, and then slapped her across the face before dragging her behind him to the interior of the hooch.

CRACK-KAKAKA-KAK-KA!

I almost had a heart attack as Reno's rifle reverberated on full automatic a foot from my ear. The man dragging the woman spun in mid-stride as the front of his chest exploded in a shower of flesh and blood. I squeezed my own trigger and the vicious little beast danced in my hands as twin converging lines of lead caught the remaining group full force as the man Reno blasted slumped against the wall, pulling the woman down with him. Dust flew in spurts across the ground as rice bowls skittered and straw flew from the walls.

A man cried out in pain. The woman screamed and covered her face with her hands as she cringed beside her slain antagonist. Our guide ran forward as Reno and I dug for fresh magazines in unison. I counted four men down with two racing for the bushes to our left. A roar engulfed them as they met the platoon head on moving up on the side. One crumpled in a heap and the other staggered back into the clearing twitching as spent bullets whistled around us. The man who had led us here spun to the ground in the crossfire, halfway to his wife and the hooch.

In less than fifteen seconds, it was over. Six VC lay sprawled on the ground and one Vietnamese man lay in pain as the woman screamed in terror. Members of the platoon appeared on the edge of the clearing as I rushed forward to kneel beside the wounded man and Reno continued on to the woman. I wrapped one of my bandages around a jagged hole in his arm that had bone showing through the torn flesh as other men circled the VC bodies and policed up the weapons. When our new medic hurried over and knelt beside the Vietnamese man I was attending, I picked up my rifle and moved to the hooch.

Boy Wonder made his report to Battalion as Lunas and Sergeant B established a perimeter around the hooch. Battalion instructed us to remain in place for the night and forgo our ambush as I viewed the four weapons, three grenades, and canvas bag of papers and maps collected from the dead Vietcong.

A chopper evacuated the farmer and his wife the following morning. Another chopper brought our new commander and a team of intelligence types out, who carted all the bodies, papers, and weapons off before we marched back to base camp.

Boy Wonder stood before us as we sprawled in the assembly area for the debriefing. "I'm damned proud of this platoon. I know I have a lot to learn. I'm beginning to see just how much. I see now what this platoon is capable of doing. I want to be a part of it. I know I will make mistakes. I hope you will ensure they are small ones." Dead silence greeted him as he turned down the trail.

Sergeant B and the squad leaders left in a group without a word and the rest of us fell in behind them. When we reached the hooch, we were joking as the strain of the previous day and night lifted its heavy veil.

CHAPTER 24

Sergeant B summoned us to formation on an otherwise uneventful day.

Boy Wonder stepped forward as we stood at parade
rest. "The 196th Light Infantry Brigade has stumbled
across a resupply base containing tons of confiscated
rice in War Zone C. Our battalion will become part of
an extended operation called Attleboro to recover the
contraband. We will airlift into Tay Ninh Providence at
1100 hours and initially establish a perimeter around an
airstrip located just outside the 196th base camp at the
foot of Nui Ba Dinh, or *Black Virgin Mountain*. We will then
conduct sweep operations in conjunction with other
units to disrupt and eradicate Vietcong forces operating
out of tunnel complexes honeycombed throughout the
mountain. The 9th North Vietnamese Army operates
from sanctuaries situated just inside the Cambodian
border known as The Parrots Beak, a sliver of Cambodia that juts out into Vietnam and fuels the main supply
route along The Ho Chi Minh Trail into our III Corps
sector. Sergeant Baker, have the men see to their gear."

We were soon descending into a small airstrip on the outskirts of the 196th base camp bordered on one side by rice paddies and the city of Tay Ninh, and on the other three by impenetrable looking jungle. We shucked our gear and began building bunkers around the narrow asphalt runway in the shadow of a monstrous mountain covered in clouds rising out of an otherwise flat plain region. The following morning we strapped on our web gear and gathered around Sergeant B and Boy Wonder.

"Our mission today is to conduct a series of heli-borne assaults in the area surrounding Nui Ba Dinh," Boy Wonder informed us. "Bravo Company will conduct a search and destroy operation along the base of the mountain, and Charlie Company will remain here on strip alert as a ready reaction force."

After an unchallenged insertion into a tiny LZ, we waded into the deathly quiet morass of vegetation single file. The triple canopy jungle overhead screened all sound and most light from the outside world, rendering the interior ominously silent and as murky as a moonlit night. We sank to our boot tops in the decaying foliage underneath, and the surrounding flora swallowed men whole in less than five feet. Movement was impossible without chopping paths with machetes. Clouds of mosquitoes and gnats swarmed in the air as rustles and unrecognized cries from undesirables on the ground kept our eyeballs moving in all directions at maximum speed in the stale, eerie atmosphere. A short time later, we emerged into our designated LZ and sank down in relief in the relatively cool 100 degree heat, our heads swimming from the sudden exposure to oxygen and light. We lifted out for a short, refreshing flight before diving back into the pit for another quick look, a process we repeated throughout the day. In late evening, we flew back to our firebase without having found anything sinister. There we sprawled in exhaustion beside our bunkers as ragged Vietnamese children lined the wire barricades outside our perimeter and entertained us as they cavorted about squealing in delight. Reluctantly we shooed them away and settled in for the night.

The kids returned the following morning. With our company scheduled for strip alert, we faced an easy day of sunbathing and getting to know the little tykes, who eagerly wiggled their way through our barbed wire entanglements to get closer to us. We shared our C-ration breakfast with them and purchased their fruit and Cokes, which they in turn helped us devour as they donned our equipment, posed for photographs, and helped us tidy up the perimeter. We learned the children came from a nearby orphanage. Starved for affection, their antics soon filled our small compound with laughter, though we knew most had seen their families killed before their eyes by both the VC and us. Many bore ugly scars and gross disfigurements from wounds they had suffered. One who had lost a leg hobbled on crutches energetically trying to keep up with his more mobile competitors. Seeing a child bearing such vivid evidence of war was almost unbearable.

I was adopted by a little girl about seven years old who had the most beautiful face on one half of her tiny head, the other side was a wrinkled mass of scar tissue containing a colorless, unseeing eye. She pantomimed a diving jet with raging fire, a product of one of our napalm attacks. Assured of a benefactor, she shyly led a small, horribly burned boy of three to me with two thirds of his body looking like crepe paper due to the scar tissue. He clung to her hand and retreated behind her with his finger stuck in his mouth when I tried to coax him near. I finally lured him closer with a chocolate bar, which he accepted and promptly handed to his sister. She broke it in half and gave part back after storing the other half in her grimy pocket. He toddled behind her as she cleaned the empty cans and cardboard boxes strewn about and placed them in the trash bags nearby. In the evening, I prepared hot cocoa and shared my meal with them. After finishing the beverage, the boy solemnly returned the tin can I had used for a cup and lingered beside me. I sent them home at dark carrying an armload of scrounged goodies.

The next evening, following a wretched day in the inhospitable jungle, we returned to the airstrip to find the kids sitting on top of our bunkers patiently waiting for us. We were shocked to discover they had policed the entire perimeter and not tampered with one single can of rations in our absence. Stripping to our underwear to wash off the day's grime became a community affair as the kids ran back and forth carrying pails of water for us. When I finished my bath, I watched the little girl wash her brother with my bar of soap, mothering him as if he were her own. When she finished bathing him, he sat where she placed him never uttering a word and waited for her to return from dumping the water.

As I lounged in the cool evening air drinking my one can of rationed beer, the girl began preparing my meal. Once the contents were steaming, she placed the cans before me and withdrew a discreet distance with her brother. I ate a few bites of each and motioned them forward. She allowed him to eat first, finished off the remainder, and then placed the residue in the garbage bags. I made cocoa at dusk and the little boy edged over to me with hopeful eyes. When I offered him the container, he crawled into my lap and wound his arms around my neck.

———

For the next week we lived a life of comparative ease. Each day we returned from our sweeps to find our group of children waiting. The little boy followed every step I made and crawled onto my lap the minute I sat down. He still made no sounds, but the joy in his eyes upon seeing me limping tiredly from the aircraft to the bunker at the end of each day said more than the other kid's squeals of delight as they found their own particular soldiers. The girl always kept my area neat as a pin.

Tay Ninh was a happy place. Each day brought routine patrols with no enemy contact. I thought of it as almost an R&R compared to past missions. We worked hard during the day, but the time spent on the ground was short. Every third day we pulled reaction force duty while Bravo and Charlie conducted their sweeps and thus were well rested as we watched long lines of Chinook helicopters ferry the loads of rice out of the enemy supply camp into the ARVN distribution points to pass back to the civilians from which taken. I was thankful for the friendly environment fate had dealt us and spent long hours dreaming of Sandy. I received a long letter from her and wrote a short one back with a Polaroid of my two adopted kids sitting in my lap as the war passed us by.

———

I greeted a new dawn with high spirits looking forward to a lazy day lying in the sun on strip alert. Bravo and Charlie departed in swirling dust storms as I cursed the choppers blowing gear around my head. Del, Jerry, Bloop, Bernie, and Reno joined me in drowsy lassitude in my sunbathing position on top of the bunker as the children squabbled and played around us. We stripped to our underwear and browned our bodies under the burning sun while sipping Cokes and swapping raunchy lies of girls we claimed to have known back in The World.

Lunch was a family affair eaten with our kids perched all over us sharing the contents of the cans. I looked fondly at my amiable companions sitting cross-legged in a rough circle jabbering in supreme contentment as they passed around cans by their jagged, peeled-back tops. These were battle hardened men I knew more intimately than I ever dreamed possible, killers who held babies with tender ease and shared meager meals with kids they would never see again once we departed. I studied their tanned, shrunken faces lit in expressions of delight, their unkempt hair plastered to sweat-beaded foreheads, their bruises and festering sores marring muscles rippling through supple bodies, as they laughed with ease and argued without bitterness and ... shivered as a sense of foreboding crept over me.

I glanced at my rifle propped against the side of the bunker, reassured by its nearness, and looked about vigilantly. Men lay in the sun as kids played nearby and an ox cart plodded down the dirt road beside the airstrip. All was peaceful and uncaring. I fought the cold tremors trying to disallow the undeniable signals I had long come to trust as I searched for a direction, a meaning. Nothing came into focus.

I looked across our happy group. "Jerry?"

His mirth-filled eyes flashed up, his grin one of pure pleasure. The grin faded and his eyes lost their sparkle as his forehead creased in a frown. "What's wrong?"

"I don't know."

The merriment of the others dwindled as they looked up one by one. Heads turned to sweep the perimeter and search out rifles before swinging back to me.

"What is it?" Del demanded.

I shrugged, helpless to explain the premonition. "I feel something."

"Take it easy, Jay," Bernie cautioned.

I shook my head in despair. "It's there, guys."

Reno looked around, eyes narrowed. "You're giving me goose bumps, for Christ's sake."

Del groaned. "Damn! Every time that son of a bitch gets one of his stupid friggin' feelings we get our ass kicked!"

"*Ump!*" Bloop bitched.

Reno searched the distant tree line. "Hell, ain't no VC for miles!"

"Ever know the bastard to be wrong?" Bernie challenged.

Reno scowled as a decided pall settled over our little group and the children squatted quietly beside us, their expressions as serious as our own.

"Should we alert Boy Wonder?" Del asked.

"Alert him to what, shithead?" Jerry demanded. "That Jay's spooked out on us right in the middle of the whole damned 196th base camp?"

Del scowled. "What should we do then?"

"What *can* we do?" Bernie scolded. "Crawl in our bunkers and pull our steel pots down over our ears?"

Reno grabbed his rifle and checked the magazine. "*Shit*, Jay!"

"It's probably nothing," I apologized.

"Sure, asshole," Jerry snarled. "You expect us to believe that shit?"

"*Ump!*" Bloop punctuated.

In the strained silence, we passed the suddenly unappetizing cans to the children, who ate from them as they watched us with troubled eyes. The far off crackle of a radio reached us, transmitting a voice garbled in excitement. One of the RTOs summoned our commander to his bunker as electric currents flashed across the perimeter.

The field first sergeant emerged from the command bunker. "Platoon Leaders to the CP!"

"Squad Leaders, Post!" Boy Wonder yelled as he rushed by.

Lunas charged by enroute to the platoon CP. "First Squad, saddle up!"

"Thanks, asshole," Jerry grunted as he ran to his bunker.

"You could've waited until after friggin' lunch," Del grumbled as he grabbed our canteens and ran to refill them.

The tranquil scene of minutes past was now one of confusion and shouting voices as men dressed in haste. I laced my boots and grabbed my helmet off the little orphan's head as Harley rushed by and dumped two hundred rounds of machine gun ammo at my feet.

"Move it, goddamn it!" Lunas shouted as he raced by. "Reaction Force, let's go!"

As I buckled my web belt, I looked down at the little boy clutching my leg with both arms and ruffled his hair. I fished out a chocolate bar, thrust it at him, and rushed off for the LZ. The little girl ran after me yelling and waving her arms. I knelt, hugged her, pried her arms from my neck, and ran on, the danger signals pulsating now stronger than any I had ever experienced.

The blades of the aircraft sitting idle on the long asphalt strip began to turn in ever-increasing revolutions as crew members looked into little doors on the side and pulled on flak vests, helmets, and gloves as we lined up, eight men to an aircraft.

Lunas ran to our group and pointed to a circle on his map. "Charlie Company is here. They've hit a large force of bad guys. Bravo is inserting here to form a blocking force. We'll be inserted here to reinforce

Charlie Company. Bravo will be the anvil, we'll be the hammer. Questions?"

"We better carry extra ammo, Sarge," I advised. "I have a feeling about this."

Lunas scowled. "Damn it, Corporal Sharpe, what *kind* of feeling?"

I shrugged. "A real bad one."

"*Shit!*" Lunas yelled as he trotted off. "Double basic loads! *Move it!*"

We broke up into running men in every direction and grabbed extra bandoliers of M-16 and belts of M-60 ammo before reassembling before our designated aircraft, gasping for breath. Boy Wonder and Sergeant B held a hurried conversation with the huddled squad leaders as we listened to the RTO's radio while Charlie Company battled it out. Lunas ran to us and pointed to his map.

"Charlie Company was inserted into this LZ at noon and ran into a wall of fire," he yelled over the whining turbine engines. "They managed to fight their way into the wood line, but now are unable to advance or retreat. They're running low on ammo and their casualties are growing by the minute. They'll be annihilated if help doesn't arrive soon. Bravo Company is in their rear here and encountering heavy resistance. The situation is desperate. Any questions?"

We skirted Black Virgin Mountain flying an erratic course to avoid the artillery line of fire. To our front, jets and gunships dove at the jungle floor releasing high explosives and angry lines of tracers into the smoldering mass below. My gut clenched as the terrible sound of rifles and machine guns locked in mortal combat reached us in a steady drum across the distance. The choppers dipped at the ground and leveled off with the skids only feet above the trees as we raced straight for the smoke and clamor before us. We cleared a row of trees and decelerated down into the middle of the roaring fight with crackling fire chasing us to the ground. The machine guns on the right of the aircraft answered back as the left side held their fire due to Charlie Company's location. Gunships flanked us, boiling smoke from their pods, as red tracers stabbed into the jungle attempting to suppress the enemy fire and protect our line of fragile birds. One of the gunships staggered as criss-crossing green lines locked onto it sending pieces of metal flying. In the next instant, a huge fireball obliterated the stricken warship as it disintegrated. A loud *WHOMP* shook our own bird as pieces of Plexiglas showered back across us. The pilot on the left slumped forward, his face covered in rivulets of blood, and we clung to anything we could grab as the pilot on the right fought to control the chopper.

The aircraft slammed to the ground and skidded drunkenly. I tumbled out and joined a ragged line of troops charging the tree line, passing several sprawled bodies from Charlie Company's initial assault still lying where they had fallen. One of them lifted a bloody hand. I struggled to pull him to his feet and attempted to drape him over my shoulder. Bloop galloped up, swung the man over his back in one motion, and ran on without pause. Mortars dotted the LZ in harsh eruptions of dirt and smoke, chasing us into the trees where the oppressive wall of noise was deafening as we joined the fight. Bullets whined and bit into trees as I crawled forward, dragging the extra ammo, as exploding mortars threw up angry geysers of dirt amongst us as our own artillery streaked overhead, adding their muffled *CRUMPS* to the din. I found a group of men sprawled in the trees with bloody bandages covering parts of their bodies as two wounded medics crawled through them doing what they could.

One lifted his head a few inches off the ground. "Alpha?"

"Yeah!"

"Have you got medication?" he begged as bullets plucked leaves from a bush between us.

"I got ammo."

He shook his head in frustration, and I squirmed off in the direction of the raging fight anxious to leave this place of misery and death behind. I crawled to a man wearing a bloody bandage covered with dirt and grime and paused next to him as he fired into the dense wall of green to his front.

He grinned. "Hey, Alpha, welcome to the party. What took you so long?"

"Your invitation was late," I yelled back, flinching as a bullet gouged bark from a tree near my ear. "Sounds like you guys have really pissed them off."

"Didn't take much to rile them." He dug for a fresh magazine. "Got any ammo or water?"

"Got both."

I ducked as a mortar blasted leaves into the air a few yards to our front, and then tossed him a bandolier of

M-16 ammo and a canteen from my hip. He unscrewed the cap, nodded his thanks, and tilted his head back to drink. His face exploded splattering blood and the canteen tumbled away. I clung to the ground in horror as a mortar exploded, leaving my ears ringing, and then jerked my rifle up and began snapping off rounds refusing to look at the gore beside me.

Mortars walked along our line whipping dirt into the air, their harsh barks mingling with the crackling of rifle and machine gun fire. A man ran screaming behind me. I looked over my shoulder as he held his arms out in front of him, one hand mangled and missing fingers, the other a bloody stump at the wrist. Puffs of dirt flew from his uniform and he slumped to the ground, eyes staring, as more rounds struck his dead body tearing chunks of skin with their impact. A raging jet passed low overhead and I pressed my face into the leaves as gigantic explosions ripped into the trees, the impact lifting my body off the ground as the percussion slammed against me. A wall of flame streaked skyward as napalm canisters skidded in after the explosives. The air disappeared and I fought to breathe in the vacuum as sizzling pieces of smoldering shrapnel showered down in the damp undergrowth around me.

For the next hour as the fight rumbled, we moved no farther than Charlie Company's initial advance. I lay flat, grimly firing through the carnage while dodging the rockets, artillery, and bombs, my mind reeling under the impacts. Finally, the jarring noise slackened and we faced only scattered firing as the enemy force disengaged. We lay stunned, too spent to pursue them.

Some men crawled about filling gaps in our line or dragging dead and wounded to the rear. Canteens were raised to parched lips as red, smoke stung eyes stared at the devastated jungle. Sergeant Lunas organized our squad as the remains of Charlie Company withdrew to the rear. I waved at a tired Jerry and Bernie moving by to regroup with their second squad as jets and gunships circled above us waiting to pounce.

Bloop and I used our steel pots to scrape out a shallow hole for the night, working in silence except for grunts and curses as we encountered roots and other obstacles hindering our efforts. Del and Reno linked in on one side of us, and Jerry and Bernie positioned themselves on the other. I eased over to Jerry and Bernie and sat with my back to a tree as they made final improvements to their position.

"We don't have any claymores or trip flares to string, or even C-ration cans to tie to bushes," I observed as the shadowy night loomed before.

"Gonna be a long night, for sure," Jerry observed as jets continued to expend their ordnance deep in the jungle before us and random artillery roamed overhead, their muffled *CR-UMPS* chasing the retreating enemy.

I laid my helmet aside, relishing the cool air circulating through my damp hair as smoke drifted through the trees from patches of smoldering brush. Jerry sat on the edge of his foxhole and fished a crumpled chocolate bar from his fatigue jacket, broke it into three equal sections, and handed one each to Bernie and me. We crunched in silence savoring each bite.

"Tough bastards," Bernie observed.

"Mauled Charlie Company bad," Jerry agreed after a pause.

I pulled myself to my feet. "See you."

I returned to my position and settled in next to Bloop as darkness descended. Flares began to make their appearance overhead, their effect diminished by the thick trees and drifting smoke. I laid my head on the rim of the foxhole and rested my stinging eyes, as the roaring jets departed with the light leaving sputtering fires and an occasional rattle of equipment the only sounds. Warmth encased me as I conjured up Sandy's image in my exhausted mind.

"Jay?" Del whispered across the short distance.

I raised my head. "Yeah?"

"9th NVA, pass it on," he called.

"*What*?" I demanded as my heart hammered. "Are you sure?"

"Intel confirms it."

"*Hot damn!*" I shouted, forgetting security in my excitement.

No wonder we almost got our asses kicked. Hell, we *still* might. I passed the word on to the next position, got the same request for confirmation, and heard the excitement in Jerry's voice as he passed the word further down the line. At last, the famed Ghost Regiment was against us. From the sketchy briefings and quick looks at the map, I knew we had them in a box and they didn't know it yet. Tomorrow we would squeeze that box until the sides crushed them. I shared my remaining piece of gum with Bloop as I whispered all I knew about their predicament in his ear. He crunched the tiny piece of gum in his massive jaw and grunted. Unable to carry on a conversation with the unshakable giant, I reminded him to keep his mouth shut so his gold tooth wouldn't give us away.

"*Ferrkyou*," a shrill voice screeched from our front as I hugged the ground in surprise. Whoever it was spoke good English and was very close. I rose to eye level with the rim of the foxhole to stare into the darkness lit by smoldering patches of coals and clicked off my safety.

"*Ferrkyou! Ferrkyou!*" the voice screamed from the right front now.

I squeezed off two rounds as other rifles spoke with me.

"*Ferrkyou! Ferrkyou! Ferrkyou!*"

Half the perimeter opened up with me as the voices screeched from different positions to our front. The shooting died down when we realized there was no counter fire and we held our breath as we searched the blackness.

"*Ferrkyou!*" the voice shouted in my left ear.

I rolled to my right in alarm and impacted against Bloop's unyielding bulk.

"*Ferrkyou! Ferrkyou!*"

We both whirled as the voice sang out behind us, heads swiveling to stare in all directions with rifles poised.

"*Ferrkyou! Ferrkyou! Ferrkyou! Ferrkyou!*"

We had two full minutes of bedlam as every man in the unit shot in every direction at the voices screaming insults from the darkness.

"Cease fire! Cease fire!" Lunas shouted. "Hold your fire, goddamn it! You're shooting at lizards!"

"Don't shoot at the voices! Lizards!" others implored and the mad minute tapered off.

"*Ferrkyou!*" one of the voices called back.

Lizards? I thought as nervous twitters broke out along the line. We held our fire. Within minutes, a hundred voices filled the night screaming the insult from our front, sides, rear, and overhead. A few gruff voices flung the insult back, obviously not lizards, as we settled back into our holes trying to hear through the clamor of the reptiles. In time they linked up with their mates and tranquility again returned to the night.

A half hour later Bloop shifted to a more comfortable position and a twig snagged his gear in a loud rustle in the stillness. A dull thump rattled the bushes to our immediate front. I pulled Bloop's head down next to mine as the night split into flame. I grabbed a grenade from our pile, pulled the pin, pushed myself upright, and heaved it as far as I could, ensuring not to hit a tree and have it bounce back into our position with us. We cringed in the bottom of the hole as it answered the sapper's challenge.

And so it went, ears strained, eyes seeking, nerves taut, each side trying to pinpoint the other's location as we exchanged grenades in the darkness. The smoke obscured sunrise found us haggard and ill tempered. Third platoon took two casualties from the dogfight, but we had no way of knowing of any we may have imposed on the enemy.

With daylight, we swept through the area to our front. Fifty yards into the torn and scorched foliage, we pulled up in stunned surprise. A large, well-camouflaged camp lay before us under the heavy jungle covering. We moved cautiously through the area and discovered the encampment stretched a half-mile from end to end and contained hooches, latrines, classrooms, a thatched hospital, and supply points. Poor old Charlie Company had landed right on the front doorstep of the long-searched-for staging area of the mighty 9th NVA. The ferocious battle of the day before took on new significance as we searched the camp abandoned in haste with discarded equipment strewn everywhere. Blood trails and blood soaked bandages littered the area in testimony to the pounding they received, but we found not a single body in the twisted mess. We established a perimeter around the prize and called for teams of Intelligence officers. As we guarded the camp, Bravo Company fought a large-scale action against elements of the enemy regiment trying to break out of the cordon encircling them. More troops flew in during the morning to strengthen the trap. Helicopters thumped overhead dropping leaflets imploring the enemy to surrender or face certain annihilation and assuring them of honorable treatment, as my pulse quickened—*we had the bastards now*!

A company from the 196th Light Infantry moved in to assume our security mission in early afternoon freeing us to continue the pursuit.

"We're to establish a blocking force in conjunction with Bravo Company five hundred meters to our front,"

Lunas advised as we prepared to move out. "Elements of the 1st Infantry Division will conduct a battalion sized sweep tomorrow from the opposite direction and drive them into our wall."

Filled with grim anticipation, we strung out through the heavy foliage to stalk the doomed Ghost Regiment.

———

Visibility was almost zero as we chopped our way into the tangled veil and paused for Bravo Company to link up with us. Radio calls between the two commanders grew heated as ours implored theirs to hustle his unit on up with us, and theirs told ours to be patient. Mustang Six intervened and ordered our commander to move on after assuring him Bravo would link up with us in the blocking position. Silverstein took point and our first squad tunneled through the mass of vegetation behind him as he hacked his way through the deep green brush. Second and third platoons flanked us thirty yards out to each side as we moved steadily in the indicated direction and drew near our blocking position, with Bravo Company still a quarter of a mile to our rear moving in to lock the gate on our left flank and seal the fate of the enemy force before us. The day of reckoning was drawing near for the gallant men of the Ghost Regiment.

"On line!" Lunas yelled as a patter of sniper fire sent us diving for cover in the thick tangle of vines.

With Silverstein pinned down to our front, Bloop and I crashed into the growth to the left as Reno, Del, Harley, and Lunas swung to the right while second and third squads scrambled to maneuver to our left and right flanks. We surged forward hampered by the unyielding jungle floor, guiding our movements by the sounds of the weapons on each side, and drew parallel to Silverstein trading bullet for bullet with the snipers.

Suddenly the whole world blew up in our face as enemy fire pelted us like heavy rain.

"*Ambush!*" an unnecessary cry sang out, as leaves and bark danced around our heads from the impacting rounds and mortars whistled from the sky sending fragments screaming in all directions. Second and third platoons fought to link into our flanks as we laid down a heavy rip of return fire to cover their advance.

We're screwed, I thought in panic as I tore at my ammo pouch for a fresh magazine.

"Medic! Medic!" voices screamed in the melee.

"Killer Niner! Killer Niner! Ambush! Fire Mission! Fire Mission! Ambush!" Boy Wonder screamed into his radio in an effort to raise the artillery.

"The trees! The trees!" Del yelled as he rolled over on his back and blasted the trees overhead. A rifle tumbled out and a body slumped after it, suspended by a rope around its waist and twisted in circles.

"The trees!" I took up the cry and rolled over, firing full automatic into every clump of green over me. "They're in the trees!"

Bodies flopped out of some and weapons slid out of others as I realized the firing from the front had masked the snipers overhead, allowing them to pick us apart with our unaware line clearly visible directly below them. Within half a minute, we eliminated the threat and turned back to the front to continue the struggle with the original group that had jumped us, as mortars rattled through the branches pounding us with deadly accuracy. Smoke hung below the heavy canopy as the ripping roar from both sides locked into a determined struggle for fire superiority. Our artillery swooshed overhead, their muffled impacts to our front seeking vengeance for the trap our foe had sprung on us. Jets thundered by with their loads ripping the jungle to shreds before us and leaving our ears numb. Finally, the enemy fire slackened.

"Jay, Lunas is hit!" Reno shouted.

"Get him to the rear, damn it," I shouted back.

I crawled to my left to link up with second squad, and Jerry stumbled by with Bernie draped over his shoulder. Two bloody stumps protruded from his trousers where his boots should have been. I caught up with him near the rear of the company where several men lay in a hollowed-out area as others brought casualties in from all directions to our medics. The brief fight had been costly I realized as I skidded up next to Jerry.

"Oh, god!" Jerry sobbed as tears streamed down his cheeks. "Oh god, Jay!"

"Shit!" I yelled in frustration as I stared down at Bernie's eyes rolled back in his head.

"It was a mortar," Jerry cried, as a medic began applying tourniquets to Bernie's legs. "It landed right between his feet!"

"Aw, goddamn it!" I screamed, the pain ripping through my gut like a bullet. I had a clear image of Bernie lying on a clean white bed with a tearful Sandy standing beside him. I knelt and grabbed Bernie's hand wanting to comfort him, to tell him everything was going to be okay, but he was unresponsive. The medic finished with his tourniquets, jabbed a needle in his arm, scribbled on a piece of paper, pinned it to Bernie's chest, and rushed over to another man. Reno struggled up dragging Silverstein and eased him to the ground. The front of his shirt was blood-soaked from a large hole in his upper right chest. A small, neat hole in his back just below the shoulder blade indicated he had been a victim of the snipers above us. Bloop hurried up with Lunas draped over his shoulder and laid him beside Bernie. I grimaced at his broken teeth and shattered jawbone protruded from his wrecked, bloody mouth and rolled him on his side as he gurgled in his own blood. Teams brought sixteen men back to the improvised aid station. The medics sent the walking wounded back down the trail to the base camp secured by the 196th and placed the disabled on litters for transport to the rear. Jerry and I watched Bernie safely off before moving back to the front.

"Corporal Sharpe," Sergeant B called.

I ran crouching to his position and squatted next to him as Boy Wonder adjusted the artillery on his radio. "How many casualties do we have?"

"Three," I choked. "Lunas took a round in the face. Bernie's lost both legs, and Silverstein's got an ugly chest wound."

"Take charge of First Squad," he ordered. "Get them tied in with the flanks and dug in, then give me a status report on ammo."

I crawled back to the line, paired the squad into fighting positions, and linked them in with second and third squads on each side. We still had more than our basic load of ammo due to the extra we had carried the day before. I reported this to Sergeant B, as steady firing erupted to our rear indicating Bravo Company was trying to fight their way in to complete the linkup. and then hurried back to help Bloop scoop out a shallow hole.

With our position prepared and our gear arranged for the night, I drank long, thirsty swigs from my canteen ignoring the growling in my stomach. We had not eaten since noon the day before, but I didn't feel the loss at the moment. At dusk, the sniper fire picked up and we stayed low in our holes returning shots randomly.

I listened in amazement as a bugle blew, followed by the shrill screech of whistles. Mortars dropped through the trees above us as a rising volley of fire swept over us. I peered over the edge of my hole and was startled to see men running through the battle-thinned jungle at us—Vietnamese men—wearing brown uniforms and pith helmets. *VC don't do that*, I thought, dumbfounded. *They aren't VC, they're Hard Core Mothers,* my mind snapped as I propped up and began firing.

Heads appeared out of foxholes on each side of me with eyes widening in shock. Rifles swung into view and a solid, unbroken mass of death spewed out before us in a river of hot lead meeting the charging troops head on, as every man fired full automatic while ignoring the blasting mortars. The enemy line faltered, stumbled, and disappeared from view under the avalanche of destruction with no attacking soldier reaching a point closer than thirty yards from our position. As our fire tapered off bodies sprawled everywhere, some moaning in broken agony among the shredded bushes and torn earth as artillery rounds clumped among them, silencing the cries of the fallen with authority and flinging the retreating remains of others in the air like broken dolls as I looked on in awe.

"Medic!" voices called as the roar diminished.

I crawled along the squad to check the damage. Harley was the only casualty, pierced through the fleshy part of his arm by a mortar fragment. I sent him to the rear. As the night deepened, flares drifted overhead to beat back the darkness, bathing the area in yellow flickering light. We traded mortar and artillery fire back and forth, with occasional mushrooms of orange muzzle flashes winking on each side.

I crawled back to Sergeant B. "We're in tight. Ammo's holding up, but we're running low on water."

"They've flanked our position through the gap Bravo's supposed to be filling," Sergeant B reported. "We're cut off from the base camp."

"Where the shit's Bravo?" I demanded.

"Settled in for the night. They'll try to link up with us again in the morning."

"*Candy asses*," I swore.

"Casualties will be kept in the improvised Aid Station until the area can be cleared at dawn," Sergeant B ordered.

I returned to the line with growing alarm, wondering who was fooling who—we were more trapped now than the enemy we were supposed to be trapping. We were in a direct line between the NVA and the safety of the Cambodian border to our rear, which was their only escape route. We were one isolated company, shot up, weary, and with a gaping hole on our left flank. All around the enemy, we had battalion-sized forces in blocking positions. Any fool could see they had to get out of our encirclement and reach the border—and we were the weak link.

The firing continued, sporadic but steady, as the night wore on. I drank the last of my water to relieve my parched throat and rinse the grit out of my mouth. I was so hungry my stomach hurt. Near midnight, I draped my head over the butt of my rifle in exhaustion as Bloop kept a bleary watch. As I dozed, I heard a bugle blow somewhere in the recesses of my mind. The shrill call of whistles jerked me upright. Men stirred and lifted tired heads as they shifted into firing positions. Whistling mortars accompanied pounding boots as flares opened overhead and artillery streaked earthward. Shadows darted ghost-like through the flattened jungle to our front. I sprayed the area as a solid line of dancing light strung out on each side of me meeting the attack with violent determination.

The surging line swept over us amid cries of pain and yells of rage, as desperation gripped both sides, one to hold, the other to break through. Caught in a searing climax of noise and confusion, I grabbed for a new magazine as a shadow closed on me, saw a glimmer of light dance off a long, wicked-looking bayonet, and lurched to my feet to meet the rush as Bloop groped in the bottom of the hole for a dropped magazine. A blinding flash sent digging needles in my face. My ears stopped hearing as welcoming darkness sucked me down into nothingness.

CHAPTER 25

A red haze enveloped me.

I'm in hell, I thought dully and attempted to draw my mind to full reality from the clutching blackness. Throbbing pain gripped my face. I sensed the dark outline of a man behind the red glow. "Where am I?"

"Aid station," a terse voice answered. "You kissed a mortar. You'll be alright."

Oh, shit, I thought in panic. *I probably don't have a face left. They always say 'you'll be alright' when you won't be.*

"Hurt?" the voice inquired, shifting the red filtered flashlight from my eyes.

"Of course," I blubbered through the saltwater in my mouth. *Blood!* I trembled, picturing my face hanging in gruesome folds as his fingers probed inside my mouth and extracted solid pieces of matter. I worked my tongue around, and discovered a couple of gaps in my gums big enough to drive a truck through them.

"Here, drink this," the voice directed. "Don't swallow. Rinse and spit it out."

I rose up on one elbow, rinsed, and spit a glob of congealed matter out.

"You'll be okay," the voice reassured me. "Nothing penetrated the skull, but you lost a couple of teeth. Lay back and rest." The weak light moved over to the next man.

I propped against a tree and spit thick blood from my mouth, gagging with the effort. The searing pain in my face began to lessen as I tried to orientate myself. Periodic firing came from my front. We must have beaten back the attack, I thought as my vision cleared and some twenty dark forms lying around me came into focus. Some were moaning as medics moved over them holding the eerie lights and talked in soft, reassuring tones as they worked. To our rear, I heard heavy fighting far in the distance and assumed Bravo Company was suffering through a similar attack. I wished them well. A medic questioned a man near me. Fear gripped me as I heard the weak reply. I crawled over and looked down in Jerry's red-tinged face as his dull eyes stared up against the glare. An ugly hole, black against his smooth skin, bubbled near the center of his chest. I whimpered, the sight searing my soul as he lay quietly while the medic worked, fighting to breathe, his efforts liquid gasps. *Not him*, I pleaded silently, *please, God, not him*!

"Jerry?" I whispered.

He frowned in concentration. "Jay?"

"Yeah, man," I choked as tears irritated the wounds in my cheeks. "Trying to get some sham time?"

He tried to smile. "So much noise ... man can't sleep ... up there." He closed his eyes.

I slumped against a tree, shaking as I stifled the wracking sobs. The medic finished dressing his wound and moved to the next man. I wiped my nose with a grimy hand and stumbled over to him. "Doc, is he going to make it?"

"Hard to say," the medic replied without looking up, his hands busy with a man below him who had half his scalp hanging over his ear. "Depends on how soon we can get him to a field hospital and how tough he is."

"He's tough, Doc, he's *Airborne*," I sobbed, sure it would make a difference if he understood. I crawled back to Jerry's inert form. "Jerry? You got to hang on for a while, man," I begged. "You hear? You're a tough son of a bitch, *now show me how tough!*"

His jaws clenched and I knew he was fighting. I sat back against a tree to keep a vigil over him, with each of his struggling breaths tearing at my heart and the momentary pauses filling me with anxiety as I willed him to live.

Sergeant B crawled back to the medics. "We've got to have all men still capable of fighting back on the line."

"You can't ask these men to do more than they've already done," the medic argued.

"If they hit us again we'll never hold them," Sergeant B replied bitterly.

Resisting the impulse to remain with Jerry, I crawled back to the front as several men fell in with me.

"Hey, where you guys going?" the medic demanded.

"Back!" Harley answered.

Feeling our way along, we reached the line and slipped into our holes. Bloop flashed a gold-toothed grin in the yellow light as I located my rifle and pulled my gear around me.

"Stop grinning at me, fool," I growled. "You'll get us both shot. Get some sleep."

His ponderous head sank down and his deep breathing soon filled the silence. I sat back with my knees drawn up against my chest, my eyes level with the ground, and my mind devoid of emotion. Peering through the ruined foliage, I knew no fear, pain, thirst, or hunger, only hope as I willed my mind back to that murky hollow in the ground and Jerry struggling with each breath he took, as random shots picked at the dancing shadows. Artillery spaced through the area in irregular patterns amid periodic whistling mortars dropping out of the sky as we waited.

———

Morning brought a scene reminiscent of trench warfare as our haggard senses took in the utter destruction. Nothing moved in the raw landscape before us other than thin wisps of acrid smoke. Shell craters pocketed the torn earth and blackened stumps stood stark on the stripped jungle floor between the NVA and us. Stiffening corpses in tattered uniforms crusted with blood littered the charred ground. A strong, sickly odor assaulted my nostrils—the smell of death—as the heat bloated bodies swelled and turned black. I shook Bloop awake, stretched cramped muscles that had been immobile through the long night, and crawled out of the hole to limp to the rear, my exploring fingers finding my face swollen and caked with dried blood. The three missing teeth left cavernous raw holes in my gums, and a dull throbbing set in as I worked my jaw to generate enough moisture to spit the clotted blood from my mouth. I approached the aid station with a heavy heart, searching for Jerry amongst the misery, and found him naked to the waist with blood soaked bandages on his chest lying rigid in the gray light. I stood looking down at his peaceful face feeling the emptiness inside my tired body. His chest heaved and a long, shuddering sigh escaped his lips. I squatted next to him as despair turned to hope. He opened fluttering, pain filled eyes to stare dully up at me. A crooked grin tugged at the corners of his crusted lips.

"Hi, guy," I whispered as pride surged through me.

He frowned, fighting for words. "You look ... terible."

I grinned around the butterfly bandages clamped to my face feeling the skin stretch and tear at the crust. "Forgot to duck."

"Fig-ures," he grunted, grimacing. "Dumb shit."

"Don't talk. We'll be getting you out of here soon. You hang on, right?"

"Want ... wa-ter." He closed his eyes, throat working, forehead creased in pain.

I limped over to an exhausted medic covered with other men's blood lying against a tree staring unseeing at the pitiful men before him. "I need water for Jerry."

He pointed to a canteen beside him. "It's the last I have."

I shook it and determined it had about an inch in the bottom, limped back and trickled a few drops of the precious supply between Jerry's parched lips. "Hey, guy, you'll be in Saigon with Gail tomorrow," I promised as he coughed and choked it down.

"Stay-with-me," he rasped weakly.

"You bet," I assured him as he closed his eyes again, breathing in shallow gasps. I moved back to the medic fighting the urge to drink the remainder of the water as the thick coating in my mouth choked me. "Doc, how long till we can move him back to the rear?"

"As soon as they clear the area to our—"

A bugle cut him short as I turned to stare in disbelief. "*No!*" I shouted, and began running to my position as whistles shrieked across the still morning air. Voices yelled in warning as heads rose above the rims of foxholes. I lunged into the pit next to Bloop as the first of the streaking mortars dropped out of the sky and ragged shots rang out. Boy Wonder began yelling into his radio as dust and smoke erupted all along our line in jarring explosions, rupturing the serenity of the morning calm in angry bursts. Then they were there, a running line of dark little men with faces stretched in fear and excitement, their mouths open as they yelled, rifles at hip level with glistening bayonets flashing in the morning light.

Our line thundered in a long tearing wail of destruction. The impact of their charge faltered and then surged forward again as we frantically reloaded. I swung my rifle, the stuttering discharge lost in the uproar, the muzzle flashing as trails of brass spit from the side. Men stumbled, flew backwards, spun sideways, and sagged to the ground. Bullets plucked the air next to my head and threw up dirt around me in spurts. A rolling yell from our line climbed into the air as darting figures closed with and swept over us in a screaming throng.

Man met man in the onrush. Rifles swung, fired, clubbed, and lunged with bayonets as men grappled, rolled in the dirt, grunted in exertion, and swore in hatred. The yelling stopped abruptly as the two lines clashed and degenerated into thumps and jarring thuds as mouths sucked air and wheezed in pain, thumbs gouged eyes, and boots crunched skulls, the scene savagely animalistic as each sought to kill or maim the other in a confrontation devoid of humanity. Bloop swung his rifle and clubbed a man. I fired straight into another's chest as he ran at me, fired twice more into still another as he slashed Bloop with his bayoneted rifle, and then knelt, firing rapidly at others near us. Bloop staggered up in front of me to club another one as I reloaded. The air filled with explosions from whistling artillery and mortar rounds. Machine guns hammered in all directions. As the momentum of the attack slackened I pulled Bloop back into the hole and resumed firing at the withdrawing men. A ragged yell of triumph rose from our unbroken line, a cry of gleeful victory as our bullets chased the attackers back to their side of no man's land. Sagging in jubilation, I shook my fist at the empty expanse of ruptured jungle as others shouted curses and screamed with exhilaration.

Voices yelled in warning amid ones of victory as I reloaded. I tuned in to wild firing behind me and turned to face the new danger. Through the shattered trees I saw a dozen NVA in the aid station. A medic rushed at one of them with his arms spread wide in a protective gesture.

A lunge from an enemy soldier sent the tip of his bayo-net through the medic's chest and out his back. A boot lifted to kick him free, sending his quivering body spin-ning backwards as other NVA shot into the ground at their feet.

"*Jerry*!" I ran to the rear as a wave of terror washed over me.

Del raced beside me as others joined in. Sergeant B jumped from his hole in front of us, followed by a bloody Boy Wonder clutching his arm, a pistol gripped in his other fist. The NVA turned to meet our disjointed attack. One fired an AK on full automatic and sent Ser-geant B stumbling back as holes appeared all along his back. Del ripped the man with a long burst as each side fired point-blank into the other. A bayonet flashed by me, missing my midsection by inches. My momentum hit the extended rifle and spun the man off balance as I crashed to the ground. The man recoiled and lunged at me again as I kicked and rolled away. Bloop towered over him from the rear with his black arm encircling the man's neck and yanked him kicking into the air. I heard bone snap as he tossed the twitching man to the side, scrambled to my feet, and ran to Jerry's prostrate form.

"*Awwwooo!*" I screamed from the bottom of my soul when I saw his right eye missing and the left side of his head a mass of broken bone and gray matter tinged with pink foam. "*You are going to die! Here and now! Every one of you!*" I screamed viciously as I turned to the withdraw-ing NVA, running as I fired, screaming my hatred, my lust for vengeance locked on their fleeing forms. I shot one in the back, paused to club him as he tried to rise up, shot him twice more in the face as he tried to cover his head, and then lurched after others disappearing into the trees. My legs flew out from under me and I struck the ground hard, chest first, and my rifle skidded away. I scrambled up onto my knees and lunged after it. Someone grabbed my ankles and pulled me down again as I kicked to free myself. Two black arms encircled my chest, crushing me, lifting me into the air as I gagged. A voice yelled in my ear, Del's voice, as I screamed in rage. Bloop's great arms stiffened, holding my squirming body in a firm vise. "*Jerrrrrryyyyyyyy!*" I gave up my struggle and slumped, sobbing in frustration.

"Easy, Jay, easy, hold him, Bloop!" Del begged, his voice filled with anguish.

Bloop inserted his hands under my arms, hoisted me onto his shoulder, and Del slipped along beside us as he carried me back through the aid station, past the riddled body of Sergeant B. Past the dead medic who had tried to protect his wounded. Past a slumped Boy Wonder crying against a tree with his pistol dangling from his bloody fist, the chamber locked to the rear on an empty magazine ... and past Jerry's lifeless form. Bloop swung me off his shoulder and pressed me into our hole, crawled in beside me, and draped a heavy arm across my shoulder.

My mind refused to focus. I knew I was blubbering as a terrible fatigue crushed me. I sought escape as my head throbbed dully. I wanted to die. I longed for the nothingness it would bring, the painless freedom it promised.

———

Slowly the world swam back into focus. My sense of feel returned. My face throbbed. I became aware of muscle cramps in my legs in the narrow hole. I felt thirst in my dry throat and gummy mouth—and the sharp sting in my heart. I wanted to live. *These sorry mothers are going to pay for Jerry!* I shifted and Bloop's arm tightened around me.

"Let go of me, goddamn it," I demanded.

He relaxed his arm, eyes watchful.

"Where's my rifle?"

He looked to the rear, and then lurched up beside me as I stood.

"Would you quit hulking over me like a goddamn ape?" I gritted.

Del came crouching over to us. "Jay? Bloop, grab him!"

"Screw you!" I shoved him away.

Del and Bloop tagged along as I stumbled back through the wreckage. Dirty, battle weary faces jutted out of foxholes in isolated locations watching our passage. Del and Bloop crouched by a tree to cover my movement through the body littered Aid Station. I located my rifle, dusted it off, loaded a fresh magazine into the empty well, and stood staring hard into the jungle, my thoughts on the demons crouched there wanting them to feel my hatred. I no longer felt the crushing anger. I was cold and empty. I did not want to rip their flesh with my bare hands. I wanted to fire my weapon in a calm, deliberate fashion and see their bodies fall in droves around me.

"Jay? Let's go back now, okay?" Del called.

I stood over Jerry's body studying his frozen features, his once slick, glistening hair now course and stiff with dried blood matting it into thick tufts. I recalled him in a tuxedo, bronze and handsome, smiling, saw him again in dirty jungle fatigues with machine gun ammo strung across his chest, his eyes full of mischief, and remembered him tipped back in the Wolf's Den holding a can of beer, his lopsided grin below dancing eyes. This mangled form with one lifeless eye staring up next to the empty socket was not Jerry. Jerry was full of life and the world around him. He was not here rotting in this stench among all the corpses lying on the ground. I smiled.

"Jay? *Please*?" Del's insistent plea tugged at me.

I walked past him and Bloop back to the line as they fell in on my heels, pausing midway to look down at Boy Wonder crouched in his hole with the radio handset near his ear. His RTO lay next to him, dirt grimed bandages covering his head, shoulder, and both arms. Boy Wonder looked up at me, his arm holding the handset dripping blood off the point of his elbow from a wound higher up. I dug through their first aid pouches for a bandage and found none, ripped a long strip of material from my filthy jungle fatigues, wound it around his arm, and tied it off.

"We've got to hold them," Boy Wonder said, his eyes seeking reassurance.

"We will, Sir," I swore.

I limped back to my position and Del slipped into his next to me. I became aware of Bloop's forehead beaded in perspiration, his eyes glazed with pain, one bloody

hand clutching his side where he had taken the glancing blow from the bayonet. I used my knife to rip the
remaining sleeve off my shirt and wadded it into a ball to
press against the gash, and then walked the platoon line
adjusting men to provide better coverage. I collected all
the ammo I could find from the bodies and redistrib-
uted it throughout the remainder of the platoon.

The sight of the bloody, grime covered men was
appalling as I took stock of our desperate situation.
Sunken eyes stared listlessly into the jungle from
expressionless, smoke blackened faces. We were out of
water, low on ammo, and had not eaten for two days
nor slept for three. We had fought almost continu-
ously since landing in support of Charlie Company
two days before, and faced three human wave attacks,
one of which involved hand-to-hand combat. Cut off
from our rear with a desperate regiment trapped to our
front, one or the other of us faced certain destruction. We had no bandages or medication with every
man here wounded in one or more ways, and all our
medics killed when they overran our Aid Station. I
grinned as I walked past the men and received bitter
grins back. *But we're not beaten yet*, I vowed as I viewed the
determined set of a chin here, an angry scowl there.
This was one damned fine unit.

I limped back to Boy Wonder and knelt beside him.
"Lieutenant, we need help."

The distant sound of battle raged on three sides of
us as he stared up at me with grime-crusted eyes. "We've
got to hold."

"We can't stand against another attack, Sir."

"Do you think ... we can ... fight our way back to the base camp ...?"

"We could never carry all of our wounded, Sir."

His jaw clenched. "We've got to hold."

"We're low on ammo. One more attack will drain us dry."

"What can we do?"

"Get help, Sir. When can we expect help to reach us?"

"Soon."

"I hope you're right, Sir," I replied as I stumbled back to my position on the line.

The firing in our area had stopped except for the lone enemy bullet that hummed overhead on occasion unanswered by our side. I caught glimpses of NVA uniforms darting through the foliage forming for yet another attack. Boy Wonder called in artillery in hopes of disrupting their staging area, adjusting fire by listening to the *CRUMPS* of their impact in the jungle to our front as the sun climbed higher and the heat intensified. My swollen tongue stuck to the grit and blood inside of my mouth. I was desperate for water and my eyes were mere swollen slits making it difficult to see as films of moisture clung to the lashes. The seriously wounded moaned from scattered locations begging for water and calling out names of mothers and girlfriends in delirium. I closed my eyes, exhausted, willing the sounds of the artillery to drift away along with the subdued whines of stray bullets as fatigue tugged me down into numbness.

I sat at a table with Sandy and held a glass of cold beer in my hand with beads of moisture clinging to the side. Jerry's echoing laughter drew me to the other side of the table where he saluted me with his raised mug and crooked grin. Then one of his eyes became a bloody socket and his laughter turned to hateful glee as his features twisted in a grimace. Sandy stood and backed away shaking her head in disbelief.

Bloop's persistent shaking brought me back into another hellish nightmare. I realized I had been twisting and moaning, and lay panting as sweat streaked down my face. All was quiet. No firing from either side disturbed the heat waves rising in the stillness.

"Are they gone?" I asked, and when Bloop shook his head, lit my last cigarette and tossed the crumpled package to the front.

Del crawled over to us. "It's too quiet."

I tried to spit and wiped the dribble from my chin. "Eye of the storm," I croaked.

"Why do they keep hitting us?"

"Because they're surrounded, we're the weakest link in the circle, and Cambodia is directly behind us," I grunted.

"At least it ain't friggin' personal," he quipped as the clear note of a bugle split the air. "Aw shit!" he swore as he scrambled back to his hole.

Rifles swung up and propped to the front. Safeties clicked off as whistles signaled the assault. The sound of mortars leaving their tubes reached us, followed by our own streaking artillery passing in the opposite direction. Running boots pounded the soft turf as explosions erupted. Boy Wonder yelled into his radio adjusting fire. A long line of yelling men broke into the no-man's-land before us. Bullets slammed into the dirt and careened off trees in showers of bark. Dots of color sparkled from the screaming line as they fired from the waist. I sank lower in my hole as my body grew rigid. My finger took up the slack on my trigger as I squinted at the running bodies through my peep sight. I opened up at the same instant as the others, squeezing rounds off instead of the wild firing of past attacks. Tracers from the machine guns arched across my front sweeping back and forth as rifles pounded the air in an angry roar. A boiling eddy of dust encased the charging line as bodies spun and dropped. I fired steadily, picking targets, leading my aim, swinging to the next form, as the air filled with burnt powder.

A gunship flashed overhead firing miniguns and rockets, ripping the enemy line to shreds, and a second gunship followed on the heels of the first. Disjointed now, our foes straggled towards us as others turned to fire up at the hell descending on them from above. A second line of determined men charged out past the stalled and fallen men of the first wave. The gunships turned and made a second pass ripping the jungle floor in front of them. The two lines converged, steadied, moved forward again as one. Our firing reached a peak as alarm swept over me. *We could not hold them!* The gunships turned like a top in the air and swooped back for a third run. The momentum of the attack faltered and then surged forward yet again as the second gunship swooped across them with guns blazing and smoke streaking from its sides. The advance faltered a second time and then coasted to a stop as the enemy crouched behind trees and jumped into shell holes, firing into us as we threw everything we had back at them.

With thirty yards between us we dueled, each picking targets and firing into the other at eyeball level. Mortars and artillery threw up smoke and dirt, striking men down regardless of uniform or belief. The two lines screamed in anger as each fought stubbornly, one unable to advance, the other unwilling to retreat, the survival of the one dependent on the destruction of the other. The noise was deafening, the moment overpowering, the determination solid as men spun, flopped, spurted blood, and crawled back to fight on.

I thought it sheer insanity and madness in its exhilarating, unchecked savagery at the most basic level of inhumanity as I emptied my last magazine and tossed my useless rifle aside. I pulled the pins on my last two grenades, flung them into the spitting line facing me, and looked wildly around for something more to fight with. Through the swirling smoke and dust, I saw Del jerk back and disappear. I raced through a storm of hornets, threw myself in a diving roll into his hole, grabbed his rifle, and popped up firing almost without pause, screaming at the wavering line of death in front of me. I dug out his last magazine, jammed it into the well, released the bolt in the same motion, and resumed firing even as it locked home. My helmet slammed into the left side of my head with a mighty blow. My vision blurred and trees reeled as I fought to clear my senses, unable to tell if I was standing up or lying down as the world faded in and out of focus.

A ragged cheer lifted and then drowned out in a thunderous roar. Yellow flame billowed from right to left across the beaten zone as a wave of intense heat rolled over me. A second jet flashed after the first, sending its canisters of jelly and fire across our front as screams of agony bellowed from the inferno. The air streamed out of my lungs as a second grinding blast of heat slapped me to the ground. All firing ceased as both sides shrank back in horror.

I sucked foul air through my raspy throat and peered out through my blurred vision as flames devoured the wasteland to my front and an overpowering stench of charred flesh assaulted my nostrils. I pulled myself up, grasped my helmet lying nearby with a large gash in the side, and turned to Del lying in a heap at my feet. I hoisted him up and laid him over the back rim of the hole, noting he had numerous small holes in his chest, face, and arms but was still breathing, and ripped his shirt into strips to make bandages to cover the worst of the abrasions.

"Easy now," I cautioned as his eyes fluttered and he tried to sit up.

"Am I hurt bad?"

"Nope, barely qualify for a Purple Heart," I assured him, thankful his voice sounded firm and his mind seemed clear.

He looked down at his blood-covered chest. "Shit, I'm friggin' *bleeding* to death!"

"Few scratches," I soothed. "Nothing serious."

Most of his wounds were superficial, although he looked like a pincushion. When I finished patching him I moved down the line to bandage others with strips of their uniforms after detailing two of the healthier men to collect the remaining ammo and divide it with those still capable of fighting. I found Harley, wounded earlier, now dead with a neat hole in the center of his chest and a jagged tear across his throat, and Reno, hit in the shoulder and across the back of his hand. I found both of our remaining machine gunners shot up with less than fifty rounds remaining between them. I pulled two of the men together and stacked the remaining half-belt beside them, urging them to make every bullet count, ashamed of asking men in their condition to fight more and knowing they would have less than ten seconds of firing when the time came.

When I returned to my position, Bloop handed me my share of the scrounged ammo, which consisted of nine bullets and one grenade. I knew we were doomed and fought the sobs building in my throat. We had nothing left to fight with, and didn't have the energy to fight anyway. The next attack would roll over us like an avalanche. I looked across the ripped jungle littered with bodies and smoke. The bastards would get through. In despair, I crawled back to Boy Wonder, who was still clutching his radio, the static weaker now as the batteries gave out and worked my mouth to generate enough moisture to speak.

"Sir, we're out of ammo and everybody's hit!" When he didn't move, I shook his shoulder. "Sir?"

"We've got to hold ... they're coming soon ..." he muttered.

"Sir, we *can't* hold!" I shouted in frustration. "We've got nothing to hold with! They've got to come *now*! Tell them!"

He stirred, keyed his mike. "Mustang Alpha Six, Alpha One." The radio crackled.

"Mustang Alpha One, this is Mustang Six," our battalion commander's strong voice answered. "Sit-Rep, over."

"Six, One. Situation desperate. We need immediate reinforcement, over."

"Roger, One. Elements are inbound to your location. Hold your position, over."

"Six, One. What is their Echo Tango Alpha, over?"

"One, Six, ETA unknown. Hold your position, over."

"Six, that's a negative, situation desperate, over," Boy Wonder sobbed.

"Roger, One. Hold your position, over," Six commanded. Boy Wonder lifted his face to me as tears streamed down his cheeks. "One, do you copy last transmission, over?" the battalion commander demanded.

I grabbed the mike. "Six, we *can't* hold! We're out of everything! Everybody's wounded! We've got to have help now!" I released the mike, shaking with anger.

"One! Do Not Repeat, I say again, *do not* repeat last transmission. Bad guys have ears too. Acknowledge," the voice chastised.

I keyed the mike again, overcome with a gut ripping rage for all the stupid brass in the world. "Goddamn it, Six! We got to have help *now*! I don't give a *shit* who's listening. These silly bastards already *know* it! They've been crawling all over our ass for the last two days! *You* acknowledge!" I released the mike and stood panting as the radio hissed and crackled. When no answering call came, I screamed in rage and threw the mike down.

Bitter frustration changed to disgust as I stomped back to my hole. All right, by god, let's get this shit over with. Nine more of the sons of bitches were going to die, *nine more*. I jacked a round into the chamber and straightened the pin on my one grenade. Make that *ten* more. I pulled my survival knife from its holster and jammed it into the ground by my hand. *Eleven.*

Bloop watched me as I sat seething.

"Jay? Is help coming?" Del called.

Heads turned to stare awaiting an answer.

"Yeah, *soon!*" I shouted back bitterly.

"Jay, we gotta *do* something," Reno begged. "We can't hold them again."

"*What*?" I snarled. "What the shit *can* we do, *goddamn it*? We'll hold, by god! Just make every bullet count!" Bloop grinned at me, his gold tooth shining. "I don't need any of your shit either," I raged. His smiled grew broader as we waited in the silence.

No one moved moments later when the bugle blew. I leaned forward on the call of the whistles and propped against the side of our hole with my rifle listening to the pounding boots. Mortars drummed around us, which I largely ignored. A thunderous firefight erupted behind us and I assumed it was our relief forces running into the snipers deployed to stop them, thinking *too little, too late*. The knowledge calmed me. I steeled my mind. *I will kill eleven more. For Jerry.* I waited as the line surged out into the no man's land. I wanted them close. Artillery flashed in ugly clouds as gunships raked them from above with pods ablaze. The bastards were brave. Or stupid. I let my peephole fill with the chest of a running man.

I opened fire at thirty yards. Our first volley tore gaps in their line from the point blank range but did not slow them. I never raised my eye from the sight and ignored the destruction around me. *"Two-three."* Concentrating on my point of aim, I squeezed the trigger. I fired twice more. Bloop stood beside me to grapple with a man as I fired into another and then turned to pick off still another one as he raced by. Bloop clamped his massive hands around a skinny man's throat choking him with vengeance. The man's helmet fell off as he squirmed and both his feet left the ground as Bloop lifted him high in the air. A flash of light spat between them and another and another as the man, an officer, fired his pistol into Bloop's stomach. I fired and hit a man thrusting at me with a bayonet, fired at another behind him, and then turned to help Bloop with my survival knife as another charged down on us. The bayonet flashed past as the man collided with me in his forward thrust and he fell across me, his breath stale and harsh as it gushed in my face. I trembled with effort as he pushed me back over the edge of the foxhole, feeling my strength leaving me. I sank my teeth into his cheek and twisted, tasting blood and tearing his flesh like an animal as he screamed and released my arm to claw at my face. I slashed with my knife and felt the blade bite into flesh, slashed again, and then sank it to the hilt in his side as his body arched and his fingers clawed into my mouth trying to tear my teeth away from his jaw. I clamped down on his fingers and felt bone break. When he groaned and sagged, I shoved him off me and stood spitting shredded skin from my mouth. Two more advanced on me from different directions as I fumbled for the grenade beside me.

The world erupted into a roaring hell. Dirt slashed against my body as splintered trees lifted into the air and numbing concussions slammed into me, the impacts leaving my senses scattered. The two men coming at me tossed into the air as I slumped into the bottom of my hole in desperation. Bloop slid in on top of me, his body whipping with the shock of the explosions. *Boy Wonder called our own artillery in on top of us*! I thought dizzily. *Bless his sweet soul*! All noise muted as my ears absorbed the shock and Bloop's body sprawled over me in the thick dust and smoke. I fought for air in a world without oxygen as my fingers clawed at the ground and pressed my face into the damp soil to escape as I waited helplessly to die, howling at the injustice and begging for mercy in the thunder of white-hot death.

The ground stopped heaving and a rhythmic crackling of rifles replaced the harsh explosions as I cringed in the bottom of the foxhole waiting for bullets to riddle my back. I recoiled in fear when a man leapt into the hole with me and covered my head with my arms as I cowered, whimpering. I gaped in shock when the man above me yelled in triumph. *American*!

I clawed my way out from under Bloop to stare up at the man firing automatic bursts to the front and pulled myself up beside him as hope surged through me to see the remains of the attacking enemy force running full tilt back into the undergrowth on the far side of no man's land. I looked around in wonder as kneeling Americans shredded the fleeing troops with streams of fire and focused on a camouflaged shoulder patch of the 1st Infantry Division realizing they had broken through. I screamed in joy and shook my fist at the retreating enemy as I cursed them with every filthy word I could conjure from my reeling mind.

The man beside me cast a worried look my way. "You okay, man?"

"You're here!" I grabbed his arm in gratitude. "Thank god you're here!"

"Hey, man, you all right?" he demanded.

I covered my face in shame as sobs wracked my body. When the firing tapered off, the man squatted down next to me and extended his canteen.

I drank in grateful draughts swallowing grit and blood as the soothing liquid spread through my parched insides.

"Take it slow, friend, no hurry," the man cautioned.

I began laughing in hysterical fits and doubled over in mirth as he stared at me. Del hurried over and squatted on the rim of my foxhole, one hand holding his arm as blood seeped through his fingers. "He says ... there's ... no hurry!" I gasped and collapsed into convulsions again.

Del began laughing with me as Reno limped over on a bloody leg and joined in, the three of us howling in the now quiet jungle as our savior stared from one of us to the other. He reached past me to turn Bloop over in the hole. The sight of his riddled body crushed my laughter as I stared down at the strange giant who had been my friend. I placed my palm over the five holes in his chest feeling the cloth burned around the edges from the muzzle blasts and saw the lifeless body of the NVA officer crumpled under him, his eyes bulging and tongue hanging.

Our rescuer grabbed the officer's pistol. "You guys mind?"

I shook my head. Del nudged my arm and extended his hand for the canteen. Tears coursed down his cheeks as he drank in deep gulps, and then passed it to Reno. I used my thumb and forefinger to close Bloop's staring eyes, placed my boot on the NVA's body to work my knife out of his ribs, and wiped the blade on his uniform before placing it back in its sheath on my side. The 1st Division man used his dressings to patch Reno's and Del's wounds as I sat on the rim of the hole and stared out across the wasteland trying to convince myself this was real … and wondering who had won.

CHAPTER 26

We limped back through the jungle to the LZ where hundreds of reinforcements were pouring in to finish off the wounded beast. I felt a deep seething revulsion for the once gallant men of the Ghost Regiment. They had fought well until the incident at the Aid Station forever dishonored them. Now I hoped they died like rabid dogs.

Droves of aircraft landed and took off from multiple locations. Del and I climbed aboard one, uncaring of its destination. As we rose above the trees, I looked down at the jagged tear in the jungle. The long, ugly scar cut a hundred yard path through the middle of the lush green with blackened stumps smoldering in desolation, the whole section leveled and the earth pitted with craters. Litter teams moved through the area like ants collecting the hundreds of dead scattered about with their stench hanging in the humid air. I savored the cool air in my face as we skirted Black Virgin Mountain and descended into our airstrip. A medic gave us a once over, decided I could wait, and directed Del to another chopper. I limped to my bunker for lack of a better direction. *Had it really been only three days since I left this place?*

The disfigured little boy and girl watched from a distance, their solemn eyes staring at my blood-crusted, filthy uniform. I sat on the edge of my bunker and watched an oxcart amble by, thinking it a beautiful sight, and opened a can of peaches to swallow the slices whole one by one, unable to chew. The little girl and boy approached hesitantly, their eyes reflecting uncertainty and distress. I offered the can to them. The little boy shrank back and began to cry soundlessly as he hid his head against the little girl's side. Her gaze remained on my face as tears trickled down her cheeks. I rummaged through the box of C-rations picking the most sought after cans and ate them unheated as I watched the more seriously wounded placed aboard aircraft. Other men met arriving aircraft to offload bodies and place them in a long line on the edge of the LZ, where teams wearing masks worked to identify and tag them before placing them in black plastic body bags. I looked away, fearful of seeing Jerry, Bloop, and Harley among them.

A sergeant herded what was left of our company together, some seventeen of the original one hundred and fifty plus who landed in that hell to rescue Charlie Company, and settled us cross-legged on the ground before a bunker, where we continued to eat with smacking lips as a skinny man crawled on top of the bunker.

"*Attention!*" some officer off to the side yelled.

"*At ease!*" he commanded before we could move.

I glanced up at the man dressed in starched, tailored jungle fatigues and polished boots as he placed his hands on his hips and stared down at our ragged little group, taking in the dirty bandages and ripped uniforms, his nose wrinkling with distaste at our putrid stench of sweat, blood, and death.

"Who *is* this jerk?" someone growled when he began to speak.

Another shrugged. "Some dandy general."

"Shit, that's *Westy* himself," another insisted as the little general droned on vaguely about bravery, the ultimate price paid, and Presidential Unit Citations.

I looked up at the little man running his mouth, thinking *so that's the Top Dog?*

"Hey, you gonna eat the rest of those beans and franks?" A filthy, bearded face with blood soaked bandages on his right arm and shoulder looked at my hands holding the can and licked his grime-encrusted lips in anticipation. I scooped out another bite and gave him the rest. He used his fingers to rake out the contents, tilting his head back to pour the juice into his mouth as it dribbled down his chin. I looked back up at the general and tried to follow what he was saying, lost interest, and rummaged for another can in my box of rations. The general stepped off his bunker and shook hands with the cluster of officers, climbed aboard his sleek helicopter sporting a plaque with white stars in a field of red, and departed in a swirl of dust as we muttered and cupped our hands protectively over our open cans to keep the debris out.

A medic walked amongst us and directed several of us to a dustoff chopper. The aircraft flew us out of Tay Ninh Province and deposited us on the hospital helipad at Cu Chi where another medic shepherded us to the emergency room. An orderly directed some of us to the shower point, where we scrubbed our battered bodies with medicated soap. He then threw our uniforms in a trash bin and made us don silly gowns with our asses hanging out before returning us to the emergency room.

With fresh blood seeping from my reopened wounds, I promptly fell asleep as I awaited my turn. Later, lying on a table under a bright light, I suffered through a doctor's probing to extract pieces of metal from my face and chipped teeth from my mouth, received half a dozen shots from dull needles, and numerous stitches to various parts of my mug. An orderly led me to a ward, where I found a sleeping Del and Reno, and issued me a bed. I climbed aboard after swallowing two pills and fell asleep almost before my head hit the pillow.

———

A nurse woke me with a tray of food. I swallowed every bite whole, still unable to chew with my wrecked mouth, waved to a gobbling Del and Reno, took two more pills, and went back to sleep. Late that night I awoke in a cold sweat and lay for a while fighting memories. I limped to the latrine to relieve myself and caught my frightening image in the mirror, where purple streaks surrounded bandages plastered all over my hideous face, with my eyes black and swollen into slits above patches of dried blood dotting cotton pads stuck all over my warped and swollen face. I went back to bed with lumps in my throat. A nurse hurried over with two tablets and a glass of water. I drifted off to sleep with visions of Sandy grimacing at my disfigurements.

The next few days were a vague recollection of changing bed sheets, taking pills, and lying flat on my back
staring up at the ceiling in a mindless limbo. I avoided
mirrors altogether. I learned they shipped Silverstein
stateside, Lunas to a hospital in Japan, and Bernie to
Saigon. None of them would ever return. I dozed and
dreamed of men chasing me with bayonets and taunting
me by sticking the tips in my face. The nurse gave me
more pills that sent me drifting again into a fog. The
nightmares left me haggard. I fought to stay awake until I
discovered the pills made me stop thinking, and then ate
them like candy, eagerly languishing in the stupor they
brought. I dreamed of Taipei, Jerry, and Sandy. I stole
more pills when I could catch the nurse away from her
station, living in a half world I never wanted to leave. I
faked pain to get more pills from a sympathetic nurse
and floated high above my bed laughing at the revolving lights. I threw a glass at an unsympathetic nurse
and went on a rampage of destruction, screaming and
cursing her and every member of her family until she
gave me more pills. After a week, they released me on
outpatient status to our Battalion Aid Station. Leaving
Del and Reno behind, I conned a prescription for the
pills to carry with me and tripled the number by forgery
enroute to the druggist. I doubled the dosage as soon as
I cleared the hospital doors and floated serenely into the
company area without a care.

I stood outside our hooch peering through the
screen door and came crumbling back to reality as I

viewed the mattresses folded back and the personal possessions removed, leaving the interior as barren as the day
I arrived. Filled with anguish, I looked down the double
row of empty cots and found only Del, Reno, and mine
undisturbed on the first squad side. Two remained on
the second squad side—neither one Jerry nor Bernie's.
I walked across to the other hooch and looked in. Two
bunks remained on the third squad side, and only one
remained on the fourth squad side. I returned to my
hooch and sat alone in the dark interior listening to the
echoes of laughter from the men who once surrounded
me there and started crying in a helpless, bitter rage.

Unable to remain with the memories, I went to the
Wolf's Den and ordered a beer, ignoring the medic's
orders not to drink alcoholic beverages with the medication I was taking. I took more of the pills to bring on
the welcome numbness as I watched the place fill to half
capacity, almost all of the men from Charlie Company,
most wearing bandages. Bravo was still in the field. Our
company was in hospitals and body bags.

In late evening, First Sergeant Black entered the
club and ordered bourbon for us. I drank steadily as
he sat saying little other than to keep me talking as he
poured booze down me. At some point, he took away my
pills. In a drunken stupor, I told him everything, crying
at times, raging at others. He let me cry and rage and
then half carried me back to the hooch, dumped me on
my bunk, and shared a bottle of bourbon with me until
I passed out.

The following morning Black summoned me to the orderly room and I sat as directed in the chair beside his desk.

He stared at me for a long minute. "How do you feel?"

Physically I'm shot up, hung-over, in a state of drug withdrawal, and feel like warmed over shit. Mentally I'm merely a drooling wreck. Otherwise, I feel fine, asshole! I shrugged, remaining mute.

"Sharpe, I'm going to level with you, son." He shuffled some papers on his desk.

Son? The bastard is up to something.

"Sharpe, you know you qualify for a rear assignment." He waited for an acknowledgment from me but received none. "Three times wounded, shit, that's more than anyone can ask of you, right? Division policy says *two* wounds and you go to the rear." He avoided my eyes as I sat impassive. "Hell, you've been through the shit as much as anybody, right?" He stood and poured cups of coffee and then plopped back down in his chair as he shoved one of the cups at me. "What I'm trying to say is—you've got experience."

I sighed. "Knock off the shit, Top, you obviously want something from me and I'm obviously not going to like it worth a damn." I picked up my cup and sipped the bitter brew.

He squirmed in his chair. "What I'm saying is, we ain't got any experience left in the unit. We've got raw recruits pouring in every day who don't know jack shit. Somebody's got to lead them." He sat back in satisfaction and raised his cup.

I blinked. "Have I missed something?"

"Today you request another waiver of the division two wound policy. I *know* I can get it pushed through." He shoved a typed piece of paper across the desk and laid a pen on it. "You start Leadership School tomorrow. In seven days you'll graduate and be promoted to Acting Jack. That means promoted to sergeant before you have time in grade to qualify and be paid as an E-4 until you're eligible for E-5. You're going to be the new first squad leader."

"Bullshit," I said. "I'm not a goddamned *sergeant*!"

"*I* decide who's a goddamned sergeant in *this* company."

"I don't know shit about running a squad."

He sat back with a smug grin. "Seems to me you always thought you could run the whole goddamned *platoon* when I was out there with you. You're a natural. You'll learn all the technical crap at the school."

"So you want to promote me to acting sergeant and make me a squad leader because you don't have anyone else left? Nope, I'll pass."

"Look, *jackass*, you'll do what I *tell* you—"

"I don't give a *hoot* in *hell* about being a squad leader!"

"—and right now I'm *telling* you to go pack your shit so the runner can drive you to the academy."

"Have you lost your *mind*, Top?"

"Your wounds will be treated by the Aid Station up there. I've already cleared it."

"I said I'm *not* interested in—"

"Now get your ass out of my Orderly Room! I've got more important things to do than sit around watching you feel *sorry* for yourself."

"*Top!*"

"You got any more of those damned pills?"

"*No!*" I glowered. "I want that REMF assignment I've got coming!"

He arched his eyebrows. "And just *who* will take care of the new men?"

"That's not *my* damn problem!" I insisted. "And *I* don't have to do it!"

"But you will." He sat back in satisfaction and jammed his cigar in his mouth.

"Why should I have to nurse a bunch of dumb assed newbies?"

"Because you're an *infantryman* who's *born* to it and you *love* this shit!"

"You're *nuts!*" I protested.

He blew a puff of blue smoke at me. "Tell you what, *Sergeant* Sharpe. You go to that silly assed little Academy. Give me a week up there. Then you come on back here and tell me you want to be a *REMF* and I'll *make* you a REMF. Deal?"

"A *week*, Top, and then I get the *hell* out of here if I want." I sat back and crossed my arms. "*And* I get to keep the Acting Jack stripes!"

"I'll even throw in four days R and R to Vung Tau when you graduate," he advised.

"What's the catch?" I challenged.

"Goddamn, son, can't I do you a *favor* without your nasty little accusations?"

"You ain't never done nothing for nothing in your whole life, Top," I countered. "You're pulling some more shit on me."

"Well screw me all to hell!" he bellowed, feigning hurt and disappointment. "Go on, get out of here! *Wait!* Sign this goddamned waiver before you go."

"When I get back—*maybe!*" I called over my shoulder and slammed the screen door on my way out.

I returned to the hooch to pack my gear and tossed it in the back of the jeep under Black's watchful eyes, ignoring him as we growled off in a trail of dust, knowing the bastard was half-crazy anyway.

———

The seven days at the Leadership Academy were a waste of time. I could have taught most of the subjects myself. The majority of it was crap I couldn't use in the bush anyway. But it was behind me now and I had the sergeant's stripes sewed on my sleeves to prove it. Now I had four days to rest and think about my future, I mused as the chopper fishtailed down to the pad in Vung Tau.

"Jay!"

I gaped in surprise as Sandy ran through the swirling wind of the rotor blades and threw herself in my arms as I stepped down onto the tarmac. "Where did you come from?"

She clung to me. "Your First Sergeant called last week and said you had been released from the hospital. He said you would be going to school for a week and suggested I meet you here today."

I steered her to the in processing point. "Bastard was pretty sure of himself, wasn't he, and how the hell does he know about us?"

"Your face!" She stared at the welts and cuts.

"Close your eyes and it's not so bad," I advised stiffly.

"Oh, *Jay*! Why didn't you call me? I was frantic. We kept getting casualties and I ... kept praying one of them wouldn't be you! Oh, thank *God* you're alive!"

"Jerry's not," I choked, my eyes filling with moisture.

"I know. I'm so sorry. Gail is inconsolable."

"Did you see Bernie?"

"He was on my ward for a week. He found out about Jerry before we shipped him stateside and was crazy with grief. He couldn't tell me anything about you."

I turned away to hide my tears. "I've got to in process."

"I've already got us a hotel ..."

————

We sat in a bistro left over from the French colonial days sipping wine. I wanted a beer. The atmosphere was close and intimate. I felt cold and hollow. Sandy stared at the wounds on my face as I studied the interior of the restaurant wanting to be anywhere but here.

"Jay, you're practically ignoring me."

"I don't mean to. I'm sorry."

"Please talk to me."

"Things don't feel right."

"Let's go back to our room. I'll make it right for us again."

I stood by the window watching the moon reflect off the gently lapping waves as the ocean breeze stirred the curtains in the dark room.

Sandy huddled in the corner of the bed, her eyes searching my outline. "I ... almost feel as though I don't know you anymore."

"Maybe you never did."

"You're hard and ... *distant* ... now, I-I feel as though I'm losing you."

I turned to her in the darkness, a soft lump of shadow in the bed waiting for me to join her there. *Why couldn't I bring myself to touch her?* "You shouldn't have come here, Sandy."

"Jay, please don't close me out. Please talk to me."

I fought against the swelling anger. "What do you *want* me to say? That we got our *ass* kicked by the *Ghost Regiment*? That everybody is either *dead* or *wounded*? *Exactly* what do you want me to *say*?"

"I-I'm sorry—"

"*Goddamn it!* Can we *please* stop saying we're *sorry*?"

"I ... don't know what else to say ... I don't know how to help you ..."

I took a deep breath to calm myself. "No one can help me, Sandy."

"I love you, Jay."

I grimaced. "For today?"

"And tomorrow!" she declared, her voice quivering.

"I don't have any tomorrows. Remember?"

"That's not fair, Jay."

"Those are the rules, lady."

"Please get out of the infantry."

"I can't ... new men are coming in ... they need me."

"Please, Jay. *I* need you."

"I have to get the Ghost Regiment—for Jerry and Bloop and Harley and Bernie."

"They're destroyed! Everyone says so."

"They're full of shit! Some of them got through."

"They say over twelve hundred of them were killed."

"*I was there, Sandy! They got through us! They'll be back! And I'll be waiting*!" I took a deep, steadying breath.

"I-I might not be, Jay ... waiting, I mean ..."

———

After an early morning flight, I caught an opportune ride back to the unit area and arrived just before dawn as the newly reforming company began stirring in a state of groggy surliness. I dismounted on the dusty road and stood surveying the twin rows of hooches bathed in weak pools of yellow light bordered by the dew covered company street. Men naked to the waist stumbled about with baggy eyes and towels draped over their shoulders as they searched out the shower point, while others drifted to the mess hall on wafting aromas of sizzling bacon and eggs blending with coffee brewing.

Black paused in the orderly room, coffee mug in hand, to stare at me through the screen side, intently watching my forlorn figure as I stood in the road just outside the company boundary. I ignored him as I assessed my emotions.

This was home now, I sensed with foreboding, the place to come to when filled with nagging doubts and fears of personal events out of control. I belonged here. I could become absorbed in the day-to-day struggle and forget the unbearable. I stared at the sagging structures of molding wood and canvas and listened to the rattle of washbasins, doors slamming, and hoarse laughter as men jabbed playfully at one another. I tuned in to the invisible throb of camaraderie offered by these strange men, the familiar sights and sounds assaulting my senses, my instincts drawn forcefully to the drama of these death dealers' everyday lives. I watched the mangy dogs drift toward me and knew every one of them by name, and who had claimed them as their own. I viewed the potholes of water and green slime with the paths beaten into the mud along the rotted and broken boardwalks that no one used anymore. I breathed the humid air, tasting the mixture of gunpowder, soap, aftershave, food, and danger.

They were a coarse and hard group living in a coarse and hard world, men who traded insults and barbed jests as naturally as others exchanged greetings, but with never a doubt they would risk their very existence for one another. The day loomed before them on tantalizing currents of adventure and uncertainty, boringly like the one before, vibrant because it could be their last. They were magnificent in their shaggy, un-groomed appearance and profane environment, 150 individuals filled with 150 opinions and private desires that the sting of a passing bullet could transform into a machine of violence and unflinching resolve to destroy. They were capable of wading through a thorn bush to avoid trampling a single flower, or of blasting another man's brains to pulp and walking through the splattered gore. They were Infantry, a dumb, cunning, passionate, heartless, funny, sad collection of ordinary men caught up in extraordinary circumstances who recognized as their only creed the need to kill or be killed.

Others might watch them with contempt as they struggled by under heavy loads with stooped shoulders, disdainful of their filthy, grime-encrusted uniforms covering unwashed bodies, when they themselves knew only showers every day and clean sheets every night. Others only guessed at the agony of raw feet and blistered hands, the misery of weeks without bathing or hot meals, the numbing bites of millions of insects, the anguish of festering sores and painful scrapes and bruises, the mindless exposure of bodies to heat, rain, cold, and drought.

These others fancied themselves as warriors as they sent their cannons booming into the air from protected bases, or banged on typewriters, drove trucks, or a hundred other things in support of the war effort. These others often forgot that their sole mission in life was to provide support to this single half-man, half-animal staring back at them from unblinking eyes.

These others would never know the sheer terror and absolute ecstasy of combat in its simplest form, of one man set against another in ruthless conflict that decreed only the better survive. None of those other warriors would ever see the sight of a rifle filled with the form of another and feel the recoil as the projectile tore skin and sprayed blood in the air.

They would never know the thrill of battle as they slew the enemy in rage, or the compassion of victory as they stood over the mangled bodies of their defeated. They would never experience the conflict within as they gazed at an enemy lying now dead and know they had killed a brother. Only these men before me would know these things. They were Infantry—and battle was their king.

I sighed, grabbed my bag, and turned to the orderly room to rejoin the brotherhood of the damned.

Black jammed his cigar in his mouth and turned to his desk with a grin.

Epilogue

America's Diplomats were born from the ashes of the first encounter with the 9th NVA and died in the ashes of the second. They were truly unique as soldiers. The replacements that followed were men of a different temperament, and though they fought as well as any ever fielded, they never seemed to possess the zeal and dedication of those fallen righteous warriors who were their predecessors. Maybe it was just as well.

Vietnam forever left its mark on our generation and our nation. We won every battle along the way to losing the war, and learned a harsh fact about ourselves— we were not invincible. Our nation launched its legions of warrior-diplomats into a conflict it was unwilling to win. It asked its citizens to be soldiers, and they were. It asked them to fight, and they did. It asked them to win, and they won. Then it handed them a political defeat that will haunt us forever. The lesson would appear to be simple: There is no truth or justice in war, no right or wrong, only *victory*. The shame of this defeat is borne by all. Millions of people died for this failure in the following years, and those still alive in that sad little part of the world today know only bondage as another section of the globe slid into a darkness that we as a free people can only imagine.

Now we can but pray that history will be kind to us for having tried and failed, rather than never having tried at all.

I served the remainder of my first tour in Vietnam as a squad leader, and eventually as a platoon sergeant, amid a great deal of controversy. I returned to serve again at the end of the war as an officer and helicopter gunship pilot. But those are stories for another time for others to tell, for mine is told.